T   N

In this colourful novel, the second in the *Sutton Place* trilogy, Dinah Lampitt continues the story of the unfolding of the curse laid by Queen Edith of England in 1045 and how its power has grown stronger with the passing of the centuries; how Giles the Fool has haunted the Long Gallery with his laughter and tears; and how the descendants of Dr. Zachary the astrologer are caught up once more into the web of wickedness spun by the doomed manor of Sutton.

THE SILVER SWAN

THE SILVER SWAN

by
DINAH LAMPITT

MAGNA PRINT BOOKS
Long Preston, North Yorkshire,
England.

British Library Cataloguing in Publication Data.

Lampitt, Dinah
  The silver swan.
  I. Title
  823'.914(F)   PR6062.A485

  ISBN 0-86009-906-7
  ISBN 0-86009-907-5 Pbk

First Published in Great Britain by Muller, Blond & White Ltd, 1984.

Published in Large Print 1986 by arrangement with Muller Blond & White Ltd, London.

Photoset in Great Britain by
Dermar Phototypesetting Co, Long Preston, North Yorkshire.

Printed and bound in Great Britain by
Redwood Burn Limited, Trowbridge, Wiltshire.

01

Once again—

To Bill Lampitt, Jacqueline Getty
Phillips and Geoffrey Glassborow
and to
Roger Chubb, Ena Daniels, Erika
Lock, Carole Restorick and Shirley
Russell for their unfailing kindness
and enthusiasm.

AUTHOR'S NOTE

Although—as in *Sutton Place*—the characters and the events in *The Silver Swan* are presented in fictionalised form, most of the happenings are based on historical fact and the principals actually lived as described.

BIBLIOGRAPHY

The Wandering Prince, L. Dumont-Wilden; *Prince Charles Stuart,* A.C. Ewald; *Annals of an Old Manor House,* Frederic Harrison; *Alexander Pope, The Letters of; Alexander Pope,* Peter Quennell; *The English Scene in the 18th Century,* E.S. Roscoe; *England and the English in the 18th Century,* William Connor Sydney; *Ghosts and Poltergeists,* Father Herbert Thurston; *English Men and Manners in the 18th Century,* A.S. Turberville.

THE SILVER SWAN

The silver swan who living had no note
When death approached unlocked her silent throat.
Leaning her breast against the reedy shore
Thus sung her first and last and sung no more.
Farewell all joys, oh death come close mine eyes
More geese than swans now live,
More fools than wise.

English Madrigal by Orlando Gibbons, 1612.

PART ONE

PROLOGUE

On the eve of her fiftieth year she dreamed such a dream. She wandered in a wild forbidden land where peacocks flew and Barbary apes laughed aloud; where the earth glinted with the colour of emerald and topaz; where through luscious trees snow-shored lakes of crystal could be glimpsed and strange white horses pawed and tossed their manes at the sapphire sky.

And in this ecstatic place where good and evil ran joyously side-by-side she saw her life spread out before her. And though she longed to turn away she was forced to go onward and upward to the place where white peaks gleamed in the sun and where redemption awaited and where all her deeds, whether they be for good or for bad, would be dwarfed to mere pygmies at the high altar of the world.

She knew that if she did not wake she would die—her spirit ascending too far for her earthly shell to contain. And so she threw herself beneath the waterfall that rolled slumberously down from the mountains, shafting into a million diamonds as it fell smokily into the river below. As the waters closed over her she gave one last sad sigh—and thus she woke, with that sound echoing about her and her soul disturbed by leaving that land of death and beauty.

For a while she could see nothing but the sparkle of the cascading stream and then, slowly, her eyes picked out the hangings of her bed and beyond them the familiar shape of her room. She was safe, she had escaped from the relentless fantasy of night and come home. But the very notion of being there made her tremble. And that small frightened movement set the bed curtains swaying, reminding her vividly of the thing she dreaded thinking about more than any other; the malevolence that had come to torment her when she was twelve turning her existence into an agony of noise and dread.

Lying there watching the dawn turn the bedroom walls to rose, she thought of Hyacinth, as she had every day of her life from the second they had met. He had filled her waking and sleeping moments for all those long years and yet she could hardly remember his face, sometimes going to an old and faded sketchbook and looking through it. But Sibella was drawn there too, and for that sweet spritely face to suddenly look up at her was a hurt she was rarely strong enough to withstand.

An orange tint was suffusing the dawn as her mind turned once more to her birthday and to the callers from London who would soon be descending upon her in dozens to toast her—the most celebrated hostess of the day and arbiter of all that was exquisite—into her fiftieth year. And so she must rise and indulge her one fancy—the

14

washing of her face and body in water from a spring that bubbled earthwards, deep from the hills of Malvern.

She had first seen it with her mother and Mr Pope, and then she had returned when she had been nineteen, and drunk deeply from the mysterious spring. And, as if she had accidentally stumbled upon the Fountain of Youth, at forty nine Melior Mary's features and body were as young and as supple as those of a woman in the early part of her twenties.

She had never revealed the mystery of the spring to anyone though secretly she doubted whether it really contained any magical properties. She had bathed in it within a few months of losing Hyacinth and on the day he had gone the fire that burns out the human body, the fire known as living, had been extinguished. And though she might charm and entertain, sit for portraits by Mr Joshua Reynolds and young Mr Gainsborough, be toasted and flattered and wooed, nothing mattered at all. Her nickname—Queen of Ice—was true.

But, nonetheless, every month one of her footmen took his place on the public stage leaving from the Saracen's Head at Snow Hill in London and proceeded to Malvern where he went quietly into the hills and bottled the water. She did not care for him to make the journey privately for, however often he would change his times or route the meanest chaise in her coach-house would—combined with the distinctive silver

15

livery that denoted a servant of Melior Mary Weston—attract the attention of such gentlemen of the road as Sixteen-String Jack or Tom King. It was not safe for a servant of the great heiress who owned the magnificent and famous Tudor mansion—Sutton Place—to travel abroad unaccompanied.

Remembering the tradition that now rested solely in her hands made her, as always, breathe slightly faster as she got out of bed, slipping a dressing gown of flowered silk over her shoulders. Before her the delicate lines of her room, decorated in white and silver, greeted her eyes as they had done every morning since her girlhood. When the malevolence had been banished and Sibella Hart had come, there had been a great change round. The old apple loft, apparently used by the original Lady Weston— her ancestress and wife of the builder of Sutton Place—had been restored as a bedroom for Melior Mary, the smaller room leading off it had been made ready for the orphan.

Now she had turned it into a dressing room packed full of clothes—enormously hooped petticoats made in richest stuffs, tumbling over gowns of French finery: beavers, hats, bonnets and scarves; yards of Spanish broadcloth and damasks, velvets and silks. Pair upon pair of high-heeled shoes jostling wig boxes and jewel cases; Turkey handkerchiefs rubbing shoulders with coloured feathers, trays of pearl pins and turbans.

As she moved towards the window her reflection in the long glass adorned with a golden unicorn echoed the gesture. She turned to look at herself and found that nothing had changed. In her angled face where the cheekbones slanted upward the same enormous eyes—swept by the jet black lashes that were part of her fame— gazed out as usual. Mr Pope had described them as the colour of April violets loved by rain—but then he had seen everything with a poet's eye, the eye of a man who loved beauty in nature.

Then there was her hair. She supposed that it was the single thing caused by the malevolence for which she could be grateful. For at the age of twelve her thick black locks had turned silver and so it had remained. And though she had wigs in abundance she preferred to leave her curls *au naturel*, sweeping them up in a mass of ringlets and jewels for formal occasions, but letting her hair hang about her shoulders like a silver cloudburst when she was alone at Sutton Place.

She leant nearer the glass and delicately traced the curve of her eye with her finger. It was an extraordinary but visible fact. Like the great courtesan Diane de Poitiers, Melior Mary had found the secret of eternal youth.

On an impulse she let the dressing gown slip to the floor and appraised herself with the cold eye of one who receives no joy in what she perceives. It was as she thought. Without a shred of conceit she saw that she was perfect; no flaw in the glittering jewel except the coldness of her soul. She shook her head watching the silver

17

sheen of her hair as it bounced about her shoulders. She would have changed it all, been transformed into a fat, greasy pig-herding slut if Hyacinth could have been hers.

She picked up the dressing gown and placed it round her shoulders, for she was suddenly chill in the early morning air. Crossing to the window she threw it open and leaned forward, arms folded upon the casement, so that she might look out all the better. The view on every side was of sweeping lawns where peacocks—introduced to Sutton Place by her mother Elizabeth—strode and displayed, their weird shriek of 'Sill, sill' cutting the stillness.

And, leaning out of the window she could see the whole of the back of Sutton Place standing in the midst of the gardens laid out by her forebears. It glowed at her in the early sun, the ember brick warm to the touch. Yet it seemed to her—as she gazed to right and left—that it was a watchful house combining a mixture of both grandeur and forebodding.

And yet she loved it. She could not contemplate life anywere else. Let the London set do what they will, she could not bear to be parted from her magnificent mansion. It had known her loves and her hates, her joys and her terrors. It had seen her conception and birth. It would, in time, see her death.

Standing there in the morning light Melior Mary was suffused with memory.

CHAPTER 1

Beneath a sky heavy with unshed snow, through a park glinting with rime and crystalline with hoar frost, a carriage wended its slow and silent way down the drive of Sutton Place. Through the windows two anxious faces peered out; one— the woman's—staring, as if her very life depended upon the great gates that lay before her; the other—the child's—craned backwards, as if it could wrest to her by sheer will power the house that, though looming overall in the bleak landscape, had just now vanished from view, as the drive bent serpentine.

Everywhere was the silence of mid-winter. Not a bird sang in Sutton Forest, not a rabbit twitched a nervous nose—yet somewhere the hunters were out, for in the distance hounds yelped for a hungry fox and the high brassy blast of a horn rent the ice-crisp air.

This far trumpeting made the woman go white to the lips and urge the coachman on to greater haste, but it gave the child a look of hope, of thoughts of rescue at hand; for though Melior Mary Weston loved her mother Elizabeth, she loved nothing so much in the world as Sutton Place—the mansion which had been in her family for nearly two hundred years, and to which she,

though nothing but a child—and a girl at that—
was nonetheless the sole heir.

Yet a stolen glance at her mother's determined
face, and the sight of the gates beginning to swing
slowly open before the oncoming equipage, was
enough to dash any idea that her father might
yet appear and stop them running away. That
even now, at this last and desperate moment, his
great red-coated figure might suddenly lurch into
view before them, holding up his arm—whip in
hand—and roar out, 'Damn you Elizabeth, what
the devil do you think you're doing?'

For all her fear of her father's moods Melior
Mary would have welcomed him. He represented
the way of life that she had always known and
enjoyed and, above all, he represented Sutton
Place. He loved the house as much as she and
was always speaking of family and tradition and
the duties of great landowners.

It was not his physical resemblance to the
Westons that gave rise to this love of heritage
however. For he stood, unlike any of the family
portraits that hung in the Great Hall, over six
feet tall with massive shoulders and a dark, swart
complexion out of which blazed two brilliant
eyes. When he was angry, which was quite often,
his pupils dilated so alarmingly that the irises
appeared pitch black. He was known amongst the
servants as the Satyr.

There was wild blood in him. His mother—
Melior Mary's grandam—had been nothing more
than a daughter of an inn-keeper. But mine host

had made good, bought land, and set himself up as a country squire. And his child, though quite the stupidest woman in the world, had been pretty enough to attract Richard Weston of Sutton Place—the fifth and the last to bear that name—as a husband. So it was this mixture that had gone to make up John Weston and it was after the strain of the inn-keeper Nevill—with its fierce, gypsy-tainted blood—that he had taken.

And, though still too young for it to be truly obvious, the inherited wildness was there in Melior Mary. She had had a restlessness about her ever since she had been born; a carefree exploring urge, not suitable for a female child. For different reasons both her parents had wished she had been a boy. And now she wished it herself for she felt that had she been male, she could have jumped out of the carriage and young as she was, have lived free in the forest.

A movement in her must have attracted Elizabeth Weston's attention for, just for a second, the mother stopped her wrapt contemplation of the opening gates and laid a hand upon her daughter's arm giving her, at the same time, a sad and earnest glance. She was so much everything that Melior Mary's father was not that it was almost as if their marriage had been one of both nature and society's cruellest jokes. The opposite of John in every way possible: short—not even five feet tall—and delicately made; her hair fair, her skin white, her eyes the light blue of a forget-me-not, Elizabeth's manner was so gentle that she could no more have been deliberately cruel than died.

And socially she bore the pedigree that for John had been ever tainted in himself by the introduction of gypsy blood from the inn-keeper. She was the daughter of an aristocrat, Joseph Gage, and his heiress wife Elizabeth Penruddock; for brothers she had Sir Thomas Gage of Firle and the rich and fashionable Joseph the second. She was unimpeachably a member of the upper class.

But now she was flying, despite the conventions of her upbringing, from her husband. For nothing had ever been right between John and Elizabeth Weston. The only things they had had in common being their child and Sutton Place. Beyond that mutual interest ceased. Her love of music, poetry and the arts were an anathema to him; she abhorred his preoccupation with hunting and energetic outdoor pursuits. From the very beginning their arranged and loveless marriage had been unfulfilled.

Yet, for the sake of a quiet existence, the two of them had—up till this fraught and terrible moment—passed several years as befitted the owners of a great estate. John had given orders, hunted, got drunk, occasionally gone to London —where he had patronised the Ladies of Drury, gone to the coffee houses and bowed to Queen Anne. Elizabeth had supervised the day-to-day management of Sutton Place, ordered new clothes, played cards with the other great ladies from round about, embroidered and sung. Their child Melior Mary—still too small for a governess according to custom—perfected her riding, copied out characters set by her mother, played with her toys and felt lonely. There was no sign of a brother or sister to add to the uneasy household.

But, nonetheless, life had not been dull during those years of truce for there were a great many visitors to Sutton Place to liven affairs. The most frequent of these was John Weston's lowborn mother. Much to Melior Mary's dismay the old lady's coach would appear in the courtyard, with what seemed the regularity of clockwork and out would get her grandmother—her once beautiful face now marred by a frill of fat— complete with an equally obese pug tucked under one arm. The pair of them would then take a seat in Elizabeth's saloon and, so it seemed to the child, remain there for the entire visit, cramming cups of chocolate and confitures—or saucers in the case of the dog—into their mouths with unnerving speed. As the animal had also acquired the mistress's unfortunate habit of breaking wind, Melior Mary's dutiful daily visit to pay her respects was an agony of dismay lest she should laugh aloud and earn a beating at her father's hand. Elizabeth sat calmly through it all, frequently leaving the room on the excuse of household matters and, thereby forcing John grudgingly to entertain his mother on his own.

On one such occasion Elizabeth, once outside the door, collapsed with laughter, throwing herself onto a window seat and stuffing her fist into her mouth. Melior Mary, coming upon her, joined in. She loved fun and gaiety and it felt awfully sweet in the sunshine to snuggle close to her mother, sniffing the sweet scents of her. Elizabeth's arms had gone round her daughter and they had indulged in silent laughter together until John's great fame suddenly loomed over them and they were given a piercing look from his dark eyes.

'And what causes this amusement?' he had said coldly.

Inwardly Elizabeth sighed. She was not afraid of him but she detested arguing so much that a thrill of unease swept her. She cast about for an excuse but nothing was forthcoming, so wearily she began to tell the truth.

'Your mother's dog...'

'Is fierce in its farting, sir.'

This last from Melior Mary.

Fortunately this struck John as amusing, and he had put his head back and given one of his rare laughs. Both Elizabeth and Melior Mary had joined in and, just for a moment, everything was as it should have been between the three of them. The husband putting his hand on the wife's shoulder and she, in return, slipping her fingers over his and the child looking upwards at the two of them and smiling too much.

Another visitor—though one that Melior Mary greeted with enthusiasm—was Elizabeth's younger brother, Joseph Gage. His arrival was always heralded by a huge Negro servant— dressed from head to foot in scarlet and gold— sprinting to the Middle Enter as if the hounds of Hell were after him, and beating upon it with a fist like a thunderbolt. This was followed, after a breathless moment or two, by the appearance of Joseph himself, riding in a carriage built for maximum sped and wearing the very latest fashion— diamonds glittering in his sword-hilt, on his fingers and about his person—while on his head he would sport the latest creation in wigs, powdered, and topped by a hat decorated with plumed and swaying feathers. He went nowhere without his slave who constantly walked ten paces behind his master.

The story was told that Joseph had bought him for a guinea when he had been only twelve years old and the Negro little older. The black bundle of skin and bone had been allowed to sleep by the fire in the kitchen, where he had been fed by Joseph with the leavings from the Gage family table. The black child grew and grew to well over six feet—and would have killed for the master who saved him from dying in the streets of London. Joseph referred to him as Sootface and treated him with the thoughtless affection usually reserved for dogs.

Elizabeth's elder brother, Thomas, also came and went during those years, as unlike his sister and Joseph as it was possible to be. A thin self-seeker with the face of a fox and the eyes of a serpent, his smile was as warm as winter, his lips tight and disapproving.

But even worse was the guardian of the Gage brothers and their sister—appointed as their natural parents had died young. With a beady brown eye that roved constantly over the younger and prettier female servants, he spoke nothing but damnation. There had never been so sinful a place as the Court according to his unceasing sermon. All the world went a-whoring, gambling and drinking. Meanwhile his wife would watch her husband with the fevered gaze of a fanatic. There was something unhealthy about them and Joseph said, quite roundly, that he would never be surprised to hear that they had murdered one another.

The rest of the social life of Sutton Place was conducted amongst the various Catholic families who lived round and about and who together formed a close and exclusive community. There was the Berkshire set—as John called them; the Englefields, the Blounts, the Racketts and widowed Mrs Nelson.

The prettiest of the women—other than Elizabeth—were the Blount sisters, one dark and saucy, the other blonde and amiable; the ugliest was Mrs Rackett who, beneath an over-large and heavily plumed wig, had thick lips, a broad nose and a hooting laugh. She made a great to-do of having a famous half-brother—the young and celebrated poet Alexander Pope—but secretly Melior Mary thought she did not altogether like him. For on more than one occasion Mrs Rackett had been heard to exclaim, 'To be plain with you my brother has a maddish way with him'. Then she would lower her voice and express her opinion that it was Alexander's deformity that was behind his eccentricities. She always had the air of one who was slightly revolted as she spoke of his minute stature and would purse her lips as if he had been born so small on purpose.

Yet it was for him, for the man that Wycherley the dramatist had described as having a 'little crazy carcass', that Elizabeth Weston was leaving Sutton Place and her husband. For it was he—the tiny poet with the handsome face and the readist wit in England—who had given her love at long last. Or so she believed.

'Oh Melior Mary,' she said now, in a sudden agony lest her child's life be ruined. 'Will you miss your father terribly? Do you like Mr Pope? Oh dear, oh dear.'

Her daughter regarded her seriously. Already, though she was still but seven years old, there was stirring in her the storm rider that all her life would never leave her in peace. The combination of the inn-keeper's blood and that of generations of the proud and fated Westons was powerful indeed. She knew, even now, that she would never love any mortal thing as much as she did the great house itself.

And yet she had a tenderness for her father. She remembered how he would swing her up onto his powerful shoulders when she was very small, the better that she might see the stained glass in the Great Hall.

'Look at those windows,' he used to say. 'One day they will be yours. Unless fate decrees that you have a brother.'

His voice always held an indifferent tone, as if he cared neither one way nor the other if her mother should have another child. But secretly Melior Mary had always known that he would have loved a son to inherit Sutton Place, to carry on the great name of Weston which—by a series of strange and remorseless deaths—had now whittled down to John alone.

Upon his shoulders like that Melior Mary could see him spread out beneath her like a countryside, every rise and fall of his face parts of a landscape. The clipped dark hair—cut thus to enable him to wear his various wigs—was a forest; the brilliant eyes, fringed by his dark curling lashes, mysterious lakes; the nape of his neck—which seemed so boyish and vulnerable—the curve of a mountain.

And when she was thus held close to him she could smell the freshness on his clothes and skin, where he had recently come in from riding, and feel the thud of his heart beneath his velvet coat. A wave of love for her father would come over her at these times. She would put her arms round his neck and wish that she could grow quickly, so that her normal view of him would not always be confined to a pair of riding boots or shoes and stockings.

'Well?'

28

Her mother was looking at her with eyes a-brim. The gates of Sutton Plae were almost fully open.

'I shall miss him, you know I will. But I must stay with you, Mother. You and Mr Pope seem so *little*.'

'Then you like Mr Pope, you funny child?'

'Of course I do.'

Melior Mary thought back to her first sight of the man that some called freak and some called god, that some pitied and others envied, yet who, it was decreed by fate, would be recognised and lionised as a genius within his lifetime.

Despite his being half-brother to Mrs Rackett he had never been to Sutton Place but the previous Christmas—the year of 1710—he had finally accepted an invitation. Melior Mary had been hidden in one of the musicians' galleries in the Great Hall, the better to see the large company arriving for the annual rout. The master of Sutton Place had thrown open his mansion to the cream of three counties and below her glided a living rainbow of colour as the ladies went past each other like bejewelled ships; the decks their enormously hooped petticoats, the sails their hair—woven à la commode into frames of wire—some two or three storeys high and covered with silk and brilliants.

Directly beneath her had stood Elizabeth in a hugely hooped dress of blue and silver, round her neck and at her ears the Weston diamonds while her fair hair was curled, powdered and woven with fresh flowers. Standing beside her, just out of vision, had been John, only the tips of his shoes being visible from where his daughter peeped.

The small orchestra—located in the gallery opposite the one in which Melior Mary was hidden—had just struck up a reel when Mr and Mrs Charles Rackett and Mr Alexander Pope were announced. Because he was celebrated—and no doubt because tales of his strangely small stature had reached ridiculous proportions—a lot of heads turned and Melior Mary stood on tip-toe in her hiding place. At first she thought there had been a mistake and Mrs Rackett had brought a child with her and then she saw that it was, in fact, a diminutive man.

But his face, as if in compensation, was handsome and striking. A finely shaped nose, a mouth that spoke of sweetness and passion, deep and large blue eyes and—from what she could hear—a delightful and charming voice. But though he was dressed fashionably with a long, curling wig and a velvet coat of cinnamon, satin lined and embroidered with silver, one side of him was concentrated and his shoulders round.

Despite all this Melior Mary saw that her mother, curtseying before the ill-shapen young man, had grown quite pink in the cheeks. And he was bending that clever head to kiss her hand. Their voices floated up to her above the sound of music.

'I never dance, Mrs Weston, but if you are not

ashamed to be a butterfly weaving with a spider then nothing would give me greater pleasure than to step out.'

She heard her mother murmur acceptance and saw John shift from buckled shoe to buckled shoe. And then as the music changed to the measured sound of a minuet and her father turned away to his brandy punch, Alexander Pope had stretched out his hand and Elizabeth Weston had laid hers in it.

Melior Mary never forgot that first union of their hands. His so perfect—the long fingers and shapely nails belying the rest of his body; hers so small and childlike. And there was something in the way their fingers lay quietly together for a second or two before they moved into the formal dance. If Melior Mary had been asked to chose a word to describe the way those hands first touched each other it would have been peacefully.

A noise behind her had made her turn round. Her uncle, Joseph, the drapery that curtained off the gallery looped over his arm, stood in the entrance. He was dazzlingly dressed in a black velvet coat and breeches, very richly laced with gold; his waistcoat brilliant with many coloured gemstones, his stockings black silk, his buckles winking diamonds. On his head he wore a white full-bottomed wig. Yet despite all the snuff-puffing hauteur of the great rake hell, empty of thought and conscious of naught but his appearance, his eyes were narrowed as he looked out over Melior Mary's head to where his sister danced with Mr Pope.

'Is he a dwarf?' asked his niece.

'No. No, he's not.'

'Then why is he like that? What's wrong with him?'

Joseph had dropped the curtain and stepped inside the gallery so that he stood side-by-side with Melior Mary looking down at the Great Hall; the hall that had been built in the reign of Henry VIII by the courtier Sir Richard Weston.

'Some childhood illness I believe,' he said, his voice faraway. 'But nature has given him genius instead. Do you believe that, Melior Mary? Do you believe that there is a law of compensation in the universe?'

'Do you mean God, Uncle?'

He looked at her.

'I'm not sure. If that is what you like to term it. But anyway Mr Pope was born to receive greatness.'

'I think I would rather be unclever but properly formed.'

'Oh so would he! Make no mistake of that, Melior Mary. He would sacrifice every poem in his soul in order to walk as straight and as tall as your father. Particularly now.'

His gaze was fixed on the dancers once more and Melior Mary looked curiously at the little poet.

'Why now?'

Joseph's eyes had been as green and as soft as

a sleepy cat's.

'Because something is stirring in his heart which attacks all mankind, irrespective of whether they be tall or short, beautiful or ugly.'

After the night of the Christmas ball Mr Pope had begun to visit Sutton Place quite frequently. At first he came with his half-sister and her husband, or with the Englefields, but then he took to calling alone, walking with Elizabeth in the gardens or exploring what was left of the Long Gallery. So that nobody could endanger themselves, John had sealed off the end leading to the ruined Gate House Wing but Pope and Melior Mary, hand in hand, and looking like playing children, would clamber through the partition to examine the place where the ravaging fire had broken out just after Queen Elizabeth had stayed with Henry Weston.

'What was it like before?' Pope had asked.

'I believe there was a spiral staircase that led into the Gate House from the gallery, which was the longest in England. The servants say it is haunted.'

Pope's deep blue eyes—almost on a level with hers—had stared as he said, 'Tell me of this ghost. Have you seen it?'

Melior Mary shook her head.

'No—it is only a sound. They say it is Sir Richard Weston's Fool.'

'Sir Richard Weston?'

'He built Sutton Place and was my ancestor.'

'So it is his initials that decorate the outside

33

walls?'

'Aye, a grand conceit is it not?'

Resisting a desire to smile, Alexander had nodded and said, 'Grand.'

And that evening sitting in the upstairs saloon, with Melior Mary safely gone to bed, he recounted the story again and said, 'She is so possessed of adult wit that it is hard not to laugh at her.'

Elizabeth smiled but John looked at him blankly and said, 'Why is that?'

'Because she is a dwarf of an adult, with all the humour that invokes.'

It was only after he had spoken the words that Pope realised he could have been describing himself and paused wretchedly. There was an uncomfortable silence during which John kicked at the log fire with his riding boot, Elizabeth bent even more industriously over her embroidery and Alexander had gulped his glass of port. Finally John had said, 'I don't care for that description of my daughter, sir,' and had got up and left the room. Horrified Pope stared after him.

'He thought I was likening her to my own deformed carcass,' he said—and before Elizabeth could stop him he had hurried out, limping rather badly because of his distress.

He had found John staring into the fire in the Great Hall, his large square shoulders hunched with unmistakable anger at his lot. If Pope had been anyone else he would have felt a moment's pity for this somewhat forlorn figure but as it

34

was he simply muttered, 'Tyrant!' beneath his breath and aloud said, 'Mr Weston, a moment if you please sir.'

John turned and ostentatiously lowered his head so that he could stare down his long straight nose at the young man who stood like an imp of paradise—chin up and blue flashing eyes—before him.

'Yes, sir?' he said.

'I apologise, sir, if you took aught amiss at my description of Melior Mary. I meant no offence.'

John hardened his mouth.

'Save your pretty talk for my wife, sir. Flowing phrases and sweet speeches have no effect on me.'

Pope had gone a little pale but stood his ground.

'Do you accept my apology?'

'No, Mr Pope, I do not. I think you trespass on my hospitality.'

Alexander looked askance and said, 'But Mr Weston I only have the greatest admiration for you and your family.'

'With regard to my wife I can believe it.'

'And what do you mean by that pray?'

'I mean, Mr Pope, that poor excuse for a man you might be but obviously the stir of lechery still abounds in your little soul.'

Alexander's pleasant voice was shaking just a fraction as he said, 'I would that I stood level with you, Mr Weston, that I might have the pleasure of striking you in the face.'

In reply John pulled the bell rope three times.

'You will leave now, sir. And if I hear aught of this from your good sister and her friends I shall not be afraid to tell the truth.'

'What truth? That Elizabeth is cast before you like a pearl before swine? That you have as much insight into her fine mind as a savage into pretty manners? Tell your truth, Mrs Weston—and be advised that I most certainly shall tell mine.'

'I hear not your squeaks, mouse.'

'Nor I your croaks.'

If I had not been so preposterous, the situation would have been pathetic—the minute exquisite, the unimaginative squire, at odds with each other for the love of a woman whose own passions lay totally unawakened.

But the argument triggered off an ill-fated series of secret meetings which began accidentally outside a bookshop in Guildford. Elizabeth was leaving her carriage to go in when, as if he had been waiting there all day, the poet was suddenly beside her and looking at her so passionately that she was taken aback.

'Why, Mr Pope!' she said, pulling her fur-lined cloak against the February wind that held the crisp tang of snow. 'Where have you been?'

It was his turn to look startled.

'Been?'

'Yes. You have not visited Sutton Place for a fortnight.

'But surely you know that I have been barred by your husband?'

'Barred? By John? Why?'

'For offending his sense of possession.'

She stood staring at him as the first snowflakes began to fall, her eyes—the blue of flowers—full of some emotion that she battled to conceal. It seemed to Pope that she was looking at him—*really* looking at him—for the very first time, and he shrank into himself. For all his fine face and melodious voice he had nothing to offer a woman in the way of physical attraction. He must charm by use of wit and words and these were of no avail to him now in the cold winter morning, where the hard white light showed no mercy.

Finally she spoke and said surprisingly, 'Why do you love me?'

'Because you are the sun, John Weston is the eternal shade, and I am the ape carried by a beauty to enhance her own splendour. Elizabeth...'

But his voice died away. He was trying too hard to be clever and her clear eyes held in them a certain pity.

'Don't look at me so. I realise that I am nothing but little Alexander for all my wordiness.'

And in that moment Elizabeth's longing for love and adoration consumed her, and she formed a passion for the man who worshipped her, his mask of accomplished and fashionable genius stripped away.

The snow was descending heavily, resting on the hood of her cloak, as she said, 'What must I do?'

His ready wit was at his lips.

'Take shelter for the immediate. There is a coffee house but two paces up the road. I will be there in four.'

Elizabeth laughed and Pope found himself suddenly unable to speak, the physical weakness which was constantly at war with his burning talent, proving too much to bear. He raised her hand to his lips and allowed himself the indulgence of tears.

After this their love, nurtured in the hothouse of secrecy, grew apace and weekly meetings turned into daily. Many times Melior Mary had accompanied Elizabeth on these bitter sweet escapades, sipping cups of chocolate and watching her pretty mother and the young man who gazed at her so intently.

It was Mrs Nelson—one of the Berkshire set—who finally brought it all to its inevitable outcome. A widow, a woman with literary pretensions, an avid collector of souls, she considered Pope part of her personal treasury and, as a neighbour and a member of the Catholic clique, she subjected him to a non-stop barrage of amorous innuendo, meagrely disguised as pity.

And it was she, having visited a shop in Guildford and gone, by chance, into the coffee house frequented by Pope and Elizabeth, who—having ascertained first that Mrs Weston was not at home—called at Sutton Place and remarked to John Weston how well his wife and the poet looked. John's thunderous silence was enough to tell her that she had hit home and she left with a triumphant swish of her hooped petticoat, larger by six inches than any other woman's in the district.

As she stepped through the Middle Enter, Melior Mary close at her heels, Elizabeth had sensed the leaden atmosphere and felt her heart lurch with fear. She had had no wish to fall in love deceitfully, would—if her life had worked out as she wanted—have been happily married and contentedly raising an enormous family.

She had not wanted John Weston from the start, sensing in him that wilfulness with which only a woman as capricious as he could have contended. But her guardian, Sir William Goring, had thought the master of Sutton Place a splendid match—and that had been the close of the matter. Her brother Joseph had been full of schemes for Sootface to snatch her—from the altar steps if necessary—and carry her off to safety. But it was as to the exact location of 'safety' that they had finally been thwarted and it had seemed easier, in the end to go through with it.

So it was with a sense of doom that she saw John standing before the fire in the Great Hall—legs slightly apart, arms behind his back—the stance he always adopted when about to argue.

'Mrs Nelson called,' was all he said.

'Who?'

She had genuinely forgotten in the welter of emotion exactly whom he meant—and it was a cardinal mistake.

'Mrs Nelson—the friend of the Racketts and

the Englefields. The mistress of the freakish poet.'

Poor unwordly Elizabeth had fallen straight into the trap snared for her.

'It does not do you justice, sir, to refer to Mr Pope in that way.'

He turned, snarling, and said, 'I'll refer to that dwarf, that rake from hell, the devil's joke, in any way I so choose, madam.'

'John, what is the matter?'

'You ask *me* what is the matter? Adulteress, deceiver, wearer of two faces...'

He had gone too far. His normally gentle wife shouted at the top of her voice.

'Be silent, you bully! There is nothing of that kind between Alexander Pope and I. That I love him is true but we have never lain between adulterous sheets. How dare you impugn my good name! I am leaving your house.'

'But not with Melior Mary.'

A look of fear crossed her face.

'A child stays with its mother. That is the law of nature.'

'A child does not stay with a woman unfit to rear it. That is the law of the land.'

'But John...'

'Say me nothing. Go to your room, Elizabeth. I do not wish to see your face.'

She had stood hesitating, then she had turned and gone up the stairs to a chamber known as Sir John Rogers's room, and stayed there the night.

For three days she and her husband had exchanged no word whatsoever, all conversation being conducted through Melior Mary or the servants. But now, on the fourth day, Elizabeth's chance had finally come. John had left at dawn for a full eight hours hunting and, when he and his grooms had finally disappeared into the heart of Sutton Forest, Elizabeth's personal servant Clopper packed as much as she could of her mistress's belongings. The two coaches that were Elizabeth's private property were brought round to the front and, leaving naught but the briefest letter, the mistress of Sutton Place and her child were now proceeding down the drive in the first of them, followed closely by the other bearing the servant and the baggage.

The gates were open at last. Elizabeth's gloved hand gripped that of Melior Mary as they passed through. She did not see that the child's cheeks were suddenly as white as the unknown world outside.

'I shall die without Sutton Place,' said her daughter, almost to herself.

'That is foolish. It is, after all, only a house.'

'But I belong to it.'

But Elizabeth did not answer and it was only Melior Mary's anguished face that peered behind them as the great iron gates swung closed again and the carriage gained speed beneath the snow-laden sky.

CHAPTER 2

The house was the smallest Melior Mary had ever seen, resembling a little pink shell into which she and Elizabeth escaped like two waifs of the sea. It stood in a trim bustling terrace beneath the very walls of Windsor Castle and was as different from Sutton Place as it was possible for the imagination to stretch. Yet, in its way it was comforting—extending to them a warmth that was not only physical.

They had two servants, Clopper—who had come with them from Sutton Place—and Tom, a thin pinch-faced boy of eleven or twelve, who did the menial tasks. Tom was a present from Mr Pope, who had found him street begging, and had decided that nobody as unprepossessing as the wretched child could be dishonest. And after having had him bathed—an ordeal from which he emerged looking, if anything, slightly worse— he had taken the boy to the house in Windsor.

There he had eaten a whole meat pie, been beaten by Clopper with her mistress's walking cane against the time he should misbehave and had stuck out his tongue at Melior Mary. For his misdemeanour he had received a bent and cuffed ear from Mr Pope.

For a man so small the poet threw a considerable blow and Tom had sat whimpering by the kitchen fire until Melior Mary had crept up and emptied a saucepan of cold water over him. With his orange hair flattened like a wet cat's and his grimy blue eyes set permanently at a squint by cruel fate he had resembled a gargoyle.

'Don't yer be emptying any more worter over me or I'll string yer up by the petticoats.'

'And what sort of language is that meant to be pray?'

'It's Dublin talk—for that's where Oi was born.'

'Then small pity they didn't leave you there and you shall address me as Miss Weston in future. Do you hear?'

And with that Melior Mary had deposited the contents of a pudding basin, which Clopper had left half mixed, over his ginger head and marched out triumphant. But Tom has waited his chance and Melior Mary had jumped into bed later that week, only to find the sheets a veritable ice pond of goose grease. She had howled, two bright pink spots had appeared in Elizabeth's cheeks, Clopper had used the walking cane once more and Mr Pope on his next visit, had grimly told the boy to go outside and wait in the carriage. At this things had come to their final head.

'No, Mr Pope, please. I am as much to blame for I put him in a nice torment,' Melior Mary had cried.

Then Tom had said the thing that moved the poet considerably.

'Oi know Oi'm ugly in me face, sirrh. But it doesn't mean Oi'm ugly in me heart.'

To Alexander, the words had such a tragic ring that he felt the tears leap into his eyes.

'Dear Heaven,' he said. 'You must not speak like that child. We are given what God wills at birth. It is only by our acts that we are judged. And if you cannot behave as a good servant to Mrs Weston, who is kind to you and feeds you, then you can only expect to be treated ill. But if you are of a sweet nature then we care nothing if...'

'You *are* ill-favoured,' put in Melior Mary, adding, 'Mr Pope, you'll not make the boy go, will you? He's company of a sort.'

Without sentiment Tom's stumpy hand was extended and she found the squinting blue gaze turned on her with something resembling affection. She had gained a friend for life.

But John Weston was like a giant with a thorn in his toe, leaving the matter of his marriage alone until it began to fester. To his neighbours and friends he acted out the role of ill-used husband with unerring accuracy—at first unwilling to speak and then, tall and brooding, standing within the admiring gaze of Mrs Nelson, Mrs Englefield and Mrs Rackett—and pouring out his heart. There had never been a more admirable man in their view than John nor a more badly behaved wretch than Elizabeth. It was their considered opinion that Melior Mary could come to no good subjected to such an influence and they strongly advised him to remove the child without further delay.

'For what benefit can come of it, Mr Weston? Who knows who might be calling upon her.'

And with that all eyes turned on the unhappy Mrs Rackett—who shared her father with Pope—and she blushed hideously beneath her redoubtable wig.

'I shall have words with her guardian,' answered John, thinking of Sir William Goring with one hand on the Bible and the other on the kitchen maid's thigh. What better candidate for a saintly exposition on the virtue of Christian marriage!

Winter passed and with the first burst of spring the daffodils flowered and Melior Mary, looking at the brave little clump in the walled garden, though of Sutton Place and the golden carpet that stretched as far as the eye could see.

But the season—even though it spoke of regeneration and birth and the old primeval stirring of blood—brought anxiety to Elizabeth. For there among her letters lay the familiar hand of her guardian and on opening it she read:

'Elizabeth,

I have been acquainted with everything you have done of late and I must insist that you have conference with me about the welfare of Melior Mary. The censure of damning lies in the hands of Him Who Sees All but...'

It went on thus for three pages and at the end of it she felt ill. In exchange for her freedom it would seem that she must return her daughter to John Weston. Her brief respite from worry was over.

* * * *

'So as she has not answered your letter, you will see her and demand the return of Melior Mary forthwith?'

'Indeed I shall, John. Indeed I shall.'

Sir William Goring patted his stomach and belched gently into his cheeks. He had just dined magnificently with John Weston feeding on various game, boiled beef, mutton pies, fruit jellies and cream custards washed down with exceptional wine and now given the final touch by a mature port and first-class snuff.

As he took a great nostrilful he thought that he had not been so pleased in an age. But it wasn't the food or drink that was gratyfing him, nor the fact that he had been called in to visit his capricious ward and take her to task—a mission he relished for he liked nothing better than to act the role of stern judge—but the serving girl who had brought him his steaming jug of water and must later run the warming pan over his sheets. She was what had set him thinking. Such a plump little thing with big dark eyes and tumbling black hair and that suspicion of a wink as she bobbed her respects. When he looked again she had been demure but he had noticed it quite surely. And for once his wife had not accom-

46

panied him to Sutton Place being at home with throbbing veins in her legs. His last glimpse of her had been sitting up in bed reading aloud from the Bible, only the frantic lurch of her eye as he had gone out of the room giving him the feeling of alarm which she constantly aroused in him.

But now all other emotions were being swamped by the contemplation of ravishment.

'...and everyone is scandalised by Pope. The Englefields and Mrs Nelson are no longer calling on him. And he has even fallen out with his own sister.'

Sir William snatched his concentration back to John.

'Pope?' he repeated.

'Yes, yes,' said John peevishly. 'That wretched dwarf Elizabeth has taken up with. She must have gone out of her senses but the fact remains they are seen together.'

Sir William pursed his lips into a very small O.

'There's a bad strain in the Gages, John. I feel I may speak frankly of it now. Somewhere—not so far back—there was something amiss.'

'What?'

'A bad marriage—low blood brought in.'

John thought at once of his own coarse grandfather.

'These things happen in most families,' he said abruptly.

'Indeed, yes. But in the Gages how clearly it may be seen. Joseph the rake hell, Elizabeth

47

playing the slut.'

'A harsh phrase,' said John.

'The truth never is pleasant. You must steel yourself. Just as I will on the morrow when I explain the wages of sin to your wife.'

He poured himself another measure of port and drank it in two hearty gulps.

'And now to bed. I shall pray, John, as you must also. If Elizabeth's sin is indeed adultery then it is grievous.'

He sighed heavily and heaved himself out of his chair. John rose also but Sir William said, 'No need to come with me. Finish your drink in peace. Goodnight to you.'

And as he crossed the Great Hall behind the footman bearing aloft a candle branch, his hopes were rewarded. Peeping down at him from one of the musicians' galleries was the sensual servant. He had just time to catch a glimpse of her before she ducked out of sight. But there was no sign of her when he finally arrived at his chamber and saw in disappointment that the bed had already been turned down and warmed. His spirits flagged. His cross examination of her was something he had been looking forward to.

He was just getting into the sheets when his door opened. Without even so much as a knock, the maid stood there. The light from the passageway blinded him for a minute but the he was amazed and excited to see she wore no stitch of clothes.

'Merciful God, girl,' he exclaimed. 'How dare

48

you? What are you up to?'

'Oh, sir,' she answered, 'I've come for your help. For I've the great sin of lust upon me and I've heard that you are a good man who prays regular—and who the Lord smiles upon.'

She smiled broadly and innocently but her eyes belied her.

'You must go away,' he said.

She advanced towards him.

'Oh won't you hear my confession, Sir William? Please sir.'

'And with that she fell on her knees before him, clasping her hands together. Sir William's tongue worked round his lips like a lizard's.

'Leave me you wanton.'

But his eyes had lit with an unpleasant glow and she said, 'Should I show you what men do to me sir? The better that a saintly man like you might understand it. For there'll be things you don't even know of I reckon.'

'All fornication is disgusting,' said Sir William. 'It is a hideous act. But perhaps there is hope of saving your soul. If you truly repent.'

'Oh, I do sir. I do.'

'Then you may act out for me how badly you have been treated in order that I may pray for you.'

She gave him the lewdest wink he had ever seen and fell to kissing his puffy white knees. And all was squeals and panting and drops of sweat as too much weight and age pursued too much depravity and youth, and Sir William in the

49

height of his appalling pleasure called out 'wicked, wicked, wicked', over and over again and she in turn clawed till she drew blood.

★ ★ ★ ★

It was not to fashionable Bath that Elizabeth repaired after her encounter with her guardian but, at Pope's suggestion the little know village of Malvern Wells where they could be quiet together and try to restore their thoughts. The poet had arrived at her house just in time to see Sir William Goring stepping into his departing coach, and inside he had found Elizabeth not in tears but in a far more dangerous state. White to the lips and unable to speak she had sat frozen in her chair and the story had come from Clopper who had overheard it all.

'I beg your pardon, Mr Pope, but he called her an adulteress and a whore and said that Melior Mary must be returned to her father forthwith.'

'And what did Mrs Weston answer?'

'She said never, never, for it would break her heart and there was an end to it.'

'And what did Sir William say to that?'

'He said they would use force if necessary and then he went stamping out and you came in.'

It was an hour before Elizabeth would speak then she said, 'Oh Alexander, they can't take her away.'

'They shall not be allowed. I have an unfinished letter to John Caryll at home and I shall add a post script. Let him try again to meditate. He is a man of great influence.'

'He has already done so once. My guardian ignored it. Alexander, they are threatening forcible removal.'

The poet began to pace the room, his face twitching with distress.

'If I were a proper man I would call John Weston out and settle the matter for once and for all. Nothing would please me more than to put a sword point between his eyes.' His naughty humour bubbled. 'But at my height, alas, all I could manage would be a dagger tip between his thighs.'

Elizabeth laughed as Alexander went on, 'Then watch out Mr John Weston. I'll cut you off in your prime, sir. And you Sir William Goring. And you. And you.'

He was dancing about the room shadow boxing and making imaginary cuts in the air, his wig flying out, his eyes twinkling like a merry fieldmouse which, at that moment, he greatly resembled; the goodness of heart, the greatness of intent, shining out from that poor little body.

And so, two days later, they found themselves bound for Malvern in the company of Joseph Gage who was heading for Bath and would deliver them at their destination.

'I shall lend you Sootface,' he had said on hearing the story of John Weston's threats. 'He shall keep Melior Mary safe.'

'But Joseph, for how long? You can't give me

your servant indefinitely and they could pounce at any time—next week or in a year. The situation is hopeless.'

Joseph had stopped to think, leaning back on his crimson coach lining, one hand grasping a cane the head of which was a brilliant aquamarine. But whether this represented a trapping or an investment to him was not known, for rumours of his wealth were both legendary and prodigious. It was said that he held a greater personal fortune—through land, houses, jewels, various monies and secret, hidden treasures—than Queen Anne herself. And yet no-one, not even his family, knew the answer.

Joseph was an enigma. Rumour upon counter rumour circulated the coffee houses of London. He was a homosexual; he was a voracious devourer of women's virtue. He gambled incessantly; he never touched cards or dice. He dined at dawn; he insisted on sleeping a full night. He had friends in high places; the inner circle would not associate with him. He was a drunkard; he only sipped wine. He was a rake hell, a devil's man, a libertine; he was afraid of women, a Catholic, a man of good character. Such was the manner of Joseph. Nobody knew him—and this was what he wanted. A certain hidden part of him was his own tranquillity. His own secret, private place to which he could fly when he felt the world to be intrusive. And all these question marks were hidden beneath a head that was always fashionably wigged but which really bore thick fair hair; heavy-lidded green eyes that seemed sleepy and often lethargic; a fairly small frame—neither too tall not too fat; and a slow smiling mouth that could charm a lord or a lunatic and yet could, when it chose, turn into a thin and cruel snarl. That was Joseph Gage.

Now he said, 'You would not consider divorce, Elizabeth?'

'Joseph, how could you ask? We were brought up in the same faith. It could not be done.'

He smiled at his sister.

'I think I am a very bad example. Do not listen to me. And yet it seems to me as sinful to dislike John as much as you do and *not* make a final break, as it is to rid yourself of him.'

Pope interposed.

'Every man—and woman—must be allowed to deal with their own conscience in their own way, Joseph. If Elizabeth's belief is stronger than yours it is her affair.'

'Surely, indeed,' said Joseph and his heavy eyes closed with the rocking of the coach and he appeared to drop asleep before them, his hand still grasping the bejewelled walking stick.

In an hour they had reached Malvern Wells, a small village with no particular distinction except for the beauty of its countryside. In no manner rivalling any of the other health resorts— least alone Bath which was the most pleasurable city in the kingdom—it was small and unpretentious and a place where one was unlikely to run into anybody from the fashionable world. For this reason Pope had chosen to go there. With his distinctive looks and early success he was an easily recognisable young man and the last thing that either he or Elizabeth wished was any further breath of gossip.

But, as fate would have it, in the one small lodging house which at its maximum could only accommodate twelve people, there were two other guests who knew them. The first of these was a small, vicious widow with artistic leanings, a deep plum-toned voice that seemed constantly to be masking antecedents of a less high-vaulting nature than she would care to pretend, and an inability to complete sentences; the other was a thin, pale girl who had known Elizabeth since childhood.

The widow encountered them on the stairs, even as Clopper was sorting out the boxes, and said, 'Why, it *is* Mr Alexander Pope isn't...? You will remember me I...Mrs Mire. My late husband knew your dear father and I have always enjoyed your work so... I am very interested in poetry, you...In fact I have been known to put pen to...Perhaps you could care to...Over a glass of claret...This is such a dreary place, Mr Pope. One meets nobody of...But then I come for the smallness of my waist and...They are the smallest in England I dare to...Will you not agree with...?'

She laughed archly and her eyes, as warm as marble, took in the fact that a woman and child stood between the poet. The glutinous voice dropped a few notes.

'Owh! Owh!' she said. 'Mrs Pope? I didn't realise you were...'

'News travels slowly,' said Alexander bowing. 'Good day, Mrs Mire. I do hope we will run into one another again.'

Elizabeth's friend was a different matter entirely. She was so quiet and shadowy that the two women had stayed in the same house three days before they came face to face. Elizabeth was alone taking the waters, Pope having stayed in his room to write and Melior Mary being despatched to walk with Clopper. Thus she was greatly startled to hear a voice say 'Elizabeth? It is Elizabeth, isn't it? Elizabeth Gage?'

She turned and looked into a face of such haggard beauty that it frightened her. Through sheer emaciation the eyes—dark and haunted—seemed three times their normal size and the white skin was drawn tightly over the bones of the cheeks. It needed no stretch of the imagination at all to picture the skull beneath. And yet the woman *was* lovely, with the exhausted splendour of a dying butterfly.

'Amelia?' said Elizabeth. 'It can't be Amelia Fitz-Howard?'

'But it is,' said the girl laughing breathlessly and putting a thin white hand to her throat. 'Or rather it was. I am Amelia Hart now. My husband died two years ago. I am a widow. And you?'

'A wife,' said Elizabeth wistfully. 'But a wayward one. I am separated.'

Amelia smiled but it seemed as if doing so drained her for she gasped and said, 'I am here for my health as you can guess and have discovered a very small but very nourishing chocolate house—though it could hardly boast the name anywhere else—have you time to join me?'

Though the request was in no way pressing it was obvious by the look in the deep eyes, that had been so fine and bold when they had both been girls, that loneliness had been her companion frequently since the death of her husband.

'What a pleasurable suggestion,' said Elizabeth. 'I am here with a poet friend who likes nothing better than to shut himself away and create works for posterity and a daughter who equally likes nothing better than to drag me round looking for trinkets.'

'You have a daughter,' said her companion excitedly, 'why so have I. How old is yours—my girl is nine?'

'Melior Mary is eight,' answered Elizabeth and they embraced each other for the sake of meeting again in that small village with its theraputic spring, remembering as they did so the joys of girlhood and the sweet memories shared.

Settled in the funny little chocolate house which was really the back of the pastry maker's shop glorified with ornate paintwork, they turned to appraise each other.

'Oh don't look at me,' said Amelia,'I know I am but skin and bone and yet I eat as much as I am able. But something wastes me away. It is

56

an ugly illness that will one day catch me up.'

And indeed, on seeing her without her cloak Elizabeth had been distressed at the skeletal quality of Amelia's frame.

'How long have you been like this?'

'Since Sibella was born. I believe it to be a consumption.'

'But do you cough?'

'No, there's the mystery. Anyway don't speak of it. I always seek the miracle cure and perhaps Malvern water will be it. Now tell me of your doings. How long is it since we met? Fourteen, fifteen years?'

'At least. But what of you? Did you not go to your Aunt in London?'

Amelia pulled the corners of her mouth down.

'I fell in love with a soldier. Didn't you hear the whisper? He was hot for elopement and they forced me—away.' She paused for a moment and then said rather hurriedly. 'I didn't really go to London. They sent me to France to keep me from him.'

'It sounds very romantic. Why didn't they like him?'

Amelia stared into her cup.

'I believe he was married already and just fancied himself more the man by maddening little girls with love.'

'Oh!'

'Oh indeed. Anyway I eventually came back with my sin atoned and was married quietly to Mr Hart, a childless widower twenty-five years my senior. A quiet man, not romantic at all, and for some reason the object of my undying love. I do miss him you know.'

The thin fingers were suddenly brushing at her eyes which over-spilled tears.

'Yes,' said Elizabeth, 'love is found in all the unlikely places.'

'I have observed that often. Perhaps because sometimes so little burns between me and death—I do not speak for sympathy Elizabeth—I see more than the proud mistress of Bath or the elegantly heeled of London. Do you understand?'

'Yes.'

'That—and the fact that my early life was so hard. I thought all feeling was dead in me till Richard Hart taught me of the gentleness and tenderness of the human spirit.'

She put out her hand and touched Elizabeth's arm.

'My friend, I believe you to be a good woman. May I entrust you with something—something more precious to me than life?'

Eliabeth stared at her and the dark eyes were suddenly fever hot in the tired white face.

'Do not hesitate. Time is on the side of no-one. Will you do as I ask?'

'Yes. Tell me what it is.'

'If I die—and that I surely will be before another ten years is out—take my daughter Sibella and treat her as your own. Her father had no family and I will not in all conscience see her go to mine. They used me ill, Elizabeth, they used me ill—and I will not allow my child to be put into their bigoted hands.'

She paused and a sudden smile transformed her serious face.

'Do you remember that old story of how my family was originally descended from the Dukes of Norfolk and that our ancestor was a great astrologer and his daughter a powerful witch?'

'Yes, you told me once.'

'That is how we came by our name—Fitz-Howard. Anyway my daughter has that gift I believe.'

'Second sight?'

'I think so. But she doesn't know it yet of course.'

Amelia stopped, short of breath.

'I have talked far too much and far too selfishly. Tell me what became of Elizabeth Gage.'

'She led a boring life in comparison with yours. No soldier lovers, no elopements, only an unkind guardian who forced me to marry money in the shape of a handsome enough man—John Weston —by whom I had a child three years later.'

The next day they found the spring that forced its way up from the dark flower-covered hills and sparkled amongst stones that had known the touch of both men and things immortal. They had walked long and slowly for Pope and Amelia found it hard in their different ways. And so it was with the shout of explorers that they first sighted the crystal brook and Pope dropped down beside it to plunge his hands into the clearness—

raising the water, untainted since time began, to his lips.

'Drink this, Amelia,' he said, 'it has the look of magic about it. Perhaps we have stumbled across the panacea we are both seeking.'

She knelt beside him, her breathing rasping painfully in her chest.

'If it were not for my child I would not bother,' she said. 'I have not been fond of living since Richard died.'

Pope smiled wryly. The war between his fragility and his genius never ceased to torture him and on days when he simply had no strength to pen the thoughts that teemed in his mind he often contemplated suicide.

'This long disease, my life,' he answered.

She smiled humourlessly—one of the few people who understood what he meant.

'Is it cold?' said Melior Mary running up to join them. 'Mother, may I put my feet in?'

Elizabeth nodded, at the same time beginning to remove her own shoes so that they could go in together. The little stream gurgled joyfully.

'How I wish I had brought Sibella,' said Amelia. 'She would have loved this. She is so happy in water.'

The sun seemed to have gone and a wind had come up from nowhere. The words 'in water' inexplicably echoed over again and Melior Mary shivered till her teeth shook. It was a strange, cruel feeling and Amelia obviously experienced it too for she added, 'You will always look after

60

Sibella won't you, Melior Mary?'

'I don't know,' the child answered truthfully, 'for I have never met her.'

'But when you do you will be as sisters.'

The sun had come out again yet Melior Mary still felt uneasy.

'Was that an omen, Clopper?' she said.

'What?'

'That echo just now—and the coldness.'

'You stuff your head too full of stories. Now help me unpack this basket—and put your stockings on.'

★ ★ ★ ★

The evening the lodging house gave its one public dinner of the week for the guests and Pope found himself seated next to Mrs Mire at the long table. Her affected plum voice gushed relentlessly into his ear.

'My dear Alexander,' she said. 'I may call you...I am a great lover of the arts I have...I know every play...Do you believe that William Shakespeare's actors were...I myself perform, you...My late husband was moved to tears and...I am, if I may boast, versatile and, so it is said...'

'Really?'

'Oh, yes, yes. Perhaps you would recite to us a...Or could I do...That would be...'

'Impossible. We are booked for cards.'

'Then I shall play with you,' she said, at last completing what she wanted to say.

61

With Pope dealing she, Elizabeth and Amelia
sat down to a game of ombre but soon grew tired
of playing and it was then that Elizabeth said,
'Amelia, do you remember the fortune telling you
did when we were girls? Would you do it for us
now?'

'Oh,' said Mrs Mire. 'Are you...? I am supposed to be...When my dear late husband was...I
knew, I tell you I knew.'

Amelia laughed.

'It is a tradition in our family that some of us
have clear sight but I think it has eluded me.'

'But nonetheless it's fascinating,' said Pope.
'Please do read the cards.'

He held the pack out to her and she in turn
passed it to Elizabeth.

'Shuffle well and cut into three.'

Though not truly gifted Amelia saw at once
from the seven card spread that Elizabeth would
never marry Pope, that for some unclear reason
she would go back to John Weston and that a
sinister force was forming itself round Melior
Mary. She did not know quite what to say.

'I am very poor at this,' she started with a
deprecating little laugh, 'but you will always be
loyal to Melior Mary, Elizabeth.'

'And my future? Will I be happy?'

'As happy as anybody ever is, I think.'

'Oh dear, that does not sound very bright.'

'You must ignore me. I do not have the family gift.'

But Mrs Mire was clamouring fruitily, her

62

lady-of-town accent growing suspect in her excitement.

'Do me, please do. Aim sure Ay'ave a...Oh, lauk!'

Amelia laid out the cards.

'More husbands for you, Mrs Mire. Two at least.'

'Owh! How shocking.'

But her wicked little eyes looked gleeful and she shot Pope a meaningful stare. And now it was his turn. Amelia saw that he would fall in love—and several times—after Elizabeth returned to John but that nobody would take his broken body to their heart forever. He would die unmarried.

'You are to be even greater than you are now sir,' she said. 'You will be quoted for centuries to come.'

'And will children be forced to learn my poems in school—and hate me for it?'

'Yes.'

They all laughed and Amelia's reading was discreetly ended.

'Then truly,' said Pope, 'I may be said to have succeeded for I shall be detested as Homer and Shakespeare and walk amongst giants.'

A few days later Amelia waved goodbye as Pope and his party climbed aboard the public-stage. Elizabeth turned to look at her where she stood, a gaunt wild loveliness about her, and one thin arm saluting them in farewell.

'Will I ever see her again?' she said.

Unexpectedly it was Melior Mary who answered. 'No. But we will see Sibella.'

The month of July 1711, was drawing to its close and John Weston was unnervingly quiet, his sole interest appearing to be a deer that he was keeping for Pope's friend Caryll which was ruining his fruits and fences.

The poet thought this a good sign but each day of silence found Elizabeth more and more nervous.

Eventually they grew irritable with one another and on one occasion when his head was throbbing with the aches to which he was a frequent victim Pope snapped, 'Oh what is the matter with you? You see that damned tyrant in every shadow. Master yourself, Elizabeth.'

She had made no reply, simply getting up and leaving the room. And, after disconsolately pleading with her to join him again, Pope eventually gave up and went home. After this coolness he did not visit her for several days and so she was alone when the knock that she had dreaded for so long came at last to her front door. Clopper's fearful exclamation as the bolts were drawn back confirmed all. Standing in the doorway of her little saloon, shrinking the house to a joke by his stature, was John Weston.

'Well?' was all he said.

'What do you mean?'

'Where is she?'

Elizabeth burst into violent tears.

'No, John, no. You can't have her. You have

no right.'

'I have every right, damn you. Melior Mary is the heir to Sutton Place and that is where she should be. Not in this miserable cot. Now where is she?'

But a cry from another part of the house told Elizabeth that John's coachman, who had been but a stride behind him, had found the child and that she was kicking and struggling to defend herself. But help was at hand, for looking beyond Weston's massive shoulders Elizabeth saw the fierce blue squint of Tom advancing silently, coal shovel in fist. Her eyes betrayed him. John shot round and sent the boy flying with a kick from his boot. Clopper appeared, nursing a bruised arm.

'You damned bully,' she said.

'Bridget Clopper be silent,' he roared. 'Don't start your familiar tricks with me.'

'You've been familiar enough in the past, John Weston,' Clopper shouted back. 'God damn you for a bastard and a hypocrite.'

Elizabeth couldn't believe what she was hearing but had no time even to think because Melior Mary—her cloak over her head so that she looked for all the world like a poor kitten doomed for drowning—was being carried past the door over the coachman's shoulder. Elizabeth flew at John.

'Leave my daughter alone, you monster,' she screamed, hitting with every ounce of her strength. But to her annoyance he only laughed, picking her up by her hair and swinging her off her feet.

'You shall never set eyes on your child again, madam. Sir William Goring and I will see to that.

'I shall go to law.'

He laughed again.

'Do, do. You'll find they are not over fond of adulterous women.'

He let go of her, throwing her down onto a chair as he did so.

'If I never see *you* again I shall be pleased,' he said and was gone from the house, his booted feet stamping in triumph. Once in the coach he laughed with pure achievement. He had put it right in one stroke. The heiress was on her way home and nobody would ever again get the better of John Weston. He was reckoning without a force so terrible that even he could have no control over the events that were destined to follow.

CHAPTER 3

The night was like a fever—hot and seething with an indefinable tension that made sleeping difficult and dreams strange and shadowy. Outside the land was bathed in light radiating from a sickly moon which veered amongst racing clouds. And with Sutton Place that same light fell on the face of John Weston where he slept alone in his large bed in the master's room, dreaming of the chase.

In his red coat he galloped on a black horse with bolting eyes which had left the rest of the hunt behind and followed a fox into a wood. But when he came up close to the animal, it was to see a vixen sitting there, brushing its tail with a small hand-like claw. And then the vixen looked up at him and he saw that it was Elizabeth, with furry pointed ears and sharp bright eyes, yet with her own legs ending grotesquely in black fox's feet.

'You see,' she said, 'you hunt me but could you kill me?'

'Yes,' he said and raised his whip but could not bring himself to strike the cowering animal. And realising his weakness the vixen fled off, loping through the forest—obscene on her long human legs. And as she disappeared from sight she let out a cry—a cry so distressing speaking as it did of terror and night-fright—that the horse reared and John felt himself falling...falling...

He woke up to find that he had actually thrown himself out of bed and was lying face down on the floor, one of the massive curtains of the four-poster wound round his neck like a rope. And it was as he struggled to free himself that he heard it again. From somewhere deep in the house that awful sound rang out once more, chilling his blood and making every hackle on his body rise.

With trembling hands John untangled himself and lit the candle that stood by his bed. He was not a nervous man, in fact he was what some people would have termed brave, but that terrible sound unnerved him bringing back to his mind something that he had long ago dismissed— the legend of the curse of Sutton Place.

He had heard it as a boy—and had laughed with contempt. It was a family story that centuries before a Viking Queen—Edith, daughter of Earl Godwin and wife of King Edward the Confessor—had called on the old Norse gods and put a curse on the manor of Sutton and its Lord for all time to come. And since then down the ages there had been nothing but a chain of disasters. Two manor houses had been built—the newer, Sutton Place itself—and nobody had thrived in either of them. Death and madness and consistent ill luck being the fate of the occupants. John had thought it so ridiculous that he had said, 'Sir, do you truthfully expect me to believe that a curse laid in 1048 could still be at work?'

His father had looked at him very directly.

'My son, a lot depends on one's deep feelings. There is a theory that each tragic event feeds the malediction so that instead of losing power over the centuries the reverse takes place—it gains in strength.'

'And how has this curse ever affected you?'

To John's surprise his father Richard Weston —the fifth member of the family to bear the name —had grown pale.

'There are things of which I never speak,' he had answered—and he had left the room abruptly.

John had dismissed it all—never given it

another moment's thought in fact. But now he was frightened. Something in his house was terrified in the darkness and he must go and find it—whatever it was—and look it in the face. Furious with himself for being so afraid he left his room, moving into the corridor and standing in silence.

From the Great Hall, below on his right, there was total stillness but by moving cautiously he managed to get himself into one of the musicians' galleries and look down. There was nothing there, only the moonlight playing on the stained glass. And then, rather guiltily, he thought for the first time of Melior Mary and wondered if she could have made that ghastly sound.

But the idea was so out of character. In the three years since he had brought her home and re-established her in his care she had been a model of good behaviour. Never speaking out of turn—in fact rarely speaking. Doing her lessons, eating her meals, never mentioning her mother— a trouble to no-one. But now he thought of her in that strange moonlight and for the first time his conscience troubled him. Had she been too well-behaved? Was the quiet way she had hiding something else? After all she would soon be twelve with the threshold of womanhood upon her.

He left the gallery and headed towards Melior Mary's bedroom which had once belonged to Catherine, one of the daughters of Sir Richard the founder of Sutton Place. There was a portrait of her in the Long Gallery—round blued eyes and golden hair—next to that of her husband Sir John Rogers. He was very dark and naughty-faced, sporting a diamond earring. Their great grand-daughter Elizabeth had married into the peerage—Charles Stuart, sixth Duke of Lennox and third Duke of Richmond. John wished briefly that his part of the family had done as well—he never had, and never would, recover from the shadow that his inn-keeper grandfather had cast upon them. But he had no time to think of that now for he had reached Melior Mary's chamber and was quietly opening the door.

He saw at once that a candle was burning and that the curtains of the bed had been thrown back but whether the mound beneath the coverlet was his daughter or a pillow he could not be certain. He hurried forward and then from the corner of the room she spoke in a frenzied whisper.

'Don't go near it, it's knocking.'

His chest went tight with fear. It was the underlying menace in her hushed tones that terrified him rather than the words themselves. He spun round and saw her sitting huddled in a corner, her knees drawn up to her chin, her eyes enormously dilated.

'Melior Mary what is it?' he said, his voice sounding overloud in the sleeping house.

'Knuckles are rapping on my bed.'

'Whose knuckles?' Who has been in here?'

'Nobody, there's nobody there. I lit the candle but the sound went on. There's something in

70

here that we cannot see.' John wanted to tell her not to be silly, that she was too old for childish fears but a look about her pinched face prevented him. Instead he said, 'One of the servants is playing tricks—or one of the farmer's brats.'

She stared at him in disbelief.

'Come search with me, Melior Mary. My stick will be across their back when I find them.'

But though they looked everywhere it was obvious that there was no intruder in the room.

'Gone,' said John. 'Slipped out of the door as I came in. Go back to bed, my child.'

He put his arms round her to pick her up and felt that she was trembling.

'I don't want to. Let me sleep with my governess.'

'No, Melior Mary. There is nothing here. You can see that for yourself.'

But the incident had shaken him more than he would admit and he decided to take a turn in the long Gallery before trying to sleep again. The windows were flooding with light giving it that strange flame-lit appearance it sometimes had. Since the fire which had broken out in Queen Elizabeth's reign destroying the huge Gate House Tower, most of the Gate House Wing and the part of the Gallery that connected with them, superstitious servants had said they could smell burning or hear the sound of flames and tonight even stolid John had to admit that it was suffused with bright light. Still he walked to what would have once been the half-way point, now boarded

71

up for the sake of safety. And then for the second time that night his scalp seethed with fright. From beyond that partition, from some point that he could not see, John distinctly heard the sound of sobbing. Something was keening its anguish in the ruined Gallery, something that he felt sure could not be mortal. Turning abruptly about John made for the safety of his own bedroom without looking behind him.

★ ★ ★ ★

Elizabeth had had an impossible three years since Melior Mary had been taken away, begging all her friends of influence to intercede with John that her daughter might be returned to her. And Pope so earnestly doing likewise that his reputation had been ruined, and he had been accused by the Catholic set of seducing John Weston's wife. The final stroke to them both had been delivered by Mrs Nelson who had made it her business to call on everyone concerned—especially Elizabeth.

'My dear I feel it is my duty to tell you...' she had started, settling herself in a chair and adjusting her lips into the tight smile that she considered a necessary adjunct to those who sit in moral judgement.

'What?' Elizabeth had asked innocently.

'I feel so sorry for you, my dear,' Mrs Nelson had replied, changing her tack.

'You have seen John?'

72

'I have, indeed I have.'

She fixed her darting brown eyes firmly on Elizabeth and her chin, slacking with the unlovely onset of middle age, wobbled with delight as she said, 'You do realise do you not, my dearest Elizabeth, that you have sacrificed your life for a worthless philanderer—a cruel jester that makes mock of human souls?'

Elizabeth looked at her blankly.

'You speak of John?'

Mrs Nelson smiled serenely.

'No I speak of that trifler—Alexander Pope.'

In her youth Jenny Nelson had been very pretty—young, fair and slim—but her addiction to the wearing of two masks, to the power of holding contrasting confidences, to the placing of metaphorical daggers in the backs of unsuspecting friends, had not served her well. The light hair had grown thin, the body thick, the nose and mouth sharp, the eyes hard. But nonetheless she could still turn a neat ankle and considered herself, in her widowed state, a good match for any man. So the festering jealousy that she had always felt for her own sex—especially for any prettier or cleverer than she—had not been allowed with the passing of the years. So to discredit, to spoil, to disrupt was her creed and her victims the trusting, particularly any who threatened her own chance with a lover.

So now she turned her attention to the putting down of Elizabeth, for had not Pope been her—Jenny's—particular pet? The little poet had said kind things about her own literary efforts and had smiled knowingly—or so she thought. And what mattered his lack of stature? Jenny Nelson was secretly a lewd woman and was not beyond daydreaming about a man's potential on a lust-hot couch. Where, she had convinced herself, Pope would not be lacking in all respects.

'What do you mean exactly?' Elizabeth had asked.

Clopper's entrance with the silver tea tray had given Mrs Nelson time to collect her thoughts.

'Pope has used you vilely,' she said as the door closed behind the servant. 'He is a rake of the worse type. *Both* the Blount sisters, Betty Marriot, Patsy somebody and they say he is mad for love of Arabella Fermor.' She paused just the correct amount of time '...and then of course there is myself.'

'You?' Elizabeth repeated.

'Yes, I. He cruelly misled me about his intentions until, frankly Elizabeth, you came upon the scene. And to think you have sacrificed your poor child for this monster.'

'I see.' Elizabeth sat very still. 'And you say that he takes all these ladies intimately to him?'

'Please!'

'Why should I mince words Mrs Nelson? You do not.'

'In that case I presume he does.'

'And yourself? Did he take your honour in exchange for a promise of marriage?'

Before Elizabeth's direct gaze Mrs Nelson's

74

eyes fell.

'Of course I would not let him have his way despite sweet words.' She looked up again and straight at Elizabeth. 'But then not everyone has my strength of character.'

Elizabeth smiled.

'Marry come up, Mrs Nelson! It's surprising poor Pope found time to pen a line with all this lechery. But I am glad for you that the respectablility of widowhood remained invulerable to the serpent and his whisperings.'

'And what of you, Mrs Weston?'

'Whatever I answer will not be believed. There lies the unhappy choice of the so-called fallen woman. If she admits a second's guilt the happy gossips of this world will clap their hands and cry 'Ah! It was written all over her face.' If she denies everything she will either be branded liar or worse—too unattractive to be asked to join in the adulterous lustings that she supposedly indulges. I do believe you have finished your tea, Mrs Nelson. May I bid you good day?'

But despite her strong stand Elizabeth was upset and the great argument between herself and Pope had started. For three weeks she would not receive him and then finally they came face to face in the street. And he had been forced to admit that he corresponded with various ladies, joking with them of his love and admiration.

'But don't you see, Elizabeth, that it is all for the salvation of my soul? I know I am but a pygmy and so I am blessed a hundred times that

75

you love me. I pretend friendship—no that is not true—*courtship* with these others merely to make myself more the man in my own eyes. Do you understand?'

Oddly enough she did. It was over three years since they had first fallen in love and she knew how his mind worked. It was typical of Pope that he would pursue other women with words while remaining faithful to her.

★ ★ ★ ★

The scream and the rushing wind became as one and in the height of an ice cold midnight Melior Mary woke to terror. The candle which nowadays she kept constantly lit beside her revealed nothing. Yet next to her own warm body something cold sat on her bed and watched her. The air in the room was so chill that her breath fluted into frost and as the wind grew to a roar the knocking began its relentless tattoo on the four-poster's wooden frame. The malevolence was here again to turn another of her nights into agony.

She heard a thin voice which she recognised as her own cry out, 'Christ have mercy on me! God have mercy on me! Leave me in peace!'

For reply the knocking increased in power, beating above her head as if it would mince her skull to baby's bones. With a sob of agony Melior put her head beneath the pillows and thrust her fingers into her ears.

76

On that first night—the night her father had heard her scream—the rapping had continued until dawn, long after he had returned to his bed. Then it had gone away as quickly as it had started. But after that it had taken to knocking both morning and evening for hours at a stretch. And always that moment of wakefulness before it began, that moment of frenzied anticipation before the knuckles of the unknown started their incomprehensible message.

But after that first week it had grown even worse. She would hear it coming to her when she was alone, hear that sound like all the winds from every land that had never known the step of man, howling together and rushing, rushing to get at her. And then when they reached their peak she would know it was in the room for the atmosphere would suddenly become as cold as death and then that terrible thing without form or shape would sit on her bed and she could feel it looking into her face with its non-existent eyes.

She has lost her only friend through it. Her governess—a shapeless, ageless woman of indeterminate brain—but nonetheless a constant companion, had fled from Sutton Place the night after the most terrible happening of all.

Melior Mary had gone to bed as usual, the midnight rushing had begun and then the thing had gone out of control. Downstairs in the Great Hall she had heard it unleash its fury as objects went hurling and crashing. Something was thrown repeatedly against the stained glass and she heard

77

the splintering of the panes as they cracked beneath the onslaught. Furniture was being pulped to fragments as it was flung violently against the floors and walls. She had leapt out of bed and started to run and run and her feet had taken her into Miss Bronwen's room and she had woken the slumbering figure with her wild, uncontrollable crying.

'What is it Melior Mary? For Heaven's sake be quiet?'

'The Great Hall is being ruined. Can't you hear it? Miss Bronwen help me.'

John had been roused, the servants had been roused, the candles had been lit. There had been nothing—absolutely nothing. Her horrified eyes had widened as she had seen that everything stood in its place, the windows not even cracked, not so much as a chair moved. John's pupils had grown black as he had turned his gaze on her and said, 'I've had enough of this trickery, Melior Mary. I'll deal with you in the morning.' But she had been saved the stick by Miss Bronwen's dramatic exit.

'There *are* such things as evil spirits that haunt children, sir. I've heard of it before. I'll not spend another night in this house.'

John had roared, 'Miss Bronwen, you are a totally brainless woman. *You* heard nothing, *I* heard nothing, *the servants* heard nothing. It stands to reason that the wretched child is merely drawing attention to herself.'

'Insult me as much as you wish, Mr Weston.

I am leaving this place forthwith.'

On the night of the governess's departure with only an old and silly servant to protect Melior Mary the malevolence had started its next stage. At about two o'clock in the morning the sleepless child had heard the Middle Enter swing open of its own accord and then crossing the Great Hall with a terrible, shuffling gait the sound had started to come up the West Staircase towards her room. Down the passage, with the noise growing louder and ever louder, she had heard it progress and then the handle of her door had turned and she had watched aghast as it had slowly opened and closed. The temperature plummeted, then something sat on her bed and she knew that she was again in the presence of evil, but that now it was walking, was growing stronger.

'Go away,' she had said. 'Go away.'

The invisible knuckles had rapped their contempt remorselessly and she knew that she was going to lose control if something did not happen to save her. She took her head from beneath the pillows and jumped out of bed, plunging headlong towards her door. She heard the sound stop and knew that the thing was going to follow her but she fled down the stairs, and on to her father's saloon where a light beneath the door told her that he was still awake.

With the malevolence just behind her she flung herself through the entrance and then stopped short. For sitting opposite her father—his legs in their fine silk stockings thrust out before him—and sipping a glass of ruby-red port, was her uncle Joseph and standing a few feet behind him and almost hidden in the shadows was Sootface the Negro.

'Oh help me,' she called out and running forward from its icy presence she collapsed sobbing at her uncle's feet. And as if he knew something, as if he—with all the mysteries of that strange coast of Africa stirring in his blood and his ancient memory—was more aware than others, Sootface leapt in fright and uttered a cry. Joseph looked at him questioningly and the slave simply said, 'The evil eye, Master. It was here.'

John began to say, 'Melior Mary, this has gone far...' but Joseph interrupted him.

'Be quiet John. Can't you see the child is half demented with fright? There's something badly wrong.'

'Joseph, she has been complaining for three weeks of a noise but nobody else hears a murmur of it. It is some childish prank gone hysteric and that's the truth of it.'

'Be damned,' said Joseph standing up and putting Melior Mary to sit in his chair. 'Have you seen her hair? Are you blind as well as foolish?'

'I'll remind you,' answered John coldly, 'that you stay in my house as a guest.'

For answer Joseph merely picked up the candle tree and held it close to Melior Mary's head. The rays fell on the lustrous hair where it sprouted as thick and as dark as her father's and there amidst the jet was the unmistakable sparkle of silver.

'What is it?' said John. 'What's wrong with her?'

'She's going white. It is a condition associated with shock. Now what do you believe?'

John merely grunted and by way of answer said, 'Did Elizabeth send you here?'

'Yes, of course she did. She had a premonition of this and she's been proved right, I'd say.'

Rather reluctantly John nodded then turned his attention to Melior Mary where she sat dwarfed and shrunken by the great chair. And the memory of her like that—the childish face pinched and haggard with suffering and made shadowy by the scarlet flames of the fire—remained with him till his last day.

'What is happening to you, my daughter?' he said.

'I am haunted,' she answered slowly, 'and if something is not done I shall die soon because it is a wild terrible thing.'

There was silence in the room broken only by the crack of burning logs and the spit of summer rain coming down the chimney and hissing onto the fire. Then Sootface spoke out of the darkness.

'Let me keep vigil with her, Master. Let me wait with her until her mother can be sent for.'

'Her mother will never set foot in this house again!'

'Many years ago, Master, when I was a tiny

boy—and before the slavers came to take us—I knew a young girl who had a demon of her own. Nobody else saw it or heard it but nonetheless her father believed what she said to him. And he convinced himself that the house was haunted not the child—and so they moved. He was a poor man and he gave up everything to take his daughter to a safe place. For three months they had peace and then one day it found her again. She was fourteen years old, Master, and she hanged herself.'

John hunched his shoulders irritably.

'What are you trying to say to me, black man?'

'Only that these children's ghosts are to be taken seriously.'

John sipped his port.

'Is this some damned scheme of yours, Joseph? Do you want me to take Elizabeth back, is that it? Because if so it won't work, do you hear?'

Joseph went suddenly and dramatically white to the lips and his eyes were as hard as swords as he said, 'I can see that you are an even greater fool than I imagined possible. For your future I give not a damn in Hell but to see you sacrifice your child to your monstrous love affair with yourself is beyond the limits of human endurance.'

And he was gone from the room, his slave behind him, without another word. Melior Mary and John sat looking at one another, the effect of what had just happened making itself felt on both of them in different ways. Eventually he said gruffly, 'You had better go back to bed.'

She did not so much faint as crumple up like a worn-out doll. She had no energy even to cry, merely putting her head in her hands, her body heaving with silent sobs. John leaned forward and put his hand on her shoulder.

'I shall come with you, Melior Mary,' he said slowly and surprisingly. 'Let this thing face me if it dare.'

She got up from her chair, moving painfully like an old woman, and put her arms about him remembering, as she did so, that time in the Great Hall long ago when he had held her high and shown her the stained glass. The faint smell of outside, of the countryside, was still about him and she felt her love for him flow—just as it had then—despite his stubborness and strange lack of sensitivity.

'Thank you,' she said.

It was very still in Sutton Place as he carried her up to her bedroom, his personal servant following behind them with a pair of candelabra held high over his head. It seemed to Melior Mary, her eyes half closing in the sleep that had been so long denied her, that the malevolence was watching them in the shadows, but by the time she reached her room even this dread thought had gone for she slept peacefully in her father's arms.

John put her down carefully on her bed, drawing the curtains round her. Then he took off his full-skirted coat and his waistcoat and dropped

83

them with his wig onto a chair so that he stood in the moonlight—gazing out over the gardens. He stayed for a long time like this, mind racing over things long ago put into the back of his brain—tales of the curse of the Westons, or rather of those who dwelled in Sutton Place, and how happiness could never be their lot. He thought of his father and wondered what had happened to him long ago; a thing so bad that he would not speak of it even to his own son. And thus with his mind on a treadmill he eventually sat down and let his head sink forward onto his chest.

At exactly two o'clock Melior Mary screamed wildly and shouted, 'It's here.'

John sprang up and threw back the curtains of the four-poster. His child was sitting upright, wide-eyed and terrified, but of anything else there was no sign. Then, without any warning a pool of water appeared on the carpet before him and he himself heard the sound of gushing as another pool became visible by the door. Finally he witnessed what he would not have believed if another had told him. Melior Mary's bedclothes were picked up as if by a hurricane and flung across the room.

'In the name of Christ begone, thou fiend,' he shouted. 'In the name of the Father, the Son and the Holy Ghost leave this room.'

There was a moment's pause and then Melior Mary heard that awful rustling gait go through the unopened door and start its slow progress along the corridor. But even as John put his arms round her to hold her tightly to his chest they heard a sound. In the Long Gallery an object crashed to the floor, followed by another.

'Is it still here?' said John. 'Is it still in Sutton Place?'

Melior Mary nodded her head, her lips forming words so faint that John had to bend his ear close in order to catch them.

'It hates you,' she said. 'It will be revenged because of you.'

He who was rarely frightened went pale.

'Then God protect us both,' he said.

*   *   *   *

'...and if he won't allow you back then I shall take the child from him by force and there's an end to it.'

Joseph stood in Elizabeth's little parlour, an elegant elbow leaning on the mantelpiece, his wig powdered and curled, his clothes a blaze of cinnamon and maroon yet his eyes—belying all his rake of fashion appearance—as hard and glittering as facets of emerald.

'But I do not wish to live with John Weston again. All I want is to save Melior Mary,' Elizabeth answered him rather angrily.

Joseph gave her a very straight look.

'I think the two things may be inseparable but in any event there is no time to lose. If the man won't come to his senses and send for a priest I hold out little hope for her.'

Elizabeth went white and Joseph shifted his weight impatiently.

'You are being very difficult Elizabeth. Get into my carriage now and go to your child. You have no choice.'

She hesitated. She was torn with the two oldest loves in the world—a man and a child—and to worsen the situation Pope, the brilliant sprite, had become like a son to her, running to her arms for protection when the world became too much for him.

'Well?'

'John would not let me in.'

'God in Heaven,' Joseph said loudly, 'you are making difficulties where there are none. I don't know which of you is the more impossible—you or your self-opinionated husband. Good day to you, Elizabeth.'

And he swept from the room, the trembling of his hand on the bejewelled walking cane betraying his anger more clearly than any words. In the sudden silence Elizabeth heard him clatter into the street, shout at Sootface, and slam the door of his carriage. Then the horses' feet were straining at the cobbles and he was gone.

Elizabeth never moved. She sat like a statue staring out of the window, not seeing the great castle that loomed over her house and all the others, nor the patch of brilliant summer sky behind it. She had no sense of time knowing only that her life had reached its watershed. That in some way that would shortly be made clear, she would see that everything had been leading up to this moment, and that the path she trod from now on would lead not only her but those around her to their destinies. She was not surprised to hear Joseph's carriage return, hear him walk slowly into the house, mutter to Clopper and then come and stand silently in her doorway.

She did not turn at first, still so acutely aware of fate's thin finger stretching out to touch her. And when she did finally move her head and see that it was John standing there, and not Joseph at all she felt the constricting chill of shock but no accompanying surprise. They gave each other a long, deep look. It had been three years to the month since they had last met.

She saw things about him that she would not have believed possible. That his eyes were puffy and red and if he had been anyone else other than John Weston she would have thought that he had been weeping; that he came bare headed, his thick short hair dark about his face; that he had not changed his shirt and a button hung loose on his coat. He turned the hat in his hands awkwardly as if it helped him somehow to speak.

'Elizabeth, I...'

She stood up and he realised that she was tinier than he had remembered—a small, fair figurine of a woman.

'I...'

'It is about Melior Mary is it not?

He dropped his gaze to the floor at which he stared fixedly and said gruffly, 'She needs you. I fear for her. Last night...so terrible...I can't...'

He dashed his hand across his eyes.

'Forgive me. I am so tired.'

'What happened, John?'

He looked at her again, neither of them moving by so much as an inch.

'Melior Mary is haunted...'

'I know. Joseph has been to see me.'

'Last night this ghost...demon...went crazed. It displaced all the furniture in the Gallery, tore down paintings, defaced those of my ancestor Sir Francis and his wife—he who died with Anne Bolyen—and threw books to the floor. I told the thing to go in the name of Our Lord—and then she called out for you, Elizabeth. I am asking you, for our daughter's sake, to...'

He could not say the words. He stood before her humbled. For the first time in her life she saw the vulnerability, the pathos of John Weston.'

'I'll come home,' she said.

Still he did not move but looked her straight in the eye and she saw that he had suffered enormously to bring himself so low in humility.

'And what of Pope?'

'I shall write to him today. I shall never see him again. But John...'

'Yes?'

'Let it be as if Pope never was.'

But there John could not control events

88

because, though he and Elizabeth vowed never to mention the poet's name again, the power that dwelled in the little crooked body could never be forgotten by them or anyone else.

John took a pace towards her and stretched out his hand awkwardly, like a blind man. She gently rested hers on his arm and wondered if the change in him would remain and as if reading her thoughts he said, 'You'll find me different, I promise.'

And as he bent to kiss her on the lips she knew that she was truly going home at last.

CHAPTER 4

'I adure thee, O serpent of old, by the judge of the living and the dead; by the creator of the world who hath power to cast into hell, that thou depart forthwith from his house.'

The exorcist stood in the Middle Enter—the name by which the great doors that led into Sutton Place had been known since the time the house was built—and looked about him. He knew, had realised from the moment he set foot in the place the night before, that he was in the presence of evil and that the frightened girl who had been introduced to him was the nucleus of the infestation. So much so that he was half expecting her to appear now as haunted children often did when he began the solemn ritual of conjuration of spirits.

'He that commands thee, accursed demon, is He that commanded the winds, and the sea and the storm. He that commands thee, is He that ordered thee to be hurled down from the heights of heaven into the lowest parts of the earth...'

Something was moving, he knew it.

'He that commands thee is He that bade thee depart from Him...'

She was hidden somewhere and watching his every move.

'Hearken, then, Satan and fear. Get thee gone, vanquished and cowed, when thou are bidden in the name of the Lord Jesus Christ who will come to judge the living and the dead and all the world by fire. Amen.'

He deliberately swept his hand upward in a gesture that set his emerald ring ablaze as he made a triple sign of the cross and, much as he thought, the sparkle of the jewel made her crane her neck. She was in the musicians' galleries above him. He could just see the top of her head. As he always did in such a case he continued with the ceremony apparently unaware of her presence.

He had been a very young priest at York Minster when he had first been called out to exorcise an evil agency from a house. There had been a child present then—a young boy—who had been dragged from his bed by the neck and pinched till the skin broke by his invisible persecutor. But it was only after another two years, and several more exorcisms of the same type, that it occurred to him that a child must always be present for this particular kind of haunting to take place. It was as if they were the unconscious attraction, the force which gave the malevolence its power. After that he had begun to concentrate on the children—praying for them, blessing them, making up his own ritual—cleansing them as well as the house. And it was only then that his exorcisms became famous. For he succeeded where others failed: he had stumbled on the way to banish the notoriously presistent demons that plagued the young. After a while be became known as the Stalking Priest and requests for his help began to come from further afield then York and its immediate surroundings. He was released from his other duties in the Minster by the Archbishop himself in order to become a travelling exorcist.

He had often wished that the law of God did not forbid the marriage of priests for he loved children, had a manner of dealing with them that was partly childlike, partly stern and withdrawn. In this he was aided to an extent by his appearance for though he was tall and thin, with the face and delicate hands of an ascetic, his smile lit up his whole appearance and made him seem boyish.

He had once had the misfortune to smile too much at a seventeen-year-old girl plagued with a cruel ghost and she had fallen in love with him.

91

And he, after wrestling with a conscience greater than any devil he had ever encountered, had reciprocated. He would never forget the shame of the passion, his disgust with his longing, his attempt to thrust away desire for her. But in the end his instinct had won and they had—virgins both—gone together to a bed of love and joy. The punishment had been almighty; his exorcism failed, the evil returned more violently than before and she, bereft of hope, had jumped from the top of Scarborough's cliffs, crunching onto the rocks below. He had made confession direct to the Archbishop and been surprised at the response.

'My son you were tempted by the Devil and punished by God. I do not intend to inflict more upon you, nor do I intend to deprive you of your cloth. I have prayed for guidance and it is God's will that you should continue to scourge evil from the souls of frightened children. Go hence in a State of Grace.'

But though his sin might be confessed and forgiven how could he help his thoughts turning in the midnight watch to that fragile body lying like a broken flower on the rocks that had served as her executioner? How could he ever forget the touch of her hand, the turn of her head, the intoxication of awakenment, his metamorphosis from celibate to lover? And though nothing would ever dismiss the memory and though it was his living torment, he had no wish for it to go. His dreams of her were all that heartened him in a rigid life devoted to calling out the devil.

The child above him was beginning to show herself as he left the Great Hall and started his slow ascent of the staircase, the skirts of his vestments rustling like leaves. As he went he recited the first five of the Gradual Psalms and sprinkled holy water about him, looking neither to right nor left yet aware that she was crouching, terrified, just behind the curtain that enclosed the musicians' gallery in this part of the house. With a measured purposeful tread he began to walk down the corridor to where the drapery hung, crimson and still. He could almost feel the beating of her heart as his footsteps deliberately slowed down.

'Do Thou, O Lord, enter graciously into the home that belongs to Thee,' he whispered.

He took another pace forward and then stopped. In the silence he could hear her frightened breathing but had no mercy for her. The evil that used her as it instrument must be driven away completely, there was no room for scruple or pity.

His voice crescendoed from a murmur to a shout as he said, 'Construct for Thyself an abiding resting place in the heart of Thy faithful servant...'

He paused, one hand grasping the curtain, and as he threw it back he fixed her with eyes glittering in a face transformed by the power that was now flowing through him. She gasped and cowered back as he roared, '...Thy faithful servant Melior Mary Weston.'

His hand with the great ring was in the air above her head and three times he made the sign of the cross. Then so quickly that she did not even flinch he had caught her by the wrist and was forcing her to cross herself.

'Thou art the servant of the Lord and no other,' he said, 'and that which comes through thee is bidden hence. Accursed demon I command thee, depart from this child. For it is I who call thee out and it is I that am God's chosen instrument.'

Melior Mary had gone very pale and he said. 'What is it? Is it here?' She nodded—speechless with terror.

'Be not afraid,' he said. 'The force of God is vested in me.'

And at that moment he had never felt stronger. Something about the child's eyes, violet dark in the height of anguish, reminded him of that long-ago love, of that sweet night voice which called him. The Stalking Priest was ready to protect, to stare the Devil out.

'Oh Lord God,' he said as the curtains were suddenly seized and shaken as if by a hurricane, 'grant that in this house called Sutton Place no wickedness or malicious spirits may ever hold sway.'

As soon as he said it he knew that something was wrong, that his voice was being drowned like that of a dwarf shouting into the wind. Yet the entity that was in his presence had recoiled. Of that he was sure. He said again, 'Grant that no wickedness or malicious spirits may ever hold sway in Sutton Place.' He felt the force surge up in him more violently than it ever had in his life before and his soul danced wildly. Beneath him it seemed that the floor began to lurch. He flung his arms out to shield the child, drenching her accidentally with holy water. He knew what he had to say.

'God of Gods, drive out the malevolence that longs for this child.'

And with that he was falling down and down into unconsciousness aware that the entity was shrieking in the blackness.

★ ★ ★ ★

In a tiny house in Islington Amelia FitzHoward put down the scuttle of coal that she was carrying and her thin claw hands went to her chest. The breath that rasped there had suddenly become indrawn on a weird gasping note. She realised at once that she had reached the end of her life, that the malaise she had been experiencing for the last few days had been the pointer to this moment. The the consumption which had emaciated her to a child's delicacy was finally gnawing at her heart. She knew that she would be lucky even to drag herself as far as her writing desk and take out the two vital letters lying there in preparation for this very moment—one addressed to Mrs Weston of Sutton Place, one to her solicitor Mr Pennycuick. But she must, for the future welfare of two people depended on it—Sibella's and...

She was breathless and blind, her life measuring out in seconds. And then she used that power which, so it was said, had always run in the Fitz-Howards. She spoke to Sibella with her thoughts.

'My poor child do not grieve for me. Go to Mr Pennycuick of Holborn and seek his help then begin your new life with the Westons. Make sure that the lawyer posts *both* the letters. I shall always love you.'

She died beneath the open desk, unable to take another step. She was thirty years old but death had eased the ravaged face to the softness of a child's and she was smiling when Sibella finally found her.

★ ★ ★ ★

'...there is still something amiss, madam. It is in the very atmosphere—and yet the malevolence that haunted Melior Mary has gone. I do not understand it.'

The Stalking Priest shook his head. He sat, out of place in Elizabeth's elegant saloon, on the edge of a gilded chair. All around him the ruched velvet draperies, the soft colours of a woman's private sitting room, were at odds with his stark black garb, his ascetic's face. Even the soft light from the many silver candlesticks could not disguise his illness of ease, his longing to take to the road and find himself once more his own man beneath God's firmament.

Elizabeth was gazing at him perplexed.

'But Father what are you saying? The child is sleeping peacefully for the first time in weeks. She told you herself that it was banished. You have seen the devil off.'

'Apparently. But yet I have never encountered anything so powerful. It was as if an ancient and terrible wickedness reached out to claw my soul.'

Elizabeth shivered and out of the shadows John spoke.

'There is something I must tell you, Father. Something that even my wife does not know. It is said that there is a curse upon this land and those who dwell here.'

In the candlelight Elizabeth's astonished face turned towards her husband and, though the priest did not move at all, a muscle suddenly twitched in his cheek. Without thinking what he was doing he rubbed it with the back of his hand. For a moment or two there was stillness and then Elizabeth said, 'What do you mean?'

As if her voice was a signal John shifted his large frame restlessly where he sat sprawled before the fire, one booted foot crossed over the other.

'Simply that. There is a legend of an ancient curse which has dogged the Westons and the families that dwelt in Sutton before them.'

The Priest spoke.

97

'And how has it manifested?'

'Death usually. Or despair and madness.'

'In recent times?'

'So they say. Francis Weston executed, his son Henry disgraced by Queen Elizabeth, the next heir dying of a wasting disease.'

'And after that?'

John poured himself French brandy from the decanter that stood by a table by his side.

'After that Sir Richard the third denounced in the Civil War as an obstinate delinquent and recusant, his sons—who bore arms for the King—arrested and imprisoned.'

Elizabeth spoke.

'But they escaped—for the elder was your grandfather!'

'Aye he lived but it was no escape to happiness. My grandmother suffered with a wildness of the brain which passed itself on to my aunt.'

'You father's sister? The one who stabbed herself as a girl?'

'Yes.'

John hunched his shoulders and the room darkened in shadow. There was another silence and then the priest spoke.

'And there has been more I believe, sir. You have told us just the bare tale.'

'There have been infant mortalities—the heir is always at risk—too frequent to be deemed normal.'

'And a child that screamed its way to dying?'

John looked at him curiously.

'How do you know?'

'He left something of himself about the place.'

'Who was he?'

It was Elizabeth speaking.

'Lord Charles Howard—grandson of the fourth Duke of Norfolk. I am kin to them through Henry Weston's marriage with Dorothy Arundel.'

The name Howard brought Amelia vividly into Elizabeth's mind and, alongside the thought of how often the Westons and the Howards had crossed each other's paths during the passing of the years, came a premonition that all was not well with her friend. Not that she had seen her since the encounter at Malvern but somehow she knew that the light had gone out on that fragile life.

The priest spoke again.

'How did the boy die?'

'In agony. Some vital organ ruptured within. Dr William Harvey was sent for from London but it was too late.'

There was yet another uncomfortable pause and then Elizabeth said, 'Why did you not tell me of this before?'

'Because I did not believe it.' John rose from his chair and began to pace before the fire. 'Because I am a man who knows what he can see or hear or touch and that's an end to it. And it seemed to me then that a string of co-incidences had been put together and made a whole.'

The priest moved very slightly.

'It is rather difficult to be a believer, Mr Weston. In truth the simplest way is to dismiss phenomena out of hand.'

Elizabeth said quietly, 'But what of Melior Mary? If it is the heir to Sutton who is at risk, what of her?'

'Perhaps,' John answered, 'this haunting was her taste of the curse. Perhaps it is done. Father?'

Remembering the spiral of power that had forced him downwards, whirling and whirring round him till he thought the drums of his ears would split, the priest answered hesitantly.

'I could not say. But I would be careful with her.'

'Should there be another exorcism?'

'No.' He surprised himself with the rapidity of the reply. 'No. Whatever it is—was—should have gone. I bade all evil leave this house.' He paused thoughtfully. 'But perhaps it is not *in this house* as such. Where was the curse laid? Do you know Mr Weston?'

'No. My father only spoke of it once—and I laughed in his face for the fool that I am.'

The Stalking Priest stood up. He was suddenly very tired. Though only forty-two years of age he gave so much of himself in his dalliance with the Devil that he sometimes felt double that. He wished that his call to God had been easier, that his rigid preoccupation with duty had been less of a rod for his back, that he could have been an ordinary priest walking beneath the soaring roof of York Minster, listening to the sound of the choir mingling with the stone as old as time.

'I will call for a blessing upon this house and upon the child,' he said. 'I must spend the night in solitary vigil in your chapel.'

'And on the morrow?'

'I will depart.' He added rather pathetically, 'I have done my best.'

But he was not at ease when the next morning his spindly horse picked its way over the cobbles of the courtyard, past the ruined Gate House and away from Sutton Place. Looking over his shoulder the house seemed to him to have almost a desolate air, enhanced by the falling masonry from what had once been a splendid and lofty tower. Yet his task was done. Melior Mary had been up and about when he had left, awaiting the appearance of an orphaned girl from London who was to follow almost immediately upon the letter which had arrived an hour before his departure.

He had said, 'I believe this to be a God-send, Mrs Weston. In every sense.'

Elizabeth had looked at him and smiled a little sadly.

'Yes, Melior Mary has been very lonely.'

'But your ward will put an end to that.'

'I hope so.'

'They will be like sisters. Our prayers have been answered.'

'And now a carriage was indeed coming into sight, the black leather work a testimony to the hours of polishing and care given by the lads from the stables of John Weston. And as the priest pulled his horse into the verge so that the carriage might sweep past him he saw the occupants distinctly—Clopper the maid and the girl she had just collected from the London stage-coach.

The child—little more than twelve or thirteen years old—turned to look at him and for a moment their gaze held. She was wearing a velvet feathered hat rather too large for her and looking, as it probably had, as if it once belonged to her mother. Into it she had thrust all her hair, so that only one escaping lock showed him that it was the colour of morning, a pinkness mixed with the gold that he had never seen before. The face itself was quite pointed, with firm cheek bones and a small chin, but at the moment it was made sadly comic by the fact that she had cried and dirt from the dusty road had become the river bed of dried out tears. To make this situation worse she had rubbed the back of her hand across her face so that she looked as smudged as a brindle pup. But the eyes themselves were cool and clear, the light green of water. And in their depths was an expression which he recognised as that of the true mystic.

For a long moment they looked at each other—the priest who called out the Devil and the child in whose blood ran ancient wisdom and power. And in that look he realised that she was unaware of her gift, had no inkling that she was different from any other girl who stood on the threshold of womanhood and felt the changes within her. Involuntarily he blessed her, making the sign of the cross. She smiled at him for that and he saw her face transform into one of a beautiful sprite, yet still with that haunting air that would always set her apart. He wondered what she and Melior Mary would think of each other—would there be great love or great hate? And then it occurred to him that if anyone could keep Melior Mary's torturing demon away it would be this girl. So God had answered his prayer more fully than he could possibly have expected. With his heart lightening within him he passed through the wrought iron gates and headed his horse to the north as Sibella Hart alighted from the carriage and looked for the first time at the Weston family —father, mother and child—who stood waiting to welcome her before the great door of Sutton Place.

CHAPTER 5

It seemed to Melior Mary that—just as if it had life and personality of its own—Sutton Place took a liking to Sibella on sight. The rainbow glass of the Great Hall glinted flirtatiously, the Long Gallery made a little whisper of greeting, the Grand Staircase gleamed importantly in the sun. The stranger had been graciously accepted. And, because she was so close to her stately mansion, the heiress opened her heart in accord.

And it was not only she who was kind. John and Elizabeth granted to Sibella the status of daughter of the house. A new-found contentment was everywhere.

But this period of innocence was to be short-lived. At the end of 1714, with the twelve days of Christmas celebrated for the first time beneath the rule of a new King, Joseph Gage came again to Sutton Place. Where he had been for the last year nobody knew. His mysterious business took him as far afield as countries old and dark like Russia, and those of bustle and adventure such as the Colonies of America. And, between those points, he would vanish into Europe for months on end, with never a word to anyone.

Now he walked with a swaggering gait into John Weston's saloon, throwing a fur cloak onto a chair and an Italian dress sword, a-glitter with turquoise, on top of it.

'Damme, John,' he said, 'how goes it with you and Hanover George? I hear you've refused to take the oath of allegiance.'

John hunched his shoulders and darkened his eyes.

'You hear too much for one who's never in England. I'll give you a toast, Joseph. To our true King—James III.'

Joseph took a sip of wine and looked at John through his golden lorgnette.

'Careful, brother-in-law—remember the Riot

Act. Don't voice your opinions before strangers.'

'You're no stranger and you're no traitor, albeit you're the biggest dandy-rake in London.'

'In England actually—or so they tell me!' Joseph's voice took on a harsh note totally at odds with his appearance. 'But hearken to me. These are difficult times. Be careful that you do not end up a marked man.'

He lounged back in his chair, one silk clad knee crossed over the other, looking every inch the cream puff. But his eyes were alert and John knew that the rake had spoken truth. With the death of Queen Anne in the previous August, the country had divided into factions.

The mighty Whig party had backed George, the Elector of Hanover, as future King; the Tories were suspected of having Jacobite leanings, of supporting the cause of James II's son, who lived in Rome and was now hailed by many as James III. But the Whigs had had their way. The Hanoverian sat on the English throne, unable to speak the language of the country which hailed him as monarch. And in his middle-aged uncouth wake came the dissension that had every true Catholic turning their eyes towards the Pretender, and the unrest that had brought about the revival of the obsolete Riot Act. If as few as twelve people met together and refused to disperse on order, they could be forcibly arrested—even at the cost of lives.

'Come to dinner, Joseph,' said John. 'Good food and good wine stop a man from thinking too much.'

So with the Negro bowing before them, the two men had descended the staircase and were just passing the side door that led into the Small Hall when it was flung open. Melior Mary and Sibella—their arms about each others waists and their faces flushed from running—stood in the entrance.

'I *knew* you were here,' said Melior Mary, flinging herself inelegantly at her uncle, 'I saw your black coach being taken round. Where have you been? It seems so long. This is my adopted sister. Sibella, this is our Uncle Joseph.'

But it was no look of little girl to older relative that passed between Joseph Gage and Sibella Hart. He knew at once that he loved her, wanted her and would possess her one day. And she, though the moon cycle had not yet started in her twelve-year-old body, was aware of his passion and lowered her gaze to the floor. She dropped a little curtsey.

'Charming,' said Joseph and raised his lognette with a hand that shook so infinitesimally that only Sootface saw it—and knew at once its cause. Sibella raised her eyes again and gave Joseph a glance that said, 'You will not hurt me, will you?' And Joseph's reply—though silent as hers—said, 'Not as long as I live.'

He adored the child consumingly at first sight.

That his fateful look lasted as much as a minute was doubtful but nonetheless something in it disturbed John for he said, rather too loudly,

'Come Sibella, take your place beside me. Melior Mary, you shall sit next to Uncle Joseph.'

He was deliberately separating his ward and his brother-in-law yet next day, when Joseph left Sutton Place hurriedly, John wondered if he was being foolish. But within two days the rake was back, a necklace of rare pearls in his hand. He clasped them about Sibella's neck.

'There—for you at Christmas. I would have bought you a doll, damme, but could see none that took my fancy.'

John frowned again but the next morning Joseph was off once more, his carriage sweeping round the quadrangle, allowing the watchers in the house a glimpes of his scarlet coat, his snow white wig curling about his shoulders, and the rubies that glinted from his fingers and sword. They were not to see him again for six months.

And during the following three years it was doubtful that he visited Sutton Place as often as a dozen times. Yet his appearances were always associated with great splendour—Sootface running ahead of the carriage, dressed in exotic robes or brilliant livery, a coach following behind that of Joseph full to the very doors with gifts from all corners of the earth. Then a flashing of jewels, a whiff of musky scent. And then gone again.

Between these brilliant interruptions life at Sutton Place appeared to resume the old calm tempo that it had enjoyed before Elizabeth's departure. But this was a total deception. Not one of the Westons was the same person they had been before. And the presence of Sibella Hart—sweeter and kinder than Melior Mary, yet with a certain quality of survival in her character—changed the balance of personalities.

Of them all John was the least affected by the presence of his ward and yet he was, without doubt, the most altered. He had developed a certain secrecy, quite at odds with his earlier years when he would have shown his mood—whether good or ill—to anyone who happened to be in his path. Even more strangely he had taken to disappearing into his study for hours on end and sometimes, in the night, would receive visitors that no-one ever glimpsed.

It seemed to Elizabeth that the midnight waking, the wide-eyed listening to the sound of a softly turning carriage wheel, the muffled clip of a hoof, happened every night. And she resented the fact that he should be smuggling women—for what other explanation could there be?—into the house where she and her daughter both dwelled. But another emotion was growing within her; an emotion that quickened her heart, tightened her stomach and made her clench her fists.

One day Clopper said, 'Why do you cry every time he—' her head jerked in the general direction of John's study, '—has late visitors? You know what he's like. Why does it upset you?'

'I don't like his doxies coming here. Why can't he go to them?'

Clopper chuckled.

'It's warmer here, Mrs Elizabeth. However well set up a Lady of Drury might be, she could never have a dwelling so fine as Sutton Place.'

'I think it is insulting, don't you?'

'Aye, I do. He should have jumped into your bed a good twelve months ago.'

'Clopper!'

But it was true. John had not truly forgiven her for leaving him. Since her return to Sutton Place there had been no intimacy of any kind between them. Elizabeth was paying dearly for her indiscretion.

Her attention was drawn back to Clopper.

'I think it's one of the maddest things. If I were you, Mrs Elizabeth, I'd have the law into my own hands, the very next time one of them comes here. You're as dainty as a doll remember—and they are but ladies of the street. Be his love only eighteen years old she could not help but look a raddled doxy in comparison to you.'

'Clopper, he would never forgive me.'

The servant looked thoughtful.

'I'm not so sure. Perhaps he stands on ceremony with you. After all, being blunt madam, you left his bed for another's.'

The truth was painful and Elizabeth was staring out of the window as she said, 'Do you think it would reunite me with him?'

'Who knows? But if it did it's worth the venture.'

And so after that Elizabeth deliberately lay awake listening for the midnight visitors but—

almost as if they knew—a week passed before she finally heard the sound of carriage wheels coming slowly and stealthily into the quadrangle.

Getting out of bed she crossed to the window and, sure enough, by peeping below she could see a woman's figure, swathed in a hooded and voluminous cloak, and alighting from a chaise. With her heart pounding Elizabeth lit a candle. In its dim light she could see her anxious face reflected in the mirror. She thought of John's eyes and how they turned black when he was in a rage. And then she though of her longing to be true mistress of Sutton Place again. She forced herself to go down the corridor to his saloon and stand, without breathing, listening to the murmur of voices within.

The clink of a decanter against the rim of a glass and the sound of John laughing softly, told her that he and the woman sat alone. She almost turned away again, but something of curiosity gave her the courage she needed to put her hand on the knob, turn it, and slowly open the door.

The scene which lay before her amazed eyes was one that she was never likely to forget. For the woman who sat straight-backed on the edge of the great wing chair was no street slattern. Nor, indeed, had she the over-painted charms of a gentleman's doxy. No, here was a woman of aristocratic bearing, with silver-grey hair swept up beneath an expensive hat from Paris, and manicured hands haughtily grasping the silver handle of an ivory walking cane. John himself sat in a more menial chair, at a lower level than that of the grande dame, and they had both been at the point of raising their glasses in a toast.

There was a fraught and embarrassed silence as Elizabeth appeared in the doorway, finally broken by the stranger saying, 'It would appear that you are being sought, Mr Weston.'

John, glaring furiously, snapped, 'What the devil's wrong, Elizabeth? What are you doing up at this hour?'

Some of her courage returned and she answered icily, 'I might well ask the same of you?'

The finely pencilled eyebrows of the woman rose and Elizabeth was violently conscious of the low neckline of her nightdress and the bareness of her shoulders. There was another awkward pause, during which John glowered at his wife and the two women stared at one another. Finally the stranger spoke.

'My dear Mrs Weston—it is Mrs Weston, is it not?—please do not concern yourself. I am old enough to be your mother and I can assure you that your husband and I are doing nothing more than talking busines.'

'At midnight?'

'Yes at midnight. It is business that we do not care to discuss in daytime.'

'And what business might that be?' said Elizabeth, in a voice undeniably hostile.

The woman looked surprised and said, 'You do not know?' meanwhile shooting John a look

111

of amazement.

'Elizabeth knows nothing,' he answered abruptly and hunching his shoulders—a gesture so typical of him—stared into the fire moodily.

'Oh!'

Elizabeth came into the room, closing the door behind her, and said with dignity, 'I do not feel, John, that this treatment of me is fair. After all I was once mistress of Sutton Place and, willy-nilly, you have accepted me back as such. And I, in return, have up till now turned a blind eye to your nocturnal visitors for, after all, a man must be allowed to satisfy his lusts even if a woman cannot.'

Just for a second John caught her eye guiltily. Elizabeth found herself in good command of her words as she went on.

'Despite my suspicions however, it would seem that you, madam, are of years too mature to allow any bad consideration to enter my thoughts. But I feel that in my position as John's wife, and therefore your unwitting hostess, you owe me—by the very virtue of your rank and breeding—an explanation of your presence.'

Both the grand dame and John stared from one to the other. Finally John rose and said, 'Lady Derwentwater, may I present my wife Elizabeth?'

Elizabeth curtsied slightly and Lady Derwentwater also rose, murmured, 'How dee do?', and turning to John said, 'Your wife has asked me for an explanation, Mr Weston. I feel that it is *your* place to give it—not mine.'

Both women stood looking at him expectantly and John, after appearing to come to some sort of decision, said, 'Lady Derwentwater, we were on the point of drinking a toast when we were interrupted. May I suggest that that toast continues?'

She looked at him very straightly, said, 'I see,' and raised her glass of claret.

'And you Elizabeth, will you drink with us?'

'If the toast is one to which I can subscribe.'

He poured for her and then raised his glass.

'Lady Derwentwater, Elizabeth. I give you the health of His Majesty. Long may he live.'

Very clearly Lady Derwentwater said, 'Our King—James III.'

Elizabeth gasped. It had never dawned on her but the explanation, now that she had heard it, was crystal clear. John had become an active supporter of the Jacobite cause and his visitors, who came cloaked in much secrecy, were fellow activists. And when she knew why the name Derwentwater was familiar. In the failed uprising of 1715—the previous year—when young James Stuart had landed in Scotland and tried to wrest the crown from the newly acceded George I, the Earl of Derwentwater had been his loyal man—and had gone to the block when the Rising failed.

'So,' she said, 'you're both for King James?'

Without saying a word, or even looking at one another, John and his aristocratic visitor closed ranks.

113

'Yes,' he said. And never had a single word held so much in it of defiance, of determination and, in a way, of threat.

Elizabeth raised her glass.

'To James III,' she said—and then she suddenly laughed. 'And to think I had you—forgive me, my Lady—lost in lechery.'

John gave her a strange look and said, 'No, you were wrong.'

Lady Derwentwater cleared her throat.

'Mr Weston, I suggest that we leave our business until tomorrow. I am staying in Guildford and will return after nightfall. I regret any discomfiture I may have caused to you, Mrs Weston. You know, you should not fear other women. You are a fine beauty and, I suspect, well loved. Goodbye.'

And she was gone, turning sideways to sweep her hoops through the door. John held the candle for her and Elizabeth took the opportunity to hurry back to her bed and blow out the light. But her husband was not to be deterred by the darkness, for, after a peremptory knock, he opened the door and walked in, still holding the candelabra.

'Well,' he said, 'you know the truth at last.'

'Yes. Why did you not tell me of it before.'

He shrugged his shoulders.

'The Jacobites are sworn to secrecy.'

'Yes—but I am your wife.'

'Are you?' he said. 'Are you really?'

'You know I am.'

114

'You betrayed me once before. Trust is not an easy flower to grow.'

'No? Neither is love when it is daily trampled underfoot.'

'What do you mean by that?'

'What I say. If you had shown me a modicum of affection in our early years then none of what followed would have taken place.'

'It is pointless to go over that. What's done is done.'

'Yes. But if I am to be anything in this house—mother to the girls, mistress of daily events—you could at least do me the courtesy of keeping me informed. I have been in torment for months imagining you servicing doxies beneath my very roof.'

John looked at her very oddly, his dark eyes glistening with some concealed emotion.

'And why should that worry you?'

Elizabeth sat up in bed, her nightgown slipping about her shoulders.

'If you really want to know I was jealous.'

'Damn you, Elizabeth. Damn you. Do you think it has been easy for me? I *never* knew how to please before you left me—and after that I had my pride. What I would have given for you—just once in our married life—to speak to me of desire, of wanting, of lechery and lust. But you were always too delicate for those things, weren't you?'

He gave a mad, wild shout.

'Oh God! I don't know if I love you or hate

115

you. But I do know that I shall possess you now. Whether you want it or whether it makes you hate me forever more.'

He tore wildly at his clothing, rending it from him so that a good deal of him was naked.

'There see me as I really am. A man—a man who desires you—despite all you've done. Are you afraid of what is going to happen to you?'

'Yes,' she said, 'you must not force yourself upon me.'

But she was feigning. She had never wanted anything as much as she wanted John Weston at that moment, and she loved the feel of his great frame upon her and his relentless hardness pushing its way within.

'You bitch,' he said, 'I'll pay you back.'

But now he was acting too. He had always loved her. Had always wanted to ravish her, to rape her, in the marriage bed and had been too afraid of her delicacy. And now surprise was his reward for she panted and sighed, receiving him with wild delight and moving like a slut.

'Elizabeth!' he said.

But she was too near ecstasy to answer him and there was nothing further said until they both gasped, 'I love you', as together—and for the first time—they swept down passion's cascade and into the pool of pure pleasure that lay quietly below.

CHAPTER 6

The lawns of the mansion house were lit by the reflection of a thousand candles; the white peacock from Araby shook his great tail feathers to the full moon; the sound of music and laughter rang out beneath the star-glistening sky. Sutton Place was en fête.

It was the summer of 1717; the summer when George I and his Court took to the Thames and listened, for the first time, to the rapturous Water Music; the summer when Great Britain was secure in the newly-signed Triple Alliance; the summer when John Weston's daughter was fourteen and to be presented, in all the radiant and unusual beauty that God had given her, to the county and to the Catholic community.

And as to who was the more pleased of the four—John, Elizabeth, Melior Mary and Sibella—who stood by the Middle Enter to receive their guests, it was impossible to say. The great landowner, with his tainted gypsy blood, calmed at last by the passion that his own wife had brought to him; Elizabeth, bearing the radiance of one who has succeeded, for had she not brought all the social set back at her feet, despite l'affaire Pope? Sibella the orphan, brought up in the direst poverty, basking not only in wealth and opulence but also the knowledge that the most fascinating man of his times—the great rake Joseph Gage—was in love with her.

But, probably, of that happy quartette it must be Melior Mary who reached the the highest point of bliss; for sheer beauty had been her gift from nature. The combination of hair silver as a winter moon, eyes the colour of dewed lilac, lashes black as jet and lips like the wild cherry, were superb in her. She outshone everybody of her time. She was born to inspire men and artists. She was the creation of a smiling and generous god.

And all those who came to Sutton Place that night, gasped at the sight of her. The Racketts, the Englefields, the Blounts—all of whom had gossiped cruelly about her mother—did homage in their different ways. Some with jealousy, some with wonderment, some with love. And then they turned their eyes to Sibella, who, with her sprite's smile and strawberry hair, would have been considered the prettiest girl in the country—if it had not been for her adopted sister. And then they said that Miss Weston and Miss Hart must be the two greatest catches this side of London—and wondered if they were rivals.

They did not know, nor could ever guess, that Melior Mary loved Sibella with all her heart. For the heiress knew that—before Sibella came to Sutton Place—her soul had once been under attack from a malevolence that had frightened even the Stalking Priest. And she also knew that this quiet,

118

smiling girl could keep ancient evils away; that the blood of old wisdom ran in her. That as long as nothing came between her and Sibella, nothing of harm could ever approach Melior Mary Weston.

They shared everything. Soon after the orphan's arrival, the old apple lofts—once used by Lady Weston, the wife of the builder—had been converted into two bedrooms. Large bright windows and a cosy fireplace had been put within each, the door that adjoined them left open almost always, and only closed on the most bitter nights when they would lie, each girl watching the fire shadows dance on their individual ceilings, listening to the owls hooting frostily in the trees of Sutton Park.

But now, this night of the great rout at Sutton Place, Sibella—at fifteen—was considered 'educated' and Melior Mary, a year younger, was not. Nonetheless Sibella still joined in their daily lessons of 'accompts'—which would later on help them with their household and gambling money —and French, drawing and painting.

Their study of the 'poetry of motion', conducted weekly by Monsieur Croix, who journied from Guildford in a velvet coat and beribboned wig and who had very excellent ability in toe pointing and all the important dances and who, furthermore, accompanied himself on the violin, she also attended.

Similarly vocal and instrumental music— played upon the harpsicord—were also a weekly

119

chore for both Sibella and Melior Mary. These lessons were taken by Signor Bussoni whose single claim to fame was that he had sung a small solo in the original production of Handel's *Rinaldo*. After this grand opera had passed him by, and he had put on so much weight through depression, that it was now doubtful if any management would engage him. When he was not teaching he helped out in the milliner's shop run by his wife, and would often arrive clutching sheets of music whilst, at the same time, anxiously balancing hat boxes on his enormous stomach.

As to reading and writing, the two girls were considered so advanced in these subjects that formal lessons had ceased and they were left to their own devices and allowed to wander freely in John Weston's library. This, then was their daily life but tonight—when not to be seen at Sutton Place on this grandest of occasions was considered a social disaster—they were the Belles of high fashion. Not little girls but sought-after young women.

Despite the importance of the occasion there were some notable absences. The most senior of these being John's mother, who was now confined to bed with what she termed a frail heart. Regardless of this disability she tackled three full meals a day and several snacks in between, her latest pug dog lying at her side, snaffling what crumbs and morsels it could.

Sir William Goring—Elizabeth's guardian—was not present as he no longer wished to associate himself with the Sutton Place 'sinners', as he termed them. From his mouth there increasingly poured forth talk of the Lord's will, but from his eye peered out a leering goat. He lived on a desert island of his own cruelty.

Neither of the brothers Gage were there. The Viscount—the elder—having been ostracised as a result of renouncing the Catholic faith for the paltry reason of saving his Flemish coach-horses, officially seized during the ill-fated Jacobite uprising of 1715. And Joseph, as always being about the world on his mysterious business. He had sent Melior Mary an emerald the size of a tiger's eye for her birthday.

Naturally Alexander Pope was not invited, though he was whispered of by half of those present. If he had been well-known when Elizabeth had run away, now he was famous. His burning talent had swept all before him as his translation of the Iliad became available in bookshops everywhere. And he also had a new preoccupation in place of Mrs Weston. Lady Mary Wortley Montagu, a woman with literary aspirations, now held sway in his brilliant heart. Jenny Nelson, who had betrayed both him and Elizabeth to John, had been dropped from the visiting list of the Westons of Sutton Place.

But, despite these absences—or perhaps because of them—Melior Mary's fourteenth birthday assembly was spoken of by all, that summer. The brilliant setting, the wealth of the host, but above all the looks of his daughter. It was generally agreed that Melior Mary was Titania incarnate.

'She shall break a few hearts,' they said. 'Think of all that beauty and all that fortune.'

They had reckoned without something; in fact did not know it. She was the heir to the Manor of Sutton and the curse she inherited with that position respected neither beauty nor ugliness, riches nor poverty. She was already in danger.

★ ★ ★ ★

The summer continued, bright and unusually hot. And on the last day of August the sun blazed, as fierce as a fireball, from the moment it rose. It was the type of day when two girls, uncurbed by their governess, might well go to the river and swim—if they knew how. But at least they could remove their stockings and shoes and cool their feet in the clear water. Seized simultaneously by the same thought, Melior Mary and Sibella slipped quietly out of the mansion and headed off through the park.

Many years before, during the reign of Charles I, the third Sir Richard Weston—grandson of Sir Henry, the Hero of Calais, and great-grandson of young Sir Francis, who had lost his head—had had the notion of canalising the River Wey to water his meadows at Sutton Place, and had made a cut three miles long, greatly improving his property.

'He was devious,' Melior Mary had told

Sibella. 'For though he appeared to be a harmless and eccentric agriculturalist he was, in truth, a fierce Royalist and a great troublemaker for the Protectorate. He was forced abroad and was labelled delinquent, so they say.'

'And he was great-grandfather to your father?'

'Yes.'

Now, on this fine morning, with the Stuarts banished from England but sympathies for their Royal House still running high in Sutton Place, Sir Richard the third's young descendant tucked her skirt up beneath her sleeves and began to wade into the canal that he had created. Sibella hung back for a second or two, her eyes—cool as the water that flowed before her—sweeping the landscape. Since first light she had had the unsettling feeling of someone unknown coming into their lives and here, by the river, the premonition was unusually strong.

Yet nobody appeared to be in sight, and she was just preparing to join Melior Mary when she heard a piercing shriek and saw her friend, tipped up like an outlandish swan, threshing wildly with her billowing dress.

Standing helplessly on the bank, skirts in her hands but unable to swim, Sibella was about to wade out, when she suddenly found herself pushed roughly aside and a man dived into the water almost over her shoulder. She knew at once that the momentous meeting had taken place—that nothing at Sutton Place could ever be the same again, that fate had caught them all up.

Downstream, the man had grasped Melior Mary beneath the arms and was swimming on his back towards the side. Sibella hurried towards them, picking up his jacket and his leather hat. And as she did so she noticed, almost dreamily, that he had pinned a bunch of wild hyacinths to the brim in the place where there would normally have been a feather.

Kneeling down, she extended her arm over the water but the young man ignored it, stepping out of the bankless canal and dropping Melior Mary on the grass, for all the world as if she had been a drowning kitten. He next shook himself so that droplets of water showered everywhere. Then he bowed before Sibella so low that his hair brushed against her naked feet.

His features were delicate—like those of the archangel Gabriel—and his look of the heavenly host was further enhanced by the same hair that had swept against her toes. For it curled about his face, thick as an aureole, the colour of wild damsons and with the same texture. By rights these things should have made him girlish, a mince-walker. But he was saved from that by a certain broadness of feature and strength of mouth and jaw, at odds with the sweep of his curling lashes and unusual eyes—the blue of the flowers he had pinned to his hat. His body was slight, elegant, but for all that strong and tough, as contradictory as his face.

Yet he could have had any looks, been as ugly as a toad and defied it. For from him pulsated, tangibly, a zest for life. That he had overcome sadness Sibella felt sure, but nothing of it showed on him. He was eager as a young hound set for the chase. Love for him welled in her heart. She recognised him instantly as the part of herself that sang and shouted, just as she had recognised in Joseph all that was beautiful and splendid and rare.

'Who are you?' she said.

'Matthew Banister. I have come to Sutton Place looking for Mrs Weston.' He peered to where Melior Mary lay coughing upon the bank. 'Surely that cannot be she?'

Sibella stared at him in surprise.

'That is Melior Mary, her daughter!'

She saw him screw up his eyes and peer more closely.

'Why yes—it's a young girl,' he said. 'The silver hair deceived me.' He smiled a little apologetically. 'I am very poorly sighted. Only vanity prevents me from wearing spectacles all the time.'

'You are right,' she said. 'You have beautiful eyes. It would be a pity to hide them.'

'Nonetheless,' he said—and taking a pair of steel-rimmed magnifiers from his pocket put them on the end of his nose. His eyes suddenly loomed large, a haze of dazzling blue.

'Do I know you?' he said, suddenly regarding her intently.

'We have never met,' she answered.

But she was not telling all the truth. She knew that she had stood like this, in much the same surroundings, seeing the thick curled head fling itself back as he watched her. They had been together before—but not in a time or place that either of them could at present remember.

'How strange,' he answered. 'You seem familiar to me.'

She would not answer, merely saying, 'So you know Mrs Weston?'

Matthew shook his head.

'No, I have never met her. It was the Banisters of Calais—my cousins—who told me that I would find employment at Sutton Place. They wrote to her on my behalf, I believe.'

They were so interested in one another that the gasping Melior Mary had gone completely out of their minds. Now they both jumped as she groaned and sat up. The Beauty was looking her absolute worst. A fact which, for no reason that she could explain, gave the usually kind Sibella a thrill of pleasure. Rivalry was in the air so strongly one could almost sniff it.

Aware of nothing Melior Mary was struggling to her feet. Her dress, which had started life that morning as pink and pretty, was a torn dishrag; her hair a witch's straggle; her eyes purplish and staring; her skin the colour of parchment.

'God's wounds and zoonters, I'm sick fit to die,' she said.

For answer Matthew laughed and Sibella saw Melior Mary's eyes—the colour of which was already becoming something of a legend—narrow.

The Beauty was mentally stamping her foot. Sibella was aware of the crossing of a bridge, of the leaving behind of total harmony, of the end of childhood. She made one final effort to restore the old ways.

'Come, you're shivering,' she said. 'We must go back to Sutton Place. This is Matthew Banister who is looking for your mother. Shall he walk with us?'

'He can do more than that,' came the sharp retort. 'He can carry me. I'm weak as a child.'

She was being deliberately imperious but Matthew simply smiled and took off his spectacles, putting them in the pocket of his jacket. It was beautiful—made of doeskin—and, as he put it on, its softness moulded to his body. He suddenly seemed very kind, as if the sweet leather had rubbed some of its gentleness off on him. Sibella found herself full of anxiety. Melior Mary had great power, even if she was not yet totally aware of it, and Matthew Banister's harmless mockery had thrown down the first challenge she had ever had from a man.

'Come along then,' he said.

He was unmoved by her. He thought her a plain child. Sibella sensed his danger and, once again, the feeling of familiarity engulfed her. She longed to protect him—as she knew she had done before. But she said nothing as the three of them set off for the mansion.

Looking through her bedroom window Elizabeth, who had woken late and was breakfasting in bed, could hardly believe her eyes as the raggle-taggle party came into view, tramping through the gardens towards the back of the house.

Throwing a dressing gown over her night attire she hurried down the stairs and so it was, with herself standing on the bottom step, that she first met the stranger who was to alter the lives of them all.

The lively hair bounced as he bowed before her.

'Mrs Weston?'

She nodded her head.

'I am Matthew Banister.'

'Ah yes,' she said. 'I've been expecting you. Welcome to Sutton Place.'

CHAPTER 7

By the light of a rather poor candle Alexander Pope was writing to Charles Rackett, his brother-in-law.

'Dear Brother,

I hope to be with you on Monday next. If you don't see me that night I desire you to send a Man and Horse (such a one as I may ride safely) on Tuesday...'

He jotted down a few more instructions but not being in the mood for one of his lengthier outpourings simply put:

'...which being all the business of the letter I shall add no more than that I am my Sister's and Yours, most affectionately,

A. Pope'

He put the date—September 7, 1717—blew out the candle and tried to sleep. But he could not. He was venturing into Weston territory, planning to stay with the sister who had resumed her friendship with Elizabeth. And for all his passion for the witty Lady Mary Wortley Montagu, for all his defiance of the world in the face of his dwarfish condition, something had taken place between he and Elizabeth that transcended physical love. He imagined that she was destined to be the great fixation of his life. He finally fell asleep with the lines of Elegy to the Memory of an Unfortunate Lady, the poem he had written to her after their parting—now, to his amusement, something of a literary mystery— going through his mind like a treadmill.

★ ★ ★ ★

With many silver candelabra throwing an excellent light on his writing desk John Weston picked up his quill pen and wrote a brief letter to his friend Charles Rackett.

'Sir,

Our Ladies do Design to wait on you and Mrs Rackett tomorrow at Dinner if not inconvenient to you. We all desire that you would make no strangers of us. In which you will Add much to the Obligations of

Your Real Friend,
John Weston.'

He wrote the date September 9, 1717—then snuffing out the candles went to bed.

The reply duly having come by return that the Racketts would be at home, the next afternoon saw Elizabeth, Melior Mary and Sibella in a flurry of preparation which drove John out to ride with Matthew Banister until the house grew calmer.

Elizabeth, standing by the window in the light airiness of her bedroom, saw them go and smiled. Since Matthew's arrival John had improved even further in temperament. It was as if he had always sought a boy's company, looked for the son that she had never provided.

And she was still smiling when Clopper walked in, bearing the great hooped and embroidered petticoat and dress that she was to wear that evening. Elizabeth composed her features and stepped out of her dressing gown so that the maid might begin the lengthy process of adorning her mistress.

Bridget Clopper had always been something of

a mystery. A pretty woman, probably about thirty years old, she had joined the staff at Sutton Place when she had been ten or eleven, and had been in residence when Elizabeth had come to the mansion house as a bride. That she had borne a child by John Weston Elizabeth had no doubt. Their intimacy had been unquestionably revealed when he had kidnapped Melior Mary from the house in Windsor.

And to add proof to Elizabeth's suspicion there was Sam, a large pleasant odd job boy with an identical build to John's and a strong look of Clopper about his face. He had, in the traditional manner, been found on the kitchen doorstep of Sutton Place in a neat, clean basket and wearing neat, clean clothes. There had been nudges and winks then as a directive had come from the master that the baby was to be kept and reared. And speculation had run high when fourteen-year-old Bridget—recently returned from a suspiciously long visit to her aunt—had been appointed his keeper. But despite all this Clopper's allegiance had been with Elizabeth, and she had risen from kitchen girl to personal maid, apparently quite unconcerned by the fact that she had once rolled around the hayloft with her mistress's husband.

The thought now being uppermost in her mind, Elizabeth said, 'How is Sam?' and the odd look that always crossed Clopper's face when the boy's name was mentioned, appeared momentarily before she said, 'He's learning to read and

131

write.'

'Oh?'

'That Matthew boy is teaching him. He's making a lot of changes at Sutton Place.'

Personal servants were as intimate as friends, so Elizabeth laughed and said, 'Is he?'

'Yes, with the young ladies too.'

The pull on Elizabeth's corset was painful and she grimaced a little as she said, 'What do you mean?'

'What I say Mrs Elizabeth. They're changing too. Haven't you noticed?'

'Don't pull quite so tightly. No I haven't really.'

She felt a little guilty. She had been too absorbed in her husband of late, had spent too many hours thinking of the particular magic they had found together, to pay much attention to her daughter and Sibella.

'How have they changed?'

'Melior Mary is quite the Beauty these days. She spends a deal of time smiling at herself in the looking glass.'

Elizabeth paused as the difficult job of stepping into her hoops was negotiated before she said, 'Does she? Well perhaps there's no harm in that. I've always thought her far too much of a tomboy.'

And it was true. Melior Mary had, in the past, developed her own highly original style of life, in tune with the wildness that flowed in her blood from generations of adventures; to say nothing

132

of the gypsies who had sired her grandfather. She had an almost obsessive love of investigation, of seeing for herself if horses were fast, if trees were hard to climb, if stable boys could be teased and not fight back. Yet the girl was charming. There was nothing in her of unkindness or cruelty and she would have given the clothes off her back to a beggar child that might come crying to the kitchens. Furthermore she was bright and amusing with a quick wit and smile that encouraged others to join in. All in all Melior Mary had the making of a high-stirruped young Beauty, destined to make a great and brilliant match, and Elizabeth was relieved to hear that her daughter was showing signs of change at last.

Clopper had begun the difficult task of lacing up the enormous petticoat, heavy with brilliants, and was clucking under her breath with the effort.

'I think you're plumper, Mrs Elizabeth.'

'Oh don't say that for the love of Heaven.'

'It is supposed to be the sign of a contented life.'

'More like middle age. Pull in as tight as you can. And what of Sibella?'

'She's always in a dream these days. If you ask me it's time a husband was thought of.'

Elizabeth made no answer. The petticoat was in place and the full trained gown was now going over her head. She made this the excuse for her silence but really she was thinking that Sibella would be sixteen next spring and after that an

133

eligible husband could, in truth, be sought.

But in her bedroom—the intervening door that led to Melior Mary's room for once being closed—Sibella, unaware of such schemes, sat quietly gazing at a small locket which she had taken from around her neck. When open it showed a miniature of her mother, Amelia, but at the moment she held it closed, simply looking at its bright gold surface. As sometimes happened when she did this, pictures would form in the reflection, and now one was coming of Elizabeth. And to Sibella's amazement it was a very plump Elizabeth. For a second or two she stared at it uncomprehendingly, and then she laughed out loud with pleasure. Her adopted mother was with child! She concentrated hard on seeing more but the picture faded. The flash of clear sight was at an end. She was putting the locket back about her neck when her maid knocked and walked in, her hands full of ribbons and feathers.

'Well, Miss, you are to have your hair put up. Mrs Weston's orders. Who'll be the grand lady, I wonder to myself. And who will be looking for a husband, I wonder to myself. And will poor old Dawkings be kept on then, I wonder to myself. Or will she be thrown out in the cold and not fit to wait upon the Belle of High Fashion with her flunkey's and her footmen?'

Sibella smiled her sprite-like smile.

'I wonder to myself if poor old Dawkings might not find herself a husband before this

Belle, and not wish to go with her anyway.'

Dawkings's expression transformed.

'Do you think so, Miss? Really?'

Sibella looked thoughtful.

'Cross my palm and I'll tell you.'

The maid stared in surprise.

'Can you do that? Do you know the meaning of hands?'

'Perhaps I do. Show me. No, not just the right hand. I want to see both of them.'

The maid crouched before her, thrusting her palms into Sibella's lap. The girl bent her head over them and, as always, found that she did not so much read the lines as use them as a channel for her ancient gift.

'Oh yes, there's a husband,' she said. 'And a long life and a jolly little son.'

'Only one?'

Sibella laughed.

'Husband or child? No, only one of both I'm afraid.'

'Can you tell me more?'

'I could but I won't or we'll be here all the afternoon and my poor hair will hang like Rapunzel's. Set too—or I'll never be ready.'

And it was as well that they started when they did, for no sooner had Dawkings woven the last blue ribbon and white feather into place, than the door to Melior Mary's room was flung open and she stood in the entrance, panting and dishevelled.

'God's life,' she said, 'I am late and now my

maid declares she's lame and I have sent her to bed. Dawkings, can you deress me? Sibella, have you finished with her? You look a vision.' She paused and said more slowly. 'Yes, you really do.' Her pace quickened again. 'Zounds and zlids, there are Father and Matthew returning. That means I'll have an hour at the most. Please!'

Her voice had taken on a beseeching note and Sibella rose to her feet. Her blue hooped gown swinging out over the taffeta petticoat.

'Yes, yes, don't worry so. Dawkings, will you help her? At least she's not having her hair up.'

Melior Mary stuck out her tongue.

'All right, grande dame. I shall have roses woven into mine. That's what I've been doing, collecting them from the garden.'

And from behind her back she produced a bunch of buds of an unusual mauvish pink.

'I hope you've thorned those,' said Dawkings warningly.

'I have—and pierced my thumb in the doing. Now can we get on?'

An hour later Elizabeth and Sibella left the small saloon—there being no sign of Melior Mary—and, wrapping their cloaks about them, sallied forth through the Middle Enter into the night air. They stood for a second till John joined them, resplendent in black velvet with a crimson waistcoat and very grand wig, listening to the sound of the coach being led round from the stable. Then, as it halted before them, Matthew Banister holding the leading rein, they negotiated

136

the difficulties of getting two hopped skirts
through the door and down onto the seats. John
was squeezed into the corner with scarcely room
to breath.

'You're gaining weight,' he said accusingly to
Elizabeth and Sibella, unable to control herself,
let out an audible giggle.

The black coach-horses pawed the ground,
their harnesses like bells in the enclosed sound
of the quadrangle; the ladies' skirts creaked as
they shifted impatiently and John Weston
thumped on the carriage roof with his walking
cane and called out, 'Melior Mary, come upon
the instant.'

And then, suddenly, there she was, as vivid and
as beautiful as a winter fairy with her lilac dress
and silver petticoat enhancing the colour of her
eyes and hair. The roses, woven into a fantastic
garland by Dawkings, only served to give the impression of somebody not quite earthly, as she
paused momentarily in the Middle Enter.

'Well Matthew,' she said quietly, 'am I in good
looks?'

For all her immense beauty she was not yet
fifteen, still only a child, and when he shook his
head her lips trembled.

'What! Am I not?'

'I cannot see you clearly,' he answered. 'Let
me step back.'

He did so and stood staring at her, seeing the
splendour of her for the first time. And he—who
had come to live so mysteriously with her family

and yet whose presence had never been properly explained by her parents, felt his heart-beat quicken then. 'You are exquisite,' he said.

'And *you* are old!' she answered, in that odd, abrupt way of hers.

'No. Eighteen. Little more than yourself.'

'Well you *seem* old.'

He smiled.

'That is because I have had to fend for myself.'

'Why is that.'

'I have no parents. I was brought up by cousins —of a sort—in France.'

'Who were they—your mother and father?'

The short-sighted eyes were fixed in her direction but she knew that, this time, he wasn't really looking at her at all.

'I don't know,' he said.

In the sudden silence the thump of John Weston's cane was almost shocking.

'Melior Mary, if you are not within this carriage in one minute we leave without you. God damn all,' he added for good measure.

'But she still stood looking at Matthew.

'Do you remember that day you rescued me? The flowers that were in your hat...?'

'Yes.'

'What were they?'

'Hyacinths. Wild hyacinths.'

'I shall call you that, for your eyes are the same colour. Exactly. And I shall think of you as my brother and that will make you love nobody else but me.'

Matthew laughed.

'But I shall love many people. I am a young man and have my life to lead.'

Melior Mary's jaw tightened determinedly.

'There shall be no other love but mine.'

And she flung herself into the carriage without another word, her self-lined cloak flying out in the night air.

'Melior Mary...' he called out.

But the mighty horses had started up and he was left staring at the disappearing coach and Melior Mary's frost-like profile, for only Sibella's light eyes turned to look at him as they sped off into the darkness.

★ ★ ★ ★

As Elizabeth slipped into unconsciousness it seemed to her closing eyes that Mrs Rackett's extraordinary wig, topped by three gigantic plumes hung about with diamond bows and flashing winkers, resembled nothing so much as a flag ship dressed overall. And as she recovered to the strong smell of salts, her hostess's anxious face only an inch or two away from hers, the impression was redoubled.

'Oh, my dear—oh, my dear,' Mrs Rackett was saying frantically, 'I should have spoken nothing. I should have held my peace. I really had no wish to upset you.'

They were alone in the hostess's private saloon, Charles Rackett and John lingering over the port,

Melior Mary and Sibella despatched to play cards.

'No, I am much recovered, please don't disturb yourself.'

'Then pray take this sip of brandy. There, that's better. The colour is coming back to your cheeks.'

Elizabeth struggled to a sitting position, leaning against a chair for support.

'You say that Alexander was here?'

Mrs Rackett looked doubtful.

'I am not sure that I should tell you again.'

'Please—I want to know—I have a...fondness... for him still—in sisterly way.'

'Well, in that case...' Mrs Rackett took a pull at the brandy flask to settle herself, '...I will. He arrived here on Sunday from Staines where he'd been at his usual tricks, visiting some poor woman—a Miss Griffin I believe—and keeping her away from church, so he boasted. Anyway he was very social and Colonel Butler called on him on Monday, and they were in wild sniggers over a letter for him which had been forwarded on here. Then John's letter arrived asking to dine and he was off forthwith—most rude I thought it—saying that he wished John's face was horned.'

'What did he mean by that?'

'Well my dear, you know how maddish and silly he is. I believe he meant that he desired John dead—and a horned devil in hell.'

Elizabeth leaned slightly harder against the chair.

140

'He still bears a grudge after all this time?'

'I feel sure of it.' Mrs Rackett's ugly face softened for a moment and she added, 'But in charity Elizabeth, he must still care deeply for you. Why else should he run from a meeting like that? Poor Alexander, I pity him in so many ways.'

'But what of his friend Lady Mary?'

'A blue stocking, a woman of letters—or so she thinks herself. They will fall out, mark my words, and then there will be bitterness indeed.'

Mrs Rackett, heavy with prophecy, took another two nips at the flask.

'But say no more of it, Elizabeth. I hear the husbands coming. Let me help you up.'

And Elizabeth was seated in the chair, albeit pale-cheeked, when John and Charles Rackett came into the room. The question as to whether to continue the evening with cards, or tell John a different version of his wife's spell of faintness, hung about Mrs Rackett's brow for a moment or two, but eventually she decided on the more sensible course.

'Elizabeth had been quite unwell,' she said, 'even losing consciousness for a minute. I believe that you should take her home, John.'

He looked shocked.

'But what was the cause?'

'Goodness alone knows. Perhaps the heat.'

And further than that she would not go as John lifted Elizabeth into the coach and settled her against a cushion. But on the way home they had

141

to stop once more, a feeling of nausea sweeping over Elizabeth, forcing her to dismount and breathe in the cool night air.

'What ails Mama?' said Melior Mary, staring out of the carriage window to where her mother stood, leaning against John, who mopped her brow with a handkerchief of white lawn.

'Do you really want to know?'

The reply made Melior turn abruptly and say, 'Of course I do.'

'I believe she is with child.'

Melior Mary's eyes widened.

'Is it possible at her age?'

'She is not yet forty. Of course it is.'

'But if that were so I would no longer be the heir to Sutton.'

'You would if it were another girl. Only a boy could usurp you.'

'Zlife—it's a strange thought.'

Melior Mary looked suddenly lost then, in a gesture typical of her, shrugged her shoulders. For the heiress adored Sutton Place. Her great inheritance meant as much to her as any brother or sister ever could.

'And you know all this through your strange gift?'

'Yes. But please say nothing. Let us see if my feeling is right.'

And it was. On John's insistence the physician was called from Guildford the very next day, and spent half an hour closeted with Elizabeth in the privacy of her bedroom.

'I believe it to be life's change,' she told him.
'There has been no flux for...'

'Twelve weeks?'

'How did you know?'

He straightened up from his examination of
her abdomen.

'Because you are about that time with child,
madam.'

'Oh, I don't believe it.'

Her eyes rolled to Heaven and she lay back on
her bed in amazement.

'It's true enough. No period of change or
cankerous growth could account for the fullness
of your breasts nor the sickness you have felt.
I congratulate you. The finest way to enter
middle life, Mrs Weston, is to have a babe to tide
you over.'

He stood up smiling to himself and wiping his
hands on a towel.

'Now all we have to do is take care that you
carry the child to completion.'

Elizabeth laughed and wept.

'It would be a wonderful thing for the Lord
of the Manor to have a son,' the doctor went on.
'A *real* heir for Sutton Place.'

Elizabeth was glad that Melior Mary was
nowhere at hand to overhear. Yet the girl appeared to receive the news well. And, after the
evening meal was over, Elizabeth found herself
escorted to her saloon as gently as if she were
made of glass.

'This will never last, tomorrow it will be

"Mother, I cannot find my bonnet", or "Where did you hide my paints?" '

But the girls simply smiled at her and left her to read a book while they went off to their adjoining rooms to be private. However, as soon as the door was closed, Melior Mary's face changed.

'Sibella, will he want me to leave Sutton Place when he inherits? Will I be without a home? Will he love me?'

Her adopted sister did not answer because a cold feeling was beginning to creep over her—something was not right, something wicked stirred somewhere.

'Sibella?'

'Don't speak of it, Melior Mary. He is as yet unborn. Leave him in peace I beg you.'

And in the master's saloon John sat before the fire with Matthew Banister and said, 'I feel like a man made young again. It is a wonderful thing after all this time.' And then because he was in his cups, he said, 'Matthew, I hope Elizabeth and I have done well by you. It was not easy to know what action to take in the circumstances. But there is no reason why you should not sleep in the house, you know. When I put you in charge of the horses I did not mean you to live in the stable quarters.'

John's speech was beginning to slur very slightly and he sunk deeper into his chair, his booted feet stretched out to the blaze, his hands—holding his ruby-red glass—resting on his

144

lap. He was always to remember that moment as one when he experienced pure contentment—something unknown to him before.

'My clerk will want to retire soon and shall have a grace-and-favour on the estate. Would you take the job, Hyacinth? That's what she calls you, doesn't she? That funny wilful girl of mine.'

In the gloaming Matthew moved very slightly, and a log shifted in the hearth sending up a million sparkling lights. The blue eyes stared intently as they focused John's face into sharp outline.

'The answer is yes, sir, to both counts. To work close to you and to speak of our true King, perhaps even to undertake missions for him, would be as good a post as I could ever wish for. And she does call me Hyacinth. I had picked flowers that day and put them in my hat. I don't know why...'

His voice trailed off dreamily and John looked up sharply at him.

'You're fond of her, aren't you?'

'Yes—and of Sibella.'

Because John was the sort of man he was he did not question this, nor did he let his mind wander down any tortuous paths but unbidden, part of an ancient song came to him. 'Three, three, the rivals; one is one and all alone and ever more shall be so.'

He cleared his throat, shifting in his chair, and Hyacinth changing the subject asked, 'Will our King come back to us?'

145

'Who knows. He was badly routed two years ago. Yet I believe he is constantly planning a return.' As if he couldn't help himself John added, 'they say there is a curse on the House of Stuart. Did you know that?' He drank a glass of port down in one. 'There is also supposedly a curse on the House of Weston.'

'I thought it was on Sutton Place itself.'

'How did you find out?'

The blue eyes looked suddenly vague and short-sighted and it crossed John's mind, not for the first time, that Matthew had a fine habit of blurred vision when he did not want to see too much.

'Well?'

'Tavern gossip—the sort that a head stable lad would overhear.'

He smiled quite disarmingly and John went 'Humph'.

'You've very pretty manners when you want, I believe you could be a rogue, sir.'

'I think we all could.'

John gave a sudden laugh.

'Well keep your tricks for the kitchen maids and away from my daughters, do you hear? They may have a brother to protect them one day soon.'

* * * *

That December saw an early frost and every morning the earth was hard and white and the branches of the trees sparkling with rime. Melior

146

Mary and Sibella wore cloaks over their riding habits and Matthew, whose job it was to accompany them daily on such excursions, crammed a hat made of rabbit fur down upon his eyebrows. Behind them, at a distance, rode Tom—he who had been saved from the streets by Alexander Pope—carrying shotgun, for the haunts of the gentlemen of the road were not solely confined to the public highways. In the great stretch of the ice-beleagured forest the iron hooves of the horses sparkled in the whiteness, and the three riders bent low in their saddles to avoid the scratching fingers of winter's branches.

And, on just such a morning, with the first fine fall of snow crisping her cheeks, Melior Mary— whose fancy it was to ride slightly ahead on the great black horse she called Fiddle—set off in the direction of the old ruined manor house, built by the Bassett family in the Middle Ages. Her cloak was the colour of cloves, the fur of her hood had once adorned an arctic fox, and she looked over her shoulder and called, 'Come on,' to the two people she had made her family, as she set off to where the early sun glowed like an orange above the stark ruin.

As usual she was at full canter so that she was lost to view by the time Sibella and Hyacinth— followed by the ever-watchful Tom—had arrived at the place where the skeleton of the Bassett's house reared above a pile of stones that had once been the hunting lodge of a saint.

It was unearthly quiet. Not a mouse moved in

the frozen grasses, the trees were bereft of birds. But the stillness was fraught—uneasy with a sense of watching and listening. Beneath his cambric shirt Hyacinth felt his spine tense, and, glancing sideways at Sibella, he saw that she too felt something, for she moved uneasily in her saddle, her long skirt trailing down to the frost-hard earth as she did so.

And then they both saw it together. Practically hidden by the long grass but glinting beneath the orb of the looming winter sun, was a frozen circle of water. Round, and as light a blue as a blinded eye, it lay hard with ice beneath the gathering snow.

'What is it?' said Sibella.

'It must be a disused well.'

'Used it to serve the hunting lodge?'

'Centuries ago.'

'It frightens me.'

For reply Hyacinth put his hand upon her arm.

They were alone in all that wilderness, nothing about them but the virgin trees and the huge, sickly sun amongst the falling flakes. And it was then that a part of his brain, not subject to his consciousness, told him that he knew her, that she had constantly been his friend through many journeys.

'Who *are* you?' he said.

But she just smiled and answered, 'You know who I am.'

To lean forward in his saddle and salute her with a kiss was as natural to him as breathing.

Yet the kiss was not that of a lover, nor yet that of a brother, but somewhere in between the two. And as they kissed, cheek upon cheek, eye close to eye, lip loving lip, the meaning of their lives became fused forever.

★ ★ ★ ★

The arrival of Sootface—black as a rook against the falling snow—told Elizabeth that, much as she had hoped, her brother would be in residence for Christmas. And sure enough, a few minutes behind the Negro—who ran barefoot in the coldness—Joseph's carriage slid softly, wheels muffled by the drifting white, into the welcome enclosure of the quadrangle. After him, as always, came two carriages, laden with gifts, and he strode through the Middle Enter and stood, looking about him, for all the world like a merchant of the East.

At his feet were heaped sweet-scented woods from the Lebanon, musks and spices from Araby and bales of cloth from Damascus; to say nothing of jewel caskets, boxes, sea chests, strangely shaped parcels, baskets of fruits and cartons of sweetmeat and marchpane. And he himself, without saying a word, was walking evidence of his year-long voyage, for his velvet coat and breeches had been stitched in Russia, his leather boots worked in Poland, his cloak handmade from the sumptuous furs that had had their origin in the traps of the American Colonies. And, even

149

more exotically still, his shirt shone with the silk of Thailand, his sapphire-strewn waistcoat hailed from Cathay and the cascading lace at his chin from Valenciennes.

Yet for all that, for all the wealth he carried upon him, for all his assurance and brilliance, his eyes were nervous as he waited for his first glimpse of Sibella. And there she was! Without any warning, crossing the Great Hall still in her riding habit, and beside her a young man with eyes blue as a springtime wood and hair as red as embers. Without knowing precisely why Joseph sensed danger, sensed that here was his downfall personified, and something about the very stiffening of his back must have alerted Soot-face, for the blackman's hand went silently to the emerald-bright dagger that hung, curved and wicked, from his silken belt.

Sibella stopped in surprise.

'Why Uncle Joseph! We had hoped that you would be here—but had no idea as to when or if at all.'

He bowed and Sootface relaxed his hold on the knife.

'Miss Hart,' Joseph said. 'You have grown up.'

With his eyes he asked her a million questions, but she chose to ignore the replies, and he knew that his suspicions were correct. That the love he had laid at her feet when she was a child was under attack from the young man, who had saluted him politely and introduced himself as Matthew Banister. With the speed of decision

150

that favours those who win the game of life Joseph knew immediately what he must do.

'And am I to be treated differently because of it?' she said, half jokingly.

'Yes,' Joseph answered evenly, 'quite, quite differently.'

But there was not time for any more for, from upstairs, came the sound of laughter and the sight of Elizabeth, plump as a partridge and rounding nicely to a child, met Joseph's astonished gaze. Holding her arm and doting with love John walked beside her. And, as if she knew that a family party was foregathering in the Great Hall, Melior Mary flung open the Middle Enter and stood, a veritable snow maiden with flakes on her eyelashes and cheeks.

'Why, Uncle Joseph,' she said, 'what are you doing here?'

Joseph looked about him aware that he had the undivided attention of everyone present. Then slowly he moved to where John stood on the bottom stair and made an elaborate bow. There was a moment's silence as everyone gazed in amazement and then, sweeping his eyes round till they finally came to rest on Sibella, he said in a quiet but extremely clear voice, 'Sir, I have come to ask you for the hand of your ward—in marriage.'

CHAPTER 8

In the silence of his small room in the stable block Hyacinth woke and instantly knew fear. It seemed to him in the hazy blur that was all his poor eyesight allowed, that something moved in the far corner of the room. He peered and for a second saw quite distinctly what it was. A funny crinkled face with hair cut as round as a basin was looking at him and shaking its head as if to say 'No'.

In one movement he had found his glasses and jumped out of bed, and yet aided by their magnification and a hastily lit candle, he saw that there was nothing. A trick of the moonlight had combined with his half-waking state to produce a weird hallucination. But nonetheless he rose from his bed and, throwing on his shirt and breeches, made a thorough search not only of his own quarters but downstairs in the stables themselves.

And as if to confirm his suspicions Fiddle, black as Hell and capricious to match, was pawing the ground and rolling his eyes whitely whilst Sibella's mare, stood trembling. Only Ranter—Hyacinth's mount remained placid in his stall.

Outside the winter moon blazed in a star encrusted sky and the snow sparkled a million points of diamond where the frost lay heavy upon it. Yet, for all the bitter chill, Hyacinth found himself reaching for his fur hat and leather coat and throwing a saddle over his horse's back. The illusion of that jester's face, grinning at him yet with a sense of warning, had ruined his repose. And now he wanted to be free in the coldness and think through the hundred and one different emotions that had become his pleasure and torment since he had first arrived at Sutton Place.

Quietly over the cobbles he led Ranter out so that the sleepers in the great house would not be disturbed. But once in the parkland he mounted and went at the gallop over the glittering ground to where the trees grew thick and dense and he felt that he was solitary with his soul.

And then what thoughts came to him. He saw again that lonely boyhood with the Banisters of Calais—who were in some remote and unimportant way connected to him; remembered only too clearly his search through the villages and towns of Europe in a quest for his parentage; recalled the shock of the extraordinary letter from England telling him that Mrs Weston of Sutton Place awaited him. And then, on arrival, learning nothing from Mrs Weston, who, for all her affability and charm, for all her kindness and sweetness of nature, either could not—or would not—give him the answer he sought. Matthew Banister nicknamed Hyacinth, and adopted by the Weston family as if he were one of their own,

153

had no more information now about who he really was than he had on the day he arrived at the mansion house.

And, as if to add to his sense of isolation—for he would have appreciated the wisdom of a father or brother so much at this point—had come the torment of passion. He was not old enough yet to know that love can wear many masks, that it can flow like a mighty river into different tributaries and brooks, that it is never the same thing twice. And because he loved Sibella as one would love a sphinx, cherishing the timeless quality of her, he was shriven with guilt because of the fascination which Melior Mary's beauty held for him.

For some mysterious reason he found he had been walking while he thought, and that he stood on the edge of a thicket. The trees there grew so dense that they leaned one upon the other, and even the infiltrating snow had been unable to penetrate the ground they covered. Why Hyacinth pushed his way through the tangled mass he never afterwards knew, but push he did, and by dint of much snapping of twigs and squeezing his body through narrow gaps he forced his way in.

And then he stopped short. For lying there was a sad solitary skeleton resting on its back, its gaunt eye sockets turning towards the heavens, its stick arms cushioning its head. That it had died there, hiding itself rather than being hidden. Hyacinth had no doubt. Yet it had not

154

suffered for there was no contortion, the body being as calmly arranged as if it had lain down for an afternoon sleep. How he knew it was a Romany gone back to the wild for his ending he was not sure.

And then he realised that at least one other person had seen this sight before him, for a hand-carved cross of wood was stuck in the ground above the skull and on it was lettering. Bending low over it Hyacinth was just able to make out the weather-worn inscription—'Giles of Guildford sleeps in peace'.

★ ★ ★ ★

It was Twelfth Night, and the great low-roofed barn that had stood on Sir Richard Weston's estate from the time Sutton Place had been built, was for this one night of the year transformed from its dark guardianship of the hay and was now a veritable palace of noise and splendour and brilliant light, thrown by the motliest collection of equipment ever seen collected in one place. Rushlight holders view with brass candlesticks from the cottages and beside these jostled silver candelabra from the big house. And all filled with a selection of candles made from the coarsest homemade tallow to scarlet wax brought from the East.

It was a scene of vivid colour, a brazier of glowing embers throwing its light over the dresses of the farm girls and wives and the flowing gown of Elizabeth, who rested on a chaise specially brought down from Sutton Place. She clapped her hands and tapped her foot to the tune of the fiddler, who sat perched on a stool above the heads of the throng, beading them with drops of sweat as he flung the bow across the strings as if Hell's host were calling the tune.

Everybody except for the very old and the very young was dancing; stamping and clapping in time and calling out the steps, echoing these shouts with cries of 'whoops' and 'whee'. And every now and then the door would open and the snow would pour in over the dancers as a man would go out to relieve himself or entwined couples would disappear into the bitterness of the night. And on these occasions there would be a glimpse of the white stillness of the home park and the breathless beauty of Sutton Place as it towered above all. But tonight it was ignored for everyone was in the barn, guests of the Lord of the Manor, feeling like kings and dancing like princes.

Against one wall stood trestle tables loaded with food. Pies and puddings crowded mammoth beef sides and giant hams spilled over haunches of game and jugs of hare. Trifle, jellies and custards nestled alongside vast tarts of fruit and great iced cakes lay waiting, white as brides, for the first insertion of the knife. Drink flowed in profusion—ale for the peasants, wine for the gentlemen and gin for those whose stomachs were strong enough. And all the while the fiddler went for his life as the dancers shrieked for tune upon tune.

Joseph, in his shirtsleeves, had removed his wig so that his cropped thick hair shone in the crimson light. He had taken Sibella round the waist and carried her half off her feet as they went skimming breathlessly the length of the barn. Melior Mary meanwhile, with holly berries in her silver hair and a dress of winter green, brought the young men almost to blows as they challenged one another for the honour of dancing with her.

And Hyacinth, galloping valiantly and fast with Old Fat Phyllis—stared at them both—and, cursing himself, collided with Bridget Clopper so that there were loud peals of laughter and his attention was distracted. So much so that he did not notice when Joseph put on his coat and, helping Sibella into her cloak, stepped outside with her to where the shrill fiddle and the laughter were muffled and the ice glittered on the farm yard stones, and little ponds shone like crystal. Nor did he see that they stepped quietly into Joseph's carriage, hidden in the shadow waiting and ready to drive them, silently and unnoticed off into the darkness of the trees.

'You know why I have brought you here?' Joseph said, as they finally drew to a halt on the edge of Sutton Forest.

And because she had old wisdom and was not a foolish empty-headed girl she simply answered, 'Yes' and waited for him to go on.

'It is because, though John Weston has agreed that you may be my wife, I want to ask you myself. I am thirty-four years old and you are not yet sixteen. Sibella, do you love me? Do you want to marry me? Or has that boy Matthew stolen you from me?'

In the great whiteness of the night every detail of their faces showed. His so worldly and strong-featured, hers so small boned and clear-eyed.

'Oh I *do* love you,' she answered. 'My love for him is as for a friend, a companion. An eternal one. Do you understand?'

His mouth sought for hers. And to his infinite joy she leaned against him. And though, to him the mystery of her love for Hyacinth deepened still more Joseph did not give it another thought, merely ordering Sootface to drive deeper into the forest where he, Joseph, might defy the laws of good behaviour and rob her of her virginity—the carriage curtains drawn against the moon—her body carried by his over the final rapturous threshold of womanhood.

* * * *

In the long barn the noise has grown wilder as drink was drained till the mugs stood empty. Elizabeth had long since been escorted back to Sutton Place but Melior Mary still whirled and turned and laughed with everyone but Matthew Banister. Like the Queen of Winter, with her green forest dress and her holly red wreath, she teased her way amongst the bucolics occasionally allowing one an extra glance, which would set him jostling and pushing to dance with her again. But at last, with the old fiddler slowing his pace and sinking his head upon the bow, she found herself before Hyacinth and bobbed a curtsey in imitation of a farm girl.

'Well, Brother Hyacinth,' she said, 'you find time for me then?'

The vivid eyes flashed.

'I had thought, Miss, that the boot was in the other stirrup.'

She tossed her head and the silver cloud of hair flew round her face.

'Well, who's to argue? Are you going to scowl or shall we dance?'

He had never held her quite so close before and the sensation amazed him. He was at once, from head to foot, on fire.

'Do you love only me?' she whispered.

He nodded the halo of curls, speechless.

She pushed him away.

'Are you struck dumb?'

And turning she started to thread a path between the bounding dancers. A premonition swept Hyacinth as he pushed and heaved his way after her and, at last reaching the coldness of the night outside, heard the thud of hooves. Melior Mary had taken one of the farm horses and had headed off towards Sutton Forest.

★ ★ ★ ★

159

Very slowly, the curtains still drawn, Joseph's coach was easing its way through the snow towards Sutton Place. Inside he and Sibella sat together intimately her head resting upon his shoulder and her eyes closed. She was weary to the bone with her first taste of a man's love. He could think of nothing but the presents he would shower upon her when she was his wife, for his latest speculations had paid of handsomely and he was amassing another fortune through Mississippi shares. It had once been rumoured that he was richer than Queen Anne, and that had not been true, but now there were even wilder rumours and they *were*—his fortune equalled that of George I.

Thinking about these things made him say, 'My darling, I must go away in January to get you a crown. When I return we shall be married and you shall wear it on your wedding day.'

She laughed and kissed his cheek. The musky scent he wore was in her nostrils and, she was just thinking how happy her life could be with him when, as if to plague her, there came a sudden beat of hooves and a thunderous knocking on the carriage door.

'Good Christ!' said Joseph, and a cocked pistol was suddenly in his hand, seeming to appear from nowhere.

Outside they heard Sootface give the cry of 'Whoa there,' and heard the four Flemish horses rear and whinny in the traces. The knocking

160

came again and Joseph, springing to his feet, threw open the door and with the same gesture thrust the pistol beneath the very nose of the intruder.

'One move and I'll blast your damnable head from you body,' he said.

But the rider shouted, 'Don't shoot. It is I—Matthew Banister. Where is Melior Mary?'

'I don't know,' Joseph answered angrily. 'Is she not at the party with you?'

'We disagreed and she rode off somewhere,' Matthew replied.

'Then you're an even bigger fool than I took you for.'

All Joseph's anger was aroused, his jealousy and resentment combining with the thought of what Hyacinth might have seen had he come upon them a mere ten minutes before.

'How could you let my niece go off on such a night? If any harm comes to her the fault lies with you. Is this how you abuse my sister's kindness to a wastrel bastard?'

For answer Hyacinth's fist shot through the open door and sent Joseph flying onto his back.

'Take that back.'

Joseph got to his feet.

'Matthew Banister—I have never liked you.'

And with that his hand too went flying, knocking Hyacinth clean off his horse and crunching into the snow. And not content with that he jumped out of the carriage and stood, fists at the ready, waiting for his assailant to rise that he

161

might knock him down again.

They set about one another, hitting like schoolboys, the blood from their noses dropping like crimson flowers upon the snow. It was Soot-face who ended it. Jumping from the coachman's seat as light as an opera girl for all his great size, he picked up the two combatants by the coat collars—one in each hand—and swung them above the ground like puppets.

'Enough Master Joseph,' he said, 'and enough from you, sir, who dares quarrel with the greatest man in London. It is Melior Mary who rides out in the darkness. It is she who must be sought.'

He bumped them painfully onto their feet. 'You, get into the carriage.' He jerked his head towards Hyacinth. 'Let your horse free.'

He fixed them all with a great dark look.

'If there is one word from any of you—and that includes you Miss—then you *walk* back to Sutton Place, for *I* go to search for the heiress and will not return without her.'

At Sutton Place John Weston strode up and down and when—in the cold, dead hours of the morning—and four miscreants returned, as wet and bedraggled as a band of gipsy rovers, he took his belt to the three young people and would not listen to one word of excuse. Joseph was requested, in the curtest tones, to leave upon the morrow and not return until the eve of the wedding.

A mood of depression fell over them all.

162

★ ★ ★ ★

In February, with her baby six months grown in her womb, Elizabeth stumbled and fell in the garden. Not badly but enough to jerk her into precipitate labour, as the life-giving bag of water in which her child dwelled was ruptured untimely and he was forced to make his entrance into the world without the strength to withstand it.

She laboured for many hours, for she was thirty-eight years old and lacked the strength of a younger woman and at the end of three days her tiny little boy was born. He lived for a few minutes and then gave up without the help that his pathetic attempts at breathing required. He was labelled John Joseph Weston and was given a full Christian burial. And, as the minute box that excused itself as a coffin was lowered into the earth, John Weston wept and thought of the curse that lay upon those that owned Sutton and how his wild and beautiful daughter was the heir once more to everything of which he stood possessed.

Spring saw the snow finally go, for it had been a long and savage winter, and it also saw the birthday of Sibella—born under the mystic sign of Pisces, that which had been marked in the sand by the followers of Christ in order to identify themselves.

The proverb of March 'in like a lion and out like a lamb' came true almost at once. The

163

weather grew suddenly warm, into full flower
came the famous lawn of daffodils where Francis Weston had once walked with Rose; his child,
Henry, in his arms. And Melior Mary took to
rising at daybreak and going to where the River
Wey ran safely and sweetly, that she might teach
herself to swim.

But for all the earliness of the hour her disappearance did not go unnoticed, for Hyacinth,
down in the stables as soon as he was dressed,
would find Fiddle gone. But yet when, some
while later, he would breakfast with the family
the heiress would be sitting with them demurely,
as neatly dressed as if she had been at her toilette
since sun up. After a week of observing this new
whim, he decided to follow her.

The morning was like a flower. Everywhere
the birds were in full throat and the scents and
sounds of spring murmured. But, as the sun tipped its golden orb up, apparently out of the river,
the murmur changed. Every creature on earth,
from small spring-legged lambs to the great three-
tonned bull that grazed alone in his pasture
kingdom, lifted their heads to sing. Or that was
how it seemed to Hyacinth. Every mortal thing
gave voice in a hymn to their god—to Pan who
piped for them his fierce, sweet notes at dawn—
and gave them a new day, a new life and the
miracle of a new season.

And she—Melior Mary—was all part of it. She
rode before him on her great black horse wearing a simple shift—and she was shoeless; her bare

164

feet thrust into the stirrup and round her shoulders her hair clouding like that of a goddess.

She reached the River Wey and he stared as she waded on horseback into the flowing stream. It was like a legend—the stark black animal, the white-clad maiden, the crystal river. They could have been making their way to Camelot! He saw her dismount on a tiny swan island where the wild flowers grew in profusion, watched as she threaded together the sweet violets to crown her head.

His heart thumped so wildly that he must have made a sudden move for she looked up and saw him. She said nothing, merely smiling as he rode into the gurgling water. He reached the island and he, too, dismounted, scooping up handfuls of flowers to throw into her lap and entwine around her in fantastic garlands.

Then she did something that made him draw breath. In one sweeping movement she threw off her shift and stood before him naked in the dawning. She transcended human beauty—she was perfection. She had been born that men might die of joy.

And after that the spilling of her virgin's blood into the dark earth, the pain of her first embrace, were all part of spring's rite. She was the maiden for sacrifice, Matthew the devouring god, as he drew her nakedness beneath his and together they became one in that bounteous and teeming dawn light.

CHAPTER 9

The air of Will's Coffee House, which stood within the bounds of Covent Garden on the corner of Bow Street, was redolent with the pungent mixture of a hundred different smells; smells interesting, smells offensive, smells pleasant, wafted one upon the other to become a distinctive and ummistakable whole—the aroma of a fashionable London meeting place.

To John Weston, entering the long room which was partitioned off into rows and rows of boxes obtainable from a central aisle—and throwing his cloak upon a heap of others that steamed wetly before a blazing fire—the smell meant more than just a coffee house. It meant to him the town, the capital, the metropolis—the place from which he would, at the earliest opportunity, make his escape that he might return to the air he could breathe.

For not for him the common meeting ground of every wit and litterateur, every politician and financier. He would as soon be standing in one of his fields, inhaling fresh air and listening to the triumphant throating of birds, than be here sniffing the various stinks of mankind odoriferously combining with tobacco, coffee and burning wax. And furthermore his ears assaulted by

166

conversation, coughs, the farts of the fat, the shrieks of the beaux. In fact he was on the point of turning and going out again when a clutch at his arm prevented him.

A pert ugly girl with protuberant eyes and no figure to speak of stood before him. Her mob cap and apron identified her as a serving girl but, despite this, she gave him a look that stripped him naked before she bobbed a curtsey and said, 'Squire Weston, sir? Captain Wogan told me to look out for you. He said that you would be a well-set-up country gentleman. Tall and broad like.'

Despite her unappetising appearance John could not help but pinch her cheek as he said, 'Really? I would not have described myself quite in those terms. Where may I find the Captain?'

'At the fourth table on the left, sir. You can't miss him—he's a big, lively fellow, like yourself. It's a change in these times to see a man of decent proportions. I can tell you. Zlife, I sometimes think I'm surrounded by midgets.'

She rolled her frog's eyes meaningfully and John cleared his throat.

'You call out to me the moment you want serving, sir. I'll be there in a trice. I'm known as Dolly—Dolly dainty foot.'

A bellow of laughter came from a hidden source and a voice said, 'And she'll serve you more than coffee if you've half a mind, Mr Weston,' and John turned to see the figure of the Captain rising from the high-backed settle that formed one side of their 'box'.

'She's mad for tall men,' he added in a lower tone, 'I think she believes it indicates vast proportions in all things.'

The stranger cracked with laughter and John was left a few seconds for contemplation of the man whose family had, since the time of the Civil War, fought to the death and bare-handed for the King that they considered God's annointed.

Charles Wogan had indeed a fine lofty carriage and the thick black hair and twinkling blue eyes which gave him the look of an Irishman. John understood the Captain's ancestors had indeed come from that island, but certainly they had been firm-rooted in English soil when an earlier Captain Wogan had distinguished himself in the Royalist army against that of Cromwell and the Commonwealth. And now his descendant emulated him. In the Jacobite Uprising of 1715—three years ago—Wogan's life had hung in the balance after James Stuart's rabble mob had savagely attacked the armies of King George I. He was without doubt one of the bravest and most loyal men in the Jacobite movement and yet to see the creature before him slapping his thigh and wiping his eyes on his sleeve, John could scarcely credit it.

Rather pompously he said, 'Do I have the honour of addressing Captain Wogan?'

The figure opposite him immediately straightened and hissed, 'Not so loud, sir, for God's sake. There is a price on my head to this day.'

Somewhat chastened John sat down saying, 'Forgive me, I had forgotten.' But as Dolly set coffee before them and went off to do Wogan's bidding as he called for a pipe, John added, 'But what of her? She knew you for who you are.'

Wogan smiled.

'There's no harm in Dolly for all her love of things large.' The corners of his eyes started to crinkle again. 'She'd as soon betray her mother as betray me. There's an—affinity—between us.'

He gave a grin and John laughed aloud.

'A man of valour in all spheres of battle it would seem.'

Charles nodded.

'So I've been told, sir. And proud of it.'

'But what of the business of today? You summoned me from Sutton Place.'

Wogan lowered his voice and glanced about him before he answered.

'It is he who dwells in Rome, sir. But you had guessed that.'

'Yes.' John's voice was equally low. 'Is all not well?'

For reply the Captain grinned once more.

'On the contrary! He is to go a-courting. He has set his mind on marriage before another year is out.'

'High time! He's played the field long enough. Who is the lady?'

'There are several in view I believe. But wherever his choice finally lands be assured that it will be one of the highest and fairest in Europe.

169

Remember that she will one day wear the English crown.'

Just for a moment the blue eyes held the blazing fire of the fanatic and John knew that however hard he might champion the Jacobite cause he could never, even in his most zealous moments, be subject to the emotion that the Head of the House of Stuart roused in the gallant Captain.

'And what part does he who dwells across the water want me to play?'

Wogan looked wry.

'The usual one, I am afraid. In order to win a Princess the exchequers must be full. He is calling upon his supporters to provide funds.'

'I'll give you my bill of hand immediately for a hundred guineas. That should pay his tailor for a new waistcoat.'

They both smiled indulgently. The thin elegant figure in Rome was their hope for the future and if he should wish to take a wife and sire a Prince so that the Stuart line might continue, they both thoroughly approved. And that their King should look his best as he kissed and courted the Princesses of Europe seemed perfectly natural to them. If he had not been asked for his contribution to the royal household John would have been astonished.

With no more to say on the matter they fell silently to enjoying their pipes and letting their thoughts wander with the smoke, and the meeting would have passed off quite happily if John had not suddenly heard a shrill voice saying from the next booth, 'He's mad, of course. I tell you Joseph Gage runs stark, staring mad.' This was followed by a high-pitched girl-like laugh and the rumbled reply of the speaker's companions.

'His latest exploit,' the voice went on, 'is beyond the pale. My dears, it is utterly outrageous.'

John's body stiffened as he pressed his ear to the settle back which concealed him, and Charles Wogan looked up enquiringly. Scribbling, 'He speaks of my wife's brother' on the bill of fare John motioned him to be quiet.

In answer to an inaudible question the speaker continued 'He has found himself a child bride, you know. He, who has been to more whore houses then I have to mass, is to wed a girl of some sixteen years. And, they say, he is crazed for love of her.'

Somebody obviously asked the identity of the girl for the prating voice went on, 'The ward of some country gentleman of means, I believe. Not that her dower will matter a whit or a jot to our Master Joseph for he has acquired such enormous wealth through his dealings in Mississippi shares that he could buy out a King—and this, my dears, is precisely what he has tried to do.'

'What?' said somebody.

'Yes, yes.' The voice was high with excitement. 'It's the talk of the Court and will be all over London in a trice.'

'He has tried to buy out the King?'

171

'No, no. Not our King.' The speaker was a trifle impatient. 'No, he has been to Poland—where they haven't two miserable kopeks to rub together so weak and inept is the sovereign—and made him an offer for the royal crown.'

There was a stunned pause and then a roared guffaw. Charles Wogan raised his eyebrows and wrote on the bill of fare 'Is this true?' John shook his head and shrugged his shoulders extending his hands outwards.

Furthermore,' the speaker went on in triumph, 'he has also been to Spain and offered to buy Sardinia from them—for thoroughly bored and depressed the Spanish are with the wretched place and like to give it away at any known second. Our friend Gage's reason being—you will not credit this—that he wants the island for a *market garden.*'

'I don't believe it!' somebody said incredulously. 'The whole of Sardinia to be used for growing vegetables?'

'That's Master Joseph for you. All wedding presents for this little girl I'll warrant a guinea.'

John was on his feet and into the next door box before Wogan could draw breath, his tall frame looming suddenly large over the group that sat there. Without saying a word his hand shot out towards the speaker—an effeminate young man with scarlet ribbons in his wig and shoes and a mouth fully pursed and pouting.

'Eh?' said the exquisite, thoroughly startled.

'You can say what you will of Joseph Gage for

172

he is a law unto himself and answerable to no man for his actions—though it is my contention that half London envies him his wealth and his strange ways—but you are impugning the good name of my ward, sir, and that I will not have. I demand an apology, sir.'

'Then you've got one,' said the young man hastily.

'Hmm,' said John. He paused not quite sure what he should do next and finally said, bringing his finger once more to within an inch of the beribboned man's nose, 'But let there be no more talk of her. She and Joseph are to be married within two weeks and I'll have no blight on their wedding.'

He turned back to Charles Wogan but to his infinite surprise where the Captain had been sitting was now an empty place. He crossed to the table and saw a note tucked beneath the candle stick.

'Dear friend,' he read, 'though my true heart lies in a good brawl I am in no position to attract undue attention to myself. Send your bill of hand to the address below in Essex Street. There are friends there and your gift will be forwarded to he who will appreciate your generosity. I remain your loyal and obedient servant, C.W.'

It struck John very forcibly just how dangerous a life it was for James III's agent in an England ruled by Hanover George. And the thought brought with it a thrill of excitement. John determined to see if anything further could be done

173

to aid the King's marriage plans.

★ ★ ★ ★

On the eve of Sibella's marriage to Joseph Gage there was a quiet over Sutton Place and Hyacinth, who had felt strangely unwell since he had risen that morning, found himself more ill-at-ease than he could ever remember.

The pain in his head grew worse throughout the day and he set himself the task of cleaning the brasses and leather that would adorn the horses on the morrow—Sibella's wedding day—in the faint hope that working with his hands might do something to ease the tension.

And then it happened. There was a roar in his ears as if his head would burst and he saw dimly that something was reflecting in the brass blinker he held in his hand. He peered at it and to his horror the mist cleared—and even with his poor sight he was able to see that a picture had formed, a picture that moved. He saw Joseph and Sibella walk down the aisle together—she fair and delicate, he exquisite in white satin coat and breeches. Behind them walked Melior Mary like a winter rose. The picture faded as an overwhelming sense of disaster gripped Hyacinth as tightly as a hand at his throat.

The reflector slipped from fingers that could no longer hold it and, as Hyacinth's knees buckled, he sat down quickly on a bale of straw. A slight sound behind him made him jerk his head round and in an almost sinister fashion—for had he not just seen her in that extraordinary miniaturised scene?—Sibella was standing in the doorway watching him closely.

'Have you got clear sight?' she said, so quietly that Hyacinth could hardly credit that those were the words she had actually used.

'What?'

The voice was louder.

'Do you see visions, Matthew?'

'I...I don't know. I saw an odd reflection, that's all.'

She turned so that her back was towards him.

'I have it you know, and always have had. It frightened me at first. Yet the gift has run in my family for centuries.'

'Who are your family?'

He had never asked her before though he couldn't think why he had not.

'The FitzHowards. We are descended from a Romany who had a child by the Duke of Norfolk. They say she was burned at the stake. She had ancient power and her son, who read the stars, knew many great things. Yet his daughter would have been the mightiest of the three had she not been struck dumb.'

'What happened to her?'

'She shut herself away from the world and became a bride of Christ—a nun. It is from her brother Jasper that we are all descended.'

'Did *he* have power?'

'No, he was a wit and a courtier to Queen

175

Elizabeth. Though I have heard it said that he was beseiged at Calais and fought bravely for Queen Mary belying his foolish manner.'

'I was born in Calais,' said Matthew softly.

'Yes, I know. An ancestor of Melior Mary's also fought in the citadel when it went under siege. That was Henry Weston. Perhaps all our forebears were acquainted one with the other.'

'If they were I shall never know of it for I believe myself to be a bastard. I only have the name Banister by courtesy of the family who raised me.'

'Perhaps your awakening perception will help you. Perhaps you will one day know the truth.'

'I hope so—and yet I dread it. I have the feeling that if ever I do learn, it will not be what I want to hear.'

Sibella turned back to look at him.

'I think that you are destined for God, Hyacinth.'

'What do you mean? That I am going to die?'

'We are all going to do that. No, I meant to study closely the true meaning of things.'

In the dim light of the stable they stared at one another, Hyacinth's hair a glowing ember in a shaft of the dying sun.

'Do *you* know who I am?' he said.

'No. I have often asked but for some reason the answer is never given. You are a man of mystery.'

Hyacinth looked at her closely.

'Do you love Joseph Gage?'

176

'I always did. And yet I love *you*. But you know that.'

He nodded his head.

'Yes.'

'I have no explanation for it. I would follow you to the end of the earth if you called. How else can I describe it? It is like two souls living in one body.'

'Exactly.' He turned away abruptly. 'It tortures me constantly because of Melior Mary.'

Thinking of the reflection in the blinker he added very suddenly, 'But, when you are married we must not cross each other's path. You must keep to your own life, Sibella, and I must keep to mine. If this strange affinity is not broken there is danger for all of us.'

'For Joseph and Melior Mary as well?'

'Yes.'

She took two paces towards him.

'Will you kiss me?'

And how well-known was the feel of her body in his arms, the brushing of that gold pink head against his shoulder, her lips upon his neck. He had kissed her once before and felt their souls unify. Now he kissed her to break the enchantment. Whatever it was that plighted them one to the other must be shattered into a million fragments.

He pushed her away abruptly, the jaw and mouth that were so at odds with his gentle beauty suddenly hard.

'Go to your wedding, Sibella. Too much is at

177

stake here.'

She straightened herself, the clear eyes losing their faraway expression.

'I pray that no ancient magic will threaten us,' she said.

'It must first overcome me,' he answered grimly.

★ ★ ★ ★

Sutton Place was alive with the sound of bells as peal upon peal from the Church of Holy Trinity, Guildford, told all the county of Surrey that, following ancient tradition, a bride was to go from the great house that day. And, just as two hundred years before when Ann Pickering— known as Rose—had married the son of the house, the mansion had been bustling since long before dawn as the Great Hall was once again bedecked with all the flowers that the June gardens could provide. Roses tumbled upon garlands of gillyflower; jasmines scented the air; the subtle blue of forget-me-nots wove amongst silver-grey lavender and the rare and exquisite morning glory had opened its bells in an indoor arbour created by the head gardener.

In the kitchen, as always with a family wedding, the cooks had worked all night and the great cake iced and shaped—by the clever use of wired and cascading beads—into the appearance of a tiered fountain, rested on its own table covered with gauze clothes. At the last moment, just

178

before it would be carried in at the end of the feast known as the wedding breakfast, the chief cook would spray sparkling wine onto the baubles to heighten the effect.

The musicians' galleries had been cleaned and now, even though it was still an hour before dawn, the players were getting their instruments and music stands into place. Gone the sackbuts and crumphorns of two hundred years ago and in their place French horns, German flutes and English trumpets, mingling with viols, basses and a harpsichord. The sheet music of Mr Handel's *Water Music* was being put on the stands. Mr Joseph Gage, the bridegroom, had apparently attended the famous *Water Music* party the year before when George I and his Court had taken to the Thames in a flotilla of sound, and the exquisite notes had drifted into the night sky until dawn streaked the river. So impressed had he been with the glory of the evening that now he had requested the music especially for his wedding day.

In the upper apartments the serving maids worked on the dresses of the ladies of the house; frill upon frill, flounce upon flounce, painstakingly pressed by a chain of stove-warmed irons brought up from the kitchens wrapped in thick cloths to keep the heat in. In pride of place hung the bride's gown—lace from Valenciennes formed the rhinestone embroidered petticoats, while the gown itself swept to the floor in a swath of rustling white satin. Beside it hung the embroidered veil brought into the family by Dorothy Arundel—kinswoman of the Duke of Norfolk and wife of Henry Weston—and worn by the brides of the house ever since. And to crown all was a sparkling diadem that had once adorned the head of a Hungarian Princess. Unable to buy the jewels of Poland Joseph had settled for another ancient symbol of wealth and power. To match it were a necklace and ear droplets that flashed out their splendour even in the pale morning sun.

And, as dawn rose over the mansion house, the army of gardeners and boys sallied forth to sweep the upper drive and the quadrangle to make all clean for the troop of carriages that would come from every part of the county, and even from London itself, as the most brilliant wits of the day rubbed shoulders with squires and country-folk, all in order to celebrate the marriage of the great rake Joseph Gage and John Weston's ward, Sibella.

And in like manner the stables and the coach house shone and the horses and carriages gleamed, that they may not be dull in comparison with the equipage and steeds of the visitors. Over-seeing this was Matthew Banister. He stood amongs the shining coachwork, his spectacles magnifying his eyes to a blue haze, as he sought for an offending speck of dust, a mane not perfectly brushed, a piece of straw out of place. He had come from Calais in mystery to an English manor house that had taken over his life;

he had found love and pain, beauty and despair, and with the ancient knowledge that was growing inside him he knew that somewhere in Sutton Place lay the answer to everything. The key to his destiny was enclosed within its walls.

At exactly ten o'clock the major domo, resplendent in his scarlet livery, threw open the Middle Enter and at that signal the carriage that was to take the bridegroom to church drew up outside. The private chapel at Sutton Place had fallen into disuse at the time of the persecution of papists and, though mass was still celebrated within its walls, so great a crowd as would attend today must go to church like countryfolk if they were to see the couple wed.

Standing waiting for his master, wearing golden robes and a turban in which flashed an emerald the size of a humming bird, was Soot-face. And as Joseph appeared in the great doorway—the doorway that had seen the arrival of Ann Pickering as a bride, had welcomed in Elizabeth, the queenly daughter of Henry Tudor and Anne Boleyn, had marked the passing of Sir Richard Weston's body to Holy Trinity—the destination of the wedding party at this moment —the mighty black man did something that he had not done since Joseph had found him as a beggar-child in London. He bowed before his master and, as Joseph gave him his hand to help him into the carriage, the Negro kissed the bejewelled fingers and said, 'Till the end of my life.' And then he was up onto the coachman's seat with the two little flunkeys jumping up behind. Inside the house the musicians struck up the grand overture of the *Water Music* and with a crack of the whip Joseph was off.

And after him went the carriages carrying the family until nobody was left except John Weston and Sibella. Standing at the bottom of the West Staircase and looking up to where she descended, her servants holding her hooped skirt on either side to make her passage easier, John sensed somebody watching them both from the shadows. For a moment he did not recognise Hyacinth for he had changed from his work clothes into a fine suit of velvet and his thick curled hair, though not bewigged, was tied back with a ribbon.

'Matthew!' he said.

But Hyacinth did not hear him. He was gazing up the stairs at Sibella with a look that struck John to the soul. For everything of tenderness, of kindness and of cherishing was written on his face. That the young man loved his ward John had no doubt for the pride of a father, the companionship of a brother and the obedience of a son were also in that long all-embracing stare.

And then as the bride of Sutton-Place reached the bottom stair Hyacinth stepped forward. From behind his back he took a sweet-smelling bunch of morning roses, scattering them beneath her feet all the way to the Middle Enter that she might leave the house on a carpet of flowers. She said nothing, putting her hand into John's as if she were still the child who had first come to

182

them in poverty. But in the doorway she stopped and turned back to Hyacinth.

'Goodbye,' she said.

And then she stepped into the bridal coach, her flowing train of satin helped in by her servants. Hyacinth made no reply as he got into the small carriage behind hers and sat down opposite John. And the Lord of the Manor obviously had no wish to speak for he immediately called out a command and, simultaneously, the two coachmen cracked the reins over the horses' backs and the little cavalcade went off at a trotting pace down the drive, out through the great gates and away to Guildford in the sunshine of that sun-filled June morning.

And at the church what merriment, as the bride's carriage and that of John Weston were brought to a halt in the town by the large crowd. For every worker—man, woman, child and infant —that lived on the estate had joined in a great procession numbering over eighty couples, all hand in hand and all wearing blue cockades to mark the occasion. In front of them, half dancing as they went, proceeded three fiddlers and a bagpipe player, scraping and blowing with all their might. And this, added to the cheers of the entire population of Guildford turned out to watch, practically drowned the merry carillon of marriage bells that rang out from the steeple of Holy Trinity.

Women in the crowd pressed forward to see the bride, men shouted congratulations for the sake of hearing their voices, children shrieked as they were pushed to one side. A fist flew somewhere and there was a scream as a hand cart bearing fish was turned over. John leaned out of his carriage window and used his walking cane on the shoulders of those pressed closest. Abuse was hurled and whips cracked in the air but finally they moved on and with the sound of the organ swelling out to greet her, Sibella alighted.

Pushing and shoving the estate workers heaved their way into the church where they stood, hats in hands and feet shuffling, at the back of the pews behind the grand assembly of London socialites who sat—powdered, patched and heavily perfumed—chattering like magpies and irreverently unaware of their solemn surroundings. And yet in all that glittering assembly there was one face above all others that stood out in beauty. In a dress the colour of damask rose and a hat of tumbling ostrich feathers, Melior Mary awaited the arrival of her adopted sister. And who could tell what emotions beset her as her black-lashed eyes searched the congregation for Brother Hyacinth who lingered a moment before he, too, swept off his hat and walked into the shadowy and history-filled atmosphere of Holy Trinity.

But there was no time to look at him for an unspoken murmur was going through the congregation. Joseph Gage had risen and, flouting convention, had turned to face the church door. As he lifted his gold-handled lorgnette to his eyes the diamonds on his hands were only equalled by those that blazed from the throat of Sibella Hart as she walked alone towards him.

In the sudden silence only the thin voice of the old cleric piping the opening words of the ceremony could be heard and, as the couple knelt before him and in God's sight were joined to one another for the rest of their lives on earth, the tears of Matthew Banister passed unnoticed amongst all the others that were shed that day.

CHAPTER 10

As the graceful trading ship, with the coat of arms of the house of Gage fluttering at its masthead, slipped from its moorings at Dover a skittish wind billowed all the sails so that she took to the water like a swan. And, standing on the deck and looking up to where the white canvas stretched joyously towards the morning sun, Sibella laughed and clapped her hands. She was a woman and a child in one, her eyes bright with excitement, her mouth sensuous with the love it had already experienced at the hands of her bridegroom. And he, exquisite as ever in a rose-lined purple cloak, laughed with her, seeing everything afresh through her eyes.

For, for all his rake hell reputation and mad wild ways, he loved her even more than before. That there would ever be a Mrs Joseph Gage,

London society had thought unlikely, but that she should be an unknown sixteen-year-old girl from a remote estate in Surrey, they would have deemed impossible. Yet Joseph cared nothing for their opinion. He knew where his heart lay and as far as he was concerned if she had been a street urchin he would have done the same thing.

Softly he said, 'Sibella, know that I will do my best for you.'

'You already have.'

And she turned in the sunshine so that part of his wedding gift to her—a great glittering zircon from Siberia set in a nest of pearls, a ruby ring from India clasped by claws of gold and emerald earrings from Turkey hung about with diamonds—flashed magnificently.

'My dear, bedecking you with jewels is not enough. That merely satisfies the whim of a wealthy man. No, I meant that I will serve you as a person.'

His green eyes had lost the languid air which usually disguised what he thought and shone at her like the gems he had bestowed.

'Sibella, do you love me? For I was determined to have you though the world go to Hell in a casket.'

For answer she slipped her arms round his waist, feeling the embroidered brocade of his waistcoat scratch against her skin. With her cheek against his chest she answered, 'I would like to stay forever like this, protected and safe from everybody.'

186

The expression on Joseph's face was unreadable as he said, 'Why is that?'

'I am sometimes afraid of the future.'

'Because of the second sight you claim to have?'

'I *do* have that gift, Joseph! It has always been there.'

His smile seemed cynical as he held her away from him looking with scrutiny into her face, but saying lightly, 'So what are my prospects? Tell me that?'

For answer she snatched up his two hands and turned them, palms uppermost, towards her. Then, just as suddenly, she released them and went once more to the ship's rail where she stood, her lips trembling, gazing out to sea.

'Well? What did you see?'

'I saw great sadness, Joseph. I saw you frightened and alone.'

She had buried her head in her arms so that she never saw the resolve that crossed the face of that supposedly most languid of gentlemen, Joseph Gage.

'Then your gift is at fault, my darling, for you are seeing my past.'

'Your past?'

'Yes. For though I may have seemed to the world the happiest of men, blessed with a great fortune and freedom to spend it as I chose, in fact I *was* afraid and lonely, A man will squander his youth on wine and doxies and think nothing of it. But when he passes a certain point that is not enough.'

'Why?'

'Because no-one wishes to die alone, Sibella. Every mortal creature must have a companion for those last declining years.'

'But you are not declining. Why you're not yet thirty-four!'

'Exactly the time when one tires of games and gaming and looks to leave an imprint of oneself behind.'

'You mean a child?'

'Yes.'

His eyes were warm again and he pulled her to him, putting one hand on her waist and with the other caressing the tumbling rosy hair that fell to her shoulders in disordered curls.

'Will you give me a son, Sibella?'

He bent to kiss her and as he did so the ocean breeze caught his purple cloak, whipping it out behind him so that he looked a fairy-tale prince stepped straight from the rainbow. But the embrace was mortal enough, his lips warm on hers, his hands slipping over the curve of her breasts. As they turned towards the beautiful cabin which Joseph had furnished as finely as any bedroom in his London house, he held her lovingly under the chin looking deep into those light translucent eyes.

'I'll have no more of your mysteries,' he said, 'It is sometimes better not to know too much. Have faith in me, my sweetheart, and seek not to examine that which is to come.'

Sibella was glad to snuggle against him like a

daughter and feel safe from all dangers whether they be those of the known universe—or something a little more intangible.

★ ★ ★ ★

On the day that Joseph and Sibella sailed for France, Melior Mary rose an hour before dawn and dressed herself in a riding habit of gun-metal taffeta. On her head she put a fine plumed hat and then, drawing on her gloves and picking up her riding crop, she left Sutton Place by a small, quiet side door that brought her out almost opposite the stables. In the darkness she crossed the cobbles swiftly, and noiselessly lifted the big wooden latch on the heavy door. Immediately the smell of hay and horsehair, the jingle of harness and the restless clip of hooves as the occupants moved in their enclosures, told her in the blackness that she was at her destination. And, reaching down with hands that had repeated the action many times, she lit the lantern that she knew always stood just within.

In the soft orange glow the outline of the stalls and the rumps of the pride of John Weston's equine collection were suddenly visible and Fiddle—used to this ritual over months—let out a whinnying sound. Rather guiltily, for she knew that Hyacinth slept in the rooms above, Melior Mary went to fetch her horse's saddle. It was not that she did not love Matthew Banister that she chose to ride alone. But the fact remained that

189

somewhere within her was an urge for certain solitary hours during the day and past experience had taught her to rise while Sutton Place slept.

The saddling done she led the horse out by the bridle. For fear of too much noise she would not mount till they reached the grass where a conveniently situated block assisted her. And then she was off, galloping through Sutton Forest in a dawn that rent the sky with finger of saffron and spice. And with each shard of light her heart lifted, for would not all this be hers one day—the forest and its creatures, the farms and buildings and, above all, her beloved Sutton Place? And was she not, at fifteen, already the toast of the county? Every head had turned when she had walked into Sibella's wedding feast and swept off her feathered hat to reveal the bountiful silver hair and the wild-violet eyes. And somewhere an unknown voice had called out, 'Here comes the Beauty,' and others had taken up the cry and she had turned, smiling to find a hundred goblets and more raised to her—Melior Mary, a daughter of John Weston and heiress to the finest estate in Surrey.

The forest was thinning a little and she realised that in the darkness she had headed her horse towards the old well of St Edward and the ruined manor house within whose boundaries it lay. She had never really liked the spot, seeming to her, as it did, too quiet and still. And this morning it had a coldness about it at odds with the fine summer sunrise. To her left the ruins reared

190

black and stark against a sky that now glowed with a tinge of crimson and she caught herself thinking how many of them there were, how she had never realised before how well the building was preserved. In fact, if she narrowed her eyes, she could almost see it as it would have been centuries ago, before it was abandoned and fell into decay.

The sound of thundering hooves behind her made her jump and Fiddle reared in terror as a grey horse ridden by a dark crouching figure seemed to come upon them from nowhere. They passed her by so closely that she could hear the man's breathing but his face remained hidden beneath the cowl of his cloak. Startled Melior Mary reined in, and then a curiosity overcame her and she urged her reluctant mount on in pursuit, for the man was on her father's property and had vanished, apparently, into the ruins.

'Ho there,' she called out after him, 'may I speak with you, sir?'

But there was no reply. Nor was there any sound except for Fiddle's snorting breath and the sudden laboured beating of her own heart. And then, at the entrance to what must have been the old courtyard when the house was first built in the reign of King John—brother of the Lionheart —the horse refused. He simply put down his head and stopped dead in his tracks and no amount of cajoling or threats would shift him. Melior Mary had no alternative but to dismount and leave him, motionless where he stood.

The glow of morning once again gave the old dead stones the appearance of life. It seemed almost that a fire was roaring somewhere and that a young suckling pig turned on a spit above it. So real was the illusion that the smell of fresh sizzling pork apparently wafted in the air. And then as Melior Mary stood there, sniffing a scent that she knew could not be in reality, she saw the man again. He stood with his back to her, his cloak—which fell from his shoulders to the ground—giving him a disembodied look, etched black as he was against the rising sun.

'Good morning, sir,' she called out, mastering the fear that suddenly came upon her, turning her blood to ice.

He did not move an inch and she was forced to take a couple of faltering steps forward and then, so suddenly that she almost died of fright, he wheeled round and she found herself looking into a face that she would never forget. Hawk-like were the features; a sharp strong nose, fierce dark eyes, a mouth that would give no man mercy. His cowl had fallen back and she saw that he wore a strange hat, flat to his head like a beret, the only ornamentation on which was a dark red brooch. On his hands were massive leather gloves and, as if to echo his appearance, a hooded bird of prey perched upon his wrist, turning its head in a series of jerks at the sound of her voice.

'Yes?' was all he said.

She had never been so unnerved. He did not move a muscle in his face or body but just stood

there, dark and forbidding, waiting for her to say
something. The sound caught in her throat as
she tried to speak again and nothing came out.
Melior Mary was paralysed with terror.

'I...I...' she stuttered.

'Yes?'

That same monosyllable again, as if it were the
only word he knew.

'I am Melior Mary Weston,' she managed
eventually in a voice that came out as a rasping
whisper.

Still he did not move but regarded her with
those frightening eyes.

'Gilbert Bassett.'

She knew that she should drop a curtsey,
acknowledge the introduction, but still the ice
of fear was in her veins. He was waiting for her
to say something more but she could do nothing
but stand like a dumb man at a freak show, her
teeth chattering with terror, her knees useless
beneath her.

Finally he said, 'Well?'

'I...I've come from Sutton Place.'

Her voice bounced back at her off the stone
walls.

'Where?'

'Sutton Place—the big house.'

He looked at her uncomprehendingly and she
thought that he must be a total stranger indeed,
for everyone for miles around had heard of her
father's mansion. At last he said a sentence and
his voice was curious—English but with an odd

way of pronouncing his words.

'Are you looking for Godrun?'

Now it was her turn not to understand.

'Who?'

His voice was irritable, his manner suddenly sharp, but still he kept that same unnerving moveless stance.

'My wife. She was brought to bed of a child last night.'

Her lips formed themselves into meaningless words of congratulation but he silenced her.

'It's dead. The midwife crushed its skull. It was a question of saving the mother or the child. And a woman can bear more children.'

There was an almost imperceptible shrug of his shoulders and Melior Mary wondered if he could really be as unfeeling as he pretended or if he masked some deeper emotion with his harshness.

A wind had come up and was freezing her to the bones as he said, 'Then who are you that rides before dawn? What is your business here?'

Her immediate reaction to put him in his place was totally suppressed by her dread.

'I am John Weston's daughter. From Sutton Place.' He still looked at her as if she were speaking another language so she added, 'From the manor house.'

The ferocious eyes glared at her.

'Don't play with me, woman. You are not from here!'

'But I am, I am,' she answered, near to tears.

'My father is Lord of the Manor.'

He drew in his breath with a hiss and at last he took a pace forward, raising his free arm as if he would smite her.

'I'll have no more of your tricks. Get hence before I have you flogged.'

'But what have I done?'

'You have mocked me as my wife lies within a thread of her life. For I am he whom you claim your father to be. *I* am the Lord of the Manor.'

And then it appeared to Melior Mary that the earth was opening up to let her fall in because as he stood there before her she realised that his cloak, which had seemed so dark and so all enveloping, was as thin as tissue and that through it she could see the outline of the wall behind him.

The scream was on her lips as he took one more menacing step in her direction and at last her limbs were free of the catalepsy. She turned and it seemed that she jumped to where her horse stood, for she had no recollection afterwards of her feet touching the earth. Somehow she clambered up into the side-saddle and with a wild shout headed the animal for home.

Behind her she could hear the noise of him leaping onto his mount, followed by the terrifying plunging of hooves as he started in pursuit. And it was only in Sutton Forest that the night-mare chase ended, for somewhere in that maze of trees the sound of the pounding horse died away and she, exhausted and weeping, at last

195

caught her first glimpse of Sutton Place.

★ ★ ★ ★

As the cry of 'land' rang out over Joseph Gage's
principal trading vessel, he and Sibella came once
more onto the deck and, in the brightness of that
halcyon day, saw the outline of the French coast
and the town of Calais—once the fortified citadel
of Henry VIII and his Court—reflecting in the
afternoon sun. Sibella, who had never left
England before, was agog for not only was this
foreign soil but was also the place in which
Matthew Banister had been born. Somewhere
amongst all those houses, dwarfed at present to
a blur, lay the very cottage or villa or even,
perhaps, mansion where the infant's first cry had
heralded his arrival. And though she would have
liked to speak of this to Joseph she had learned
better.

She had changed, at her bridegroom's request,
into a travelling dress of brocade and he—slightly
to her consternation—was now adorned in a full-
skirted coat of the lightest pink, heavily laced
with lilac threads; a rose-coloured waistcoat bearing embroidered flowers; shoes with very high
red heels; and a cravat in which was placed a
large and twinkling diamond. To crown the effect
he had tied ribbons of matching pink upon his
walking cane.

After a few moments of silent contemplation
Sibella said, 'Joseph, your ensemble gives the

wrong impression of you.'

He turned an amused face towards her and said, 'Oh? What impression would that be, my dear?'

She hesitated, too young to be subtle, too old to come out with what she was really thinking.

'Well?'

'It makes you seem womanish, too pretty and mincing,' she said at last.

'You think so?'

He raised his lorgnette and peered carefully at his waistcoat and breeches.

'Yes I do. I would not like the French to think you a flip-flap.'

Joseph laughed.

'Do *you* think of me as one?'

Sibella's response was immediate.

'You know I do not.'

'Then, my darling, I care nothing for what the rest of the world imagines. They may think me as dainty as a powder puff if it pleases them.'

'But I would not like it said that I was married to such.'

Joseph's smile disappeared, and with a firm hand suddenly under her elbow he was propelling her back to the cabin saying, 'There is something you must know. It is only fair that I tell you everything.'

Sibella gazed at him anxiously.

'You are *not* a...?'

'No, I am not. Sibella, does it occur to you that in Europe I dress more...daringly, is that the

197

word?—for a particular reason?'

She looked at him blankly.

'I see that you have not considered it. Well, to come straight to the point there *is* a purpose. It is simply that I wish to appear the grand fop, the fool with scarce two twopenny wits to rub together.'

'But why?'

His whole demeanour had changed; within that pink coat dwelled a man as tough as leather.

'Because I am a spy.'

Sibella was so astonished that she could not utter a word.

'An agent for James III, my darling. I should have told you before—you have married an active Jacobite.'

Sibella found her voice.

'But you are often at Court—an associate of King George!'

Joseph's eyes twinkled.

'I am what some would term a traitor. King George's Court regard me as a harmless, rather eccentric, man of wealth, and then I cross the Channel where I am regarded as a man of dubious inclinations. My real purpose is to pass on information to the Court of King James.'

'And is it my role to play the child wife of this monstrous dandy who flaunts himself in all the capital cities of Europe?'

'Just so. And you will forget our conversation if you are loyal to me. Not one word to anyone of it, not even Melior Mary or...' His voice took

198

on a harsh note. '...or your beloved Brother Hyacinth.'

She would have liked to say then that he need never worry again, that he—Joseph—with his strange sweet courage and wild kind ways, was everything to her. But the words died on her lips. Always, gnawing at her contentment like a cancer, was the fact that Matthew Banister lived and breathed. And she knew that as long as they both walked the earth there would never be any true and lasting happiness for her.

★ ★ ★ ★

In the sudden chill of the roseate sunset that ended that strange June day, Brother Hyacinth saddled up Ranter, the strawberry mare that had been assigned to him by John Weston, and headed for the ruined manor house that lay within the limits of the Manor of Sutton. Even before he had risen that morning, just as he was stepping from his bed. Melior Mary had burst into his room like a fury and wept where she stood. It was so foreign to her nature, so strange to see Elizabeth's capricious daughter humbled in any way, that he had taken her in his arms.

'What ails you, sweetheart? You're trembling like a hare.'

The strange tale had come out in frightened whispers and as he listened Matthew had felt his spine prick with terror and the scalp seeth upon his head.

'So someone's a-walking there?'

'He said his name—Gilbert Bassett. He's dead—and yet he looked at me with his fierce hawk eyes.'

'They have always been strange—the ruins and the well. Sibella...' his voice was suddenly too casual, '...she was frightened of the place.'

As if this reminded her of something Melior Mary suddenly thrust her hands forward. 'Hyacinth, can you read palms? Tell me if I will ever get my heart's wish—if you and I will be married and run Sutton Place together.'

He laughed without humour, Matthew's jaw—the only mar to his looks—grew set.

'And is that what you really want? To be saddled with a bastard for a husband? A man with no name and no money save that which he earns as your father's secretary.'

Her eyes deepened to purple and Melior Mary took him by the shoulders.

'If I cannot have you, Hyacinth, then I shall have no-one. I would rather decay to rot in spinsterhood.'

For answer he pulled her hands into his. A whirring sound was already beginning to throb in his eardrums, the walls of the room pulsating in rhythm with his heartbeat.

'It frightens me—this magic,' he whispered.

'I *knew* you possessed it.'

'How?'

'You have a look of Sibella sometimes.'

But her voice was far away for—beneath

Hyacinth's feet—the room was changing and he, for the first time in his experience, was out of his body. He stood, seeing but unseen, in the midst of a great group of men and realisd from their cockaded bonnets, their roughspun kilts and fiercesome two-handed swords that they were clansmen of Scotland. Bright red strips crossed by four green and one yellow was the tartan in the sunshine; and a thousand voices were raised as a banner of white silk with a crimson surround suddenly floated free in the Highland air. A legion of swords flashed up in salute, the pipes skirled a greeting and a great cry of 'Prionnsa Tearlach' seemed to sweep over the lochs and rumble in the foothills of the mountains. In the distance a solitary figure clad in scarlet breeches and waistcoat snatched off his yellow bobbed bonnet in acknowledgement. Who he was or what the occasion signified Hyacinth had no idea. But he knew one thing, he was seeing so far into the future that this man was not even born.

He dropped her hands. He was back in his own room and she was gazing at him with frightened eyes.

'Hyacinth, I thought you were dead upon your feet! Your soul seemed gone for a moment or two.'

'It was.'

'Where?'

'That I cannot tell you.'

'And did you see my future?'

'I think you have the power to become a

201

Princess if you so choose.'

She gazed at him in amazement.

'But that can never be. I am quite determined upon you.'

He smiled sadly and her hot wild blood rose in her.

She had made an exasperated noise, thrown her riding crop upon the ground and swept from his presence in a fury. But long after she had gone Hyacinth had stood stock still gazing at the open door and wondering how future events would fall into place and what role, in the play of Kings and Princes, was destined for Prionnsa Tearlach.

Yet now, with his horse slowing beneath him and the ruins of the ancient manor house coming into view, his mind was completely on the present and what lay waiting for him amongst the rapidly lengthening shadows. He had gone, that very afternoon, to John Weston's library and there—hidden amongst all the old and precious documents—he had found the key to Gilbert Bassett's haunting. It was the anniversary by date of the man's death. Over five hundred years before when King John Plantagenet—he who had signed the Magna Carta—had bestrode the throne of England and the thirteenth century had been but a mere babe-in-arms, on this day, Gilbert Bassett had ridden to his death.

In his mind Hyacinth could see the great falcon sweep up from the leather gauntlet, could imagine the craning of his neck as Bassett watched it beat its wings against the glow of the sun; could almost feel the sudden rearing of the horse, startled by a yapping hound, and sense the catapult into oblivion. And then—was God turning his back?—the milk-sucking babe, the third that the Lady of Sutton had produced but the first to survive its birth, puking and choking in its crib and growing white as wax, even as the messenger's feet ran the flagstones to tell her the other news. Hyacinth shivered. It must have been too much for her to bear. Had she run demented from her child-bed into the forest and thrown herself down in the green darkness to scream out her anguish? Or had she turned her face to the wall and accepted her cruel fate? No-one would ever know. Only the silent stones that rose before him so enigmatically had witnessed what actually took place.

It was with a sense of fear that he realised that, from a walking pace, his horse had now actually come to a halt. He looked down and saw by the carriage of its head and the pricking of its ears that something, somewhere, was moving. And then he realised what it was. From out of the ruins, soaring in an arc of power, a falcon rose into the air and fluttered, seemingly, above his head. With a sound of terror Hyacinth's mount bolted, shaking him out of the saddle and up onto its fore-quarters, his arms clinging to its neck. And then—just as Melior Mary had described— he too heard the beat of hooves behind him and knew that Gilbert Bassett had stepped through time and was reliving that last terrible hour when he had gone to hunt and had himself been the quarry.

He glanced over his shoulder but could see nothing; yet still the clamour of pursuit grew louder and even louder in his ears. The sweat of his horse was slippery beneath him and foam appeared at the mouth of the frantic animal. Desperately Hyacinth wound his fingers into its mane. He knew that if he was thrown now it would mean a broken neck. And then, as if from nowhere, another two pairs of hooves added themselves to the din. And these were real and mortal enough. Behind him came a voice.

'Hold on Mr Matthew, sirrh. Holy Moother of Chroist, the booger's goin' a hell of a lick.'

It was Tom, Melior Mary's squint-eyed companion of childhood, bent over one of John Weston's finest mounts and lathered like a jockey as he strove to catch up. And, after a few minutes, a string of Dublin expletives and the beating down of his riding crop actually brought him level. But there was nothing he could do about it and they charged side by side, as if in some ludicrous race, towards Sutton Place. Behind them the sound of their pursuer filled the air and Tom shouted, 'Who's that in the name of Chroist?'

Hyacinth could not answer, feeling at his last gasp. He was aware that another minute would see him done for, that he would simply let go and fall beneath the tumbling hooves.

'Gilbert Bassett,' he shouted. 'Rest in peace I

command you. You've no right to this forest. You are dead, man! Dead!'

The sound of pursuit ended so abruptly that the silence was shocking. At one moment there had been the noise of a slavering horse at full gallop, at the next nothing but the stillness of the deep forest.

'Are you all right, sirrh? What in the name of God was it? Glory be, me old moother told me of the Hounds of Hell but Oi'd never have believed it if I hadn't heard it with me own ears. What with her doying of the gin and all.'

Hyacinth wiped his sleeve across his forehead as his horse, gasping near to death, finally came to rest.

'Well, anyway sirrh, you're out of it! And with nothing but a sore arse to show—if you'll pardon the awkwardness of that phrase, sirrh. Shall I take the poor devil...' he jerked his head in the direction of Ranter, 'back to the big house, you looking as if you're about to drop down on your hunkers, sirrh?'

Hyacinth shook his head.

'No! I'll see to her. Tom, thank you for saving my life.'

The squinting leprechaun grinned.

'It's a damn good thing that me old moother didn't believe in ghosts, sirrh. Good day.'

And with that he disappeared once more, whistling, into the forest.

★ ★ ★ ★

The trading ship had berthed at Calais, the great anchor—which held her riding in the wind some distance from the shore—down and secure in the seabed. A rope ladder had been lowered to a small rowing boat which lay tossing like a shuttle-cock on the full swell below. Seated in the boat was a very pretty young woman, dressed in a fox fur mantle, whose clear green eyes and strawberry hair would normally have attracted attention and shouts from the ragged bunch of sightseers who leaned against the harbour wall. But today all eyes were on an amazing personage which was lowering itself down the rope on high teetering heels that would have been more suitable at a Court levée. On top of its head was a tricorne hat that sported a ruby brooch shaped like a sickle moon, and beneath this a huge wig hung about its shoulders; a wig whose curls lifted menacingly as the sea breeze caught it—making the owner temporarily resemble a startled spaniel—and which seemed in imminent danger of lifting off and floating wildly out to sea.

From the personage's shoulders hung a velvet cloak of the colour known as cyclamen, the lining of which was violet satin flecked with silver. And startling though this colour combination might be the personage had seen fit to carry it through his complete ensemble, for his many skirted coat was violet, his waistcoat silver encrusted pink, his breeches lavender. Long purple ribbons hung from the silver cane that was now being passed to him over the ship's rail and which, despite a great deal of shrieking in a high voice, he seemed quite unable to grasp. In fact as he stretched his hand out one of the red-heeled, diamond-buckled shoes slipped and he appeared in momentary danger of plunging feet first into the ocean.

Sibella did not know where to look. If she had caught Joseph's eye she would have laughed, so she contented herself with looking slightly to her husband's right, a fact which could not be observed in the distance.

'Zlife!' he was screaming, 'I warrant I'd as soon have the Great Pox as hang here like a monkey in extremis. Can none of you salt scalders get me down? Zoonters, one would think I pay you for looking, you do stare so! Sibella, do something.'

As if it had life of its own the rop ladder swung away from the ship's side so that Joseph's feeble struggles were suddenly redoubled in effort.

'Dear God! Am I to end up drowned with me prinkum-prankum all gone for naught? Drag me in, you sons of...'

Fortunately the last few words were drowned by the sound of a distant cannon fired inshore. With a mighty effort, that could have been mistaken for extreme agility if it had been executed by anyone other than the enfeebled fop. Joseph jumped free of the ladder and landed in the rowing boat. He wiped his brow with a musk-scented lace handkerchief.

'Odds Life, Sibella, I've aged ten years. I

207

should have followed my instincts and stayed in London. Europe's fit for nobody 'cept those who stare jackanapes at decaying ruins and unclimbable mountains. God's wounds, I must be running demented.'

And with that he wrapped himself in his cloak, pulled his hat down over his eyes and fell to grumbling into his gums. It was with some measure of consternation that Sibella looked across at him, for even she had not been quite prepared for such a to do as was now making the sailors snigger and the rowing party gaze steadfastly at the floor.

'Joseph?' she said quietly.

'Don't talk to me, I'm quite put about,' came the reply—but from the folds of the cloak an eye bright as a water rat's looked into hers for a second and then slowly winked.

'Very well, sir. I shall not,' she replied—turnig her head away to hide her face.

As the boat made fast to a ring, set in the harbour wall by a flight of steps, a man detached himself from the crowd and stood waiting at the top, his hat in his hands. His twinkling eyes appraised Sibella in a manner that she considered bold but his unabashed delight in her left no room for annoyance, and so it was with a laugh that she first set foot on French soil. The stranger came forward and bowed over her hand, raising her fingers to his lips.

'Mrs Gage?'

'Yes.'

'Captain Charles Wogan at your service, ma'am. May I humbly say that Joseph is a very lucky man.'

Behind them a peevish voice was raised in a high pitched moan as the impossible red heels minced up the steps amongst the disgusting flotsam of a French harbour.

A white hand with long thin fingers flapped a handkerchief and then pinioned it firmly over quivering nostrils.

'Zblood!' came the feeble cry.

'Mr Gage, I have ordered your carriage, sir. If you and m'lady would be good enough to step this way.'

'God a'mercy,' Joseph shrilled. 'I warrant if it is more than two paces I shall be dead with exhaustion. Everything is slipping away. Sibella, Wogan, take my arms if you'd be so good.'

He fell limply between them, his heels making a tap-tapping sound as they dragged him to where a closed spring coach stood at the ready, its driver peering anxiously in their direction. The Captain gave the man a nod—saying nothing about their destination—as he and Sibella bundled in a Joseph whose face had turned an unpleasant green colour. Exhausted Sibella sank back against the seat only to see Joseph cautiously open one eye.

'Is the coast clear?' he muttered.

'Aye, you son of a dolly-mop—begging your pardon, ma'am.'

Joseph sprang to his feet, shouted 'Whee!' like

a schoolboy coming out of class and threw his hat and ridiculous wig aloft in the air. Sibella gaped astonished as the Captain executed a nimble dance step or two and then fell down upon one knee before her, clasping one of her hands in both of his.

'Why bless your little heart,' he said. 'Sure, Joseph, if it isn't the prettiest little thing that ever drank milk. I love it—I do, I do.'

And with that he rained kisses on Sibella's fingers.

'And will you be coming with us, my pretty?' he went on. 'There'll be nothing but the finest for you at the Polish Court. Why they'll be stuffing sweatmeats in your little mouth all day long.'

'The Polish Court?'

She was utterly bewildered.

The Captain tried to look contrite but was forced to grin as he said, 'And hasn't it the sweetest voice! Why, Joseph, you're the luckiest man alive. But the Polish Court it is, my precious little ma'am.'

He burst into song.

'A frog he would a-wooing go, hey ho said Rowley! Whether the Captain would let him or no, with a roly-poly gammon and spinach—hey, ho, said the bride of King James.'

Joseph said, 'So you've found her?'

'I think so.' The captain slapped his thigh. 'By Christ—begging your pardon, ma'am—I've seen some of the ugliest women in the last few months. The Princess of Furstenberg has a nose

210

like a drunk's, the one from Saxony is fair, fat and forty-five, and the Princess of Baden's a dwarf with the pox.'

'Truly?' said Sibella.

'As true as I kneel here. But now I've found three little beauties—and all sisters. Poland has produced a merry nest of turtle doves. But which is it to be, that's the question. So we'll let your handsome husband decide, ma'am, for he can speak to them in their lingo and find out who's the sweetest of nature.'

He hummed a few more bars and then said, 'That is if you don't object, ma'am.'

Just for a second Sibella hesitated, for she had no real desire to waste time while her bridegroom courted other women, albeit on behalf of King James. Then, in a great flash, she knew that they must go; that it was right; that one of the Polish Princesses would make a brilliant bride for the King and would bear a child that might easily regain the British throne.

'Object?' she said. 'Why I can't wait to see them. Come along Joseph, we can't keep the ladies waiting.'

And with the sound of Wogan singing at top voice about them the horses leapt forward and the spring coach took the road to the French border.

CHAPTER 11

'...and so if you could go at once, sirrh, for himself is sweating loike a pig and his toes fairly lapping he's in sooch a foine state of agitation.'

Tom was panting, having just run from the house to the stables, his squinting eyes so screwed up with concentration that it was quite impossible for Hyacinth to know in which direction he was looking.

'What's it about, do you know?'

'Oi haven't an oidea in me head, sirrh! Unless of course...' the crossed eyes took on a sly expression, '...it would be about herself.'

He leered, gargoyle-like. Hyacinth, overcoming a wild desire to throttle the life out of him, said, 'I have told you before to refer to the young mistress as Miss Melior.'

Tom pretended to look contrite and Hyacinth, in one of his rare black moods, kicked a stone. Ten months had passed since Sibella's marriage to Joseph. Ten months during which Melior Mary had celebrated her sixteenth birthday and the gates of Sutton Place—closed previously as etiquette demanded to the suitors who would come from everywhere to try and obtain such a brilliant match—had been thrown open with an official assembly.

212

Young men had been there in droves—from London the usual collection of fops and beaux led by Lord Chesterfield's handsome son; from the county a fine selection of stalwarts, the tallest and most dashing of which was squire Roderick's eldest boy Gabriel; the Catholic contingent en masse, with one or two eligible youths amongst them; and then the relatives. And in their midst, determinedly eyeing Melior Mary for all he was worth, her chubby cousin, William Wolffe.

Hyacinth had not met him before as William's mother—John Weston's sister, Frances—disliked socialising and preferred to lead a life of quietness at Haseley, amongst the beautiful gardens planted nearly two hundred years earlier by Margaret Weston, daughter of Sutton Place's builder. Margaret and her husband, Walter Dennys, had gone, after their wedding, to live at Haseley Court and had created great walkways and water gardens, mint scented knots and rose-entwined arbours. By co-incidence Frances Weston had also found herself there as a bride—for the place had long since passed out of the hands of the Denny's—and had set to work with devotion to restore her ancestress's home. The house—badly decayed—had been gutted and rebuilt in what had become known, of late, as Queen Anne style, only one wing remaining of the old Tudor building. And the care and attention of the gardens had become her passion.

Now she looked about her as if she could not wait to get back again, her eyes scarcely taking in the fact that her son and Melior Mary were pounding about the Great Hall in time to a fierce gallop. And at exactly that moment Hyacinth, who had been glaring helplessly at the whirling couple, had felt a tugging at his sleeve and had heard a lisping voice say, 'Mither Banither, if you pleathe thir, I have no partner for thith danthe.'

It had been William's sister Arabelle, as tiny as a doll and with a childlike personality to match, who stood shaking her powdered curls as she put her head back to look at him.

'I'd be tweeibly pleathed,' she went on. 'I do feel thuch a doltard when I thtand out. I twuly believe is is becauth I look like a little girl but I am theventeen—older than Cousin Melior—weally I am.'

Hyacinth had smiled down at her and offered her his arm, acutely aware that Melior Mary's great eyes were resting on him. Because of this he had raised Arabelle's fingers to his lips and been rewarded with a blush and a downward flutter of the eyelids from the pretty simpleton.

Ever since that night William Wolffe senior had taken to visiting Sutton Place every two weeks, bringing William and Arabelle and another child—an obnoxious, smelly brat of some thirteen years, called Beavis—with him. Frances Wolffe stayed behind, pleading indisposition though everyone knew that she was, in reality, walking about her gracious lawns, sighing in sheer ecstasy.

To the horror of Matthew—and the delight of

214

John Weston and William Wolffe senior—Melior Mary seemed to find some amusement in the presence of her round cheeked cousin and was forever riding off with him, presenting her backview to Matthew as he gazed after them. But never far away was a lisping voice.

'Are you buthy, Mithter Banither? I thould enjoy *tho* much to go widing with you. If we huwwy we can escape Beavis for he ith occupied thwowing thtones at the horthes.'

An involuntary oath had escaped Matthew's lips as he had headed for the stables and the unlovely sight of Beavis, sitting aloft the hay bales, pinging pebbles from a catapult at the hapless beasts. One jump had got him up alongside and before the boy could move Hyacinth had swung him in the air by his collar.

'Right, you little snot-blower, I'm going to smash your eyes out.'

Beavis started to shriek and from the ground below Arabelle launched into a series of shrill and meaningless cries.

'Be quiet, you stupid girl,' Matthew had snapped—quite furious with the whole family—but this set her off all the more and her howls, coupled with the yelping of her brother, must have been audible for some distance for into the furore walked Melior Mary, with William one step behind.

'God's wounds,' she had shouted, 'what's this to-do? A thieves kitchen in Hell most like! Arabelle, stop bellowing; Matthew, put the boy down; Beavis, shut your mouth; William, fetch help.'

They all stared at her for a second and, though both Arabelle and Beavis were suddenly silenced, nobody spoke. It was Hyacinth who shouted out, 'No Melior Mary, I will *not*. I intend to take him within an inch of his life. And if William wants to put his fists over it—he may!'

'Damn you!' said Melior Mary.

'Your temper runs imperious, madam. And you may order others—', Hyacinth's eyes swept over William in a cold stare, '—but never me. If you were a boy nothing would give me greater pleasure than to step outside with you.'

That day had ended very quietly. William and Arabelle—the one plumply sulky, the other in copious fits of tears—had returned to Haseley early whilst Beavis, sullen and limping, had sat in the homeward bound coach for three hours, refusing to come out even for dainty cakes and lemonade. John and William senior had parted rather gruffly and Hyacinth had been sent to the stables where, after eating some cheese and drinking a bottle of rough red wine to himself, he had gone to bed.

From that time on he had been in semi-disgrace. John's manner had become abrupt, the old fatherly way vanished. As for Melior Mary, she would not even look at him. Since that day, over a year ago, when she had given her body so freely, she had dismissed the incident as if it had never happened. He thought sometimes that

216

she had forgotten the miracle of that morning when all the animal kingdom—he and she included—had felt the stirring of nature's dark and relentless compulsion. Though she sometimes spoke of love she had never since shared with him its joy. She seemed to have chosen the role of innocent. And yet he would sometimes catch her looking at him with hidden fire in her glance. He often wondered if she enjoyed taunting him with her games.

And now she was angry with him and, for once, he was bored. If she wanted to play the minx with him, let her. To Hell with her! He could have Arabelle if he so much as raisd his little finger to beckon, for she still gazed at him adoringly with vapid blue eyes.

And now this! Summoned on the instant to see a John Weston who had not thawed in his manner at all. If it had come to her father's ears that Melior Mary had lost her virginity... For, no doubt, John was full of the idea of uniting the houses of Weston and Wolffe in marriage. If Melior Mary should die without issue her heirs were the two Williams—father and son. How neat to tie the inheritance back into one. But who would want a wild-blooded girl who had once given herself to a stable boy?

The knock on John's door and the following 'Enter', rang in Matthew's ears like a funeral bell. His master was standing with his back to him, facing one of the windows, in his hand a letter which he was reading with some apparent excitement. For a second or two he did not look up and Matthew stood waiting for retribution. He even opened his mouth and said, 'Sir, I...', in order to break the silence, but John suddenly turned round with determination.

'Matthew, damn you, I am furious with you for the beating of my nephew Beavis. I nearly threw you out of service...but now...'

He tapped the document with his other hand.

'Sir, I know it was wrong. That she...'

'What the devil are you talking about? Matthew, you have been sent for!'

'Sent for?'

'Don't stare at me witless! This letter is from the King's emissary—Captain Charles Wogan. He wants you to travel to Europe immediately. Have you the stomach to do a service for King James?'

Dumbfounded, Hyacinth nodded.

'Well, it's this. You know Lady Derwentwater who calls here from time to time?—she whose husband was executed after the '15 uprising.'

'Yes.'

'Do you recall curing a lame horse of hers with one of your special ointments?'

'Yes, I do.'

'Well, she had apparently written of it to Wogan. And now he wants you to join a rescue party.'

Hyacinth could do nothing but stare as John continued, 'King James wishes to marry Princess Clementina Sobieski but she and her mother are prisoners at Innsbruck. On their way to Rome from Silesia they were captured and the British Government has now brought direct pressure to bear on the Austrian Emperor who is only too anxious to please. So, the royal bride is in a convent, guarded night and day. It is the Captain's plan to lift her out of it and for this he must be sure that every horse in his team can run. You will travel to Strasbourg under the name of Captain O'Toole and take orders only from Charles Wogan. You must leave in the small hours of tomorrow and sail on the morning tide, in order to catch them up.'

Hyacinth nodded. He was more excited than he had ever been in his life before.

'I shall ride with you to Dover and see you aboard.' John's voice took on a rather wistful note. 'Further than that I dare not proceed for fear of contravening the Captain's wishes. But you shall have two hundred guineas and I want you to hire a stout coach to take you to Strasbourg. Trust nothing ram-shackle or ancient. Speed and reliability are of the essence.'

'Yes, sir.'

Hyacinth found himself at a loss for words.

'You are fluent in French?'

Hyacinth nodded again.

'That's all to the good. Now Captain O'Toole—forged papers accompany this letter as proof of your identity—not a word of this to anyone. Particularly Melior Mary.'

John turned to stare out of the window and

his voice was measured as he said, 'I don't want her upset. She is considering a proposal of marriage from her cousin William, and you know what a headstrong, flighty Miss she can be when she puts her mind to it.

'Now, you will find a uniform belonging to a captain in Dillon's Irish Regiment hanging in my dressing room. A tailor from Guildford—a loyalist—will be here as soon as it gets dark to ensure that it fits you. Go to the chamber known as Sir John Rogers's room. You will find that your personal things have already been put there.'

'So it is all arranged?'

'Yes.' John turned and looked at him very directly. 'Matthew, I am sorry that there has been bad feeling between us. I was angry with you not just because of Beavis—who deserved a whipping for a more snivel-mouthed repellent boy I have yet to meet—but also on account of Melior Mary.'

Hyacinth's heart sank again.

'Melior Mary?'

'I know her temperament and once she has her mind set on something—or someone...' He paused then added slowly, 'It is imperative that, with the responsibility of this great inheritance, she marries—wisely. Do you understand me?'

'Are you saying it would be better if I did not return from Austria?'

'Yes.'

There was a hardness in Matthew's eyes as he

answered, 'Then so be it.'

In the silence that followed, the rustle of another human being in the corridor outside made them jump. But, though John hurried to the door, all he found was Melior Mary on the point of knocking. Ignoring Hyacinth she said, 'I am sorry to disturb you, Father. I had just come to say goodnight.'

'Goodnight, my child. Will you not bid Matthew the same?'

The eyes were the colour of amethyst as they gave Hyacinth a cool glance. A pale hand extended itself.

'Goodnight Matthew.'

And with that she was gone.

The moon was up and skittish, as the small fast chaise—unmarked with the Weston crest—turned out of the great gates and headed for the coast. Beside the coachman Tom rode shotgun for, though both John and Matthew were armed they were, with no postillions or accompanying servants and travelling in such dark hours of the morning, a tempting target for gentlemen of the road. And sure enough as they left the village of Sevenoaks in Kent there was a distant thud of hooves behind them. Turning, Tom could vaguely make out a black figure but it melted into a clump of trees as he peered at it. To be on the safe side he fired a couple of warning shots and, thankfully, no more was seen of the villain.

They arrived at Dover just after eight o'clock on a fine spring morning, with the tide running at full swell and the ships, waiting to carry those wishing to journey across the Channel, already swarming with passengers. Hyacinth had only time for one large nip of brandy at the post house that stood on the quayside, before he too embarked. Then it was anchors up, canvasses into the wind, and hats off to wave at those left on shore. Turning his face into the morning, realising that he was probably seeing John for the last time, Hyacinth pulled his cloak about him and leant on the rail. He was returning to the land where he had been born with no further clue to his identity, no real progression in his life, and it was bitter gall. He was just making his way to the cabin below, where he might sit with the others and drink himself into a stupor, when there was a touch at his elbow. A black cloaked figure, hidden by its hood, stood before him.

'Do I know you?'

Matthew felt vastly irritable.

With a laugh the figure threw off its covering. Gun metal taffeta was the riding habit, wild lilac the laughing eyes.

'I should sincerely hope so,' said Melior Mary—and she dropped him a curtsey.

★ ★ ★ ★

The Hotel Coq d'Or which, though larger than its more humble rivals still remained only a posting inn as far as the average traveller was concerned, was—for the time of year—very heavily

222

booked indeed. In fact there were no available rooms left at all and those journeyers who arrived late on the evening of April 16, 1719 were told that they would have to content themselves with the floor and a blanket or, if that did not please them, go on and cross the French border that night.

And a motley collection the party of guests— who all seemed to know one another—were, as they sat down to dine on that chilly spring night. First there was a loud contingent of three Irishmen—all officers—who drank a great deal of champagne and slapped each other on the back. The leader of these appeared to be a Captain Wogan, the only army man to have brought a servant with him—a Scotsman with a great gashed scar running down his left cheek to his jaw and an accent that the landlord found totally incomprehensible. As well as the other two—Major Gaydon and Captain Missett—a fourth officer, Captain O'Toole, was expected that evening and his room was being jealously guarded against all would-be hirers. Nor was the gathering exclusively male for Mrs Missett had accompanied her husband—and this despite the fact that she was expecting a child—and she, in turn, had brought a maid.

By ten o'clock the meal was cleared, brandies were drunk, and the carefree chatter told the landlord that the next day he would receive a handsome tip. Therefore it was with an ominous feeling that he handed Wogan a note—brought a few minutes before by a boy from the village. Something about the very look of it told him that the message did not contain good tidings. The Captain, too, seemed to sense this for he ripped it open without ceremony and scanned the contents. Then he screwed the paper up into a ball, said 'Mother of Christ!', and threw the offending pellet into the fire. The landlord, guessing that he had been right, bowed over the greasy white cloth that hung from his extended arm, and discreetly withdrew.

But before he could even close the door Mrs Missett had said, 'What's the matter Charles?' and Wogan had answered, 'It's O'Toole—he's got a woman with him.' Fortunately for the maitre the rest of the conversation was lost to him.

'Wha'?' said the Scotsman—whose role as a servant seemed to slip from him as the room became private to the assembled company—'has he gone oot his head?'

And Major Gaydon put in, 'What the devil's he playing at? Who exactly *is* he, Charles?'

On top of which Captain Missett had boomed, 'Is he to be trusted? Who recommended him?'

They all leant forward as they spoke, head inclined towards head, and at that moment—on that particular date in that particular year—they were, without doubt, the most exciting group of adventurers in Europe. Gaydon—grey and distinguished—from his years of active fighting service; Misset—tall, humorous, the sort of man who would laugh while he killed; Wogan—the Anglo-

Irishman whose family had fought for the Catholic Kings since time immemorial; the man-servant Mitchell, probably the most interesting of them all—he who had assisted the Jacobite Lady Nithsdale in the rescue of her husband from the impregnable Tower of London after the 1715 Uprising; Mrs Missett—considerably younger than her husband, tall for a woman, but bright-eyed and quick, ready to serve her King even though a child kicked within her; Jeanneton the maid, known as Jenny, born sulky and with a certain large-toothed aggressiveness, yet included in this enterprise because she was to play a vital role—a role the truth of which would be properly explained to her. All-in-all a strange collection of humanity, yet not so if one realised the common wish—to see the House of Stuart re-established upon the throne of England. To see the German Elector gone from British shores and an Englishman take his rightful place in the land that by ancient heritage was his.

'The note says she's John Weston's daughter,' Wogan went on.

'Who?'

'John Weston of Sutton Place. He is a loyalist and active supporter. O'Toole—alias Banister—is his servant and comes on Lady Derwentwater's say-so.'

'But why bring anyone—least of all a young woman?'

In reply Mrs Missett laughed and rolled her pretty eyes, saying, 'Oh la la!' to Major Gaydon.

But Wogan answered him shortly, 'She will have to remain here. There is no way that she must be allowed any further.'

They relapsed into a brief and worried silence broken only by the fall of charring logs in the fireplace. And into that ember glow, into that crimson light, which warmed the faces of King James's most loyal subjects and transformed their clothes to shades of flame, walked Melior Mary. She stood before them with the shimmer of an opal, the watered silk of her dress reflecting pinks, blues and mauves, her hair gleaming like fire on snow. There was not one of them that did not catch a breath, even the tough and scar-faced Scot. In fact there was, for him, a strange tightening in his chest that he had, up to now, only associated with danger and challenge.

'My name is Melior Mary Weston,' she said quietly, curtseying humbly before Major Gaydon as the most high-ranking office in the room, 'Here to explain my unwanted presence amongst you—and to make amends.'

Into the shocked stillness Mrs Misset spoke, yet no-one else moved or made a greeting.

'Jeanneton, would you take Miss Weston's trunk to my room if you please. Is it outside, Miss Weston?'

She smiled and nodded, her eyes a-tilt.

Apparently inconsequentially Mrs Missett said again, 'Jenny, see to Miss Weston's things.'

'And while you're there ask Captain O'Toole to step inside.' It was Charles Wogan speaking.

226

The girl bobbed and went out and as soon as the door closed behind her Wogan said angrily, 'I don't know how much you know of our enterprise, Miss, but nothing must be discussed in front of Jenny. She is not party to the plot.'

He had been frowning, gazing down at the toe of his boot, but now he looked up and into the eyes that were fast becoming the toast of the day. Despite himself, despite all the trouble that she was causing, his twinkling Irish grin burst forth, creasing his nose.

'Well, well,' he said, 'you're as pretty as a flower in morn I'll grant you that. But I'll wager you could be a devil given half a fighting chance. God help us!'

He shook his head, laughing, and she smiled back; there was an instant affinity between them. Yet still she chose to remain silent, saying nothing as she swept another deep curtsey and looked slowly from one to the other. Beneath the dazzle of that splendid gaze each one capitulated. Gaydon fatherly; Missett amused; his wife pleased; Mitchell afraid. Afraid of the lurch in his heart which made him unable to look at her and forced him to turn his scarred face away after a moment or two.

Mrs Missett, who suddenly seemed bold and not worried to any great degree if she spoke out of turn, said, 'For myself, I'll be glad of your company, my dear. It is difficult for me not being able to converse freely before Jenny and yet longing to talk to another woman. These men, they think they're brave. But let one of them go on such high adventure with a babe kicking their ribs and we'd soon hear a moan, I'd warrant.'

For answer Melior Mary, in that strange unashamed way of hers, put her hand on Mrs Missett's stomach and felt the rounding that lay hidden beneath the fully-cut skirts.

'I'd be proud to be the companion of you and your passenger, ma'am,' she said.

But now all attention was on Mitchell who cleared his throat and addressed himself to Wogan in particular, and the assembled company at large, though all the while keeping his eyes averted from Melior Mary's face.

'It's my feeling, sir, that you should tell Missie... It'll no be fair on her, nor on Mrs Missett neither, if you don't.'

His influence over the others was considerable—the hero of the Nithsdale escape commanded respect wherever he went in Jacobite circles.

'I am thinking of it,' said Wogan. 'What do you feel, Major? Missett?'

The two Irishmen nodded in agreement and as if he had been listening at the door—which indeed he had—Hyacinth chose this moment to come in. And with him into the room, like a physical presence, came everything that they loved and cherished and sought in the Jacobite cause. Youth, vitality, that consuming interest in life all rekindled by this, his greatest adventure. He was the son for which the Missetts longed; he was Wogan's brother; Gaydon's lost youth. Only Mitchell felt the old deep Celtic stirring of hatred and knew that his soul was dark against this man.

Without preamble, as if he had known them always, Hyacinth said, 'Madam, gentlemen; I have come here to help you. What is your plan?' And, strangely enough, it was Mitchell who told him that the Princess and her mother were in desperate straits; that they lay imprisoned in a convent at Innsbruck with nobody to help them but a gentleman usher.

'There is nothing we can do except snatch her away and substitute someone else in her place. If we simply abduct her without covering our tracks we'll all be done for. We must get out of Austrian territory and into Venetian before the alarm goes up.'

It was Gaydon who spoke.

'But who will you substitute?'

Hyacinth had questioned and Captain Missett answered him.

'My wife's servant, Jeanneton. She has agreed to do it in exchange for rewards. But she believes that you, O'Toole, are eloping—rescuing your light-of-love from an odious marriage. She has no idea of the true identity of the Princess.'

'If it works,' said Hyacinth, 'this will be remembered as one of history's greatest escapades.'

Wogan bellowed a laugh.

'What do you mean *if!* I'd like to know the name of the bastard who can stop me now. I'd kick his arse from here to the Ring of Kerry.'

The next morning saw the party up and about early. As soon as a repast had been snatched, bills were settled and a heavy berlin, acquired by Wogan, was trundled round into the courtyard. Mrs Missett, Melior Mary, Jenny and Major Gaydon climbed inside and into the pillion went Hyacinth—the shortest of the men. Mitchell coiled a great lash of rope to the coachman's seat and then took up his position on the box. Captains Missett and Wogan rode escort, leading the two spare horses.

They had never endured anything so tortuous. The enclosed coach—essential to shield the escaping royal bride from prying eyes—lumbered through the mountains like an ox, and eight days had passed by the time they at last came within sight of the Austrian border at Kempten.

Tamsin Missett, accepting every jolt with as much of a smile as she could muster, occasionally exclaimed 'Odds Zlife!' and once she growled to herself, that, 'the wretch would be born in the hedgerow'; but she escaped without mishap and sailed serenely into the inns at night, where she would wash herself and then go straight to bed; her supper being brought to her on a tray and her evenings being devoted to cards or reading with Melior Mary. She was a great laugh and a great flirt; full of mischief, despite her condition, and ready for any jollity or diversion. She had found in herself a fondness for the wayward heiress, and during one of their more intimate

230

conversations said, 'What is there, my dearest, between you and O'Toole, In my romantic way I had quite cast you as the heroine in an adventure—running away with the groom in order to avoid a forced marriage.'

Melior Mary had laughed.

'It is not quite like that. I have not really absconded because I intend to return when this daring scheme is all played out.'

'But what of your father? Will he not thrash you to within an inch of your life?'

'Quite probably. But he will forgive me in the end.'

'How can you be so sure?'

Melior Mary had turned to look at her and Tamsin had seen a tear form in eyes that had grown dark.

'Because of Sutton Place. Because of the house. I am the heiress and my father would do anything rather than see it pass from my hands. He wants me to marry my cousin to secure the inheritance, but he would let me stay single rather than take from me what is rightfully mine.'

'And what of O'Toole?'

'Hyacinth? I want him to share the mansion house with me.' Her face grew hard. 'But *I* must be the mistress—I'll never play second fiddle.'

'Sutton Place means a very great deal to you, doesn't it?'

The tears spilled over the high boned cheeks.

'I am part of it. That is how I feel. It is more than a building—it has life. It takes command.

231

One day I think it will consume me.'

Mrs Missett shivered.

'I am not sure that I should altogether like that. But what if your father makes you give up Hyacinth in order that you may inherit?'

'Then give him up I shall, for the man is not yet born who could be more important to me than the house.'

Mrs Missett shook her head, bewildered and perturbed.

Early the next day, soon after sun-up, Captain Missett and Mitchell rode off alone and were back by nightfall. Contact with Chateaudeau—the Princess's Gentleman—had been made and the date for the rescue fixed; two days hence, on April 27. Now there was nothing to do but wait and anxiously watch the deteriorating weather. By the morning of the day on which all their brave hopes were pinned it was snowing heavily.

It was Mitchell, who had ridden out in the disguise of a knife grinder, who came back with a message from Princess Clementina's mother.

'Sir, I managed to mutter to Chateaudeau while I sharpened up the Mother Superior's killing blade...'

Wogan looked surprised and Mitchell allowed himself the rare experience of a smile.

'It's for chickens—or so I was told! It would seem that the old Princess is oot her mind with worry about the icy conditions.'

Wogan snarled.

'Then she'll have to worry on. The rescue proceeds tonight. Mitchell, go back and get word to Chateaudeau. Tell him snow hinders everyone, not just us.'

'She'll no like it!'

'And neither do I like it,' said Jenny, from the door. 'I knew that this was no ordinary elopement, Captain Wogan. I knew that you wouldn't have all these people together and my mistress putting herself out, simply for a friend. If you think I'm getting into trouble just for you lot and your precious King James, you can think till the last trump. I'm off and nobody can stop me.'

And the pert slut would listen to neither please nor threats. She packed her belongings in a tablecloth, pocketed the money for her part in the affair, and hitched herself a ride in a haycart with a handsome farm lad. She was last seen leaning against him heavily, swearing that she did so to keep out the cold, and all the while her hand plucking at the material of his breeches in a way that left none of them in any doubt as to where she would sleep that night.

'The stinking whore!' shouted Wogan, bringing his riding whip down onto a chair. 'I hope she finds herself at the bottom of a ravine.'

'Too late for that now,' answered Gaydon. 'What the devil we do is more important.'

It was as inevitable as if it had always been meant that Melior Mary should step forward. In fact Tamsin Missett wondered if she was being fanciful in thinking that this was the hand of fate, that destiny had sent this wild and beautiful girl, full of passion and courage, to bring Princess Clementina out of prison, instead of the clod-hopping and surly Jeanneton.

And that night as she wrapped the girl in a cloak of fox and tied a hood upon her to conceal the silver hair and shadow the face, she wept in gratitude. God had answered all their prayers. A worthy substitute would be smuggled in past the porter's lodge, posing as Chateaudeau's amorous conquest.

But, though all the men stepped forward to lift the heiress onto her horse, it was Mitchell who shouldered them aside, pushing Hyacinth quite roughly as he did so. His strange scarred face was within an inch of Melior Mary's as he put her into the saddle.

'I'll no ride with you, Missie,' he said, 'for it is Captain Wogan's perogative to rescue Her Highness. But don't think I'll leave you rotting there. Just give me two days and I'll have you oot.'

He raised her hand to his lips and she felt his mouth hard against her fingers.

'I'll never let you go,' he said, so quietly that even she had to strain her ears to hear him.

But she could not answer for Wogan had swung onto his horse, which stamped as impatient as its rider. But long after the others had turned back into the warmth of the inn, Mitchell still stood there, frozen to the bone, watching where Melior Mary had vanished into the million crystal flakes that rent the blackness of that momentous evening.

It was the bleakest of cold midnights and Melior Mary was alone in the whiteness, only the gleam of a lantern from the porter's lodge showing her that anyone in the world was alive at all. From where she rode the convent in which Princess Clementina and her royal mother were incarcerated was black as pitch against the snow sweep of the valley and Melior Mary's brain ran fancifully for a moment over those huddled figures that slept in their meagre cells or prayed in the darkness with nobody to see them but God. She imagined gnarled fingers telling beads that they could only feel and tired old knees bent like sticks in the ancient attitude of reverence. What were they praying fore? A hot fire; warm tasty soup; someone to put their arms about them and tell them that this endless sacrifice had been worthwhile? She pitied them even though they kept the Princess and her mother in their midst against their will.

'You must go straight to the lodge,' Wogan had said. 'Chateaudeau has already given the porter a bribe. He believes you to be a...' His voice had hesitated and then he coughed. '...a girl from the village going in for an hour or so.'

Despite the cold and despite the danger of it all Melior Mary's smile had gleamed in the darkness.

'And this Chateaudeau—my supposed lover—is

he the kind of man who would smuggle in a woman? Suspicion has not been aroused?'

Wogan had laughed in his unbridled way.

'God bless your heart no. He's a dandy-cock if ever I saw one. Nobody would think twice of him having *two* little doxies in a night. Begging your pardon, my dear.'

'I hope he will take me straight to the Princess!'

Wogan laughed again. His immediate rapport with Melior Mary had grown into something else. Despite the difference in their ages he knew that for this woman he would have given up the life of a roving spy and settled for King James's service in Rome if she could but have been his reward for doing so.

He squeezed her waist where she sat next to him on her black horse and said, 'You little box of sauce! If you've any trouble with him kick his arse and remind him that business always has the advantage over pleasure.'

She smiled up at him beneath her snow covered hood. She thought him one of the most captivating men alive. And now as she crossed the short distance between the thicket—where he lay hidden and watching her—and the lodge, she wished that he could be with her.

'Jeanneton?'

The voice at her side was a whisper but nonetheless she started. She had not seen the black-cloaked figure detach itself from the shadows and take hold of her bridle.

'No, it is not she. I have taken her place.

The man hesitated, peering up at her, and Melior Mary pulled the hood protectively about her face.

'You are Chateaudeau?' she asked.

For answer there came an exclamation and then a voice said, 'Damme odds my life! I don't believe it!'

'It is true. She ran away. I was the only person young enough to substitute.'

For answer there came a muffled laugh and the voice continued, 'You may be young, Ma'am. But for all that you've got silver hair.'

There was no way he could have known. The fox fur hid her entirely.

'Who *are* you?' she said suspiciously.

'Someone who's getting his prinkum prankum damnable wet in this blasted blizzard.'

There could be no mistaking that voice. As he looked up in the moonlight Melior Mary's astonished gaze looked straight into that of her uncle Joseph Gage.

Beneath that same frost-streaked moon Sutton Place lay icy, the reflected beams shining through the Great Hall windows and casting blobs of colour on the cobbles of the stone flagged floor. Not a creature stirred for miles and yet suddenly in that cold strange hour before dawning both John and Elizabeth Weston woke and were at once alert, sitting bolt upright in the darkness and straining their ears for the noise that had disturbed them. It was an odd sound—so faint that

237

it was impossible to tell what it was or from where it originated—but for all that insistent and a little frightening.

Reminded rather too sharply of Melior Mary's haunting—five years ago now—John swung his legs out of bed.

'What is that noise?'

Elizabeth's voice was fearful in the blackness.

'I don't know.'

'It sounds like a banging cane.'

'I'll go and find out.'

But she insisted on accompanying him and together they left their bedroom, crossed the Great Hall and went towards the Long Gallery, climbing the East staircase.

Despite all John's intention to have the Gallery restored it still lay, partly sealed off, very much as it had done since the fire that had part consumed it during the reign of Queen Elizabeth. And now it had that odd light look which the servants said was the blaze re-living its fury but was, in reality, the first streaking rays of dawn reflecting in the mullioned windows.

And, to add to the strangeness, from beyond the partition that cloistered off the most damaged portion John and Elizabeth could hear the sound. It was a clattering—rather like a child running a stick along a wall—and very faintly, combining with it, it seemed to them that a man was humming a tune. And then, to make Elizabeth grow pale and turn into the protection of John's arm, the noise came through the division, though nothing was visible, and the stick rattled along the wall just beside them.

'Is it the Fool?' whispered Elizabeth, for the story of the jester who wept whenever disaster was to strike the family was well-known.

'Aye, I think so. But I've never heard tell of him like this.'

That strange, long-dead voice was like the crackle of dried leaves as it moved away from them in the direction of the musicians' gallery. And then Elizabeth, just for a second and even then not sure that it was not merely a blink of her imagination, saw him. He was skipping nimbly round, his back towards her, his head on one side and then the other, running his Fool's stick with its funny belled head along the walls as merry as a small boy free from lessons.

'John, look!'

But the Fool had gone and the sound was suddenly stilled.

'Did you see anything?'

'He was happy, John. He was happy. I do believe that something momentous is going to take place.'

And John, knowing for sure that his spirited daughter had gone off with Matthew Banister to rescue a bride for King James, put his head back and laughed aloud.

★ ★ ★ ★

'But you're only a girl,' Melior Mary exclaimed.

239

She had not meant to be rude to a Princess of the blood but the bouncing ball of energy into whose miserable cell she had quietly slipped while Joseph stood at the door to watch for any late walkers was so unlike her preconceived idea of a royal personage that she was unable to help herself.

Clementina giggled into her handkerchief. She was amazingly pretty with eyes like dark suns and bobbing brown curls. She could have been no more than seventeen but with her tiny frame and delicate features could have passed for considerably less.

'I am zo happy to see you,' she whispered. 'We shall change clothes you and I. No? Here is Mama to help us.'

If the two Princesses had been put into prison any hope of rescuing the bride royal would have been impossible but despite their longing for England's support the Austrian government would not have dared such a slight even to a minor power like Silesia so the two women had been placed in mean, but adjoining, rooms in a remote convent lying on the outskirts of Innsbruck.

Melior Mary curtsied as Joseph hissed from the corridor, 'Silence I beg all three of you. If anyone should chance upon this we are lost.'

Princess Sobieski nodded her head. She was a very serious looking woman with none of her daughter's vivacity, though they had in common the same sparkling eyes. She fixed these now on

240

Melior Mary and made a sign for her to disrobe but as the heiress threw back her fur hood the older Princess's eyes widened in disapproval. The abounding silver hair was so unlike her daughter's that it seemed impossible that the two young women could masquerade as one another.

'Mr Gage,' she said beneath her breath.

He looked in at the door and seeing the Princess Mother pulling faces he walked—quiet as a stalking panther—into the room.

'Your Highness?'

'Zees girl will not do. 'er 'air! It eez quite the wrong colour.'

A grim expression crossed Joseph's face and he said, 'Highness, this is the only girl brave enough to take on the mission. The other one defaulted for fear of the consequences. My niece shall wear a headdress and with God's will the substitution may go unnoticed until the Princess has left Austrian soil.'

'Will zere be reprisals against us? I am no coward, Sir, but what will 'appen to those left behind?'

'You'll be set free, Madam. There is no bargaining power in you once your daughter has escaped. And Melior Mary and I must take our chances of imprisonment.'

'Oh, eet is all so terrible.'

The elder Princess moaned and wrung her hands. She was a natural worrier and could not have been a worse person to face up to imprisonment and subsequent rescue parties.

'I shall build a church—no, a cathedral—if we all come out of zis alive.'

But nobody looked at her for Joseph was suddenly sprinting back to the doorway as silently as he had come in. They all turned their heads and a second later he was back in the room dragging with him, his hand clapped over her terrified mouth, a mouse-like little nun who struggled hopelessly in his arms.

'Oh my God,' said Princess Sobieski, 'we are undone, we are undone!'

And she sank down heavily upon her daughter's bed.

'Nonsense,' said Joseph. 'Get your daughter changed, Highness. And in silence too.'

The three women then began to enact a scene which—Melior Mary thought long afterwards—must have seemed more than funny should anyone have been there to observe it but which, to them, was one of the most terrible of their lives. Without saying a word Clementina and Melior Mary began to exchange their uppermost clothes while, at the same time, watching with a horrid fascination Joseph stripping the wretched nun's cowl from her head and gagging her with it.

Over the top of the black band her sad little eyes rolled piteously and the expression on what could be seen of her face was pathos itself as Joseph tore off her habit and trussed up her arms and legs like a chicken. Melior Mary stared in frank astonishment. She had no idea at all what her uncle could be doing here; he whom she had always considered the greatest rake hell of his time and far too lethargic to even be interested in the Jacobite cause, let alone take an active part in the rescue of the Princess.

But on the matter of his lethargy she realised she had been totally wrong. The man who stood before her now rending the miserable nun's garments to shreds was a merciless machine. If he had had to kill the Bride of Christ in order to save the Princess he would have done so.

Eventually Melior Mary could bear it no more and—having dressed herself in Clementina's golden taffetas and pushed every lock of her hair into a lace coif—she crossed to his side and whispered, 'What's to be the Sister's fate?'

He tied the last knot into place and said rather savagely, 'They have a remote attic here where they keep rummage. Nobody will hear her there though she shout till Kingdom come.'

'But she can't shout in that gag.'

'Precisely.'

Melior Mary looked at him closely and said, 'Why do you hate her so?'

Her uncle stared at her in surprise.

'I don't hate her, she just got in our way. It is as simple as that, I feel rather sorry for her in truth and when they discover the substitution I shall tell them where she is hidden.'

'I have never seen you like this. I always thought you so foppish.'

'You are young yet, my girl. In every one of

243

us there dwells two people—often quite opposite to the other. In some there are more than two.'

'In *everybody* there are these separate characters?'

'Oh yes, without doubt. The strongest can be made weak by their love for a child, a woman. The weakest wretch with no will power of his own can fight like a rat for what he considers rightfully his. You have much to learn, Melior Mary.'

Princess Sobieski groaned quietly.

'My daughter will nevaire be saved. See, she is shorter than your niece. She will nevaire, nevaire get past zee porter.'

'Then put high heels on her for the love of God,' snapped Joseph. He was bundling the weeping nun—clad only in her shift—over his shoulder and had no patience at all even for a Princess. 'Now I want no sound from any of you while I dispose of this poor creature. Highness, put what you want to take into an apron and hold it under your cloak. When I return I shall walk with you to the porter's lodge and lift you onto Melior Mary's horse.'

Clementina's face fell.

'Then I shall not need my rope ladder? It was so difficult to get the butcher's lad to bring me one.'

'No,' said Joseph firmly. 'You will not need your rope ladder.'

'Perhaps another time?'

'With God's good grace there won't be another

244

time.'

The three women stared at him contritely and did not utter a word, only Melior Mary having the audacity to pull a face at his retreating back.

Wogan thought in after years that the hour he waited alone in the cold—only dismounting once to relieve himself—was the longest of his life. In the convent nothing stirred. He had seen Chateaudeau—the code name of his old friend Joseph Gage—meet Melior Mary and walk safely past the porter. And after that—whether it boded for good or ill—total silence.

But now, at last, his horse was pricking its ears and—by straining his eyes—he would see two figures, arms wound round each other lover-like, ambling past the porter's lodge. Whether it was Melior Mary with Joseph or whether it was Clementina he had no idea; the fox fur concealed the face completely and he thanked God for the blizzard which the old Princess had said would spoil it all but which he had maintained would be to the advantage of the rescue party.

He watched as Joseph and the girl approached Melior Mary's tethered horse and then he saw something which set his heart racing. The girl had stumbled, as if she was not used to her shoes, and one of them had fallen off. Melior Mary had gone in wearing riding boots—this was the Princess trying to make herself look taller.

Without bothering to look for the missing footwear Joseph lifted her onto the sidesaddle and kissed her on the cheek. Wogan saw the Princess throw her arms round the great rake's neck and kiss him exuberantly. Then in a flurry of flying snow she was off—heading towards the thicket where the Captain still lay hidden.

And then he watched as she turned to wave, saw Gage's arm raise in response and then saw his friend turn back into the yawning blackness of the sleeping convent. Would he ever see him alive again—or the Beauty who had so deeply stirred his soul? But no time to think of them, the pretty little thing had reined in and was peering anxiously amongst the trees.

'Is zat you Chevalier Wogan?' she said as he called her name softly.

He couldn't help himself.

'It is, me little darlin'. Glory be to God but you're free. And isn't Jamie the Rover just the luckiest man this side of Dublin.'

He let out an involuntary Huzzah for his heart sang. The dynasty was secure—the royal bride had started the journey to her wedding.

CHAPTER 12

'She's gone,' said the Mother Superior. 'She and the Princess's Gentleman. They were traitors—they rescued prisoners of the Emperor—they got what they deserved.'

Hyacinth went cold.

'She's not...?'

The woman of God looked at him as unsmilingly as only a zealous Christian could. She had long ago forgotten what charity meant, knowing His way and His laws and caring nothing who might be crushed while divine rights were executed. She was a merciless machine devoted to dogma and she looked at him narrow-eyed and tight-mouthed as she said, 'Dead? No. They're both in prison. But you can pray for their souls' in there.'

Hyacinth turned away, his riding boots sounding over-loud on the stone floor.

'Then I shall go to them.'

She shrugged her shoulders.

'As you wish.' She had already lost what little interest she had in him. 'Let God's will be done.'

The walls of the room were formless, the drums of Hyacinth's ears were at bursting point; again a thousand voices called out for Prionnsa Tearlach; a brave young figure floated free the standard.

'It has, madam,' he said, turning in the doorway. 'Princess Clementina is on her way to Rome and to marriage. And by King James she will bear a son who will come to reclaim his father's throne. He will be the pride of Scotland—of all of us.'

The nun's habit was black against the snow-driven window. She had taken hold of the crucifix from round her neck and was bearing it aloft.

'Begone,' she said, 'back to whatever monster of Hell spawned you.'

'God have mercy on your pitiless soul,' he said in reply. Then he turned and walked, without once looking back, from the house of the brides of Christ.

* * * *

'God damn it,' said the prisoner in a reedy voice, 'but I do swear that this pox hole is ruining me prinkum-prankum, so it is.'

He stood, for the simple reason that his legs were shackled to the wall, and any other position would have been impossible for him, with his back against the damp-running stones, his arms behind him, his head lolling to give his neck what rest it could. He was in the cage that passed for the communal dungeon lying beneath the fortress of Innsbruck.

'Shut your woman's mouth, dandyprat,' growled a voice from beside him, for though he had spoken in English the meaning of the words was clear enough.

'Don't speak your lingo, damme.'

For a reply a lump of human dung was flung at him, staining the prisoner's once exquisite turquoise satin breeches. With an amazing suddenness his arm shot out from behind him and a fist like a flint crunched into his assailant's guts, causing him to groan and slump, winded, upon the stinking floor. Without seeming to pause for

248

breath the prisoner resumed his original stance.

And that was how Matthew Banister found him, peering in the light of goaler's candle, his handkerchief pressed to his nostrils to stave off the stench of human waste.

'Chateaudeau,' he called out in French, 'I've come to see you. My name is O'Toole. I am a friend of Captain Wogan's.'

At the sound of his voice a curious transformation took place. If the word alert could have been applied to anyone in that dread place, it would have described the prisoner's attitude. His head pricked like a hound's, his aching back tensed, his manacled legs straightened.

'Well, well, Banister,' he said drawling. 'I've been expecting you. How dee do?'

Amazed Hyacinth screwed up his short-sighted eyes and found himself staring straight into the face of Joseph Gage.

★ ★ ★ ★

It was like March in May, the wind roaring up the Channel and the sea wild with spume. Most of the passengers had gone below, sick to the stomach. But on the deck, standing beneath the sprit, a woman watched the waves with dancing eyes while beside her, standing protectively between her and the spray, a man with a great gashed scar watched every expression on her face. To a casual observer he would have seemed emotionless, in some ways like a hunter watching his

249

prey; quiet and still, betraying by not so much as a flicker his presence. But that would have been a rapid impression. For anyone who cared to study the man more closely would have seen that, rather than being a stalker, he would have killed without compunction or hesitation any living thing—man, woman or child—that approached the girl in anything other than respect. Mitchell of crag and glen, the man of lochs and waterfalls; Mitchell of the hard-heart and sword-edged spirit, loved fiercely. And all the more because the emotion was foreign to his experience; the mother that bore him dead within the hour, the father tough and harsh as leather. No warmth, no tenderness, no human caring ever; and then, like a cloudburst, the meeting with Melior Mary. Mitchell was overawed with the immensity of his own feeling.

'Look out there.' Her voice interrupted the jealous contemplation of her eyes, her skin, her hair. 'Do you see? The waves are like white horses. Is that possible; that great white horses could dwell out there and swim in the sea's race?'

He thought silently for a moment or two and then said, 'Who knows, Missie. There's a legend in Scotland of a beast that dwells in a loch. They say the blessed Saint Columba was called in to exorcise it—but even he could not do so. Perhaps horses *are* out there, dwelling in fathomless caves.'

A lock of silver hair escaped from beneath a burgundy hood as she turned to look at him, the great eyes—the colour of mist in that storm tossed day—wide and credulous.

'How wonderful it would be to capture one and return with it to Sutton Place and watch as it went like a thunderbolt through the forest. You will love my mansion house, Mitchell. I hope you will stay long.'

'A great deal depends on your father, Missie. Who knows what kind of reception he will give me?'

Melior Mary laughed, turning her face into the wind.

'Oh *you* will be welcome! You are a servant of the Earl of Nithsdale and a friend of King James. In his eyes you could do no wrong. It is *I* who will have to look to my hide.'

'He'll no touch it.'

The reply was very quiet and Melior Mary stared at him.

'Why do you say that?'

'For one reason you risked your life for the Princess—and for the other I would kill him first.'

But this last part he murmured so softly that his words were blown on the breeze and were lost to her.

'You're such a friend, Mitchell,' she answered —and she tucked one of her small, strong, hands into the crook of his arm.

★ ★ ★ ★

'But I promised John Weston that I would not
251

return to Sutton Place.'

'Damn you, Banister—all I ask is that you see Sibella safely there. She is alone and bewildered, with no word from me since I went to conduct the Princess and her mother to Rome. And if I had guessed then that it would have led me to this hell cave I would never have entertained the idea.'

Joseph sat amongst the filth, his leg irons removed at Hyacinth's shouted insistence to the goaler, his beautiful clothes indescribably digusting, his hair—grown to his shoulders—alive with lice.

'First taken prisoner in the damned convent—and now this!' he went on. 'I doubt that I shall come out of it alive, Banister. You *must* take her to the only other family she has.'

'But Melior Mary—she is safe?'

'Aye—and no thanks to either of us. She would be rotting here beside me if that fellow Mitchell had not cut down six men where they stood and snatched her aloft his horse. No, it is you who must take my wife back to John and Elizabeth. Do I have your word on it?'

Why he hesitated Hyacinth never knew, but hesitate he did. And a second later that familiar feeling of danger, that even the mention of Sibella's name could arouse, stirred itself within him. Nonetheless he covered the minute pause by coughing into his hand, so that Joseph only heard him say, 'Of course. I shall go straight to London.'

252

'She will be in my Berkeley Square house. Tell John to see that it is closed up and so, too, my places in Bath. Don't let Sibella worry, Banister.'

With a lurching sense of betrayal that did not sit easily upon him, Hyacinth said, 'I'll take care of her.'

And as if sensing the guilty tripping of Matthew's tongue, Joseph lowered his voice and his last words came out like drops of venom, 'And if you—or any man—should take advantage of my position and lay so much as a fingernail upon her, you are as good as dead. I will personally string you up and watch you dance. Now begone. If they kill me or let me decay to the end I shall somehow have word taken to the Ambassador. Meanwhile, silence means that I live, Banister. Remember that. Silence means I live.'

* * * *

May had passed and with it the celebration of Beltaine; and now the mighty sun lay at its furthest point from the equator on the very fringes of the tropic of Cancer. Beneath a translucent sky the world quivered with the power of the summer solstice and, as if in accord with the old rhythms that stirred in the earth's magic heart, the fabric of Sutton Place was warm in harmony with the ripening land.

It was the eye of midsummer—the night when the sky was always light; the night when the ancient stones of Salisbury glowed again with

253

energy; the night when those who were near the timeless secrets of the cycle of life and after-life, lit fires that the death of the sun might not let evil hold sway. And—as the sun finally went down and the moon goddess rose in the heavens —old, wild prayers were said for the year that was now condemned to die.

And, at last, the coil of destiny, that had lain in wait so long for Sibella and Brother Hyacinth, was sprung. And they, hapless creatures, must take part in all that had always been planned; must act out the next sequence that the pattern of birth, of pain, of despair, had relentlessly set for them. There was no hope; they could not break the ancient spell even if they had been aware of its existence.

In a moon trance Sibella rose from her bed and crossed to the window—mullioned were the panes, moulded the sill—as vigorous still as the day when English craftsmen, directed by the Italian master, da Trevizi, had put them in place. Beneath her the silvered garden rolled away, with nothing but the moving droop of a peacock's tail to disturb the night. Yet she saw none of it, only feeling the stirring of a long-forgotten ritual; only knowing that she must go to he who was her soul's partner or die before the ailing sun struggled once more into the heavens.

In the room next to hers Melior Mary tossed in her sleep, near to waking but not yet ready to open her eyes. She had known no peace since her return to Sutton Place. Strangely through no

254

fear of retribution at the hands of her father who—on hearing her part of the adventure—had said no more of it.

No, her trouble lay further than that; in a deep-rooted anxiety with her own wild ways. She knew that she would never feel contentment's comfort if she could not harness her spirit, control the fierce emotions that sometimes raged within her; knew that she must no longer torture Matthew Banister by witholding herself from him. She had given him her virginity, allowed him to possess her exquisite body once. But then she had become afraid, not of love itself but of the pleasure she had found in it. For in that pleasure lay dependence upon another. She had sensed her one weakness. Matthew Banister had the power to master her—and in mastering her so, too, Sutton Place.

Yet now she could no longer risk losing him. She sensed that he had had enough of her cruelty; within the week he planned to leave the mansion house forever. And that she could not allow—Brother Hyacinth was her chosen consort and must remain at her side always. She must gamble on her taste for passion devouring her.

But as Sibella glided past her door Melior Mary heard nothing. Nor did John and Elizabeth, who had grown more and more alike with each passing year; speaking the same thoughts at the same moment, laughing at the same things, striking the same attitudes over matters of the day. Middle age had ironed out all the fire of youthful diversities; they had turned harmoniously into a boring country landowner and his wife.   But, in his room in the coach-house block, Mitchell woke and knew, with the dark Celtic blood that was his birthright, that ancient mysteries were at work. And he rose and dressed for fear that his Missie—the girl for whom he had left the Earl of Nithsdale's employ and gone instead to act as bailiff at Sutton Place—could be in danger. Like a dog he waited in the darkness, sniffing for trouble.

And for Hyacinth, just waking, there was the sense of a net's closure. He had heard that rare thing, the sound of the great wheel of fortune coming to rest. But with it followed no elation, no joy that he could leap on before it began its next mighty cycle and be carried forward to a completely new bridge of life. Only a quiver of foreboding, over which he had no control, seized him coldly.

Melior Mary's voice came back to him with the words she had spoken after his reappearance at the mansion house.

'There is that in me—detestable though the emotion is—that cannot share anything. Do you know that when my mother lost her poor sad babe, I was glad? No, not glad that she was unhappy or that the mite never knew God's daylight, but glad that I would not have to share Sutton Place. Glad that the inheritance was still to be mine. There is only one person with whom I can share the house—and it is you! That is why it is so important that you love only me. For if you fail me I am doomed to be an old maid and never produce the son that will save the Weston line.'

She had looked such a stormy petrel as she said those words, the big eyes smouldering in her face, the silver mane tossing.

'I think it is better if you do not say that, Melior Mary,' he had answered. 'I am a man from nowhere. Your father's wish is that you should marry William Wolffe, his sister's son, for the sake of heirdom.'

'Never,' she had whispered. 'Sutton Place is mine without need for that. And you are to be my consort. Remember what I say to you—you must love nobody else.'

And now, in the silent enchantment of midsummer Eve, he knew that she was coming to him. That the other side of her extraordinary personality was teasing its way across the quadrangle to slip into his arms and surrender to him what he had craved for two tormenting years; the sensual witchery of which only she was capable. She would cloud his senses and raise him to heights of eroticism with her love; she who had been scarce more than a child on that one wild occasion when she had been his, was coming back to him at last.

The knock on his door was disturbing, not the light tap that he had been expecting but a measured three strokes, as if a cane banged down upon a stage at the start of a play. And then he knew that he had one last chance, that if he did not answer fate would give him another opportunity to wrest round circumstances. But he was a runner in a maze. Every corner presented him with the same alley. He could no more have lain there, silent in the shadows, than ended his life.

'I'm here,' he called out—and very slowly, as in the way of portent, the door swung back.

The figure that stood there was bathed in silver from the moon that shone through the window on the stairway beyond. Even the face, scarcely visible beneath the silver clouding hair, was frozen in a mask of argent. It was Titania come on her dream night; it was Diana the goddess with her silver hunter's bow; it was the earth's oldest mystery here to take him in its inevitable embrace.

His passage to her arms was a return to his mother's breast, the nursing of his child, the absolute union with his eternal wife. And then because, at last, he knew what she had always done, Matthew Banister dropped to the floor and—as ritual decreed he must—made obeisance before Sibella.

★ ★ ★ ★

In the filthy stench of his prison cell Joseph Gage woke with a shout from a mad, bad dream and into the blackness muttered, 'I still live, Matthew Banister. Remember I still live.'

Nobody paid him any attention except that in

England—in Sutton Place—his sister Elizabeth sighed in her sleep and his neice awakened at last and, putting on a velvet cloak, left the house by the great door called the Middle Enter. And as she crossed the quadrangle—silent in the stealthy shadows—Mitchell stiffened. He had heard nothing, seen nothing, but he knew that she was at hand. Everything was ready for what must remorselessly be done.

If Hyacinth had been in his right mind he would have heard the creak of a stable wicket, the light step upon the wooden stairs. But as it was he wandered beyond the stars with his immortal woman, blending his arcing spirit with hers. He never knew, never heard, the door opening and the gasp that followed as the heiress stood framed in the same splash of cruel moonlight. Never realised, or ever could, that she fled down and out to where Sutton Place reared against an indigo sky. Nor that her headlong dash was suddenly halted by arms that gripped like a trap about her shoulders.

'Missie, where are you going?'

'Mitchell, damn you, let me go.'

The hard voice was like the beating of a drum.

'Where are you *going?*'

'Into Sutton Place.' Her answer was flat, without emotion. 'He has betrayed us both—both me and the house. He has to die for it.'

'I'll beat you to a pulp first. You'll be no blood spiller, Missie.'

'Let me go, you Scottish mountebank, or I'll

claw your eyes from your face.'

'Mend your wilful ways, do you hear me? You have no prior claim on the man.'

His fingers were cutting her wrists and she struggled like a frantic cat.

'I have! I have! He belongs to Sutton Place.' She broke, in a storm of despair. 'Oh, Mitchell, I love him. I *have* to have him! How could he do this terrible thing?'

'Because it's a magic night, Missie,' he answered softly. 'A night when good and evil are walking side-by-side.'

'God help me,' she muttered into the rough cloth of his jacket, 'But I'll never forgive him. He has broken my heart.'

In the stillness Mitchell laughed wryly.

'No, he hasn't, Missie. There'll be others.'

His arm was round her shoulders, his hand stocking her hair, until she had cried herself silent and the first rays of midsummer sun had finally shattered the predominance of sister moon. Then—and only then—was he able to walk her back through the dew pools to Sutton Place.

★ ★ ★ ★

There had never been such a triumphant sound, never a more glorious moment, than when the choir of St Peter's in Rome, soared forth with the great 'Gloria' that heralded the marriage of a King of the Royal House of Stuart. Beyond the highest altar in the world, beyond the vaulting ceiling and up to the very bell tower, rose the sound. And in response the joyful carillon sent the tidings from the mighty basilica to all the other churches in Rome. And they in turn burst forth so the whole world might know that, in the face of all danger and plotting, the Pope had just pronounced King James III and Princess Clementina Sobieski man and wife.

There was no-one who did not weep. Sir Charles Wogan—who had bowed the knee before His Holiness and been made a baronet—and Sir Roger Gaydon and Sir Michael Missett, knighted by King James, felt the warmth of tears on their cheeks and were not ashamed. Wogan had seen Clementina run from the convent in thick snow, minus a shoe, but had heard her laugh with joy as he had bundled her bodily onto a horse that would take her to freedom.

'What eez the name of she 'oo 'as taken my place?' she had asked breathlessly.

'Melior Mary Weston, Highness. She is an Englishwoman and loyal.'

'Then may God's blessing be hers. If she eez ever in Rome she will be granted the freedom of the city.'

But the solemn speech had been too much for the girl—barely seventeen years old—and she had collapsed giggling with relief and shock. For a moment Wogan had wondered if she would shout hysteric but the discipline of the ancient House of Sobieski had triumphed and she had turned her attention to riding side-saddle in that desperate and wintry night.

Now she stood, delicate and tiny, beside the elegant bridegroom who bore on his shoulders the hopes and desires of every Catholic and royalist in the world. Slowly they turned from the altar and with measured tread, with the organ declaring in all powerful voice that history was made, they walked in progress—the Holy Father before them—towards St Peter's Square.

In the congregation Tamsin, Lady Missett—great with child—was too near her time to do much more than move her eyes but she caught the gaze of the little Princess—now Queen of England in the eyes of the Jacobite cause—and they smiled fleetingly. Tamsin had put muffs upon Clementina's feet to combat frostbite and for reward she had been created Maid-of-Honour. Nor had King James overlooked the futures of his loyal servants forbidden, by their very daring, to set foot in Britain again. Wogan had passed down to posterity the code names of Jenny and O'Toole so that Melior Mary and Matthew Banister might be free to come and go from England as they pleased, but he and the others must bear the brand of exile for the rest of their days on earth. Yet life—and a good life at that—awaited them in Catholic Spain. Colonel Sir Charles Wogan was to be Governor of La Mancha; Colonel Sir Roger Gaydon to command the garrison of Manzanilla; Colonel Sir Michael Missett had been given Oran.

All was gaiety, all was youth and splendour,

as King James walked in a shower of rose petals out of the cathedral beneath which the bones of Peter the Fisherman lay—old and magical.

* * * *

'You can go,' said the gaoler.

In the dimness that was the world to which he had become used, Joseph Gage stirred himself, rot was his daily familiar, decay his companion. He could do nothing but blink as an unfamilar shaft of light fell across his vision.

'Don't gape at me, man!' The voice was rough but not unkind. 'I'm telling you you are free. The Emperor is tired of you. James Stuart is a married man—the cause of your argument is long since talked out. Go!'

Like an owl, yet like a mouse, Joseph blinked slowly.

'Then will you release my chains?'

'Yes—now—they're undone. A chaise is waiting for you outside; it bears the Ambassador's crest.'

But Joseph could only turn his head very slightly.

'Then help me, if you will, into the daylight. By God, I do swear that this incarceration has spoiled my...'

'Prinkum-prankum?'

Despite himself the gaoler smiled.

'Yes, damme.'

The words ended in a groan as the prisoner

crunched onto his knees, his legs, chained up since the beginning of May, too weak to carry him.

'Must I crawl to freedom?'

The warder shook his head.

'No, there's someone in the chaise awaiting you. I shall send them in.'

'I pray God it is not my wife. She must never see me like this.'

But the gaoler had gone. And when he returned what light there was in that terrible cell was suddenly blotted out. For there, filling the doorway was his huge body, dressed in riding clothes of black and silver and wearing a tricorne hat with a crimson cockade and one golden earring, was Sootface the Negro.

'Oh, master, what have they done to you?' was all he could say.

Joseph managed a faint smile.

'They've ruined me pri...'

But his voice died away and the sudden looseness of his limbs told the blackman that Joseph was almost unconscious. Nevertheless there was one more whispered sentence.

'Sootface, don't let Sibella see me so wrecked. I beg you to restore me to health before you take me back to Sutton Place.'

CHAPTER 13

A mile away from Sutton Place, in almost exactly the spot in which Sir Richard Weston and Sir Henry Norris had once stood with Master da Trevizi seeing the manor house take shape before them, John Weston sat astride his chestnut hunter with a set of plans in his hands, gazing in the same direction. It had been his intention some years before to repair the damage to his house but the stillbirth of his son had driven all such ideas from his mind. But now he felt it was time to consider doing so again. The only problem really being what action to take over the Gate House Wing.

When Henry Weston—son of Sir Francis who had died beneath the executioner's blade—had been restored in blood by Edward VI, that he might inherit his grandfather's great house and no longer have to suffer for his father's attaintment, Sutton Place had been glorious. But for the hero of Calais—it was legend that Henry Weston had been one of the last half dozen men to leave the citadel, fighting Frenchmen till the moment that he leapt onto his horse and cut his way to freedom—glory had been short-lived.

He had been knighted on Coronation Eve by Queen Elizabeth—just as his father had been at

the Coronation of her mother Anne Boleyn—
and had, in the same year—married the sad, dark,
beautiful Dorothy Arundell. Her father Thomas
Arundell and Henry's father Francis Weston had,
by chance, both become Knights of the Bath at
Anne's Coronation and had both been beheaded
for treason. On her mother's side Dorothy had
been a Howard—one of the Duke of Norfolk's
clan. In fact her aunt had been Catherine
Howard, Henry VIII's fifth wife—another accused of vice and adultery.

The web of blood that had joined Dorothy and
Henry Weston to Elizabeth Tudor had been too
unbearable to think about. In fact there were even
those who said, in cruelty, that Henry and
Elizabeth had had the same father. But Dorothy
had worse to bear than wicked whispering.
Twenty-two members of her family had either
been beheaded or attainted at the whim of kings.
So it had been with the wildest feelings beating
in her breast that the closed, secretive face of
Dorothy had looked into that of her cousin, the
red-headed and clever daughter of Henry VIII
as she walked for the first time into the Great
Hall of Sutton Place.

The fire that broke out three days later—on the
hot night of August 7, 1559—had been a strange
affair. Nobody quite knew how it started. But
some said that the figure of a woman, wearing
a hooded cloak, was seen creeping away from the
Long Gallery half-an-hour before the alarm was
raised. And there were whispers that Dorothy,

Lady Weston, had decided to avenge herself on the Queen and burn down the cursed manor house all in one stroke. Yet it was Dorothy, in her nightdress, who had struggled to help her husband put out the blaze that was to ruin the far end of the Long Gallery and destroy the interior of the Gate House.

But now, looking at the exterior in the late September sun, it appeared in good order; only a small amount of falling masonry to give away the truth that it was a burned out shell, an empty facade.

'What do you think?' said John to Elizabeth, who sat in a small chaise beside him. Ever since her miscarriage he had refused to allow her to ride anywhere and she had grown sweetly plump, at thirty-nine, with lack of exercise.

'How dangerous is it?'

'Not at all. It has been well shored up.'

'Then should we just restore the Long Gallery and leave the Gate House until a later stage?'

John contemplated, sticking out his lower lip in typical pose, as he did so. He was almost forty-five but tall and strong as ever, only the fast greying hair and the slight bulge where he had once had a flat, lean stomach showing that there had been any passage of time since the day Elizabeth had reluctantly become his bride. Yet no-one could have guessed that there had ever been ill-feeling as the Lord of the Manor and his wife looked critically at their mansion and then back at the plans. Their unity was complete.

And it was as well, for in their household there was an illness of ease that wore at them like water on pebbles. And nether could point to the cause, for no specific thing was actually apparent. It was simply as if, since the return of Melior Mary and Matthew from Austria, a great silence had descended everywhere. No more the heiress's quick impatient step as she hurried about her hundred and one preoccupations; no more Sibella's light fluting voice as she teased a servant girl about reading her palm; no more Hyacinth's laugh as he joked with Tom or brought a wayward horse under control. Everything seemed so still and sad, as if the house were listening to them all.

'Is it because Joseph is away?' said Elizabeth suddenly.

And because they had now become the couple they were John knew exactly what she meant and said, 'I don't know. It's damnably rum. They've all changed so much.'

'Perhaps you should have refused to take Matthew back. It has ruined Melior Mary's reputation that she went careering off with him.'

John went 'Humph' and said, 'Her reputation may be shredded with the Wolffes but it is as fine as ever it was in the county. Gabriel Roderick is a constant caller—though she can do better than that! She merely ran off to help her King, that is all.'

'You don't think it is the influence of that man Mitchell?' Elizabeth said, as they turned towards home.

And once again John read her thoughts.

'No, it can't be. He is a great man—he was involved in Nithsdale's escape from the Tower, you know...'

Elizabeth nodded her head; she had heard it a hundred times.

'...and that's a mark of his worth. No, I think the trouble stems from Sibella. She hardly has a word to say for herself these days. The girl's lost without Joseph.'

And as John's mount and her one-horse chaise came into the quadrangle there was, once again, evidence of the canker that was eating at the fabric of their lives. Hyacinth came out to take the horses and Elizabeth—looking, perhaps, more penetratingly than usual—saw how changed he was. The abundant curls, the delicate nose, were still in evidence but his mouth bore a sad and anxious look. It seemed as if his love affair with life was over. He had a hopeless air as he stood before them.

And, as he led the horses away, Elizabeth knew that that was all they would see of him for the rest of the day. His way of calling with the family when invited or calling across to visit John of an evening, was over. Now his only appearance in Sutton Place was if particularly asked.

And, as if to put all her thoughts into deeds, at that moment Melior Mary appeared on horseback returning from the direction of the forest. Without a word, without even looking at the man with whom she had once run so happily through girlhood, she slipped from her saddle, tossed the reins over the horse's head and handed them to Matthew as if he were a lackey.

'Good day,' he said.

'Good day,' she answered, but her eyes stared straight in front of her, and without uttering again she stalked off in the direction of the house. Hyacinth smiled at Elizabeth a little apologetically, as if to say 'Oh, it's just one of her moods,' but neither of them believed the other and he turned and walked away again, his back hard with misery.

But worse was to greet Elizabeth when she went indoors. Having removed her cloak and tidied herself from the excursion, she made her way to her saloon, where it was her ritual to serve a dish of tea to her daughter, her ward and any other ladies who might be visiting Sutton Place. But on ringing her bell and Clopper appearing she was informed that Mrs Gage was lying down unwell on her bed, and that Miss Melior Mary was not thirsty.

'Not thirsty indeed! Tell her that I wish to see her,' said Elizabeth, firmly put out. 'And Clopper see that a tray is taken to Mrs Gage. Not thirsty! Whatever next?'

But when Melior Mary appeared in the doorway a few minutes later Elizabeth stopped short, the angry speech she had prepared dying away on her lips. That she—Elizabeth— beauty of the day that she had been, could have given birth to this fairy thing still brought emotion to her throat and the strange feeling of pain at her knees. Her daughter stood before her in the afternoon light—platinum the hair, brook violet the eyes, damask the cheeks; whilst over the slanting bones of the face dropped the dark lashes with all the delicacy of the stamens of a flower.

'Oh Melior Mary, I shall be so happy to see you wed,' said Elizabeth without thinking.

For answer her daughter gave a little shrug and a laugh that was not a laugh at all but a cry of pain, if her mother had been but able to interpret the sound.

'I don't feel I am right for wedding,' she said. 'I shall stay Melior Mary Weston, spinster, of Sutton Place, I think.'

'Nonsense!' Elizabeth spoke roundly. 'I know that all you lack, my dear, is a season in London —and another in Bath should that fail.'

With a smile her daughter crossed to her. She was three inches taller than her mother, whose minute stature had been one of her principal attractions for Mr Alexander Pope, and she seemed—at that moment—the more adult of the two, as she put her arm about Elizabeth's shoulders.

'Should that fail? My dearest, attempts to marry me will I fear. I am too undomesticated of the routine of smiling at some boring man each day and ordering his ridiculous meals with stupid cooks. And as for sharing a bed with unloved flesh...'

271

'Melior Mary!'

'But that is what it is, isn't it? Year in, year out—patient but aggrieved.' She turned to look out of the window. 'Unless there is love, Mother. Unless there is passion to turn day-to-day living into joy.'

Elizabeth regarded her in silence. There seemed no reply that she could make. Instead she said, as she saw Melior Mary give a small salute with her hand to someone who walked within the garden below, 'Who is that?'

'Only Mitchell.'

It was a relief to change the subject and Elizabeth answered her too quickly, 'I cannot state that I altogether care for the man. He seems to me a deal too taciturn.'

Again that laugh that had no joy in it.

'Oh, he can speak enough when the occasion demands.'

'I think I would prefer it if he returned to Rome.'

'He won't do that, Mother. For he *does* know the meaning of love and loyalty. He would have died for the Earl of Nithsdale. Now the focus of his attention is me.'

'What are you saying?'

'Nothing! Nothing that need give you any alarm. He is my dog, my slave, my right hand—call it what you will.'

Elizabeth sat down.

'I had thought that role to be played out by Matthew Banister.'

The look that turned on her was as cold as winter frost.

'Then you thought wrong, Mother.'

With a gesture of pushing something away Melior Mary also sat and—obviously determined to be questioned no further—said, 'I am parched for tea. May we begin without Sibella?'

'Sibella will not be joining us. She is indisposed.'

'Oh?'

There was a meeting of eyes; Elizabeth's suddenly and strangely defensive, Melior Mary's sharp and unrelenting.

'What is wrong? How long has she been ill?'

Elizabeth adjusted the folds of her dress.

'She has not been herself of late. But this present malady seems only to have occurred today.'

The pause between them was alive with questions that Elizabeth had never considered.

'I wonder what the trouble can be,' Melior Mary's voice would not have disturbed a sleeping child.

'I don't know. Melior Mary why do you stare so? What are you thinking?'

The heiress of Sutton Place looked to the tips of her nails, the pleat above her knee.

'Nothing, Mother. Nothing at all.'

But it was a 'nothing' that meant the reverse, and in the enforced silence that followed two of the maid servants bearing aloft the silver tray and all the accompanying sugars and spices that went to the serving of tea, Elizabeth found herself of a sudden counting upon her fingers. Joseph had last been in England at the beginning of April— now it was September. Could it be? But if he had left Sibella in that condition surely some visible sign of it would be showing?

She decided to be direct and, fixing her daughter with a very firm look, she said, 'Has Sibella confided in you? Come, you may tell me. If there is to be a babe at Sutton Place I should dearly love to know of it.'

'A babe?' said Melior Mary, all shock and innocence. 'Why, Mother, that was not the impression I conveyed, I trust. But now you speak of it—perhaps.'

Elizabeth had never been more honest than when she said, 'Look, my girl, do not mince with me. That is what you implied—and you know it.'

Melior Mary dropped her gaze.

'Perhaps I did. You are wiser than I. If my thoughts bubbled over themselves and the truth came out—then you would know.'

Elizabeth's pause was only momentary as she answered, 'There is only one way to find out the answer—and that is to ask Sibella direct.'

★ ★ ★ ★

In his room above the stable block Matthew Banister wept. He wept for the anonymity of his life, for the fact that he had known neither the love of mother, strictness of father, nor the companionship of brother or sister. He wept for the

274

division of his heart between Melior Mary and Sibella. He wept for the fact that he had finally been led to betray them both.

If he could only have understood; been able to speak to Sibella; tried to comprehend what took place in that remorseless blaze of moonlight. But that was not allowed him. As if a play had ended and everyone had acted out their roles to the full, Sibella seemed no longer to have any time for him. The Midsummer ritual had turned to ashes in both their mouths.

And, as if she guessed what happened that night, Melior Mary's unremitting cruelty pursued him like a hound of hell. Somehow, he felt sure, she knew that he and Sibella had been lovers.

A step on the stairs raised his hopes for a minute but it was not Melior Mary but the scar-faced Scotsman who stood in the doorway.

'What do you want with me, Mitchell? I am ill. Leave me in peace.'

'You're no ill. You've been caught out. You and Joseph Gage's wife in your bed and Melior Mary saw you.'

Hyacinth sat up.

'Then she *does* know?'

'Aye, and she came running down the stairs and wept as if her heart would burst. I could kill you for it.'

For answer Hyacinth said, 'I don't suppose you know anything of compulsion, Mitchell.'

The eye that glittered where the livid scar ran

down was fierce, as it fixed itself on Matthew.

'Aye, I know of it,' he answered savagely. 'I've seen men compelled to kill others, inch by inch; I've seen raiders compelled to swing babe's aloft and crunch their skulls down on pointed rocks; I've seen soldiers compelled to rape women until their legs were broken and their wombs torn out...'

'For the love of Christ be silent. I spoke of magic's compulsion—something you would never understand.'

'I am a Celt, Banister. I know of magic—and of the thin line that divides good and evil. I think that somehow evil is at work here.'

Hyacinth's long suppressed anger flared.

'Then if that is so, it is not of my making.'

The scarred face turned towards him expressionlessly.

'Whatever force holds sway is old and rooted in the earth. But from wherever it comes, my only care is that Missie remains protected. As far as I am concerned the rest of you can go hang.'

Hyacinth stood up to face him.

'A fine credo! Well do your worst then. Mount guard over your Missie—who might let you kiss her foot in exchange for your life—and be damned to you. It is true that the Manor of Sutton, its lords and heirs are accursed—fight off that!'

'I come from a country, laddie, full of strange tales—a secret room in the Castle of Glamis in which dwells a monster born to the family; phan-

276

tom bagpipes, beasts in lochs—oh yes, I believe in the hands of Mitchell and the power of my fists.'

'They won't help you in the face of a curse!'

Mitchell made a sound of contempt and was gone without a backward look.

★ ★ ★ ★

It was the end of September, 1719—a day of seasonal mist swirling so coldly that Sutton Place lay entombed amongst the vapour. Nothing moved anywhere and it did not push fancy too far to imagine that the house was cut off from the rest of the world, the inhabitants forced into a confinement of unbearable closeness. With each passing day the tension in their relationships, one to the other, had grown tauter. They were like maypole dancers whose ribbons had woven incorrectly; their only hope to unthread and start again if collision were to be avoided.

John—the least affected—sat this day in his study before a largely stacked fire, a glass of port in his one hand, his mass of share certificates, at which he was glancing at random, in the other. Encouraged and advised by Joseph—whose fortune had been quadrupled by his investment in Mississippi stock—John had bought liberally into the South Sea Company. Immense profits were anticipated from South American trade and, so far, John's dividends had been most rewarding. In fact so strong was the South Sea Company—

277

incorporated in 1711—that to buy in these days cost £100 a share. But he and Joseph were already situated comfortably, between them accounting for a high percentage of stock ownership.

And, on this same day, Elizabeth and Melior Mary sat on either side of the library fire, each with her nose in a book. Beneath a portentous cover that bore the inscription *Mrs Herron's Manual of Petit Point*, Elizabeth sighed over the collected works of Alexander Pope, whilst Melior Mary was at far less pains to hide *The Mad Abbess of Rookwood* beneath the sleeve of *Fauna and Flora Peculiare to Surrey*. Occasionally one or other of them would throw a log on the fire thus obviating the need to constantly ring the bell. In this way the greyness of the day left them unaffected, and it was only Elizabeth's saying, 'Is Sibella resting?' that brought them back to the realities of Sutton Place.

'I believe so,' answered Melior Mary, scarcely raising her eyes.

'Well, with the child due in four months she must take full care.

'Yes.'

Just that. A flat one-worded response and a faint raising of the dark brows. But enough to set Elizabeth thinking that the situation was odd indeed. For a woman who was to bear a child in January Sibella still remained very small. She —Elizabeth—would have thought her ward more likely to give birth in the spring judging by her appearance. But, of course, that was not possible because Joseph had left England on April 23. And thoughts of that made her say, 'You know your father has heard from the Ambassador? It seems that your Uncle will be back any day.'

Melior Mary cleared her throat.

'He must love Sibella very much to stay away until now; until his appearance had improved sufficiently for her to see him. Any other man would have come flying home to his wife regardless if he be a veritable skeleton, in my opinion.'

Elizabeth looked up quickly. She often got the impression that Melior Mary liked nothing better these days than implied cruelties with Sibella as the subject. Her verbal knife would twist and turn like a snake and yet, in actuality, not one thing she said was truly amiss. So much so that Elizabeth wondered if she imagined it and the fault lay in her own mind.

'Joseph does love Sibella, it's true,' she answered slowly. 'But I believe it is in a very protective way. I can imagine him hiding until he is once more the great man—the great rake hell, if you like—that she has always known.'

Melior Mary's voice shook very slightly as she answered, 'It must be a wonderful thing—to have this capacity to arouse such depth of feeling in others.'

And just for a moment she was vulnerable, as weak as she had been when the malevolence had tormented her. Elizabeth, misunderstanding, rose

from her chair and went to her daughter's side
so that she must kneel down beside her and put
her arms round her waist.

'My darling, you shall have such love,' she
said. 'It is a shame, in one way, that Sibella—
your sister—' Did she feel the body harden and
pull away or was it only her imagination?
'—should have married so long before you, but
you have still to see your eighteenth birthday.
You will break so many hearts, my dearest.'

Again that strangely gruff little voice said, 'I
have no wish to inflict pain upon others. But
Mother...', the great eyes turned on Elizabeth
fiercely, 'swear that you will not make me marry
just for the appeasement of neighbours and
gossips. Or so that Sutton Place might have a
man about it. I would rather stay an old maid
than have to compromise.'

'An old maid indeed!'

'Don't laugh at me. Promise that I shall never
have to enter a loveless match.'

'Very well, I promise.'

Only then did Elizabeth sense the girl grow
calm and feel able, after stroking the silver hair
a while, to return to her place beside the hearth.
But above her head, in what was left of the Long
Gallery, another soul was in torment. Shivering
with cold, for no fires were lit now that the great
room was so little in use, Sibella trudged back
and forth in the silence and the strange dim light.

Beneath her clasped hands the baby that—had
she spoken the truth—should have been leaping

with life by now, lay still as the tomb. The most terrible—and yet the most predictable—of all things had happened to Sibella. In that wonderful, ecstatic conjoining of bodies; in the wicked, joyful thrust with which Matthew Banister had claimed her as his own; in the shared culmination which they had enjoyed without shame, a child had been conceived. Hyacinth's seed had sprung within her and she had welcomed it. Only now, with the magic of that night nothing but a memory, did the shame eat at her spirit. She had betrayed Joseph Gage—one of the truest hearts ever born.

She had reached the end of the gallery and was about to turn back when she hesitated. What made her climb through the small hole in the partition she never knew. But climb through it she did and was not altogether surprised to see that she was not alone in the room that had been made by the division. Outlined against the windows where Rose Weston had watched for the messenger bearing the tidings of Francis's execution, where Catherine Weston had dreamed of her love for Sir John Rogers, where Lady Weston had sat with her maids watching for that very same Catherine to appear, was a gaunt figure. It turned as Sibella came and raised one thin hand to its face. There was no mistaking its haggard splendid beauty. It was Amelia—her mother.

Despite the fact Sibella had loved her, despite the fact that she was at one with things supernatural, she could not move a step. She knew that she must be in the direst danger if her mother had taken the immense leap from the darkness to come to her. Yet even as she watched, the spectre was fading, melting into the mullioned windows as if it had, after all, been only a trick of the light.

Sibella found the movement in her limbs returned and involuntarily took several paces forward. But there was nothing. Her outstretched hand touched the glass and the moulding of the window sill. And then as if the history of all those who had stood before her was a compulsion, Sibella found herself gazing out over what, on a clear day, would have been a fine view of forest and parkland.

Strange mist floated past her face. She thought that she was lost in the sky and that she looked down upon a grey seat out of which a great red dragon was convoluting its way towards Sutton Place. And then she was suddenly alert, all attention. Very dimly, almost invisible in the fog, she saw that a cavalcade was indeed on its way towards the manor house. And the scarlet and gilt coach could mean only one thing—Joseph was coming home.

She forgot everything as she clambered back through the partition and, so it seemed to her, traversed the vast space without touching the floor at all. Then down the Grand Staircase, through the Great Hall, to wrench and tug at the bolts of the Middle Enter. Startled, the major domo appeared and then Elizabeth and Melior

Mary. But she cared nothing for any of them.

The door was open and she was running out into the mist, her arms outstretched. And then, just for a second, she stopped in her tracks; conjured from nowhere, apparently, Matthew Banister stood before her. He had sought her out at last.

'Sibella,' he said in an urgent undertone, 'for God's sake speak to me. I can't go on. I have been cast out by both you and Melior Mary.'

'Hyacinth,' she answered, 'what we did was wrong. It is best forgotten by us both.'

A wave of sickness from the child that he had implanted within went over her—but she stood her ground.

'It *must* be,' she said, 'for the sake of us all.'

His beautiful face was within an inch of hers so that she saw every detail of eye placing, of colouring, of the spring of hair on brow and temple.

'Damn you, Sibella,' he said through gritted teeth. 'You have used me ill. How can such a thing ever be forgot? Go to Joseph then! You'll hear no more from me.'

The wild blue eyes had blurred with anger and she wanted then to take him to his rightful place in her arms, and hold him like that until all her life—and his—had wound down to total peace. But from out of the fog came the sound of carriages and then halting wheels and banging doors; and then foolish, silly, beloved, crazy high heels came clip-clopping over the cobbles.

283

'Joseph!' she called.

'Damme, Sibella. Think I'll go back to Italy. Damn foggy this country.'

And there he was, thinner than she remembered, more lined about the eyes, but still Joseph—in a brand new brocade suit of the latest style, with a curling wig beneath his tricorne and a great satin bow on his cane.

'Zoonters, I...' he started, taking a mincing step forward. But he could not go on. 'Oh Sibella,' he said. 'I never thought to see you again. And I love you so much. God help me—but I do.'

And with that he took her against his heart and wept like a child as Brother Hyacinth turned on his heel and walked off alone through the greyness of that dismal day.

CHAPTER 14

In the early February afternoon the cry of a newborn infant seemed to wail thinly in the corridors of Sutton Place. No 'Here I am world, come see me stretch my toes', as there had been in the introductory howls of Giles Rogers—the first baby to arrive in the mansion house: nor the lusty cheerful shouts of Henry Weston—son of Sir Francis and Rose and the first heir to be born within the walls. Nor, indeed, the persistence of Melior Mary's cries as she had greeted the house that was her inheritance. No, these poor little gasps sounded tired and dismal, as if their perpetrator had no energy or will to fight for his survival.

In the darkened room that had, centuries ago, belonged to Sir Richard and Lady Weston the fragile figure of Sibella lay on the great four-poster bed like a wax effigy; while in the crib at her feet her minute son seemed merely to be a toy. That either of them would survive the next thirty minutes was unlikely and as he listened to the mother's feeble heartbeat the unfortunately named, but brilliant, Dr William Smellie—brought especially from London at the cost of several hundred guineas by Joseph Gage—shook his head.

He had not really understood this case. Or rather he had understood it only too well and been forced to hold his peace. That Mrs Gage was not as advanced in pregnancy as she would have him wish, he had absolutely no doubt. The growing child was too small, the womb too high, the movements too few. But where with a woman of the streets, used for demonstration to his students, he could have shouted, 'Don't try and fool me, madam. I am the doctor remember. This pregnancy is not yet thirty weeks!' he felt constrained with a member of the upper classes—and wife of one of the richest men in the Kingdom—to keep his thoughts to himself.

That Gage was not the father and that the child had been conceived while he had been abroad was absolutely certain. But, just as the doctor was puzzling how he could protect his patient's honour and yet still tell the great rake that the birth would not take place till March, Mrs Gage had gone into labour. And how furiously; from the start the contractions strong and severe and the mother shaking with uncontrollable convulsions. Once again Dr Smellie was suspicious. If he had not brought with him from London Mrs Thacker—the midwife he trusted above all others —he would have suspected that some substance, probably ergot, had been introduced into the case.

But Dawkings—Mrs Gage's girlhood maid fetched from her cottage on the estate to help with the accouchement—had not proved forthcoming. A furtive look and a denial had been the only response.

'Dammit, woman, Mrs Gage's life is in danger. Have you given her anything?'

'No, Doctor, I have not. I wouldn't know about things like that. I'm not a woman of medicine.'

But as she had left the room she had wanted to turn back and blurt out, 'Yes. She made me get the stuff from the midwife in Guildford. The one who gives young girls physic to abort their unwanted babes. But she swore me to secrecy on my son's life. So how can I tell?'

It had been two nights ago, when she had taken Sibella's supper tray to her, that the whispered voice had said, 'Oh Dawkings, do you remember the days long ago, when Miss Melior Mary and I were carefree?'

She had answered, 'I do well, miss. But it's my belief that you ought to be carefree now, instead of lying in your room with the curtains drawn all day. I think you're a regular sulk. You have the finest husband in the land, so many say, and he brings you to your parents and your sister for your confinement. And what do you do? Take to your bed like a milksop.'

For answer had come the sound of bitter weeping and Dawkings, regretting her sharp tongue, had taken her mistress into her arms.

'There, there, my dear. Poor old Dawkings did not mean to sound so cross. It's just that the whole house is gloomy with you in the miseries.'

Sibella's warm tears had fallen into her lap.

'But they don't want me with them. Mrs Weston prefers hunting to "women's business" and Melior Mary hates me. Only Joseph—'a convulsive sob on the mention of his name, '—really cares about me.'

Dawkings had been so startled by this that she had said, 'What do you mean Melior Mary hates you? What wicked business has passed between you? Why, you were like babies from the same womb.'

It was then that Sibella had looked up, her eyes swollen and streaming, and said, 'Dawkings, swear to me on the death of your son that you will never speak of what I am about to tell you.'

'Oh, Miss—Mam—I don't like to do that. It's such a terrible thing to swear.'

'But you must! Do you know the real reason why I came back to Sutton Place? It wasn't to be with the Westons at all. I made that my excuse. No, it was so that you could help me. I must have help, Dawkings. Or my husband will be shamed for the rest of his life.'

'Oh Miss, what have you done?'

'I have let another into my embrace. Matthew Banister is the father of my child—and Melior Mary knows it.'

'Holy Mother, forgive me. How could you do such a thing? Is Joseph Gage not lusty enough for you?'

'It was when he was abroad, may God help me. It was only once, Dawkings, and yet, do you know, it was the sweetest wildest pleasure I have ever felt.'

'You ought to be ashamed, Sibella. You have brought yourself low.'

'In your eyes, perhaps. But in my own heart I do not regret a moment. If I had to relive it—I would do it again.'

Dawkings had turned away from her.

'I feel you to be a traitor, Miss. Mr Joseph has given you every gift that a man could lavish— why you were married in a Princess's crown! and he has given you his love. I think you have be-haved hatefully and I don't care if I *do* speak my mind.'

For answer Sibella had put her arms round the servant.

'You are loyal—and you are right. But I am

to pay dearly for it. In inducing the child to come early, I think it will cost me my life.'

Dawkings had stared at her.

'What's this mad talk?'

'I want you to go to that midwife in Guildford —the wicked old baby killer. She has the stuff—it comes from poisoned rye—to make my baby be born ahead of his time. Then Joseph will never know.' Her voice took on a frantic note. 'He *must* never know. You do see that, Dawkings, don't you? Even if you hate me for my treachery, do not punish Mr Gage.'

'But if the babe is born untimely it will die.'

Sibella's grip had been painful as she had said, 'Do you remember the games we used to play in the past? How I would look at the palms of the servants and the farm girls and tell them what their future would be? Well, I know my own. I won't live to see this year out, Dawkings. I know it for sure. But I also know that the baby will survive the ordeal. Therefore help me. I beg you. Let Joseph's memory of me remain kind.'

So the ergot of rye had been smuggled into Sutton Place in Dawkings's apron and swallowed down with the breakfast chocolate. That it could kill, madden and blind was well-known but Sibella had grabbed for it as if it were her last hope.

And now, as Dawkings bolted from the room beneath the doctor's penetrating eye, the tragic consequences lay behind her; Sibella scarcely breathing, the tiny mite gasping for life. But the doctor who, for all his silly name was a tough Scot and London's leading 'man midwife' was shouting behind her, 'Damn you, woman, get the finest brandy in the house. And send that wet nurse up here as soon as she's had a bath.'

Dawkings turned to stare at him in the doorway.

'What?'

'Are you deaf? Strip that girl of her clothes and wash her in hot water, then send her up here in a clean shift. If I can't save Mrs Gage I intend this poor premature thing to live. Don't stare like a lunatic. Get about your business. Mrs Thacker, what do you make of this?'

'This is a seven-month child, Doctor. Brought on by ergot I wouldn't be surprised. But for what motive?'

The doctor touched the side of his nose.

'I think Milady has a lover. But if she had, she's paying the price. Thacker, warm this poor scrap of flesh by the fire and don't let him stop breathing. I'll do what I can for my patient.'

And throughout that night, as Sibella convulsed with poisoning, he held her to the heat of his body and administered the medicines that slowly brought the shaking under control. But still, an hour before dawn, the Weston's priest brought the paraphernalia of ritual into the birth room and christened Sibella's son Garnet, before administering to her the last rites.

Only then was Joseph Gage allowed in. He stood for a long time gazing down at his wife's

290

drawn, white face before he turned his attention to the infant that lay in Mrs Thacker's arms, fed upon a mixture of breast milk and brandy put upon its tongue by a dropper.

'I had not realised he would be so small,' he said at last.

Mrs Thacker said, 'Yes, sir,' but made no other comment and it was the doctor, standing up wearily for a moment, who said, 'The first born often take after their mother. And she's only tiny, your wife.'

'But he looks minute. Will he live?'

'I'll do my best, sir.'

'And—Mrs Gage?'

'I fear she's slipping away. I think it best you ask her family to come to the bedside.'

John and Elizabeth were duly roused but when they went to get Melior Mary she had already left her bed. She must have heard the commotion for five minutes later she appeared, wearing a cloak, and bringing with her Matthew Banister.

'I went to fetch him,' she said abruptly. 'I felt he should see her.'

The doctor thought it was a strange business—the young man with the plum-coloured curls bursting into tears, and Miss Weston, who should have wept, standing there dry-eyed. And then, quite suddenly, he guessed the truth. It was ridiculous to say that that scrap of humanity, fighting for its life in the midwife's arms, resembled anybody. And yet, just for a second, he saw the likeness. As sure as fate he knew that here stood the poor babe's father.

But if it were the case—and the doctor was certain—the man either did not know, or did not care. For he did not even glance in his child's direction, but knelt instead by the bed, taking Mrs Gage's hand in his.

'Sibella,' he said, only just above a whisper, 'you are not to die.'

He could not say more because Joseph was approaching and making obvious, even in these tragic circumstances, that he did not care for the young man's proximity to his wife. But the doctor's experienced eye had already caught a flicker of response in his patient.

'Mr Gage,' he said urgently, 'she moved. If, with your permission, the young man could speak to her again.'

It was the strange silver-haired girl who made the decision.

'Let them stay together, Uncle Joseph,' she said. 'If anyone can save her it will be Hyacinth.'

For answer Joseph merely nodded his head and silently went out, followed closely by his sister and brother-in-law. Melior Mary lingered in the doorway.

'Hyacinth,' she said, 'I had vowed to myself that I would never speak to you again.'

'I know,' he said, without looking up.

'But if Sibella dies it will be on your conscience.'

'What do you mean?' he answered angrily.

But she would not say and swept from the room. Dr Smellie was furious. So much so that he rose and followed her into the corridor outside.

'Is it your custom, Miss,' he said, 'to conduct personal arguments in the presence of the sick and dying?'

She turned her wonderful eyes on him.

'Doctor,' she answered, 'when the elements clash they cannot always choose the exact location.'

But he persisted.

'Have you no feelings for your dying sister?'

She looked at him squarely.

'It is true she was my sister once,' she answered, 'but she renounced me. I loved her, you see, and she played me false.'

'And have you not the charity to forgive her now?'

'I sometimes think,' she said as she started to walk away, 'that death-bed pardons are for the weak minded and superstitious. I cannot forgive what she did because her act put into jeopardy the future of Sutton Place. And that was intolerable to me.'

'You're heartless,' answered the doctor. 'A cruel little bitch.'

'Probably,' she said.

But by the morning the crisis was over for both Sibella and Garnet. It seemed that Hyacinth had summoned her back to life. And, as for the child, some strength appeared to go into him from the very presence of his real father in the room. It was, in truth, a miracle as the day's first light brought a glow of pinkness not only to the awakening sky, but to the cheeks of Sibella and her sleeping son. Rising from his knees Hyacinth turned to face the doctor.

'Is she out of danger?'

'The next twenty-four hours will tell—and with the babe too—but you have brought her back from the brink. That's for sure.'

'Then I shall go. There are certain things that must be said now, certain acts that must be done.'

And without saying more he turned and left the room, heading out of the house and back to the stables. All about him the morning was like a glass bowl—as fine and as clear as the point where the land met the sky beneath the sun's new rays. But he saw none of it. He was full of purpose as he walked back to the stall in which Fiddle was kept and waited in the shadows for the horse and its rider to return.

★ ★ ★ ★

Joseph never knew why he went back to his chamber from the sick room, instead of to priest and prayer as John and Elizabeth had done, but go he did. And there, waiting for him, clad in white from head to toe, stood his servant Sootface. In the mood of mourning that was creeping over the house the sight of the huge Negro so arrayed was shocking to him and, for the first time in many years, he raised his voice in anger.

294

'Why are you dressed like that, damn you? Sibella lies a-dying upstairs. Have you not enough respect to put on black?'

Sootface's grimace was a mask of determination.

'Master, there are bad spirits in this house. They are lurking, even at this moment, to catch the soul of your wife and your son. But do you know something? They are afraid of light. They are afraid of me when I dress in my white things and say "Off with you, old spirits. I'm not sad. See, I'm in my best clothes and I'm on my way to celebrate the birth of the new little master. You've come to the wrong place. Must hurry along—there's nobody dying here.' So, Master Joseph, I'm asking you to get on your prinkum-prankum and then go a-walking with me to show them that we know everything's all right.'

Joseph shook his head warily.

'I can't. I am going to lose her. And Garnet as well.'

'Is that what you call him? Garnet?'

'The priest has admitted him to the Church for he is too tiny to survive. Garnet is a family name.'

'Master, stop it, please!' Sootface's expression was barely controlled. 'Look, look here Master. Look what I have ready for him.'

He thrust a hand-carved figure into Joseph's hands. It was a grinning black monkey of particularly repulsive aspect.

'That's no ordinary monkey, Master. That is

a god-monkey. Once he possesses him Garnet can never be in danger again. Come on, Master Joseph, put on your dandy frills and take me to your son.'

Joseph was so tired and miserable that it was easier to let his slave bedeck him than to argue. And so it was that half-an-hour later a figure dressed in shimmering cloth of gold; a large sapphire winking in the lace at his throat, a dress sword with sapphire encrusted hilt hanging at his side, allowed himself to be led by the arm into the Great Hall.

The fire had been alight all night and the atmosphere seemed warm and comfortable belying the tragic circumstances of the morning.

'Stay there.' The Negro's voice was booming as if he addressed anything evil that lurked. 'Don't be afraid, Master Joseph. I'm going upstairs to bring that baby down here, just you wait and see now.'

And he was gone, dark as a panther, up the staircase—his robes visible in the musicians' gallery for a second before he disappeared from sight.

★ ★ ★ ★

In the gloom of the stable Hyacinth heard the clattering in the courtyard that heralded Melior Mary returning from her morning ride and shrank even more into the shadows that hid his presence. He had come to the moment of his life when all stood at bedrock. He could endure no more. He was like a trapped animal—snipping and snarling and ready to kill or be killed. He could no longer go on as fate's plaything.

Her quick light step and the clipping hooves gave him one second to draw breath before the wicket was abruptly thrown open and there she was, leading her mount in. And then he was before her, leaping out from his hiding place to face her, one hand grasping her shoulder so that she could not run away, the other gripping his hunting crop.

'You are less than the dust,' he said, not pausing for her to speak. 'You have defied the law of humanity. You left your sister to die and went to ride. Melior Mary Weston, I sicken that I ever loved you.'

Her startled eyes were enormous as she wheeled round.

'Take your hand from me this instant! It is *you* who have defied all that is decent. Here, in these very stables, you betrayed me with my so-called sister. I saw you locked in your lust. You know nothing of loyalty and goodness.'

'How dare you! What happened between Sibella and I was an hour of madness—never to be repaired.'

Her sound of derision turned to a gasp as he shook her violently, lifting her feet from the ground so hard did he grip.

'You laugh! It shows how little you know of life. It shows what scant kindness dwells in that wretched heart concealed beneath the mask of beauty. But you do not deceive me, Melior Mary. I know you for the merciless bitch you are.'

For answer her riding crop flashed in the air, only to be knocked from her hand by an answering blow which caught her on the cheek. A trickle of blood ran down the soft skin and into the silver hair.

'I never thought that I would lay my hand on you but now I've a mind to kill you. Did it never occur to you to forgive? No, you of the mighty stirrup must act as judge and jury in one. Who are you to pronounce sentence on others?'

'But you knew you had to be steadfast for the sake of Sutton Place.'

'Damn Sutton Place and damn your wild notions. It was just a caprice that I had to be yours. You could make a glittering match amongst the nobility and still have your wretched manor house.'

She glared at him, her fury boundless.

'You can speak ill of me, you can curse the world, but say no thing of the mansion. You know I would drown in a bucket to save one brick.'

He caught her beneath the chin, forcing her face close to his.

'Then hear this. I hate the place. It has brought me to ruin. I came with every hope high for the future and met a conspiracy of silence. And to add to my torture I fell in love with you. No, more than that. I grew to worship you, to treasure you, to cherish you beyond words. And you stamped on me for the unfeeling bitch that you are. I should beat you to a pulp for your wickedness.'

'Then why don't you?' She thrust her chin forward defiantly. 'Go on, vent your spleen. I'm not afraid.'

For a long moment she stood in danger of her life as the blood drained from Hyacinth's face and his hand raised the hunting crop above her head. Then, with a gasping sob, he threw her from him.

'Get hence. Go on. I never want to see you again.'

'You were afraid to do it.'

'Yes, yes,' he answered, his head in his hands. 'I was afraid because, God help me, I love you still, for all your unkindness.'

It was the hunch of his back that made the burning tears flow. But still she would not be humbled, preferring to turn away rather than let him see her weep.

'Go away,' he said again.

'No, I will not. I cannot. I pledged my life to you when we first met. It was no whim, no child's play on the part of some spoiled chit. I truly loved you—and that is why I hated you for what you did.'

He lowered his hands.

'You love me still?'

'Love, hate—everything; all confused.'

'Then if you love me, forgive Sibella.'

'That I can never do.' She had turned round to look at him and her eyes were the flash of distant storms. 'I once told you that there is that in me that cannot share. It is true. And yet I hate it for I know it will bring me happiness. But if I forgive you...' Her voice broke and her lips trembled and the tears came gushing too quickly to hide. '...then I can never pardon Sibella. Don't you understand that to justify your acquittal I have to blame her? Oh, it is such a terrible thing to be as I am, Matthew. I swear that only you and Sutton Place know the dark corners of my soul.'

'But if she dies?'

'Then die she must.'

'But the child—surely you will not hate the child?'

Despite all her suffering Melior Mary was still aware of the strangeness of the remark. Not in the words spoken but in the way in which they were said. It occurred to her with immense clarity that Hyacinth did not know the truth about Garnet's parentage.

'Well?' He waited for her reply.

She stood very still, her mind darting like a caged mouse. She knew that she could break him now, finish him and be avenged for all the hurt he had given her. But why? She wanted him and somehow—however hard she must fight, however great the cost—she would make him master of Sutton Place. It was better by far that he never knew the sickly babe was his. Let Sibella's deception hold sway.

'I shall love the child as my cousin,' she said. 'He has come into the world innocent when all's said.'

She took a step towards him. She had gone very pale but her expression was one of the great determination as she said, 'Hyacinth, in June— on my eighteenth birthday—I want you to marry me. We shall elope and let the world go hang. Will you do it?'

'But I have no family...'

She stamped her foot.

'God's life! You will drive me to insanity yet. There'll be family enough when you take me on. Now, will you have me or not?'

There was no need for him to answer. The storm bird was in his arms where she had always truly belonged. And oh the precious feeling of her! The sweet body, so delicate and yet so strong; the hair rippling like silver satin; the sweep of the great lashes against his cheek.

'Oh, my darling,' he said, 'forgive me.'

'There is nothing to forgive. I had already forgotten the past.'

'Nothing—and nobody—shall ever come between us again. Melior Mary, my love, my joy— Queen of Beauty.'

Their kiss was the plighting of a lifelong troth; a bond that would last forever.

★ ★ ★ ★

301

Past the musician's gallery, down the staircase, into the small hall and finally into the Great Hall, came the tiny procession. First Sootface, dancing a little as he went; then Mrs Thacker, a tiny bit stiff, a little highly starched, a fraction too much of the goffered cap and crinkly apron, but for all that bearing aloft, in a mass of swaddling, Garnet Gage.

'He's alive!' said Joseph.

'Yes, sir. He saw out the night vigil and he's fit to come and greet you—but only for a minute. He must be kept warm at all costs.'

The rake hell bent over the tiny creature held high for his inspection. One long finger, decked with a rainbow opal, reached out to touch the slumbering cheek, the long fair lashes.

'My son,' he said.

'Yes sir, if you please.'

'He shall have everything that I can possibly give him. But more than that—he already has my love.'

'Yes sir.'

'If you can guarantee he survives I shall give you a pension for life.'

'Nobody can guarantee mortality, sir.'

Joseph could not answer her. His heart was too full of the old, wild love of father for son; at the joy of creating a creator. He was fulfilled; a man through his boy.

'Here are five gold guineas, Mrs—'

'Thacker, sir.'

'Cherish him until he is big enough to deliver

302

into my arms. I am the proudest father in the land.'

Mrs Thacker's eyes were turned to the floor as she curtsied and said, 'Oh, thank you, sir.'

★ ★ ★ ★

It was May time again. May, so great with joy and sadness for the House of Weston and the Manor of Sutton. On May 21, 1509, Sir Richard Weston had first been honoured by Henry VIII—and made Keeper of Hanworth Park and the Manor of Cold Kennington; Steward of Marlowe, Cookham and Bray; Captain, Keeper and Governor of Guernsey, of the castle of Cornet, and the isles of Alderney and Sark. And all to celebrate the young King's coronation.

Then on May 17, 1520, the Duke of Buckingham had been executed at the Tower and Sir Richard granted the Manor of Sutton as his sinister reward. In May, 1530, Francis had been married to Rose and three years later—again in May—made a Knight of the Bath at Anne Boleyn's coronation. And then the springing of the trap. On May 17th, 1536, Francis had been beheaded on exactly the same spot at which Buckingham had died. Sir Richard's prize had turned to ashes. Old evil, old violence, had reached out over the centuries. And now it was time again. There had been no blood sacrifice since the death of John Weston's infant son. Reparation must be made.

But none of them knew how close they all were, how only a few hours lay between them and the end of their way of life. Only Sibella, wondering how she had escaped the death which she was certain had been lying in wait for her, felt cold as the doctor—returning to Sutton Place from his London practice—pronounced her fit to travel home; felt that it was not her destiny to escape like this.

Yet what could be wrong? Joseph, in a state of exaltation, had been refurbishing and redecorating their house in Berkeley Square, buying solidly into the South Sea and Mississippi companies, all to give the child he believed his own an inheritance worthy of a prince. Melior Mary had not seemed so joyful in a year—though she had yet to look Sibella direct in the eye—and with the lightening of her mood, catalyst that she was, the atmosphere of Sutton Place grew cheerful. All of them, all of the family, were in their own kind of peace.

So, putting her fears aside, Sibella Gage at last rose from her childbed and allowed Dawkings to dress her in a travelling gown of green and leaning on Joseph's arm—for her legs were as weak as water—she had come slowly down the staircase and into the Great Hall.

They were all there waiting for her; every character in the scene that must shortly be enacted. On either side of the fireplace stood John and Elizabeth, as pleased and as proud as if this were Melior Mary's child that was being carried down to them by his nurse. And, seated on a chair near to them, Melior Mary herself made a pretty picture in the afternoon sunshine. Hyacinth stood in the entrance leading to the Grand Staircase and Sootface bowed before Joseph's advancing feet. Only Mitchell was missing but, even as she thought this, Sibella saw the Scotsman's scarred face and brilliant dark eyes in the shadow of the small hall. They were all in place.

And at that moment fate could have gone two ways. It would have been possible for Joseph and Sibella to bid farewell to the others, to take Garnet and put him in their travelling coach, and for them to leave Sutton Place with no more than a wave of the hand. And then they could have gone on to another life. Sibella would have borne more children, Joseph would have turned his attention to his speculations and seen the deep water into which he was getting, and the whole history of the House of Gage, and the great rake who led it, would have been different.

But the circles of life were poised and the happiness that could have been theirs teetered on the brink, as a moment of destiny was enacted. Melior Mary said, 'May I see the baby?' It was as simple as that. There was no malice, no recognition of what might lie ahead. The heiress spoke in love, with no thought of her old mad anger.

Afterwards—ever afterwards—she relived that moment a million times. She saw the nurse turn to Sibella for permission, saw her adopted sister nod her head. Saw Joseph's adoration of his wife and child, saw John and Elizabeth's indulgent exchange of glance. Might it be that their own wild girl was feeling the first instincts of motherhood, they seemed to be thinking.

And then the little bundle was in her arms and she was gazing down into that tiny face complete with Sibella's nose and mouth and hair of a reddish, pinkish shade. But then he opened his eyes and Melior Mary knew she had never seen anything so beautiful.

'Why,' she exclaimed with joy, 'he is the most perfect child in the world. Have you seen the colour of his eyes, Mother? They are the blue of wild hyacinths.'

A great black spiral was at her feet and she was falling down into it. She would have given anything then—even Sutton Place itself—for those words never to have been spoken. She saw Elizabeth frown at John, saw Sibella go white to the lips, heard Hyacinth gasp behind her, saw the roll of Sootface's eye and the step forward of Mitchell. But it was on Joseph that there was the most profound effect of all.

She observed him realise the truth. He turned to look at Sibella and then at Garnet and then, over her head, to where Matthew Banister stood. Then he lost all colour and for one moment she thought he was going to drop where he stood. But he recovered and in a voice completely unrecognisable as his own hissed, 'Kill him.'

The cruel bladed knife was in Sootface's hand

instantly and the Negro was running forward, pushing aside John as he went. Melior Mary rose to her feet to throw herself in his way, but too late. The blackman had reached the bottom of staircase and if Hyacinth had not turned and sprinted up them and into the Long Gallery, he would have been dead.

Melior Mary could only think of one thing to do.

'Mitchell, for God's sake save him,' she screamed.

She had never seen anything happen so quickly. As if her voice had been a starting gun everybody started to run in different directions; Joseph, Mitchell, John and herself up the stairs, the nurse and the baby out of the Great Hall; Sibella towards the Middle Enter, followed by a slower Elizabeth.

But Hyacinth, with just a second's start, was making for the hidden door behind one of the four fireplaces and the priest's staircase that led to the grounds below. Yet he was not quite fast enough. Sootface's great hand had him by the collar and the knife flashed in the air. Then in that echoing gallery there was a cry, a scream— and a shot. Mitchell's voice rang out, 'If anyone of you moves I'll blow your brains across the ceiling.' There was total and utter silence.

★ ★ ★ ★

They found Sibella in St Edward's Well, looking

such a sad tiny little thing. It was Joseph himself who went down to get her, lowering six feet to where she had drowned in the deep tunnel. Her golden pink hair floated like weed upon the surface, her face just below the level of the water, her eyes open and staring to the sky above.

He had carried her all the way back to Sutton Place in his arms and it was he who had laid her on the bed in which Garnet had been born. And then he had gone. He had simply picked up the child, called out to Sootface to follow him and jumped into his carriage. There had been no word for Elizabeth no backward glance, no attempt to seek out Hyacinth—nothing. The curse of the manor had taken away everything he loved and had pride in. He was never to see the house again.

CHAPTER 15

On the night before her body was due to leave Sutton Place Sibella came and stood outside. Her sightless eyes seemed to gaze at the mansion that had loved and killed her, her immobile stance undeterred by the savage rain that lashed at her dress and turned her hair to strings. She continued this ghastly vigil for an hour and in that time Melior Mary, who saw her from her window, gave a scream that sent a shiver through all those who heard it; and Matthew Banister, who glimpsed the phantom as he walked alone and aimless in the grounds, seemd to lose his reason and went running through the dusk shouting Sibella's name over and over again.

They brought him in at midnight, semi-conscious. Mitchell had found him at St Edward's Well, white and shaking and saying something of a woman who had writhed at his feet. But despite all this, despite the fact that his spirit was almost done for, Elizabeth and John waited for him and asked him to speak to them alone. He knew that he was about to learn what he had always wished and always feared—the truth about his parentage.

John, his face dark and savage, was the first to speak.

'Matthew, in view of what has happened you must go from Sutton Place and it is my wish that you never return.'

He had turned to face them both as gravely as he could.

'Mr Weston, madam—you must believe I did not know, until Melior Mary spoke, that Garnet was my child. And you must further believe that Sibella did nothing that she could help.'

Elizabeth drew in a breath.

'If anyone else uttered that I would scorn them but in a way I credit what you say. Matthew, to a certain extent I take responsibility for what happened. I should have foreseen it years ago and spoken out. But you see I had given my word never to divulge the secret.'

John shifted from foot to foot and said, 'We were wrong not to tell you, Banister. It put you in great moral danger. But here is the fact and take it like a man—you are Sibella's brother.'

Everything in place! The strange bond that stirred ancient memory, the love so different from that for Melior Mary. But, oh God, what terrible consequences.

'Then I have broken God's most basic law,' Hyacinth said, in despair. 'I have committed incest and Garnet is the child of brother and sister.'

Elizabeth burst into tears.

'Dear Jesus, to hear you speak those words is like a knife in my heart for I could have warned you. But I had sworn to protect a good name. You see I had a friend—many years ago—Amelia FitzHoward. When she was just a girl she ran off with a soldier and he left her with child. Her family were in deep shame and sent her to Calais, where there was another branch of her family descended from Zachary FitzHoward and his mistress Rosalind Banastre. I speak of two centuries ago, Matthew, but it had always been family pride that they had such an ancestor. You were born there and given the name Banister— which is how it changed in time—by your cousins. But when she died Amelia left instructions to Mr Pennycuick, her lawyer that you should be sent here that I might take care of you. And she also requested me to bring up Sibella. I had both her children under my roof—one a bastard, the other

310

by her husband Richard Hart—and it was written in her last letter that I should never tell either of them. Now look what tragedy has come out of it.'

'And Sibella never knew? She died without realising?'

'As far as I am aware.'

With the knowledge that in the cool of midnight when the sun begins to die, he and his sister had created a child, Hyacinth saw himself for what he truly was. An instrument of some greater destiny. He had loved life so much to start with, would have enjoyed its light and shade so greatly. But really all that had been required of him had been to father Garnet. He and his wishes had counted for nothing.

He turned in the doorway and said, 'I bid you both goodbye. I shall never return. All I ask is you tell your daughter I will love her forever.'

But even as he said it he knew that they would not. Would rather let the wild grieving creature that lay upstairs, sobbing upon her bed, grow to hate him. Would believe that time would heal her passion and that she would make a safe, comfortable marriage that would secure Sutton Place and the Weston line for centuries to come.

A thought struck him and he turned back again. 'It is the curse on the heir, isn't it? Melior Mary is to be deprived of her true love.' Just for one burning second, for the very last time in his life, his clairvoyance came back. 'All these events have led to one thing. Melior Mary will never marry. The direct line from Sir Richard Weston is to die out.'

John said, 'It is best you go. You have caused enough trouble here. You will never set foot in Sutton Place again.'

'Be sure of that. The house has seen me out and it has seen Joseph Gage out and it has caused Sibella's death. I wish you joy of it.'

He was so bitter as he left them. He who had had so much exuberance and gaiety to offer the world was finished at twenty-one years of age.

'Where will you go?'

It was Elizabeth that spoke.

'God knows. To try and find peace—whatever that may be.'

The short-sighted eyes were a blur of hyacinth blue the damson curls were deep about that arch-angel head.

'I will pray for you, Matthew Banister.'

He gave a despairing empty laugh—and was gone forever from their sight.

The next day saw the black-plumed cortège leave Sutton Place for its wearisome journey to the home of Viscount Gage—the family seat where Sibella would be laid to rest within the vault. But though Melior Mary—who had not spoken a solitary word since the day they had brought Sibella in—had allowed Clopper to dress in her starkest black, now she refused to leave her room. Elizabeth and John could do nothing with her and finally, in desperation, they sent Mitchell—dark as a rook in his mourning clothes.

The heiress was standing with her back to him,

staring out of the window across the gardens. Even without looking round she must have sensed who it was for she said, 'She stood out there last night and looked up at me. Do you know that, Mitchell? She blames me for it all—and rightly so. If I had said nothing she would still be alive.'

Hands strong as whips were on her shoulders as he said, 'Missie, take care! You tread a dangerous path. She would never blame you. She was probably looking for her babe, poor lost soul.'

'But she was out there in the pouring rain, looking up at me.'

'She was looking at the house. Now come to your senses. There's a long journey ahead of us—and a grief-stricken man waiting to be comforted.'

'You speak of Matthew?'

'I speak of her husband—Joseph Gage.' There was a note of irritation in his voice. 'Missie, you cannot indulge yourself like this.'

The eyes flashed in his direction.

'What do you mean?'

'What I say. Arrant selfishness allows you to behave in this manner. You care nothing for your mother's suffering—nor that of your father. You stand here in martyr's pose and let the rest be damned.'

She flew at him but he caught her wrists and held them above her head.

'Listen,' he hissed. 'We all have to live with

313

guilt—there's not a man nor a woman born who does not—but it is how we master it that matters. And yours, Missie, shall be private. You can scream and cry in the quiet of your room till your heart bursts open. But you'll no inflict your dark soul on the rest of the world.'

She pulled her hands away from his grasp and stood rubbing the newly sprung red marks.

'Hyacinth has gone, hasn't he?'

'He left at dawn.'

'I shall follow him.'

'And give up Sutton Place? For your father will never let you marry him now. He'd as soon disinherit you—and that's the truth.'

She looked at him slowly.

'Is it?'

'You know it is. Think carefully. If you play the bitch forever you will have nothing.'

'But I am stricken with guilt.'

'When you spoke of the baby's eyes did you mean to draw attention to the likeness between it and Banister? Did you deliberately set the cart of death to roll downhill?'

'No.'

'Then brace up, Missie. Be strong. For you can have your heart's wish. But I tell you one thing. I'll watch you—and your behaviour—like a raven. You shall never act the shrew while I live. The great lady of Sutton Place must be worthy of her title.'

'And if I dismiss you from service?'

'That you'll not do. Only a ghost can live

314

without its shadow.'

And with that he held out his hand to her and led her down to the black carriage and the sound of the single tolling bell that rang out for Sibella from the steeple of Holy Trinity.

★ ★ ★ ★

The letter to John was brief:

November, 1720

'Dear Brother,
I am ruined! The South Sea Bubble has burst and the Mississippi Company collapsed. Everything has been sold to pay my debts. I shall be at the Posting Inn in Dover the night after tomorrow and if you would see me again before I leave England I would pray you to be there.
Your affectionate brother,
J. Gage.'

John's worst fears had been confirmed. His own investment in the South Sea Company had been heavy enough. Earlier in the year the organisation had underwritten the English national debt on a promise of five per cent interest. Shares had risen to ten times their value and speculation had run wild. And Joseph with his enormous holdings in both that and the Mississippi Company in France had trebled his already vast fortune. But he had been too full of the death of Sibella to do little more than nod his head when informed of the fact.

In better times might he—or even John who was far less shrewd—have seen the potential ahead? But neither had—and the government attempt to halt speculation, the consequent fall in the price of shares and the inevitable bursting of the bubble had savaged them both. The long-awaited restoration of Sutton Place had been cancelled and many of the pictures and much of the silver had gone from the mansion house. But that Joseph had been actually ruined John had not realised until this moment. Though perhaps he should have guessed for, simultaneously with the English disaster, the Paris based Mississippi Company had gone tumbling as well. So Joseph had lost everything—wife, fortune, the right to call Garnet son. Without a moment's hesitation John ordered his coachman to take him to Dover.

As he entered the inn on the waterfront he remembered that the last time he had set foot in the place had been eighteen months earlier when he had seen Matthew Banister off to Europe and the rescue of Princess Clementina. What a change in that short space of time: when Sibella a merry bride; Melior Mary as full of fire that she had run away to take part in the adventure; Joseph—unbeknowst to anyone—already at the Polish Court and ready to adopt the guise of Chateaudeau, the Princess's Gentleman. And now Sibella cold in the Gage family tomb; Melior Mary withdrawn from the world; Joseph a ruined man in every way. And of Hyacinth himself, not a word. He had walked out of Sutton Place into the rainy May morning and had never been heard of again. John thought of the curse that dogged them all and shivered as something walked over his grave.

A voice at his elbow said, 'John! So you've come!'

He looked round but could see nothing of Joseph. And then, peering more closely at the man who stood beside him, he gave an exclamation of surprise. He had thought to find the great rake at his most distraught, sighing into his lace kerchief, but the figure beside him exuded vigour and a certain restless desire to go out and wrestle with the world.

And not only that. If John had passed his brother-in-law in the street he would not have known him. For gone was the prinkum-prankum, the frills, the lorgnette and the walking cane; and in their place were doeskin breeches, a linen shirt and a leather coat and riding boots. Discarded was the great curly white wig and the thick hair had been allowed to grow from a short crop to the shoulders, and was now tied back with a small black bow. The cat eyes had a look in them that no man would cross and the mouth was hard. Joseph was unrecognisable.

John could only say, 'You've changed!'

'Aye, the fop has been dismissed. He's a pitiful figure without the fortune to back him, would you not agree?'

'But where are you going dressed like that? What are you going to do?'

'I have ten guineas between myself and starvation. Enough to secure passage for Sootface, Garnet and myself to France. I have connections in Paris that will help me raise cash and—after paying my respect to the King in Rome—I intend to join Wogan, Missett and Gaydon in Spain. In short I'm going for a soldier, John. In the service of the Spanish King.'

Weston was dumbfounded. It was the very last thing that he would ever have expected.

'And you are taking—', he paused, inwardly embarrassed '—Garnet—with you.'

'Of course. He is all I have left in the world beside the Negro. Don't look so bewildered. They have children in Spain you know. I hear that Tamsin Missett gave birth to a fine girl for whom Queen Clementina herself has stood godmother.'

John shook his head.

'But what do you know of soldiering?'

'Nothing that I cannot learn. I'm still three years off forty, John. Don't put me past taking up a new life.'

'And where's the child?'

'Here. Come upstairs where he sleeps.'

And sure enough in a tiny cramped bedroom in which John could not stand erect, Sibella's son slept in the arms of the slumbering blackman. He was nine months old and more like Banister than ever. Joseph said, as if reading John's thoughts, 'I see Sibella in him—and that is all that matters to me. He loves me as his father. His first smile in this world was for me. He and I shall stick together through this lean time until I can make a new fortune for him.'

And John knew then, with no second sight or power of that kind, that Joseph would. That from this disaster would rise another Joseph even more successful than the first.

'I wish you both God's blessing,' he said.

'Thank you.'

From the harbour came the call 'Tide, tide,' and it was the moment for Joseph Gage and his party to embark. And so it was with the winter sea shouting of storms and the November wind biting to the bone, that John stood once more to see a ship make for France.

And long after the vessel bearing the man who had been one of the greatest of his day—the richest, kindest, most eccentric person that John had ever grown to love—disappeared from view, the Lord of the Manor of Sutton stood where he was. He was cold to his heart. With his very title he had inherited the agony of a long-dead Queen and all those most beloved to him had become immeshed in its coils. But two had escaped. Joseph Gage and the child he called his son had sailed for Spain and a brave new life.

As John Weston turned for home he prayed not only for Joseph's safe deliverance but for those whose destiny it was to remain at Sutton Place.

PART TWO

CHAPTER 16

She had remembered; strung together all those beads of thought of which the necklace of her life consisted. There, in the early morning sunshine on her forty-ninth birthday, she had stood by the bedroom window, looking out upon her peacock-jewelled lawns, and had re-lived it all. Even to the ultimate agony; to the extraordinary sensation of freezing that had gripped her from the moment Sibella's poor drowned body had been carried into the Great Hall to lie with the stained glass windows splashing pools of colour onto her newly-dead face.

It was a sight Melior Mary could never forget and when she had eventually emerged into the world again, she had won the nickname of Queen of Ice. Even George II who, as Prince of Wales, had come across a portrait of her by Sir Godfrey Kneller and had tried his hand at making her his mistress, had been refused. And those seeking the pleasure of capturing beauty so unique—princes, dukes, earls and statesmen who had thrown their hearts and their fortunes at her feet, had only heard Melior Mary laugh politely and spurn them. But she was clever in her refusing. She had few enemies—in fact invitations to stay with the great hostess at Sutton Place were prized high indeed.

It had been Mitchell who had finally decided what role she would play in life, for she had planned to do little. A visit to Malvern to improve her ailing spirits—so desperately worried over by John and Elizabeth—had had no apparent result. Though, in fact, she had found again that magic spring which she had first seen with her mother and Mr Pope and Amelia FitzHoward; and, shortly afterwards, had discovered its extraordinary effect upon her appearance. But other than that she returned to the mansion house as wretched as ever.

But John's interest in re-building the family fortune after the bursting of the South Sea Bubble had caught her attention. He had begun to deal in the buying and selling of property and found that his nineteen-year-old daughter was a shrewd and energetic business woman. Only too glad that something aroused enthusiasm in her he allowed her to participate and, within two years, the refurbishing and restoration of Sutton Place was once more in hand.

But she was the despair of her mother. Melior Mary seemed almost mannish in her approach to life. Riding and business dealing were her only sources of interest and suitors could be paraded till Elizabeth dropped. And quite suddenly—she did. In 1724, aged only forty-four, she grew weak one day, lay down upon a sofa, smiled at John and died. She had not lived to see her beloved house completed and was laid to rest, wearing a sad, puzzled expression, in the family vault at Holy Trinity. Alexander Pope—now acknowledged leader of the literary school of the day—wrote to Melior Mary from his house in Twickenham sitting, as he penned in his exquisite grotto. She condemned his manuscript to the flames.

A few months later the work on Sutton Place was completed. At last the Long Gallery, spoiled so long ago by fire, was re-opened and made beautiful. The dining room and staircases were re-panelled and additions made to the stained glass in the Great Hall. But there was no Elizabeth to see it; no husband of Melior Mary's to ride with his father-in-law and love the house; no grandchildren to fill all those empty echoing spaces with their fun; no word from a brother-in-law gone long since to a foreign land. John took to drink and to riding. And one day the two combined to send him flying and he was for evermore lame. He lived to see the death of the man he hated above all others—the Hanoverian, George I—and himself died three years into the reign of George II. His last words on earth were, 'Support the boy in Rome, Melior Mary.' For Princess Clementina had been fruitful. James III had been blessed with an heir—Charles Stuart.

And then the house had been deserted. Melior Mary had come back with Mitchell from the freezing misery of John's funeral and had stood warming her hands at the fire of the Great Hall.

'Well,' he had said, 'that is that. It's all yours now. You are the mistress.'

She had looked at him impassively. 'Yes.'
'And what do you intend to do about it?'
'What do you mean?'
'Just that, Missie. Are you going to live here like a hermit or are you going to open the house to guests? Are you going to live as befits the Lady of the Manor or are you about to rot alive?'
She stared into the fire depths.
'I am not very interested in people, Mitchell.'
'Selfish as ever.'
She turned angrily, stung by his remark.
'Remember that the power of dismissal lies in my hands solely now! You have no right to speak to me so.'
'I have every right because I love you. Yes, and as a man loves a woman too. A million times I have wanted to possess your body but was prevented by my position in your father's household. Oh, don't look startled. You must have known it.'
'I have never even considered it. Hyacinth took my virginity and my love with it, that is all I know. You must leave Sutton Place forthwith. You have no respect.'
He had taken a step towards her and she had looked at him properly for the first time in years. The great livid scar ran down his cheek behind the still brilliant eyes, but his black hair had become sparkled with white here and there. Yet the years had not been cruel. His lean frame—fairly small in stature—had gained no weight and he was still as strong and tough as he had ever been.

'You may ask me to go—and go I will,' he had said earnestly. 'But consider this, Missie. What do you have left? Bridget Clopper, Sam, Tom? A handful of servants to occupy the mind of a clever young woman who has set her face against men? You'll be dead—in your brain if not in your body—within ten years. And then what price Sutton Place? What future for the mansion house with no firm hand to guide it?'

He had hit home as well he knew.

'But I have sworn never to marry.'

'And you need not break your vow. But you must go out into the world. Look at you! You are twenty-seven years old but by some miracle still appear ten years less. Society is yours to conquer!'

Even Mitchell did not know the secret of Malvern's hidden spring and Melior Mary's eyes flickered a little.

'Show the world your beauty and move in Court circles. They say the King never recovered from his infatuation for you when he was Prince of Wales, and would still make you his confidante. Remember your father's dying words. How else can you serve Charles Stuart?'

He had got her trapped now.

'What should I do?'

'Go to Bath immediately. It's the season and you will take the place by storm. If you wish I will accompany you as major domo.'

She put her hand out to him.

'You will never mention that again, will you;

your desire for me?'

'No, never.'

And it had been as he had said. Admittedly, on the first morning when she had attended the baths during the early hours, attired from head to foot in bathing clothes—her little tray carrying her handkerchief, snuff box and puff box attached to her waist—she had caused no stir. But at the taking of the waters in the Pump Room afterwards—accompanined by the playing of music and the animated chatter of fashionable visitors—everything, including the orchestra had come to a stop.

Melior Mary, as befitted her mourning, had advanced to be greeted by the Master of Ceremonies, Richard Nash, in rustling black taffeta and a black straw hat, hung plentifully about with trailing silk roses. Turning from his conversation the beau had actually let his mouth drop open in amazement.

He had seen lovely women in his enviable role as the Master of Bath. But the creature who stood before him now was incomparable. Eyes like flowers gazed steadily at him. And, as she swept her curtsey, the brim of her hat threw a shadow onto cheek bones that were both hard boned yet softly skinned. He bowed and took the proffered hand—small and white—and brushed it with his lips.

'My dear madam...', he said, but could manage no more. He was lost for words. Finally he said, 'I believe you are more beautiful than anyone else alive.' And it was then that every voice was hushed and the music died away. Beau Nash had just created a new fashion and polite society stood thunderstruck.

After that Beauty and her Beast—as Melior Mary and her scarred servant became known—were the talk of the town. And it was the frustration of every hostess; of every beau, fop and dandy; of every theatre manager; of every charlatan, rogue and thief, that mourning for her father forbade her to do little more than take tea and dinner. Cards, theatres and routs were precluded and, as a result and as the Scotsman had nicely judged, she went on everyone's list for future invitation when the London season began and her period of grief was at an end.

And that was how it had started. Melior Mary had gone from triumph to splendour. She had been presented at Court where the King had whispered to her tenderly; in fact she had become the object of desire for all men of blood and imagination. Furthermore fashion had copied the wide-brimmed hats and trailing feathers that she wore so well and the phrase 'à la Weston', had been born. And, at last, Sutton Place had rung with laughter as it had not done since Sir Richard the builder had laid the great red carpet beneath the feet of Henry VIII. Naturally George II could not follow suit and grace with his presence the home of a Catholic hostess, but this did not stop him casting his heavy-lidded German eyes in her direction, and wishing that the dictates of high politics could have been otherwise.

But he—the King—must never forget that in Rome the Stuart child was growing up; that the hope of the Jacobites was now in his teens and a delightful youth by all accounts. For all their apparent acceptance, no Catholic—not even one with the charm and grace of Melior Mary—could ever quite be trusted. And, while Royal George thought these things, she obeyed her father's wishes and gleaned information from the highest sources, passing it on to the ever present, ever watchful agents of James III, just as her uncle had done before her.

And what of Joseph? The last sight Melior Mary had ever had of him was snatching the infant Garnet into his arms and running from the Great Hall.

But then came an event guaranteed to bring every true Jacobite, old and young, rich and poor, crowding to the cause that they had secretly believed was hopeless; Prince Charles Edward begged permission to attempt to regain the throne.

In 1744 Jacobite agents everywhere—including Melior Mary Weston—had been informed that Charles was on the move. He had already gone through Italy disguised as a Neopolitan courier, changed to the guise of a Spanish officer to pass through Tuscanny and was now living in terms of greatest secrecy in France, awaiting passage to Scotland. Secret meetings became the order of the day and in the excitement of dark midnights the Lady of the Manor received Lord George Murray—exiled after the uprising of 1715—and Sir Hector Maclean, who left the mansion house for Edinburgh and was thereupon recognised and arrested.

But London was at play, choosing to ignore the growing rumour of a pending invasion. Even the King had been heard to remark 'Phew! Don't talk to me of that stuff!' And, as Melior Mary had made her way to one of the little alcoved tables at Vauxhall Gardens, her mind had been full of teeming ideas. It was March 1745 and she knew that the Prince was now at Nantes. A movement from a chair on her left had, at that point, attracted her attention. Reluctantly she had glanced at the man—half hidden in shadows—who sat there and had, as quickly, looked away again. But there was something of familiarity about him. The manner in which he held his head, the fluttering of his lace kerchief as he raised his wine glass to his lips.

She turned to stare. He had bowed his head to her, a mocking smile playing about his lips, and his face had come full into the candlelight. Her hand had flown to her mouth and her eyes had grown wide. Age had added some more lines, bagged the eyes and increased the girth a little, but there could be no doubt.

'Uncle Joseph!' she had exclaimed.

He had risen and once again she had gasped. Clad all in claret brocade, a diamond order, set in silver upon a blue riband, sparkled on his chest.

'My dear,' he had said, rising and joining her table. 'I was told that I would find you here tonight. But I can't say that I would have known you. Age has not withered nor had time decayed. It was your hair alone that I recognised.'

'But what of you?' she had said. 'The last I heard you had gone for a soldier with nothing in the world but ten guineas and now...'

The spread of her arms took in his splendid appearance. Joseph had laughed.

'Oh, me prinkum-prankum do you mean? Well yes, I fought hard for King Philip and Queen Elizabeth Farnese...'

Melior Mary had smiled. Elizabeth of Spain and her chief minister Cardinal Alberoni were the two most ambitious people in Europe and the Cardinal was a committed Jacobite. Small wonder that Joseph Gage had found favour.

'Yes?'

'...rewarded me with a silver mine.'

'A silver mine!' Melior Mary had burst out laughing. 'Uncle Joseph, you are incorrigible. I do vow and declare that no bitter circumstance could ever master you.'

He looked suddenly grim.

'There was a time when I thought it would, niece. When Sibella drowned, when I discovered that Garnett was not truly mine, I wondered if my heart might stop with grief.'

'And what of Garnet?'

His good temper restored itself.

'Why he is landed in Scotland my dear. He

332

raises troops for the Prince.' His voice had lowered to a whisper. 'I tell you, Melior Mary, that when he comes the clansmen will rise in their thousands.'

She had leant forward, peering earnestly into her Uncle's face.

'And will the Prince succeed, sir? Will he get to London?'

'If his nerve—and that of his advisers—holds out. He must not weaken. He must march straight through and I do swear that if he does so there will be a Stuart King upon the throne of England before the year is out.'

She had put her head back and laughed for joy and Joseph had wondered at the unlined neck and small firm chin. He remembered everything about her youth so distinctly—the terrible ghost that had haunted her, the wild independence that had given his sister fits of despair, and the lion-hearted courage that had almost imprisoned her in the fortress of Innsbruck. He had loved her then, but when she had revealed the true identity of Garnet's father he had never really forgiven her. At the back of his mind there had always been the thought that perhaps she had done it on purpose.

And now she had transformed into this. A timeless beauty who ran Sutton Place with equanimity; a society belle of fashion who had laid both London and Bath by the heels; a Jacobite agent who had King George's ear; a shrewd business woman who had accumulated a fortune in property; a confirmed spinster. And it was this last that stuck in his throat. Somehow it did not quite fit with the rest. Or did it?

Without really meaning to say what he did Joseph asked, 'Did you ever hear again of Banister?'

Her whole manner changed. The laugh had died away and she had looked at him with a sad, distant expression.

'No.'

'Nothing?'

'No. He left Sutton Place on the morning of Sibella's funeral. I never saw him again.' As if this reminded her of something she added, 'Do you believe that the house is accursed? Is that why you didn't visit me there?'

A chill wind had come from nowhere and blew round the tables at Vauxhall as Joseph answered, 'I think it is a fearful place. Full of shadows and unspoken threats. I have vowed that I will never put my foot over the threshold again.'

His niece gave him a strange, unreadable smile. 'It has consumed me,' she said. 'It demands that I never leave it.'

'Is that why you do not marry?'

'Partly, perhaps.'

Changing the subject, but not really doing so, he had said, 'Garnett has been a wonderful son to me. It is for him that I have worked for this.' He tapped the order on his breast.

'What is it?'

'The Spanish equivalent of a knighthood. I am

a first-class Grandee of Spain.'

She had leaned across the table and kissed him on the cheek.

'I am glad that life recompensed you for all that you endured.'

'The prize of Garnet was enough,' he had said. 'I pity Matthew Banister that he never knew his son's sweetness.'

She had made no answer and they had fallen to talking of his reason for visiting England, and the funds he hoped to raise from the great Catholic and Jacobite families to support the army of Prince Charles. She wished then, as she had done so many times but particularly now, that her father was still alive. He would have been seventy—eight years older than Joseph.

'How my father would have enjoyed this,' she had said as they parted.

He had kissed her hand. 'Let us pray that the adventure ends with a crown.'

And with that he had gone and she had never seen him from that day to this, her forty-ninth birthday. Whether he—or even Garnet—was still alive she did not know, for many good men had fallen in the rising of 1745.

And it had worked out exactly as Joseph had said. Prince Charles Edward and his Highland army had marched as far south as Derby, where Lord George Murray had advised retreat and the Duke of Perth advancement on London. It was tradition that on that December day the Prince had been in despair at the very idea of turning back. He was all for pressing forward and to victory. Melior Mary wondered if Garnet Gage had been with him and, if so, what he would have said. It was not difficult to guess.

But perhaps he had not been present for Charles Edward had turned back and lost the crown that was there for the snatching; in London King George had prepared for flight and the banks were paying out money in red hot sixpences to those preparing to leave the capital.

As she turned from the window to be dressed splendidly for her birthday rout, Melior Mary thought that if Prince Charles had made the other decision he, without doubt—as son of the ruling monarch and she as a principal supporter of the Stuart cause—would be coming to visit her today; would be pressing gifts upon her from his father James III and himself; would be mentioning his mother, Queen Clementina, who had died young —only living fifteen more years after her escape from Innsbruck.

But fate had decided otherwise. Charles Edward had crossed to France with only his life and the clothes he stood up in, after a frenzied manhunt that had lasted five months. King George's son, the Duke of Cumberland, had without doubt harboured a personal grudge against the son of the rival King across the water thinking, perhaps, how near he—Prince William —had been to being deposed. The Highlands had been ransacked for Charles Stuart and thirty thousand pounds had been the price on his head.

But he had escaped and now buised himself with pleasure in the capitals of Europe. Or so Melior Mary had been told.

The knock on her door told her that Lucas, her personal maid, had arrived to dress her, but calling 'Wait', Melior Mary delayed a moment longer, as she splashed on her face and body the water from Malvern. It might well be that she was forty-nine and that no King's son would visit her this day, but society looked on Melior Mary Weston of Sutton Place with a fervence beyond belief. Both she and her manor house must appear at their very best even though, since the day that Brother Hyacinth had left them, they now had only each other to love.

CHAPTER 17

The sky had been grey all day with a heavy bulging look that had made Sam—John Weston's bastard by Bridget Clopper—scratch his head and say, 'It'll snow, I reckon, when it gets warmer.' Tom, uglier in both looks and temperament with the passing of time, had answered, 'Of course it will, you stupid booger. Doesn't it always when the Missus has her Christmas party? And don't Oi always have to sweep the courtyard so that the horses don't slip? And don't you always say the same thing year in and year out. Be off with

337

you, you lumbering idjut.'

Sam had put his fists up but had then decided against it and had ambled off towards the kitchens to see if his mother, in her sixties now but still with something of the old pertness about her, would give him something to eat. But she had merely boxed his ears and told him to get out of her way, for was it not all hands to help the cooks with Miss Melior Mary's grand card party tonight? Grumbling to himself and looking for a moment uncannily like John, he had eventually headed for the stables where he had hidden some ale, and could sit and think of the old times when Mattthew Banister had been in charge, Golden days—all gone now.

Inside Sutton Place it was the usual Christmas scene of activity as, by tradition centuries old, the Great Hall was prepared for guests. Over two hundred years before, Sir Richard Weston had headed his feast on the high table, looking to where his servants had crowded the trestles to join the family. Now his descendant, hostess of a more elegant age, oversaw the setting out of her card tables and chairs, purchased from the Chippendales—father and son—so that her guests might play whist and piquet or even the dangerous faro—at which a man might lose all he possessed in one night.

And if they should tire of that then they might wander in the Long Gallery and listen to the musicians, or if thirst and hunger called, a feast was laid out in the dining room. Melior Mary

had a reputation for giving one of the finest enter-
tainments during the Twelve Days and carriages
would set out as early as morning from the more
distant points, the only fear that snow might stop
them getting there. And as the grey clouds
loomed ominous, coachmen urged their charges
on to even greater efforts in order to defy the
weather.

As the first glittering flakes began to fall,
Melior Mary, too, looked with some anxiety. Her
estates and gardens were fast taking on the air
of a treacherous paradise on this winter day of
1752. But yet she must consider that her forty-
ninth birthday had gone last summner—and with
the King's grandson now Prince of Wales,
following the death of Prince Frederick, youth
was the order of the day. She must be seen to
be as beautiful and as lively as ever.

It was with extra care that she slipped a gown
of silver tissue over her hooped petticoat, and
oversaw her hairdresser weaving violet ribbons
into her hair, and draping great plumed ostrich
feathers à la Weston over her diamond-encrusted
shoulders. Only then was she ready to take her
place in the small hall and greet her guests as
they arrived.

Mitchell, as silver-haired as she these days,
stood outside her bedroom door and offered her
his arm as she came through. This love for her
was tangible though he had not spoken of it since
the day of John Weston's funeral, his scarred and
savage face impassive as he appraised her un-

339

changing beauty.

'Well?' she said.

'Well enough, Missie! They say you practice
the black arts and have found the secret of eternal
youth.'

'Perhaps I have.'

Mitchell looked at her wryly.

'Nothing would surprise me about you.'

She laughed.

'You're a miserable Scot and I've a mind to
dismiss you.'

'You've been doing that for the last thirty
years. Come to your guests and stop your foolish
prating.'

They went down the staircase with the silence
of old acquaintance: she, blissfully unaware that
she had come to depend on him for everything;
he only too sure that if he were to die her mer-
curial spirit would disintegrate.

But what a success the party! With the fire in
the Great Hall stacked halfway up the chimney
and the logs a-crackle; and the musicians playing their sweet sounds to lull the dullness of
silence and let the conversation flow free.

The brilliant noise of laughing and chatter
swelled and died again like the sea as the card
players concentrated and relaxed by turn. And
amongst them Melior Mary was as gleaming and
as cold as a gemstone. She seemed no more than
twenty-five in the warm, glowing candlelight but
yet there was rumour spoken of her behind the
fluttering fans and lace-heavy handkerchiefs.

Why had she never married! How old was she in truth—and was it so that she was a virgin?; that the most prestigious men in the land had offered to no avail? What secret lay behind those dazzling eyes? Who held the key to Melior Mary Weston?

But she heard none of it and sat down to cards as joyful as a girl, light with champagne and compliments. Opposite her was grumpy Lord Barraclough, glaring at his hand as if it had been dealt by the devil, but beside her the Marquis of Bath could scarcely concentrate for raising his quizzing glass and squinting at the curve of her sweet throat.

'If the snow worsens we will have to stay the night,' he said—while his wife, older than he and with the face of a hatchet, glared furiously about her.

'Damme, I hope not,' answered Barraclough. 'Can't sleep if I don't know the bed. Got to know a bed before I get a wink. Took my bed with me during the French wars, you know. Damnable Frogs burned it up. I never forgave 'em. Why I'd as soon share my bed with a heathen as I would a Frog.'

Lord Bath gave a hoot of laughter in reply to this and Lady Bath frowned severely, while Melior Mary giggled in a manner unknown since her youth.

Barraclough rattled on, 'No offence to you, my dear Miss Weston. I'm sure that your bed would be most comfortable.' Unaware of the double

341

entendre he persisted through Bath's shouted mirth, 'In fact if I had to choose a bed in all this land I would probably elect for yours. But the fact remains that if the snow thickens I shall leave. So be so good as to inform me, Bath, should the weather worsen.'

How my Lord was supposed to know should this turn of events come about he did not stop to examine but played a card with a flourish, quite oblivious that the Marquis wept for laughing and his wife had swelled up like a puff adder. And it was with this scene about her— the old man shouting, 'Play on, Bath, play on!', the Marquis snorting wine up into his nose; the Marchioness almost ready to walk from the table—that Melior Mary saw something that made her half rise from her chair.

She was sitting near to the fire, her card table one of two dozen crowded for play, but one of the few that could see into the small hall beyond. The clanging of the bell had told her of a late arriving guest but she had done no more than glance up, knowing that two footmen and Mitchell hovered in attention near the hall door. For tonight the Middle Enter, opening direct as it did into the Great Hall, was not in use.

As she glanced she saw that Mitchell stood in the entrance archway, his dark eyes and clothes black as a raven's, his manner watchful and slightly alert, as if he suspected ill of he who came through the darkness to the heiress's house in the hour before midnight. And so it was, gazing at him in an abstracted way, that Melior Mary saw the extraordinary thing that happened. Without any warning at all the hero of the Nithsdale rescue dropped onto one knee and bowed his head. At one moment he had been standing ready to see off the late arrival if need be; at the next he was bent in an attitude of deepest respect.

Melior Mary gazed in astonishment. And then she saw a hand—a tough, strong hand yet with fingers that tapered to elegant and manicured nails—extend itself. A dark red ring gleamed as Mitchell raised the fingers fervently to his lips. She rose in her chair to see better who it was but the man had drawn back into the shadow. There was nothing for it but to leave the Hall and find out for herself. And as she did so she felt her knees grow suddenly weak. For no reason at all she was excited—and yet afraid. She knew that destiny was about to play a great game with the Queen of Ice.

★ ★ ★ ★

The chapel in Inglewood Priory was very cold under the first snowfall of winter. In fact the little monk who knelt alone in the hour before mid-night, preferring to pray rather than lie shivering in his narrow cell, felt his fingers numbing on the beads of his rosary and could see his breath frosting as he mumbled the time-worn words.

He did not know why they called him Little

343

Monk. He wasn't very short; in fact not short at all really. Nor was he senile or even particularly mad; just of some indeterminate age and harmless as a flower. He had forgotten how long he had been there, for one year was very much like the next. But it seemed to him that he must have knelt to pray at Christams time on at least some thirty occasions. And, after it was done, he would, year in and year out, rise up and perform the same ritual. He would go out into the darkness and slay a dozen of the geese that formed part of his flock and then take them to the kitchen and pluck and draw them, that the Brothers might eat them on the morrow. For the two fast days were over and now they could feed on fowl without offending against the will of the Lord.

But he—the Little Monk—did not enjoy eating them very much, picking at his food and then passing it to Brother Augustus who sat on his left in the refectory. For he loved his geese very much and knew them all by name. To take the life of one of them was like killing a child to him. But though he loathed the duty he could not shirk it, for he was the goose boy—and the goat herd. And he also looked after the six dairy cows who gave the monastery its milk each day.

He had always loved animals and when he had wandered into the priory, half starved and raving, all those years ago, the thing that had brought him back to his senses had been a sore on the leg of the Abbot's horse. Something in

344

his memory had stirred—for he had no idea who he was or where he had come from, however much the monks would question him—and he had mixed up a paste of herbs and flowers and had daubed it on the animal. When its leg had grown strong and better they had put him in charge of the monastery livestock, for it was quite obvious by that time that, unless somebody came to claim him, he was destined to stay with them and enter holy orders. After all they couldn't just turn him out again onto the King's highway.

But the old Abbot had liked him and given him his own special name when he had been received into the Brotherhood. But nobody called him that now except the new Abbot, who was tall and thin and mean of spirit—a purser of the lips, a wringer of the hands. In truth a bit of an interferer with the dreamy sun-filled days of gaggle and herd. For what better than to sit where the mill stream flowed and the wheel plunged eternally into foam, gazing at the world from beneath the brim of a battered straw hat?

'Brother! Brother!—what are you doing?' would come the rude interruption.

And no amount of explanation that he was keeping his eye on hatching goslings would suffice. But he must up, onto his feet and back to the monastery to busy himself with milking, and sweeping the yard, and all the million and one things that occupied his harmless, meaningless days.

And even now, as he knelt to pray in his own

345

private time, he looked anxiously over his shoulder lest someone should come to nag him, to send him about some errand or other. But all was still. The monastery snatched an hour's sleep before the rigours of midnight prayer in the bleak harsh darkness. Yet he was right—somebody stood there even now. He turned to see properly, his thick pebble glasses dim in the candlelight.

'Father?'

'No, it's Brother Augustus. What are you doing, Little Monk?'

'Praying—and thinking.'

In the darkness the fat man chuckled.

'Thinking, my brother? What are you thinking about?'

'I don't know.' He sighed. 'Of a time I can't properly remember. You wouldn't understand.

'Oh, wouldn't I?'

Brother Augustus had been a Jacobite once, in those mad wild days of the 1715 Rising. He had fought like a savage, clawing the throats from his adversaries and then—when his name had gone on the wanted list—he had disappeared into this backwater, this dreamy priory in Berkshire. And there he had turned to God and to fat. Both his escapes to forgetfulness.

'Wouldn't I understand, my brother?'

But the Little Monk was rising to his feet, muttering to himself and to the Almighty. It was goose killing time. Brother Augustus looked at him for a moment with genuine affection. Harmless, sweet man.

346

'You don't know what it is to really kill,' he said, just beneath his breath.

'Oh but I do,' replied the Little Monk surprisingly.

'What?'

'It was my fault that she drowned herself in the well. Ding, dong bell—my poor girl! But I can't remember who she was. Brother Augustus, *I can't remember who she was.*'

The fat man had stared at him as the Little Monk had gone out to slay the Christmas geese.

★ ★ ★ ★

Even judging by English standards it was a cold Christmas. And Joseph who was used—albeit that he lent too heavily upon his walking cane when proceeding along—to personally plucking an orange from his grove during the celebratory Twelve Days groaned a little.

'Are you old?' said the wide-eyed granddaughter.

'Of course, damme. Don't I look it?'

'Yes and no. You're made exciting smart by your prinkum prankum.'

She was everything that he could have wished had she really been his. Bright—the child of Tamsin Missett's daughter, Sarah; for Garnet had united in marriage with one of the oldest and most famous Jacobite families of all. Beautiful—for she bore Sibella's clearwater eyes and Mrs Missett's dark, bountiful hair. Loyal—for she had

347

Matthew Banister's honest heart and Michael Missett's fealty to his true King. Magic—for there was something in her of the old ways, of the FitzHowards, and their dark mysteries.

'Pernel, you talk vastly. What do you know of the bad days and the great rake, Joseph Gage?'

He stroked his hand on the thick black hair as they walked along together, wanting to be remembered, wanting to recreate for her the image of himself as it had once been in the eyes of London's fashionable society.

'Only what they tell me—Mama and Papa. How you were the most daring trickster in Europe. How you would take any disguise. How you and Grandmother Misset both took part in the most astounding rescue of all time. The night, with the snow curling thickly upon the ground, you took from the convent the imprisoned Princess Clementina and smuggled her, as a bride, to King James.'

Her eyes were bright with the fervent tales of childhood, of deeds told a hundred times and cherished in each telling.

'Grandfather?'

'What, Miss Prattle Mouse?'

'You did do all those things, did you not?'

'Aye, and more. Did you hear tell of how I left England with not a penny to my name and how your father and Sootface and I lived on naught but bread on our journey to Spain?'

'Yes. And how you pleased the King so greatly with your bravery—and the Queen with your courtly ways—that they gave you a silver mine and you became the richest man in Spain and a Grandee.'

Joseph smiled. What a pageant it had been. And yet he had paid dearly for it. His wife dead before she was even nineteen; Matthew Banister the father of his beloved Garnet. But Joseph had kept the secret to himself. His adopted son had never suspected for a second that he was anything other than a true Gage. And when jokes were made in the family about his deep blue eyes and his curling hair, Joseph would simply smile and say that those looks came from the FitzHowards, from the line started by the sorcerer known as Dr Zachary. And that, after all, was the truth.

'You're dreaming,' said his grand-daughter accusingly. 'You have the look of faraway in your big pussycat eyes.'

She jumped up at him and tried to land a kiss on his cheek. She loved him more than anyone else alive; more than her parents, more than her twin brothers, younger than she and so alike that only Sarah Gage could tell them apart. More even than Sootface who dozed in the wintry sun like an old black dog.

An elegant hand bearing a blazing emerald ring flapped at her. 'Zounds, child! You've ruffled me cravat. Foolish creature.'

But he didn't really mean it for he picked her up in his arms.

'I love you, Grandfather,' she breathed noisily into his ear. 'You won't die yet, will you?'

'Most certainly not,' said Joseph. And kicking Sootface into wakefulness he handed her over his head to the yawning Negro.

'I'm too old to carry children about,' he said, pretending to be peevish. But he couldn't keep his face straight for Pernel answered, 'Anyway, it ain't done for a rake hell to be seen with sniffy children. It might spoil their grand ton.'

The laughter of the three of them rang out as they headed into the orange grove.

★ ★ ★ ★

Melior Mary could not believe what she was seeing. Mitchell, on both knees was crouched before a young man who stood, partly concealed by the dim light of the fire, in the entrance hall of Sutton Place. And as he knelt the Scot repeated over and over again in a kind of chant the words, 'Mo Phrionnsa.' Furthermore he sobbed as he spoke and shook from head to foot with some overwhelming emotion. The air was alive with excitement, with challenge and with a peculiar feel of ecstasy.

'What's to do?' said Melior Mary abruptly.

She was afraid. She could sense danger about her. There was something in the very way the stranger stood there, so still and so calm, that set her heart beating fiercely. She felt that the time might be near—after all the frigid years she had imposed upon herself—

when she could give her proud spirit once more to a man and thereby, the pain and glory of it all.

'Who are you?'

She knew that she sounded rude but was too nervous to care. And it seemed that he was not offended, for in the gloaming he chuckled. She would always remember that in the years that lay ahead of her; that the first thing she ever knew of him was laughter in the darkness.

'Well?'

He stepped forward at that and she drew breath. It was he whom she had sworn always to serve; he who, by the very nature of his birth, could demand her loyalty to death. She sank into a curtsey and when her knees touched the floor, remained kneeling. Prince Charles Edward Stuart had come at last to Sutton Place.

He laughed again, but very gently, and said, 'Madam, Mitchell—I beg you rise. I am here incognito. My assumed name is Sir Humphrey Morris. I would prefer that you greeted me as such.'

Despite the greatness of the moment Melior Mary's lips twitched into a smile. The Prince's enthusiasm for disguises and pseudonyms was lovingly joked about amongst his followers. He liked nothing better than to dress up and walk about a town, delighting himself with the fact that he passed unrecognised.

'As Your Highness commands,' she said and

351

stood, though not daring as she did so to look up into his face.

Nonetheless she was aware that he was smiling as he said, 'We had heard rumours—even in Rome—of your prodigious beauty and, do you know, my father has a painting of you? But it doesn't do you justice, ma'am. It doesn't do you justice.'

His reputation with women was alarming. Madam de Guémenée had taken him as her lover almost by force, and had parted company with him only after a ridiculous scene. The forty-year-old Princess de Talmond had started off by honouring him in society and had ended up being honoured in his bed. Mesdames de Vasse and de Montbazon had succumbed, along with Mademoiselle Ferrand and a score of actresses. He was the Prince of hearts—followed in the streets of Paris, cheered at the opera. He held a fatal fascination for women and played it to the full.

And when she finally looked tentatively into his face, Melior Mary saw why. It was not that he was conventionally handsome—a tall slim body, a thin face with a pointed chin, a broad strong nose—it was that he had the eyes and mouth of a sensualist. And this was so at odds with his enormous physical bravery—proved beyond a shadow of doubt during the bitter fighting of '45 and the ghastly privations of being hunted down like a fox—that it was tantalising. He was a contradiction within himself. He was a soldier and a philanderer. A powerful and deadly combination.

But now he seemed mild enough as he said, 'While we are still private let me send you the good wishes of our Royal Father. He would have you know that every effort you make, every thought that you spare him, is most highly regarded in Rome.'

Melior Mary curtsied again and said, 'While we have life and wit, sir, we shall continue to strive for the cause of King James.'

The fighter stirred in his eye.

'And I too, ma'am, you can believe. But more of that when your guests have departed. Now be kind enough to lead me in.' He looked a school-boy for a second as he added, 'As Sir Humphrey Morris.'

And with that he walked, as coolly as if he were going to play cards in the safety of his own home, into the Great Hall and sat down—nodding his head and introducing himself politely to Lord Barraclough and Lord and Lady Bath—in the place recently occupied by Melior Mary. And when she looked again he had been dealt in and was leaning back in his chair, one leg crossed over the other with a great deal of nonchalance, study-ing his hand and flicking at an imaginary itch on his nose with a lace-edged handkerchief.

She turned to Mitchell who was once more in control of himself.

'Had you any idea of this?'

'None at all.'

'What has brought him to England, do you suppose?'

Mitchell smiled.

'There'll be a plot afoot, Missie. Mark my words. You'll hear it all before the night is out. Prionnsa Tearlach will not rest till his father is retored to his birthright.'

'Prionns Tearlach?'

'It's Gaelic for Prince Charles, Missie. That's why he's called Charlie. The English Jabobites misheard Tearlach.'

'Bonnie Prince Charles—he is, isn't he?'

Something in her voice must have been soft for Mitchell looked up sharply and said, 'He's still young, Missie. You were a friend of his mother's.'

She gave him a dark stare and just for a moment the old bad Melior Mary, who went her way and cared for no-one's opinion, peeped out at him.

'Hold your tongue,' she said.

He shrugged his shoulders and walked away and her glance went again to the Hero of the '45 —her true sovereign Prince—who sat chattering like a bird with Lord Bath, laughing and taking his ease in Sutton Place as if he had known it all his life. Conscious, perhaps, of her gaze the large heavy-lidded eyes flicked up and looked straight at her. They seemed to have the quality of a topaz about them, and an aureole of amber around his pupils. But it was the expression in them that riveted her. They held a dreamy alertness that made his thoughts quite clear. He found her beautiful and probably had no idea of her true age; it was obvious that he desired her.

For a moment she forgot who he was and turned her head as if he were any jumped up-dandy staring after her, and by the time she had recollected herself he had looked away again, giving the impression that he had not noticed the rebuff. But he was smiling to himself as he trumped Lord Barraclough's ace. She had not disturbed the equanimity of King James's gallant son.

The evening passed splendidly, the snow holding off long enough to allow those who lived nearby to return home in safety, and those who were staying in Sutton Place to contemplate the pretty sight of flakes swirling past the windows as they climbed into beds made cosy by vigorous use of warming pans. At last even Lord Bath was gone—very drunk and singing cheerfully—and Melior Mary was alone with the man known to his enemies and supporters alike as the Young Pretender.

She found that he was contemplating her in a rather curious manner, a puzzlement about his brows. As courtesy demanded she waited for him to speak first but it was a long time before he finally said, 'It was told by my mother that it was you who took her place when Captain Wogan led her to escape.'

'That is true, Highness.'

'I find it difficult to believe. Frankly, ma'am,

you look too young to have been involved in such an enterprise. Were you a child at the time?'

She laughed quietly and smiled at him where he sat in a high-winged chair before the fire in her white and gold saloon.

'I wish that I could say I was. It is true I had not then seen a great deal of life but...'

He interrupted her, the heavy lidded eyes suddenly kind.

'Forgive me, ma'am. I did not mean to pry. It is not my business and there's an end to it. It is just that you are so remarkably youthful.'

The Prince who had stared at her so boldly had vanished, and in his place was the warm-hearted King's son whose boyish enthusiasm had won the hearts of the tough and worldly Scottish Chieftains and their fighting clansmen. In his concern not to offend her he had leant forward and put his hand on her arm, not in any way flirtatiously but just as an offending dog might put out a tentative paw. She had forgotten, in all the long cold years, how the touch of Matthew Banister's fingers could once make her blood race hot. Had thought that that sensation would forever more be denied her. Until tonight that is, when she had sensed something of the calibre of this most unusual man.

Now *his* touch had her mind disconcertingly spinning. She could not breathe properly as she said, 'My Prince, I *am* old...it is just...that I...'

He put his finger to his lips.

'It is not our wish that you speak of it again,

ma'am. We all of us grow older from nine months before our birth. Age is of the heart. Some people are old when they are but five years; I have met them, tough little Highland children who are already small adults. Others, like a chieftain of ninety whom I also came across in the '45, are sparkling with the joy and eagerness of true children. You are in this last category. Because of your beauty and your wit if you were twice my age, you would still be younger than I am.'

Prince Charming! Her heart was thudding with joy. What greater compliment could she have ever been paid?

'Thank you, sir.'

She was at a total loss for words and lowered her eyes and gazed at the floor like a tongue-tied girl. And he, who had been taught the art of love by older women, read the signs aright and most cleverly changed the subject that she might regain control of herself—and be forever in his debt as a result.

'Madam,' he said briskly, 'I am in England on the business of King James. There is a plot to bring down Hanover George.'

She looked up, startled. 'There is to be another rising?'

'In a way. Even as we speak Macondonald of Lochgary and Dr Archibald Cameron are in Scotland to raise the Highlanders.'

'And will they march south?'

For a moment the Prince looked a trifle

fox-like.

'Er—no. They will be there as a back-up force, should it be needed.'

'I am afraid I do not quite understand, Highness.'

He grinned, as cheerful as a boy again.

'Oh tis a great scheme, ma'am. Alexander Murray—he is Lord Elibank's brother—dreamed it up with me in Paris. He is to raise a company of one hundred loyal men in London. I am to lie low at Lady Primrose's house in Essex Street and then, when the time is ripe, he will march into St James's Palace and take the Hanoverians prisoners—and I will proclaim myself.'

Melior Mary stared at him incredulously.

'And that is the entire plan?'

'Yes. Do you not like it? Where is the flaw?'

A cloud had gone over his face, in fact he suddenly seemed fractionally cross, Melior Mary found it almost impossible to make an answer. She knew already that he would alter the rest of her life, even if he went from Sutton Place this very night, never to see her again. He had melted the frost that had possessed her, had rekindled the bright ember that had once been the reckless spirit of Melior Mary Weston.

'Well, madam?'

'Highness, is Lord Elibank sure of his ground? Can a hundred men be raised in the capital?'

He rose from his chair with an impatient movement and began pacing up and down, his full skirted coat swishing as he walked.

358

'What! Are there not a hundred loyal hearts and true in the city that should be mine? Tis a poor day for the House of Stuart if that is the case.'

Melior Mary rose to her feet also.

'Oh sir, there are! You know how well you are loved. It is only that I fear for *you*. The army are organised and true to George. I think your gallant band might be slaughtered and you along with them. Butcher Cumberland would sacrifice much to see you dead.'

The Prince stopped in his tracks and gave her a forceful stare.

'Ah, Melior Mary,' he said, 'you don't know what it is like to be in exile. You don't know what it is to live every day with discontent eating at your heart and at your guts. I would say this to no other person alive but you—my father has lost heart. It is *I* who am Regent of England; it is *I* who risked my life to regain the throne; and now it is *I* who plot and scheme and bear depression's cold hand when I am thwarted.'

She saw him finish his glass of wine in one swallow. It was a gesture typical of him. Drink fired him when action could not. It was a habit that would eventually bring the hero of the '45 to ruin and despair. But now neither of them could envisage such a thing and she automatically poured out another glass.

'My Prince,' she said, 'do you need funds? I know I can be of little help in this latest enterprise but your men will need paying, will they not?'

The large eyes twinkled a little ruefully.

'Madam, have I ever not needed contributions to the royal exchequer? How tired you must be of it.'

For answer she snatched off the diamond necklace she wore and put it into his hands.

'My ancestor, Sir Richard the agriculturist, brought these into the family from Holland. I believe they once adorned a Queen. Now let them serve a Prince.'

He bent to kiss her fingers and when he looked up she saw that his eyes held some lazy expression with which he had regarded her earlier.

'Of all our subjects,' he said, 'I can truly say that you are the most beautiful and the most loyal. May I salute you with a Prince's true kiss?'

The lashes swept down as he put one hand beneath her chin and drew her mouth to his. And as the warm sensual lips tasted hers he drew her into his arms. She knew then why women fell in love with him wherever he went; for he kissed her as if she was the most precious creature on the earth. He had in him the art of making a woman feel delicate, cherished, a thing of beauty and fragility.

And there was no hope for her. She who had been without love for so long was more vulnerable than most. The Queen of Ice was melted and banished as the loving lips brushed her neck like a butterfly.

'Melior Mary Weston,' he said quietly.

'Tonight I must leave you, for there is much to do in London. But I shall think of you while we are apart. Will you wait for your Prince?'

'Sutton Place and its owner are your servants,' she said.

And it was only time and the breaking of the dawn that brought their conversation to a close. She walked to the Middle Enter with him—for she was determined that he should leave by the door through which so many of the Kings and Queens of England had trodden. Outside a wintry sun blazed over the glittering snow and there was a dark excitement about the land. The Prince of the House of Stuart was astride his black horse, furs wrapped about him, his eyes bright in that stirring daybreak.

'I shall return—and soon,' he said. 'But even if I am delayed, remember me.'

And then with a wave of his hand he was gone, and she turned back into a sleeping Sutton Place and did something that she had not done since the day Matthew Banister had also ridden off into the harsh and remorseless light of morning. Standing in the engulfing embrace of her mansion house, she wept.

CHAPTER 18

There could be no doubt that the ball at the London home of Lady Suffolk was a great success. The young Prince of Wales was there, masked and wearing pink clothes and a pearl embroidered waistcoat; Mr Pitt had been in, run a beady eye over the assembly, and gone again; the Duchess of Marlborough's daughter had grown quite giddy through dancing and had been forced to sit out amongst the older ladies; and Miss Melior Mary Weston, looking as youthful as ever and clad in midnight blue and a mask of silver satin stood, surrounded by admirers, holding her own private court.

But, as far as the men were concerned, the height of elegance was achieved by two gentlemen who arrived late—though not late enough to cause embarrassment to their hostess —for they outshone all as to the manner of fashion. The old man, clad in deepest burgundy, wore thin shoes with pinchbeck heels and on his breast bore the twinkling order of a Grandee of Spain; while his son, tall and well-made and with a glimpse of dark-red curling hair beneath his wig, wore gold encrusted powder blue and covered his face with a mask sewn with brilliants. And when they saw Miss Weston it was as if she had met them before—or at least the elderly gentleman—for she embraced him and then stood, quite still and staring, at his masked son.

'Garnet—at last!' she was overheard to say.

And he replied, 'Cousin Melior Mary! You are far more beautiful than I expected.'

And then the trio had become quiet and had just stood looking at one another as old memories had been allowed to flow free, for Joseph was seventy-one now and Melior Mary fifty, while Garnet had recently celebrated his thirty-fourth birthday. Yet the great rake's eyes were as bright and alert as they had been the first time he had seen Sibella, while his niece still held the secret of eternal youth. As for Garnet he was, without doubt, a remarkable man.

He stood taller and broader than Matthew Banister had been, harking back in looks to the Duke of Norfolk—the founder of the FitzHoward line—and also, though none of them knew this, to the soldier who had run away with Amelia FitzHoward and left her shamed and desperate. In the way of nose and mouth he had a strong look of Sibella, but the lustrous eyes and hair could leave no doubt at all as to whom his true father had been. It was almost painful to Melior Mary to see him, so much did he stir in her of old love and sadness. She wanted at once to embrace him and yet run away. But feeling her uncle's eyes watching her sharply, she finally made a curtsey and said, 'I hear you married

Tamsin Missett's daughter Sarah. I knew her—in a manner of speaking. Tamsin was with child when we took part in the Queen's rescue—all those long years ago.'

Beneath his mask Garnet smiled.

'Yes, my mother-in-law speaks of you still.'

'She is alive?'

'Yes, and Colonel Missett also.'

'There is a great colony of us in Spain,' said Joseph quietly, for even now it did not do to speak aloud of the old Jacobite days.

'Sir Charles Wogan?'

'Alive and merry. And I have three grandchildren, Melior Mary. The houses of Gage and Missett have been united forever.'

She looked just like a sad little girl as she said, 'How much I would enjoy seeing them. I always wanted to have children, Garnet, but I decided—when I was young and prone to that sort of thing—', she gave a humourless little laugh, '—never to marry unless it was to a man who would love Sutton Place as I did.'

Garnet said, 'Sutton Place?' and Melior Mary gazed at him aghast. It was incredible—but he did not know what she was talking about.

'My home. My mansion house.'

Smooth as silk Joseph said, 'I don't think I have ever spoken of it to Garnet. It never really came into the conversation. You will think us most parochial.'

She wanted to say, 'How could you? That was where his mother was brought up. But you hate the house and because of that you have never even told him it exists.'

And not without malice she said aloud, 'You must come and visit me, Garnet. It is a beautiful place. Your mother and I spent many happy hours of girlhood within its walls.'

The masked face turned to her intently and she felt Joseph stiffen with anger.

'Of course! It is the house I was born in! My father *did* speak of it—once.'

Garnet patted Joseph's arm to remind him and Melior Mary marvelled for a moment at the great love and concern that Matthew Banister's son had for a man with whom he had not an ounce of shared blood.

'We do not mention it because my mother died at my birth. But you know that,' he added in an undertone.

Beneath his visor Joseph's face was closed and still but Melior Mary knew that he was looking at her with a gaze like stone. Just for a moment she re-lived that scene long ago. Sootface leaping the staircase like a cat; Hyacinth running for his life; the screams of herself and Elizabeth; the smell of gunsmoke; and poor sad Sibella making for the Middle Enter and for the end of her life.

She hesitated for a moment and then said, 'Yes—she died when you were born. It was a black day for all of us.'

She felt Joseph relax once more and turning to him Melior Mary, in order to change the conversation and speaking in little above a whisper, said, 'And what of His Highness? What's afoot?'

This apparently non-committal question that any Jacobite might ask another, hid a multitude of emotion. She had not clapped eyes on Charles Edward since the Christmas before last, when he had ridden from Sutton Place to London in the dawning—and to another hope of the crown. But of course the preposterous scheme of Lord Elibank's brother had faded to nothing and, after staying in hiding at Lady Primrose's house for a while, the Prince had slipped quietly across the Channel and into obscurity. It was rumoured that he had been seen in Paris, heavily disguised—his face painted red, his eyebrows black and a handkerchief obscuring his countenance— but after that, nothing.

A source close to Sutton Place had whispered to Melior Mary that the Prince had been drinking too heavily and that he had taken up with a woman—Clementina Walkinshaw—whom he had met in the '45 and who had followed him to Europe. Melior Mary had wondered at the time why she had taken this remark so badly. In fact a feeling of fury had possessed her and she had gone to the stables, saddled up her horse, and ridden off into the forest—just as she had done when she was a girl.

It has only been when she was too close to St Edward's Well to stop, that she had realised what she had done. She had not been near the place in over thirty years—since the day Sibella had died in fact—and now it was a horrid shock. There it was—just a crude hole in the earth— but she noticed that someone had rolled a great stone over the opening, presumably as a safety measure. The temptation to push it back, kneel down and peep into the narrow tunnel that plunged darkly into the earth, was overpowering. And she had been just about to dismount when her horse had reared suddenly and she had had difficulty in bringing him under control. When she had looked again it had seemed to her over-active imagination that the stone had moved slightly—as if something were coming up out of the well to stare at her—and she had given a wild scream and headed for home. And that night it had started to rain and Sibella had come to Sutton Place to look for Garnet and maintained her sightless vigil for what seemed like hours on end.

Even now, even here, at the warmth and gaiety of Lady Suffolk's rout, Melior Mary shivered and Garnet, totally misunderstanding, said, 'Do not be afraid. All is well with the Prince. He is here in England.'

Melior Mary gasped. 'Here?'

'Keep your voice low, Cousin. He has several plans afoot—' Garnet smiled affectionately, '—you know what he is like for schemes! He intends to use me as his aide-de-camp for I can pass freely about the countryside where he cannot.'

'And he?'

'Will stay somewhere. Perhaps at Sutton Place. He speaks of you with great affection, Cousin.'

The hot blood was uncomfortable in her cheeks. She knew that both Garnet and Joseph were looking at her and was only glad that the mask hid her face.

'Ah well,' she said, 'I expect it is because I knew his mother.'

Garnet put his head back and let out a great roar of laughter and in that movement, in that sudden burst of exuberance, the young Matthew Banister was in the room and stood beside her as he had once used to do, before his vital spirit had been thrust from him by life's cruelties.

'I hardly think that is the reason,' said Garnet. 'I believe he has purloined his father's portrait of you and that it hangs to this day in his bedroom. Would that be out of loyalty to his mother, do you suppose?'

She could not help herself, she was not thinking. She said, 'Oh, Matthew, do not tease me so.'

* * * *

In his tiny cell the Little Monk stirred in his sleep. He had been dreaming such a strange dream. It seemed to him that he was walking in a parkland and that in the distance he could see a great house that loomed over all. It had been a warm, amber-bricked house with many mullioned windows and yet it had a huge gate house tower that soared eighty feet into the air, dominating the countryside and giving a sinister impresssion that detracted from the rosiness of the brickwork.

It also seemed to him that the house was watching him, sometimes approvingly and sometimes with a frown, and he supposed this to be caused by the shadows of the clouds that played sportingly with the small high sun. But what he did not like was the way in which—turn away and take a new path through the trees as often as he might—the house always lay before him. He could not get away from it and with each renewed look he became more and more aware of a yawning arch in the gate house wing, and another that lay behind it like a dark mysterious pit. The great door was open and lying in wait for him.

How strange are dreams! In his night mind he gave a little whistle and thrust his hands into the sleeves of his habit to show the place that it could not frighten him. And then it laughed at him. Quite distinctly he heard it laugh. It had neither a man nor a woman's voice but more a roar, like that of a lion's. But a chuckling lion. And then a girl said, 'It is very naughty of you not to come inside. But then you always did tease me so.'

And with that—with that unknown and invisible female sounding quite mutinously cross with him—he woke up and peered round to see where he was. But the putting on of his pebble glasses—which made him look silly in his mind but only sad and gnome-like in reality—revealed nothing but his stark little cell and the crucifix beneath which he always slept.

★ ★ ★ ★

The letter was waiting for her when she returned
from London. It was dated May, 1754, and read
as follows:

'Madam,
I have come once more to England on matters
with which I would speak with you but must not
write. I have been at Meath House, Godalming,
these two days past and would care to visit you
on the morrow, after nightfall. The rider awaits
your reply.

Charles P.'

Picking up her quill she wrote:

'From Sutton Place,
May, 1754
Highness,
My home and I are, as ever, yours to com-
mand. I hope that you will honour me with your
presence to dine tomorrow.
Assuring you always of my loyalty,
Your devoted Subject,
Melior Mary Weston.'

She folded the paper and pressed her signet
ring into the hot wax so that the Weston crest—
the Saracen's head and the words 'Any Boro'—
stood out clearly, then she took a pinch of snuff,
a habit of which she had grown fond of late, and

despatched the letter back to Godalming.

To say that her heart was in turmoil was to understate the case. She was in an ecstasy of excitement. And also of anguish. That she had fallen in love with Charles Edward Stuart—or perhaps with the *idea* of Charles Edward Stuart—she had no doubt. But gnawing at her excitement was the fact that she was seventeen years older than he; that if she had married at the age when it was seemly for most girls to do so, she could have easily had a son as old.

It seemed to her that, except for when she slept, she spent the next twenty-four hours either draped before her mirror, checking again and again that she looked at least twenty years younger than her actual age, or berating her dressmaker who—poor woman—to ensuere that a new gown would be ready, had sat up all night with two young sewing girls to assist her.

To add to the tension of the household, Mitchell too, was in a strange and savage mood. He strode through the house like a dark angel, assuring himself that the very stones of the floor were fit to bear the feet of Prionnsa Tearlach, but for Melior Mary he had nothing but glares and freezing looks. In the end she tired of his evil disposition and took him to task.

'What's the matter, damn you? I would have thought you to have been in Heaven in view of our guest, but you look sour as a virgin deserted at the bed post.'

'Mind your tongue, Missie!'

'And you mind yours! Why are you so sullen?'

'Because of you and your foolishness. You're in love with His Highness. It's written all over your face for everyone to see.'

'And what if I am?'

'You are seventeen years older than he. And anyway he is of the Royal House of Stuart.'

'Neither of those things have any bearing on the case. He does not love me and is not likely to.'

She remembered the look that Charles Edward had given her when he had sat in the Great Hall and she had turned her head away; the fatal fascination he held for women had annoyed and captivated her simultaneously.

'But even if he should—flirt—with me...' Her tongue played over the word. '...what of it? I have loved no-one for years. All warmth and affection went when Matthew Banister left. What is it to you if I know happiness once again before I die. Are you jealous, Mitchell?'

'You know I am,' he answered fiercely. 'I have devoted my life to you and your welfare, Missie. Thrusting down all the powerful desires that you aroused in me and making myself feel half a man because of it. And now you expect me to sit by and watch you make a fool of yourself? And of the Prince as well. Well, I'll no be a party to it.'

'What are you going to do?'

'I am going to leave Sutton Place this very day. Oh, don't jump up like that. I may be old but a better bailiff, a better servant, you'll not find for many a mile. Someone will employ me, never fear.'

'How can you talk so foolishly? We have been together for thirty-five years! That is a lifetime to some people.'

'Yes—and you have been my life's work. I guided a wild girl that would have shut herself away—peeping at the world like a novice nun—into becoming a Beauty of two generations. And now she rewards me by arrant foolishness over a man whom I regard as heir to the throne.' And with that he was gone from her room and ten minutes later strode from the mansion house carrying no more than a bundle of belongings. At any other time she would have been inconsolable, gone after him and begged him to return. But this was the wrong moment. In four hours the hero of the '45 would be stepping over the threshold after eighteen months away.

It struck Melior Mary with sudden amazement that it was one of the manor's fateful dates. It was on May 17, 1521 Sir Richard Weston had been granted the Manor of Sutton; on May 17 Sir Francis Weston had been executed for adultery with Anne Boleyn; and now on May 17 the Young Pretender was to come once more to Sutton Place. She wondered if it meant anything, wondered if the curse that had taken Hyacinth from her and left her to die without a child of her own, could be about to strike again. For a long moment she felt thoroughly despairing and then the fire in her rekindled and—as one hand stretched out for her powder puff—she turned

373

once more to the contemplation of her ravishing reflection.

★ ★ ★ ★

The Little Monk jerked awake as a fish tugged at his line, his battered straw hat falling down over one eye making him look for all the world like a rakish angel as it did so. He guiltily pulled it straight, cramming it down over hair that, for all its whiteness, was thick and curling. He should have been at peace, here by the mill stream, if it had not been for the fact that he had just woken from another dream. A dream of the great house, the second in as many weeks.

He did not like it very much. It disturbed the sunny world of flock and gander and gurgling brown trout and left him with a sense that something was about to happen that would leave the idyll of his life forever changed.

Not that this dream had been as sinister as the first. On the contrary there had been people in it; jolly, laughing people who had given him the time of day as he had passed wondering, perhaps, who the meek figure in the roughspun brown habit and comic pebble glasses could be.

'Good morning,' he had said to them.

And they had answered, 'Good morning, Father,' for they had probably thought that he was an abbot—more important than he truly was—and he, may his worldly pride be forgiven him, had not disillusioned them.

Two jolly girls wading in a sweet river had waved to him as he had trotted past and a big, dark man with the look of a squire about him, had reined in his horse and raised his hat. Then a pretty woman gathering morning roses had smiled and bowed her head. That part had all been very pleasant. But he hadn't liked meeting the youth at all. Not that he—the young man— was malevolent or threatening in any way. On the contrary, it was his very familiarity that had been so frightening.

The Little Monk, in his dream, had stared and stared at the nimbus of damson-coloured hair and the flower-blue eyes and wondered where he had seen them before. But nothing had come to mind so eventually he had settled for 'Good morning,' and a quick nod.

'Good morning, Father.'

Even the voice had been recognisable. And then the house had loomed into view, as big and as inescapable as ever. He had turned his back on it and it had played the silly trick of being in front of him again. In his day he had grumbled into his gums and the young man had said, 'It is very difficult to leave Sutton Place, Father.'

And then the fish had tugged on his line and he had woken up disconcerted by the house's omnipresence, the young man's look of old acquaintance. He heaved himself to his feet with a sigh. Something, somewhere was not quite right and though he once might have been able to tell what it was, now all he could do was scratch his white, woolly head as he toddled off in response to the monastery bell tolling at the end of another May day.

★ ★ ★ ★

'A toast, ma'am,' said Charles Edward Stuart raising his glass. 'I drink to the most beautiful woman in the county of Surrey; in fact the most beautiful in England. I drink to you, Melior Mary.'

He stood up and downed the port that shone like a ruby in the firelight, then he automatically refilled the glass from the decanter that stood at his right hand. Dinner was over, the servants had been dismissed and the Prince was very slightly drunk. But, nonetheless, there was a coolness between him and the chatelaine of Sutton Place that had not been there when they had last met. He had hoped to come back straight into her arms but, instead, found himself being kept at a discernible distance.

He had changed somewhat in the eighteen months since he had last been in the manor house. Thinner, paler, there was now an air of seething discontent about his mouth, which occasionally twitched of its own volition. But those strange heavy-lidded eyes—the colour of topaz—were unaltered. Everything of his nature was in them—adventurer, the soldier, the malcontent, the sufferer, the sensualist. A complex man, brave as steel and unhappy as a beggar. The crown of

376

England should have been on his head and then he could have developed into the bright charmng King that nature had intended at his birth. But the wound of pretence was in his heart, exile was corrodingh is soul, hopelessness had begun to hold him in its iron fist.

And tonight he felt unusually depressed. His beautiful subject with eyes like the Parma violets he had picked as a child was, for no reason, unfriendly; the wine was making him irritable and somebody, had hatched another useless plot to kidnap George II.

'I am not happy here,' he said suddenly and abruptly—and drained his glass again as if to endorse the feeling.

'I am sorry, Highness.'

'But I would like to stay for a few days if that is acceptable to you ma'am. Gage can run my affairs. Yes, I think Sutton Place would make a very good headquarters.'

He paused, his mood veering in direction, and then said, 'And of course it has one irresistible attraction.' He had decided to try his luck with her again.

'And what is that?'

'You as my hostess.'

He leant back in his chair, one satin clad knee crossed over the other, and gave her a slow and deliberately charming smile. A smile of which he had first discovered the devastating effect amongst the bonnie Scots lassies who had thronged round him in their bright colours during the '45. And which, after that, he had simply practiced about the Courts and salons of Europe. Everybody liked his naughty grin—peasants, aristocrats, whores—everybody that is, except Miss Weston who did not seem to respond particularly, merely repeating an earlier saying.

'My house and myself are you servants, sir.'

She was an enigmatic woman. He had desired her enormously at their first meeting and was only sorry that he had had to leave the same night for she had seemed to respond warmly to him—in fact he would have thought of her as an easy conquest. But enquiries amongst the Jacobite agents with whom he was on more intimate terms had yielded up a puzzling picture.

'The woman's a freak,' young Lord Atholl had said roundly. 'No-one is permitted her bed. I tried; my father—in his time—tried. They say even Hanover George and his son tried. She's known as Queen of Ice, you know.'

Charles Edward had stared at him in astonishment.

'Your father—and Hanover George! I know she stood in for my mother but how old *is* she for God's sake?'

'Some say she's sixty—but I believe around fifty is nearer to the truth.'

'I suppose she must be, yet she looks only half of that!'

'I know—they also say that she has discovered the Fountain of Youth! One of her maidservants was bribed and said that she washes in and also drinks some heathenish water each day.'

'Good God!'

'Good God indeed! It is said, too, that the man is not born who could pull up her skirts.'

It was crude talk before a Royal Prince but Charles and Edward Atholl were no strangers to this kind of badinage.

'Shall I try?'

'You, my Prince?'

'Why not. Unless she has anatomical difficulties...'

'Neatly put.'

'...I wager I'll be first man.'

Lord Atholl had laughed.

'If it will be anyone it will be you, sir.'

But now, sitting here, with this flower-like creature looking at him down the length of the dining table, Charles Edward remembered the conversation and was vaguely uncomfortable. She was no cheap opera girl to joke about with other bucks; he sat in the presence of beauty, of something a little magic in its rarity.

'Have you ever been in love?' he said, with that extraordinary abruptness he had used earlier in the conversation but which was really quite foreign to him. She gave him a quizzical look and he writhed with embarrassment. He really did not know what possessed him. He began to apologise but she was already speaking.

'I was once, Your Royal Highness.'

Was she being over-formal because she was annoyed?

'There was a tragedy in both our lives and he went away—forever. Since then I have not been profligate in my emotions.'

'I meant no offence, ma'am. It is just that you are an exquisite. To be honest I am quite bowled out by you.'

She laughed and Charles took a mouthful of port wishing that some of his old style with women—and his previous easy manner with her —would return. What had he said just now was true. He had totally changed his mind. He found her presence too disturbing to reduce her merely to the status of another bedroom conquest.

In a voice deliberately non-committal she changed the subject.

'Would you care to retire to the Long Gallery? It is very fine despite the fact it stood many centuries damaged by fire. My father had it restored about twenty years ago.'

He knew that she was waiting for him to stand up but he remained where he was, leaning forward over the table so that she looked at him in some surprise.

'Why are you so cold with me?' he said. 'I have no wish to upset you.'

She looked away again.

'How could you? You are my Prince and my sovereign Lord. It is not my place to be upset.'

He jumped from his chair, his depression turning to the anger that could make him wild with rage and was now only just held in check.

'How can you speak so? You know me—you

know my deeds. Has being a Prince ever made me less the man? I care about my subjects—I care about *you*. I am not yet so numbed by frustrated monarchy—nor the drink that relieves the pain of it—to ride roughshod over the feelings of others. Nor, I hope, would you. Tell me why you are treating me so coldly.'

There was a long pause while she stared at her plate and finally, when she spoke, it was in a voice choked with despair.

'Sir, when we last met we exchanged kisses. You may believe it—or you may believe it not— but there has been nothing of passion in my life since the time when my sweetheart left me. And that was over twenty years ago. But yet you aroused love in me. How dare I speak like this— but truth must out? I must fight against my feelings because the fact is I am old enough to have borne you. This year I shall be fifty-one.'

She wept before him, humbled to nothing by her wretchedness. It took him only two strides to run the length of the huge table and to kneel by her side. From where he was he saw the great lashes masking the shine of her eyes, watched her hand sweep up to brush away the springing tears. His heart groaned within him that he had over-joked about possessing so delicate a creature.

'I do not ask you as your Prince,' he said, 'but as a man. So the freedom of refusal is yours by right. Melior Mary, it would pleasure my soul more than anything I could name—and that includes the crown of England—to taste the ecstasy

381

of your body. Will you yield up to me what you have refused the whole world?'

'But I am too old for you, sir.'

'You could be a hundred years for all I care. I am in love, Melior Mary—I am in love. Now, will you have me?'

Her wonderful smile was his answer and he bowed his head before her. He was a boy again; his spirit danced as he picked up the hem of her dress and smothered it with kisses. And then into the room came exultation—as fevered and as raw as anything that either of them had ever felt before. A frenzy was upon them—a frenzy that both recognised as heart's wish, as journey's end, as great love.

The mistress of Sutton Place wept with joy as the man for whom the Scottish nation had raised ten thousand swords now, most humbly and quietly as if he were the minion, led her by the arm towards the consummation of shared adoration.

And oh what fulfilment to lie naked in her bed and feel—after all the lonely years—the warmth of his arms about her, the press of his firm flesh against hers! It was spring encapturing autumn as he raised her flowing hair and pressed it to his lips; it was the regeneration of earth by rain as he covered her body with his bountiful kisses; it was the bonding together of every star in the firmament as he at last made her his. Every bell in Christendom rang out its silver peal as that long-forgotten explosion of rapture took first her, and immediately him, to the feet of enchantment.

Melior Mary Weston and Charles Edward Stuart were at one. The differences of age, of birthright, of upbringing were not even considered by them. If God had let him be born merely an English aristocrat and she what she was—daughter of a country landowner—nothing could ever have parted them again. But he was heir to an ancient and accursed line of Kings and she mistress of the strange and haunted Manor of Sutton. Their paths were not destined to lie to together.

CHAPTER 19

Down the sweeping path—that had become known by tradition as Lady Weston's Walk—wearing a gown of mulberry velvet and a hat that trailed black feathers from its brim, came Melior Mary. Half walking, half running, she laughed to herself with the simple enjoyment of a child's game of hide-and-seek. She had left Charles Edward behind gathering wild flowers for a nosegay and it seemed a pleasurable thing to dodge behind a great oak—one that had stood in Sutton Forest even when Edward the Confessor hunted there—and watch him first smile, then frown, as he tried to find her.

She had never thought this kind of bliss possible. A glance from him, a touch from his smallest finger, was enough to make her dizzy. Joy bubbled abroad at the sound of his voice. She wondered that the human frame could withstand so much heightened feeling. And yet, somewhere deep within, was a gnawing sense of guilt. For now she realised how profoundly she must have hurt Brother Hyacinth. She had driven the poor wretch to despair for little more than a girl's determination to have what she wanted.

She had spoken of her guilt to the Prince as they sat, side-by-side before the fire in the Long Gallery, and his reply had made him seem the wiser and the older of the two.

For he had said, 'You should not think in that way because for everyone that one gives one's heart to—be it only for a second—a change is made in the balance of life.'

'What do you mean?'

'That paths are crossed, emotions are honed, nobody is quite the same again.'

'And you believe this, who have had so many women, some of them most casually?'

'Yes. Even the experience of lust is not wasted.'

Melior Mary had sat and thought. 'But my childish grasp on Matthew Banister spoiled that part of his life.'

The Young Pretender had said, 'Melior Mary, people *allow* their lives to be ruined. What others do to us is, in the end, in our hands. Come love, come hate, come passion, come revenge—there is always a moment when we can tell them to stop.'

She thought about that conversation again now, peeping round the trunk of the oak tree, imitating the cry of a cuckoo. Had Brother Hyacinth allowed himself to be ruined—or was it what fate had intended?

The Prince had spied her out of the corner of his eye and came running forward, bunch upon bunch of wild flowers held in his arms, thrown at her feet with a flourish. Then he dropped upon his knees and kissed the hem of her skirt—an extravagant gesture.

'Highness, it is I who should be kneeling to you. Please rise, sir,' she protested.

'No, no—for you are my Princess, my Queen. Don't you understand that I love you Melior Mary?'

She laughed with happiness and was horrified to see him go pale and start to shake.

'What is the matter?'

'Somebody has walked past. I felt a skirt swish against me.'

'But there's nobody!'

'Yet her fragrance is still in the air. Can you smell it?'

'No, what do you mean?'

'Perfume. A scented lady has gone by.'

Melior Mary laughed.

'Then we have a ghost.'

'To add to your others?'

The tone of his voice was grim. Physically brave though he might be, the hero of '45 had a dread of things unknown.

'We have Giles the Fool,' she answered lightly, 'and he is harmless, enough, Heaven knows.'

'I think there is more than he,' he answered, rising to his feet and staring her in the eye. 'A dark woman, heavily veiled came out of one of the bedrooms and made me a curtsey before she vanished.'

Melior Mary gasped. The legend of Anne Boleyn's ghost—she who would appear only to royalty—came crowding back into her brain. It had been seen only once before—when Charles I had visited Sutton Place during the Civil War—but undeniably it was a bird of ill-omen. The King to whom it appeared would never gain, or re-gain, his throne.

'Her black eyes followed me everywhere, full of foreboding.'

As the Prince said this the day grew progressively more chill, and Melior Mary took the Pretender's arm, saying, 'Come, sir. I am tired of this sylvan game. Shall we go into the house and take a dish of tea?'

But Charles Edward was not in a mood to be cajoled for he pulled away and said, 'There is another thing of which I must ask you. A thing that disquieted me when I heard it. It is that the Lord of the Manor of Sutton is accursed. That he and his heirs are doomed to death and despair. Is it true?'

Melior Mary had turned her head so that the brim of her hat masked her face as she answered.

'Oh yes! Throughout our history one can see the evil thread of it.'

'Even to you?'

She laughed bitterly.

'I in especial. I gave my heart—then lost it and swore that I would never marry. And now I am to die childless—the last of the direct line.'

'So how will the estate be settled?'

'My uncle William and his son—also William—were the heirs but they died. So now my cousin John Wolffe—William's eldest boy—is due to inherit, yet I often doubt he will.'

'What do you mean?'

'He is bloodless—a sickly creature—and his brothers are not strong. Something eats away at all three of them.'

'And are there no girls to succeed?'

'They all became nuns—even my silly cousin Arabelle. We are a doomed family.'

Charles Edward turned to look into her face and she saw that his eyes held, just then, the sad doomed look of the Stuarts.

'Then we share an unkind fate,' he answered, 'for there is a curse on the Kings of Scotland also! James I murdered; James II killed; James III doomed to fight his own sons and be assassinated; James IV to fall at Flodden; James V to go mad; the Queen to die beneath the blade at Fotheringay—not one of them to end peacefully in their beds, do you realise?'

All the warmth had gone out of his face. 'I want to triumph,' he said. 'I want to be King

387

of England but there is a bane upon me. My great grandfather, deposed: there's no hope for me! I am the child of a fated house.'

She did not know how to answer and he went on, 'Just as you are. Wicked thoughts, old hates, lay in wait for us at the moment of our births. Who can save Charles Edward Stuart and Melior Mary Weston for God's pity?'

They stared at each other in bleakness.

* * * *

Garnet had not felt well since he left London. In fact though he had considered taking the public stage for his journey to Bristol, the thought of bumping over villainous roads, squeezed close to stale smelling squires and frowsty farmer's wives had made God's air seem preferrable. He had finally set off on horseback.

He had said goodbye to Joseph some days before, for, though the recent disappearance of Charles Edward had puzzled them, it had been nonetheless decided that Garnet's visit to Bristol should proceed: Captain Segrave, a one-armed Irish officer and an old associate of the Pretender, had arrived in the city and was engaged upon rallying the Jacobites.

'And what do I say if they enquire for the Prince's whereabouts?' Garnet had asked as Joseph had minced, in scarlet beribboned shoes, up the gangplank of the ship headed for Spain.

'Say that you cannot tell—that you are sworn

388

to silence.'

'But where is he in truth?'

'Garnet, you know him better than I! He is having an affaire-de-coeur, obviously. He's bored to distraction with Miss Walkinshaw, and is practising his charm on some beauty. He will contact you through Lady Primrose when he begins to tire, never fear!' And with that Joseph had kissed Garnet affectionately and they had parted company.

But almost within a day of Joseph's leaving the first symptoms of some kind of sweating sickness had seized his adopted son and now, rising after his first night's stop in the town of Reading, Garnet found himself unable to face the mighty breakfast of ham, beef and onion pie, jugged hare and the mess of mussels that was set before him. He contented himself instead with a pint of ale. But this sat uneasily upon his stomach and, by the time he had reached the village of Theale, he was taken ill and was forced to dismount, where he vomited behind a tree.

After that his horse led him. He leaned forward over its neck, his body drenched with sweat, his eyes closed in a face white and drawn. He could not remember ever having felt so ill and wondered if he was host to some tropical sickness, contracted in Spain.

If it had not been that his fingers were woven into the horse's mane he would probably have fallen off, landing in the River Kennett along whose banks his mount was placidly plodding in the lazy afternoon. His last hope before he plunged into oblivion was that the creature might take him into a village before nightfall—and after that the earth and the sky merged into one and he fell a million flights into darkness.

Waking again was strange because, though he was aware that he lay in crisp lavendered sheets, he was unable to say a word nor see clearly where he was. Garnet knew that he was awfully near death and could hear the murmur of prayers from the little hobgoblin figure that piled him in a mount of blankets and held his wrists when he tried to throw them off.

'Oh God!' he groaned.

And a funny little face—the only feature discernible a pair of thick pebble glasses—put its mouth close to his ear and whispered, 'Drink this, my son. If you will co-operate with God, He will co-operate with you.'

And then some liquid with the after-glow of wine but the sweet smell of herbs was poured down his throat, and he slept again more comfortably.

When he finally woke up it was midsummer, the sun high in the heavens, the air droning with bees, the smell of June roses wafting through the tiny mullioned window: the light from which showed him that he lay in a small stone chamber, the little hobgoblin sitting on a rough wooden chair at the end of his bed and peering at him anxiously through a mane of white curls.

'Oh, my son, are you restored?' it said.

'Yes, with God's help—and yours,' answered Garnet. 'Tell me where I am.'

'At Inglewood Priory.'

'And where is that?'

'Not far from the River Kennett. Between Kintbury and Hungerford.'

'And how did I get here?'

'You fell at my feet, my son. I was fishing and your horse stopped beside me to drink—and there you were! That was over two weeks ago.'

'Two weeks! I was due in Bristol on June 6.'

The Little Monk smiled, resembling a merry barn owl.

'Well, that's an appointment you've missed. Today is Midsummer Night—when the fairies play tricks.' He looked sad for a moment and added, 'It can be a cruel time of year.'

'And who are you?' said Garnet.

'Oh, nobody important. Just a member of the Brotherhood whose job it is to tend the animals and catch the fish. I am not the Abbot if that is what you thought.'

Observing his homespun habit and worn-out sandals, Garnet had not for a moment suspected that the little fellow could be anyone of standing in the monastic hierarchy but he said with kindness, 'You are obviously highly regarded that you are in charge of the hospice.'

The Little Monk looked rueful.

'I think that is because, in truth, I am good with horses and their complaints. I had a way of making up little brews and ointments to soothe

391

them and then I went on to experiment with the medicaments for the human species. They have proved successful over the years.'

'And what may I call you?'

'Little Monk. Everybody does. The old Abbot gave me a name when he received me into the Brotherhood but nobody uses it.'

'And what is your real name?'

The little man shuffled his well-worn feet.

'I don't know. Like you I came in here through the charity of the Brothers. They found me raving and starving on the highway and they nursed me back to life. But when I regained my senses I had no memory of what had gone before.'

He suddenly looked vulnerable and pathetic and Garnet had a ridiculous urge to comfort him. Very vaguely the little man reminded him of someone.

'And how long ago was that?'

'Over thirty years. It seems to me I've been here forever. And what of you, sir? Do you hail from London?'

'No, no. I live in Spain—in Castile. I am in England on—business.'

The pebble glasses turned towards him anxiously.

'Oh dear! Should we send word to your family? Will they be worried that ill has befallen you?'

Garnet shook his head.

'No, I am often away for long periods without communication. They will have no cause for alarm.'

The Little Monk's face brightened.

'Then you will be able to stay here for your recuperation! Nothing would do you more good than to rest in the sunshine. I could take you to the river and show you how to cast a line.'

Garnet smiled at him. What a curio the man was! Slightly mad, with a knack for healing—and yet with such an endearing way about him. Like a crazy archangel with that great halo of white hair.

'Would you enjoy that?' he said. 'Teaching me how to fish?'

The Little Monk looked down at his toes. 'Yes,' he said. 'If I hadn't been a monk I would like to have had a son. It would have been so jolly to have walked with him and shown him all the wonderful things of the countryside.'

Garnet could have wept.

'Well, Little Monk,' he said, 'as soon as I am fit to move about you must introduce me to the splendours of the English landscape. For though I was born in England my father took me to Spain when I was a mere babe-in-arms. It would be a rare experience to see my homeland through your eyes.'

The little man's smile was a beam.

'It would be as rare for me Mr...?'

'Gage. Garnet Gage.'

★ ★ ★ ★

In Melior Mary's beautiful gold-appointed bed-chamber, within her softly curtained four-poster, she and Charles Edward lay clasped together in sleep. An hour after midnight he had loved her body with his and now he lay, one arm round her, the other resting on the pillow, whilst woven round one of his fingers was a lock of her silver hair. They were perfect as they slept. He, so slim and delicate featured; she like a piece of sculpture in the moonlight.

Yet his rest had not been quiet. He had dreamed that the sweet, haunting fragrance of a scented lady was in the room; that he had opened his eyes and seen her watching from the end of the bed. He had dreamed too that the curse of the House of Stuart was catching him up. That he was doomed to failure, to idleness, to drink. He had woken shivering in the greyness of dawn and come to a decision. He must end his idyll at Sutton Place. He must return to the outside world and make one more final and desperate bid for the throne. He must rally Scotland, he must march south and this time not turn back.

But yet could he do it without the woman who lay, sleeping still, beside him? If Helen of Troy had launched a thousand ships could not his face, combined with his strength, raise against the clansmen who had once been prepared to die for him? And, moreover, he loved her. He cared nothing at all for Clementina Walkinshaw who had followed him from Scotland to France and who—though his mind veered away from the stark fact—had borne him a child ten months ago.

He would pension Clementina off and establish Melior Mary Weston as his official mistress. Even his father could not object. And then if he was forced to marry some dull European Princess he would have his beautiful love set up in her own house—for by now in his imagination he had conquered England and was the Prince of Wales —to comfort him and relieve his brown of the cares of monarchy.

The Young Pretender drifted back to sleep with his mind at peace. His days of foolishness were at an end. He would show the world what he could do with a beautiful Englishwoman as his consort. The crown of England was there for the grasping and nothing would stand in his way.

★ ★ ★ ★

'Well?' said the Little Monk.

A gurgling trout with the iridescent scales of a rainbow lay at his feet. Garnet clapped his hands.

'Well done. It must weigh ten pounds.'

'Easily. There's a good supper for you and the Father Abbot.'

'Not you?'

The Little Monk smiled. He had a very beautiful nose and mouth but, rather at odds with them, a tough jaw line that suggested that, in his youth, he might have been quite a formidable fighter. He was not, thought Garnet looking at him closely, as small as his nickname suggested.

In fact he was really of average height though rather stooped about the shoulders. Nor was he that old. Probably not a great deal more than his middle fifties. But the quaint spectacles and the mass of white hair gave him the appearance of someone much older.

'No.' He sighed a little. 'I don't think I would enjoy eating that particular trout somehow. You see, he and I are old friends. I've chased him round this river many a long day and now I've caught him just to show you. I would feel that I was munching a companion. I'm the same over the geese. It is very foolish.'

His battered straw hat had been pushed back in the excitement of the catch and now it fell off and into the fast flowing Kennett.

'Oh dear,' said the Little Monk. 'I was rather fond of that.'

The trout gave a frantic wriggle lying, as it was, in the warm sunshine.

'Throw him back in,' said Garnet.

'What?'

'Throw him in. He's a friend of yours. The Father Abbot will never know. Come on, quickly —let the poor devil live.'

'Oh my son, my son—you think very much as I do.'

And with that the Little Monk freed the fish from the hook and cast it back into the bubbling stream, where it floated—hopeless and flat—for a minute or two, before giving a great bursting leap that told them that it still had life.

'I fish a little in Spain,' said Garnet, 'though I have none of your skills. My father sometimes comes with me—and really is quite good, though he would never admit so to anybody for fear of ruining his impression in the eyes of others.'

The pebble glasses turned towards him uncomprehendingly.

'What do you mean?'

Garnet laughed.

'Well, in his time—when he still lived in London—he was the great rake of his day; a beau and a dandy-prancer. But this masked a man of true courage; a man prepared to fight for the causes in which he believed. However, he would never show this to anyone except those closest to him, and is always at great pains not to spoil what he calls his prinkum-prankum.'

'He is still alive.?'

'Very much so! Over seventy but actively involved in everything to this day.'

'And you mother?'

'No, she died at my birth.'

The Little Monk stared out to where the fish cavorted with the joy of living.

'How sad for you—never to know her touch.'

'She was a great beauty. Look—there's a likeness of her in this locket.'

Garnet flicked the clasp open and bent down to the level of the monk's face. The funny pebble glasses moved themselves to within an inch of the delicate miniature and stared for a long moment. Then in the heat of the afternoon, the

Little Monk staggered.

'What is it, Brother?'

'Nothing, my son. I felt a touch of faintness, that is all. The sun is probably too much for me without my hat. Tell me, what was your mother's name?'

'Sibella.'

'What a pretty word,' said the Little Monk, and with that his face turned towards Heaven and he fainted like a sack at Garnet's feet.

★ ★ ★ ★

There had never been a more splendid day at Sutton Place; midsummer, June blazing, a house—built by a courier for Kings to visit—happy that a royal Prince was dwelling within its walls. And outside in the glorious parkland, beyond the gardens where the summer peacocks stretched, the Lady of the Manor and her lover played at shepherd and shepherdess. A lutenist, hidden behind a clump of trees, plucked an air that could have been written for her ancestor Sir Francis; while a hound that might easily have belonged to Sir Richard the builder, snaffled up food idly thrown to it by a King's son.

Melior Mary was arrayed in pink brocade, with beribboned lover's knots upon her sleeves and shepherd's crook. On her hat were pinned fresh roses and, round the base, she had woven the green willow to show that she loved truly. The Prince wore a shirt and breeches, that he might ride with her later in the day, and had taken one of her ribbons and tied it around his neck to show that he, too, was in love.

Their happiness had made them the two most beautiful and brave people upon the earth. At that moment Charles Edward would have forsworn liquor forever if she had so commanded; would have marched upon London with a hundred loyal Scots and stormed the citadel; was made young and strong, prepared to wrest round circumstance by her love for him. And she, in turn, was ready to sacrifice anything for him; anything that is, except the one thing that he was shortly to ask.

'Shall we ride?' he said. 'Shall we go to this accursed well of yours and exorcise its evil with our love? Is that possible?'

'I don't know,' she answered. 'I know that good is stronger than bad, but that we could have such power I doubt.'

'But I love you so much. You have brought back the courage that was in me once. I am on fire with ambition. I feel hope's breath in my throat.

She smiled.

'Than I shall take you to the place. It is time my courage also came up.'

They were characters from fairy-tale as they trotted side-by-side through the dappled forest; Bo-Beep had found her shepherd, Daphnis his Chloe. All around them the sounds of June chorailed in abundance, then grew suddenly

399

silent at the point where the trees thinned away.

In front of Charles Edward and Melior Mary lay all that was left of the old manor house. To the right the ruins of the hunting lodge, beyond those a solitary cottage, before them the well of St Edward.

'But I can see nothing,' said the Young Pretender. 'Just a stone lying on the ground.'

'That covers the well. It was put there after a drowning.'

She had never spoken to him of Sibella's death, of how they had found her with her hair floating out like a sea anemone.

'And what's that beyond?'

'The old manor house, built in the reign of King John. I saw a ghost there once.'

She spoke without thinking but Charles Edward gave her a sharp look and said, 'This is haunted land, Melior Mary. And Sutton Place is alive with night walkers. Did you hear Giles cry last evening? Is that not meant to herald disaster?'

'So it's said.'

He did not reply, giving her an unreadable glance from his heavy-lidded eyes, as he dismounted and walked the few paces to where the stone lay uncompromisingly before him.

'I'm going to move it back.'

'I'd rather you didn't.'

'Nonsense.'

He turned to her and smiled and she saw, in that instant, how he must have appeared at the famous entrance into Holyrood, when Edinburgh had bowed before him. His skin tanned by the winds of Scotland, his eyes bright and gazing warmly at James Hepburn of Keith—proud and respected old man—who had come out of the crowd, gone down on one knee, and tendered his drawn sword in homage.

'Mo Phrionnsa,' she said.

But he did not hear her, too preoccupied with removing the stone.

'It's very deep,' he said as it shifted. 'I cannot see the bottom.'

Slowly and reluctantly she walked to stand beside him; a tunnel of blackness dropped sheerly before her feet. Charles Edward tossed in a pebble and after a while they heard it splash in the darkness.

'Melior Mary,' he said without looking up at her. 'I want you to leave this place and come away with me.'

Not understanding she answered, 'But I thought you wanted to see it.'

He gazed at her over his shoulder from where he knelt.

'I don't mean that. I mean that I want you to give up Sutton Place and come to live with me in France.'

She stared at him wide-eyed and he stood up so that he could look down at her, his hands on her shoulders.

'So many things are in my heart, Melior Mary. My crowding ambition, my love for you, my dread of things dark. But they all converge in one thing. I want you beside me, helping to win back my father's crown. And it is not just for that reason that I ask you to renounce your manor. I believe that we both come from cursed lines and that if you cast free—make Sutton Place over in favour of your cousin and heir—the spell will be broken. Will you do it?'

His grip on her had tightened and she was unable to move as she answered, 'Highness, I cannot. Sutton Place is part of me. Don't you understand?'

'No I don't by God! It is a house, a building. Nothing more.'

'But it is my birthright.'

'And the crown of England is mine! Would you let your Sovereign Prince lose his inheritance in order that you keep yours?'

'No, no.' She was frantic. 'You can regain England without my giving up the Manor. I can be at your side without that.'

'Can you? Can you dwell in France as my wife and also be the chatelaine of Sutton? I am the Pretender's son. You will have to live according to my station.'

His well-known temper, notorious for appearing in drink, was beginning to flare without the spur of wine.

'Well, madam? I am offering you my hand—albeit morganatically. Will you have me?'

'But I was born for Sutton Place,' she answered.

He brought his eyes down to a level with hers and she saw that the amber coronas were as fierce as those of a god of war.

'Then keep it,' he said through gritted teeth. 'May it keep you warm on a winter's night when you have grown old—even as *you* must, Melior Mary, when your pact with the Devil to keep age at bay is at last played out!'

'But, my Prince...'

'Say nothing more. You have rejected me. That is enough. I bid you and your accursed house goodbye.'

He turned and ran for his horse. If he had stayed another minute he would have struck her. She was everything to him—beauty, love, his hope for the future—and she had thrown him aside in exchange for bricks and mortar. He would not look back, even in response to her pleading cries, but in his mind's eye he could see her standing, the most perfect creature on whom he had ever gazed, defenceless and alone by the well at which she, and all who inherited Sutton Place, had been eternally damned.

★ ★ ★ ★

'I will do my very best of course,' the doctor had said, 'but frankly I can offer you little hope.'

He was one of the new breed of physician, trained at Glasgow by William Cullen, and come south to exercise his skill in clinical medicine because of his attachement to a Berkshire girl.

403

He had married her and set up practice in Newbury and become quite celebrated thereabouts as the teaching of his revolutionary tutor had been put into action amongst the inhabitants.

'If anyone can save his life it will be Dr McGregor,' Brother Augustus had said to Garnet. 'You'd better ride over and fetch him. None of the other monks can help.'

So Gage had gone immediately and two hours later Dr McGregor—who had been out calling—had arrived at Inglewood Priory.

The Little Monk had not really regained consciousness since he had fallen at Garnet's feet on the sunlit river bank. He had murmured a couple of times during the journey back to the monastery —slung across Garnet's shoulder like a child— and after they had put him to bed and removed the funny glasses, he had flicked his eyes open once, only to close them again immediately. But other than that there had been so sign of life in him. He appeared in a coma, the symptom of sweating—the dreaded thing that had almost drained the life from Garnet—soon starting its accompanying and relentless process.

'Did he catch this from me?' Garnet had asked.

'Without a doubt.' Dr McGregor's voice had been flat. 'He nursed you through a similar thing you say?'

'Yes. I thought at the time it was a malarial condition.'

'I think not. It seems to have all the signs of the old Sweating Sickness of the past. It is my

404

guess that you contracted it in London.'

'But I recovered!'

'Yes, but you have youth on your side, sir. This poor fellow will have a far greater struggle.'

Garnet had looked down at the curling white hair on the pillow, on the beautiful nose and mouth, on the archangel's face—dignified now without its spectacles—and said, 'If he dies because of me I shall never forgive myself. He is a truly good man. A little saint really.'

Dr McGregor had washed his hands in a basin and said, 'The day will undoubtedly come, Mr Gage, when medicine will be invented that will cure almost everything. But when that hoped-for event takes place I doubt that the transmitting of disease—one person to the other—will ever be curtailed. We should all have to walk round constantly clean and scarcely breathing. Think upon it. You may have killed six people already, quite innocently, by passing on illness to them. It is something that simply cannot be avoided.'

He had gone then and left Garnet alone with the figure that burned in an ever-growing pool of sweat. And it had seemed utterly right to hold the little man in his arms as he sponged cool the poor fevered body. He had been doing that for several hours when Brother Augustus had come and said, 'Mr Gage, you must take some rest. You have only just recovered from the same illness. Go and see to yourself and I will sit with him.'

And so Garnet had left them and Brother

Augustus—the old, hidden Jacobite—had sat beside the bed of his friend and said, 'God—I haven't been a very good monk as you well know. I used the monastery to hide-out and took the habit because it was expedient. But this little creature *is* good. Of course I have no idea what sort of life he led before he came here. He could have got up to anything. And, if it is impossible to save his life, let him know peace and happiness before he passes into your immense care.'

It wasn't like the old warrior to weep but he had felt tears spurt then onto his cheeks. If he could have been said to feel affection for anyone at all it was the Little Monk. Augustus had had his head in his hands and had indulged in a fit of weeping when Garnet had come back into the room.

And now it was evening on the third day of the little Monk's illness and Dr McGregor was shaking his head.

'I'm sorry—there is no hope left. I doubt if he will last till morning. You can give him this physic and he will feel nothing. Just let him slip out quietly.'

Garnet turned to stare out of the window. The late June sun was setting like a ball of blood behind the priory's west face so that everywhere he looked was glowing crimson.

'I feel that I've always known him,' he said, without turning round. 'This is unbearable. You are sure?'

'Sure,' said McGregor. He was already thinking about his next patient—a farmer's wife with a complicated labour which he suspected might result in twins. 'Where do you wish me to send my bill?'

'I shall pay you now. I am leaving for Spain as soon as...'

'Quite. That will be one guinea.' He slipped the money into his waistcoat pocket. 'Goodbye to you. I wish you a safe journey.'

'Heartless wretch,' said Brother Augustus as the door closed behind him.

'That is the modern man. But they do good, you know. They pioneer.'

'Um! I suppose I should fetch the Father Abbot now. The prayers had better be started.'

He went out leaving Garnet alone to stare at the dying man. In the unusually bright evening he looked younger—his hair taking on a red tinge that reminded Garnet of his own. In fact his features were quite reminiscent of those that Garent saw in the mirror each morning. A ridiculous fact but one that became more undeniable the greater Garnet thought about it.

He sat down beside the bed and put his arm round the Little Monk'a shoulders and to his surprise the eyes opened and gazed into his. Garnet had never seen them before, masked as they always were by those clown spectacles, and now he exclaimed out loud. A flash of blue, as vivid as his and dimmed only by the encroachment of age, was staring at him with an expression of adoration.

'Garnet?'

It was a cloud that spoke, so light and vaporous was the sound.

'Yes, Little Monk?'

'Oh, my son, a wonderful thing has happened to me...'

The gasp died away as all about the room came the dreaded reverberation of the priory bell tolling out its requiem for the dying.

'Garnet...'

The whisper was lost beneath the bell's great voice and Garnet bent his ear to the pale lips, lifting the monk in his arms as he did so.

'Yes?'

'All the mist has cleared. Do you understand?'

Garnet shook his head and the blue eyes intensified in their loving stare.

'While I slept I dreamed. And when I dreamed I knew the answer.'

Next to Garnet's chest the heart beat was growing fainter. The inevitable parting could only be a second away.

'I love you, Little Monk,' said Garnet. 'Go to God in peace, sweet man.'

'Oh my son,' came the answer. 'You see you are...Oh, Garnet...*my son*.'

And with that he put his head against his boy's shoulder, smiled up at him, and died.

He was buried two days later in the priory's graveyard; row upon row of humble graves marked by tiny headstones. Above the Little Monk they erected one with the words 'Brother

Hyacinth'.

'Was that his real name?' said Garnet, as he knelt to say his final farewell.

'No,' said Augustus. 'Nobody knows what that was. Hyacinth was what the old Abbot called him. He said he had eyes that reminded him of wild flowers—a foolish fancy, I suppose.'

'Brother Hyacinth,' Garnet smiled reflectively. 'Do you know, I think he regained his memory before he died. He looked at me so earnestly—as if he had remembered something after all these years.'

'Did he really? Well, well, well!?' Brother Augustus's mind was already on what he would eat for supper that night—funerals had a terrible way of making him ravenous. 'I hope it made him happy—he deserved that.'

'Yes,' said Garnet. He mounted his horse and turned it towards the priory entrance. 'I wish I had known him longer. He was so easy to love.'

'Indeed. Well, goodbye Mr Gage. I don't suppose I shall see you again.'

'No. It was fate not design that brought me here. I shan't be returning. Goodbye, Brother.'

He nudged his horse's sides and trotted towards the gates but at them he turned, waved his arm, shouted 'Goodbye,' and then added beneath his breath, 'Farewell Brother Hyacinth.'

CHAPTER 20

That was when she began to hate the house; the moment she stood by the windows at the far end of the Long Gallery and saw Charles Edward Stuart become a dot amongst the distant trees of the home park; the moment she skimmed, on lightning feet, down the staircase and out to the stables to find her horse, Thunder, unharnessed, but Tom's mount ready to be ridden. Without pausing for a second she had clambered onto the mounting block and struggled into the unfamiliar saddle, transformed by despair—as wild and impetuous as she had always been.

She must have stood by the well, motionless, for five minutes after the Prince had ridden off—and then she had plunged after him, only to learn that he had returned to Sutton Place to collect his belongings but still she was too late. The view from the gallery had told her that she must go at full gallop to catch him up.

But now, having driven the beast without mercy and with the great iron gates in view she could see him ahead of her. He was calling to the lodge keeper to open up and the man was hurrying to obey. She watched in horror as the gates began to swing back.

'Your Highness,' she called. 'Charles Edward.

Don't! I'll come with you. Damn the house, damn everything. I'll leave it all.'

But he could not hear her and the massive iron-work was opening wider and wider. She saw him kick his horse's sides, where he had reined in while he waited.

'No, no, no,' she shouted in full voice. 'I have changed my mind. I'm coming with you.'

He must have heard something because he glanced back over his shoulder but at that moment she was hidden by a tree. So fate played his trick on them both. The gates were open and Prince Charles Edward—the fated heir to the House of Stuart—cantered through them and to a life destined evermore to spiral downwards. The hero of '45—the best and bravest of all that line of Kings—had lost his moment of hope.

Behind him the gates began to swing to again and, as Melior Mary hurled up to them, they finally shut in her face. She jumped from her horse, twisting her ankle as she did so, and wrenched at the bars with her bare hands.

'Come back! Come back!' she screamed.

But there was no sign of him. He was riding as if the Devil was in his soul.

'Oh God help me!' she said—and she sank to the ground sobbing. The gates loomed above her like the portcullis of a prison, the words 'Sutton Place' picked out above them, the Tudor rose emblazoned in gold.

'God help me!' she shouted again, regardless of the lodge keeper's face staring at her in shock.

'So house, you've shut me in have you? You've caught me at last! Well, we'll see. If you can ruin my life I can ruin you. Be damned to you, Sutton Place.'

She was still moaning, 'I hate you,' when they carried her back to the house and laid her on her bed.

'Get a doctor for the love of God,' said the old woman that Bridget Clopper had turned into. 'She's taken an hysteric that's like to kill her.'

But Tom—Melior Mary's childhood companion—said, 'There's one who'll do her more good than a doctor. I'll go and fetch him. He's never been far away from her.'

'And who might that be?'

'Mitchell, of course.'

'Mitchell! Yes, he'll know how to deal with her.'

★ ★ ★ ★

Joseph said, 'So you're back. Damme, boy, you had me worried. I thought some ill must have befallen you.'

It was July and Castile languished beneath a heatwave but in the courtyard of the villa that belonged to the Grandee Gage fountains trickled coolly and a vine—old, gnarled and as greatly respected as its owner—cast a lush purple shadow over the place where Joseph sat at his ease, fanning himself with ostrich feathers. At his feet Sootface lay like a curled dog and, as Garnet

412

approached, Joseph pushed the Negro affectionately with his shoe.

'Damnable fellow can do nothing but sleep
these days. Step over him, Garnet, will you. Sit
here. Tell me what news of the Prince.'

'None at all. I didn't see him. I was taken ill
on my way to Bristol. That's what delayed me.'

A hand that shook a little, but still thin and
elegant for all that, stretched out and poured
some wine from a cooler.

'Drink some of this. I think you'll like it. I laid
it down when we first came to Spain all those
years ago.'

His love for Garnet was painful in its intensity.
He would have given his life instantly and
without expression for him. He adored him as
he had adored his mother. Yet Joseph's face held
its languid expression and the green cat eyes did
little more than flicker as he said, 'What happened exactly?'

'Apparently it was the Sweating Sickness, contracted in London. I was taken ill on the journey
and would be dead I think, if it had not been for
the charity of an order of monks.'

'Whereabouts was this?'

'Inglewood Priory. It's in Berkshire—near
Kintbury.'

Joseph shook his head. He had left England
so long ago that if he had ever heard of the place
he had forgotten it.

'But the story has a sad end, I'm afraid. The
Brother who nursed me caught the illness—and

413

died.'

Joseph sipped his wine.

'Was he an old man?'

'It's rather difficult to say. He had an oldish
air but was probably not yet sixty. But he was
gentle, so good. A little maddish. The monks had
found him years before, apparently, wandering
with his memory lost.'

Joseph made a 'Tch, tch' sound.

'He wouldn't have harmed a fly—but I killed
him.'

'Oh come, come Garnet. You cannot hold
yourself responsible for nature's progression.'

'What do you mean?'

'If it was meant to happen—if it was the time
when he was destined to go—it would have taken
place regardless of you.'

'Do you really believe that? Did you think that
when my mother died in childbirth?'

Joseph hesitated and in his sleep Sootface sighed and scratched.

'Yes and no. She went before her allotted span
but perhaps there was no other road open to her.'

'I don't understand.'

'No.'

The word was final, a trifle crisp. In the great
vine's shadow nothing stirred but the tinkling
silver of the fountains.

'He was a kind man,' said Garnet quietly.

'If he nursed you back to health I am eternally
in his debt. What was his name?'

'No-one knew—he couldn't remember it himself. But he had a name in the Brotherhood.'

'And what was that?'

Everything was very quiet as fate hesitated. Should Joseph Gage who had put so much into life, who had been ruined in so many ways and who had fought back and so nobly won, be the victim of further pain? And Garnet, who had none of the old great gift of both his parents and of the family that had sprung from Dr Zachary, shifted a little in his chair as something of the weight of the moment rubbed off on him.

'Little Monk,' he said slowly. 'They called him the Little Monk.'

'God rest his soul,' answered Joseph—and there was no sound in the courtyard but for the bubble of the wine, the splash of the fountains and the snores of the Negro, Sootface.

★ ★ ★ ★

'Get out of your bed,' said Mitchell. 'Get out and draw back these curtains. You must, Missie. For everybody's sake.'

She had been like it for a month; lying in the shadows, staring at the wall and eating nothing but a piece of bread a day. Nor had she bothered to drink her water from Malvern and consequently age had caught her up apace. There were wrinkles round her eyes and on her cheeks; the glorious silver hair had lost its lustre and hung in tatters about her shoulders.

She turned to look at him and the great violet

415

eyes were dull and hollow.

'What do you want with me?' she said in a voice he could not recognise.

'I want you to come back to life, Melior Mary. For you may as well be dead, lying there like that. And dead you certainly will be if you don't stand up soon.'

But he was old now and lacked the power he had once had over her. Only the livid scar and the brilliant eyes were left to show the ferocious man who had once dwelled within.

'Go away,' she said.

'I can't do that. I can't leave you to rot. I love you, Missie. I want you to live again.'

'That I can never do.'

'No, perhaps not. Not as the great Beauty. But you can get up and lead your daily life as Lady of the Manor. Sutton Place needs your care and attention.'

She gave a wicked laugh.

'Does it? Good! Then it shall not have it. It has ruined my life with its demands. Now it can suffer in its turn.'

'What do you mean by that?'

'It blinded me with its old heritage for a while. I thought that it mattered more than love. But it doesn't—nothing does. And the hesitation was long enough for me to lose Charles Edward. Now there is nothing for me but to rot into old age.'

She turned her head away from him and wept bitterly into her pillow.

'Oh don't, Missie—don't. It breaks my heart

to hear you. Those are such tragic words.'

He felt broken, defeated. He could think of no way to bear up her spirit. Down the hardened cheeks his own tears trickled in anguish.

'Mitchell stop!?' she had looked up and seen him cry. 'Please!'

But he could not answer her. He felt that his fighting days were over.

'Mitchell.' Her voice had a softer note. 'Will it please you if I get up today?'

'Yes.' His answer was muffled. 'Yes, if you will promise to act out your life properly.'

'Never in society.'

'That's probably to the good.' He looked at the ravaged face before him. 'But here, Missie. You may hate Sutton Place now but you will learn to love it again in time.'

She turned a hard look upon him.

'We shall see,' she said.

* * * *

It was December and it was snowing in Castile. Pernel Gage and her brothers—the twins James and Jacob—had never seen such a thing before, and they rushed out of their grandfather's house and into the vined courtyard. Big white flakes fell out of the sky towards them and they laughed and tried to catch them in their mouths.

'Are they cakes?' said James, and his brother, who was so like him that even Pernel was sometimes deceived, echoed, 'Yes, are they cakes?'

417

'Yes,' answered Pernel. 'They are snow cakes—though Mama called them snowflakes. I shall catch you both one.' But her attention was attracted by something else and she said, 'Look at the fountain. It's a little frozen palace.'

They hurried to where the courtyard's big central cascade hung in tiers of glass-like pendants.

'Why, it's lovely,' said James, and then he added, 'What's that?'

In the largest sheet of ice a reflection was forming that was visible to all of them.

'It's Sootface!' Pernel exclaimed. 'What's he doing in there? Look, he's waving.'

They all turned to stare at each other—the identical boys and their dark-haired sister. They were magic children. Full of the ancient lore that had by-passed their father and come straight to them.

'He's saying goodbye, isn't he?' said James.

'Yes,' answered Pernel. 'Don't go back into the house yet. Grandfather's crying.'

'Leave him in peace. We shall kiss him better later.'

And, sure enough, in his seat by the fire Joseph sat in tears. At his feet Sootface lay curled up in the soundest sleep of all.

'Oh damme, damme,' said Joseph. 'I loved him so. My faithful brother dog.'

Garnet said, 'He died how he would have chosen—in his sleep, by a roaring fire and at your side.'

He gently removed the Negro's turban and

418

beneath it the white woolly hair sprung up like fleece.

'He was quite old,' he said wonderingly. 'I never thought of him as that somehow.'

Through his tears Joseph said, 'We're all getting old, Garnet. Time passes you know. Time passes.'

★ ★ ★ ★

In that same bleak winter Melior Mary sat before the fire in the Great Hall and grumbled aloud.

'I'm very cold,' she said. 'I don't know why we sit here Mitchell. Is it just for the look of it? The mistress of Sutton Place in residence. Is it for that?'

'I don't know, Missie,' he answered. 'It was your instruction.'

'Well it wasn't a very good one. I'm frozen to the bone.' She pulled her shawl more tightly round her shoulders and added, 'And I do wish you wouldn't close your eyes when I'm speaking to you.'

'I can't help it, Missie—I'm greatly tired.'

'Well you're boring company, boring and old. I think I shall walk round this wretched house of mine. Try not to be asleep when I come back.'

She lit a solitary candle from those that burned in a candelabra at her side and set off slowly towards the west wing. Night after night she did this, walking round from room to room—her only light the small flickering flame. But she

419

always ended her solitary perambulation in the same place—by the windows of the Long Gallery. There she would stand for an hour or more, gazing out into the darkness, her candle a beacon on the windowsill.

As Mitchell watched her departing figure his heart bled for her. He knew, without her ever having said a word to him, that the sole purpose of the vigil in the gallery was to look for the Young Pretender. To see if the lights of a carriage or the moonlit figure of a horseman might be piercing the blackness which fell like a pall over Sutton Place at night. Poor tragic woman! She had turned—in the six months since Charles Edward had gone—from a great glowing Beauty to a thin wispy-haired old woman. Whatever secret she had found to preserve her youth—and she had never confided in Mitchell what it might be—she no longer cared to exercise its art. The wonderful girl, the fire maiden for whom he had transformed his entire life, was gone.

And now as he sat in the shadows of the Great Hall, alone by the fire, he felt again the pain in his chest which was so familiar to him and which, with his ferocious strength, he had fought off so many times before. He knew that it was the Grim Reaper whistling in the dark for him, that the time was coming when he must answer the tune. But how could he forsake Melior Mary? She had nothing left but his devotion. Everything had been taken from her but Sutton Place—and against that she had developed a loathing which seemed to grow with each day. He sometimes felt that only he stood supporting the thin wall that divided her unruly personality between stability and madness.

Yet now the pain was growing more intense—it sat on his heart like an iron crab. Mitchell closed his eyes. It seemed to him then that he was back in the Jacobite uprising of 1715. He heard the sound of grapeshot; the roar of the Highlanders at Braemar as Jamie the Rover—James III—was proclaimed King by the Earl of Mar; stood by his master, the Earl of Nithdale, as they fought barehanded with the English troops; felt once more the wicked thrust of the dagger that had ripped half his face open, leaving him scarred for life.

In his death dream Mitchell saw once more the famous Nithsdale rescue. Saw Lady Nithsdale and two of her friends pass in and out of the Earl's room in the Tower until, in the end, the guards were so bemused with the comings and goings of the three veiled weeping women that the Earl—dressed in female clothes—had walked straight past them and out to where Mitchell waited with the carriage below. Then to Rome and to freedom and to a life of enjoyable exile— had it not been for Melior Mary! Everything changed; nothing the same any more.

He had loved her as only a hard man could. With the intensity that was part of his iron soul. For her he had been humbled, made a shadow before boys like Matthew Banister and the Prince himself. And now he could feel nothing but an overwhelming misery that he was not to die in her arms, that even at this vast and final hour he was not to be allowed one moment when his love for her should reign paramount above all others.

'Melior Mary,' he called out—but his voice was a cobweb in the Great Hall's loftiness. 'Pray for me—as I shall for you. Love your house, Missie, for in a few moments there'll be nothing else left for you.'

But she did not hear him and it was an hour before she quitted the Long Gallery and descended the stairs to where the fire burned low in the dimness.

'You've let it get even colder,' she said to the slumbering form in the chair. 'Why didn't you throw on a log?'

But Mitchell did not answer and she saw that his head had slumped forward onto his chest.

'Mitchell?' she said sharply, 'are you not well?'

She reached over to shake his shoulder and as she did so he fell sideways against the chair's arm with no more life in him than a cloth dolly.

'Oh no!' Her cry was a shout direct to God's face. 'Not that! Not Mitchell!'

She pulled him against her, kneeling down by his side so that she could hold him closer.

'There's too much death about,' she said. 'Too much separation and pain. I can't bear it, for he was my rock and my anchor. How could you do this to me?'

And then as she wept into the dead man's hand, which she held against her cheek as if it were the petal of a flower, a look of fear crossed her face.

'So that's to be the way of it, is it?' she said. 'That is how the curse unfolds. Not only childless and the last of the line but now to be immured here alone. Was ever a house so wretched, was ever a dwelling so cursed as you, my inheritance, my torment—Sutton Place?'

CHAPTER 21

Riding before George III in procession, the King's champion, armed cap-à-pie and mounted on a magnificent charger, flung down the gauntlet in accordance with ancient tradition— and just for a minute the huge crowd at the coronation of this honourable young man were totally silent, the only sound the jubilant carillon from Westminster Abbey. For this would be the moment, if moment there were to be at all, when the Jacobite sympathisers—quiet for years now as their King James III slipped into senility and their Prince became a hopeless drunkard—might make some last, brave, desperate demonstration of their loyalty to the Stuarts. Nobody really expected it, but the Jacobites were an unpredictable set. Was the gauntlet to lie where it had

423

been thrown?

The girl, when she stepped forward, was the greatest shock of all. An old dour Highlander perhaps, but not this dark-haired creature with eyes like clear water and probably no more than fifteen years old. She gave the champion a mysterious smile—a magic smile almost—and then the gauntlet was in her hand and she had vanished into the crowd so quickly that it was obvious that her accomplices were dotted everywhere. There was an audible gasp and the young King turned his honest German face to his equerry and called through the carriage window, 'Who was that?'

'A Jacobite loyalist, sir. A fanatic. She will be arrested immediately.'

'If you can catch her,' answered the King.

And he was right—there was no sign of the girl anywhere. But now something else caught George's eye. A hooded abbot standing amongst the spectators had moved slightly forward and was gazing to where the newly-crowned King rode in his golden coronation coach. The hood fell back and a bitter face out of which stared eyes like molten amber looked at the monarch. George III drew in a breath. Surely not! But yet in that ravaged countenance there was more than just a passing resemblance to Charles Edward Stuart.

And as he gazed at the man who should, by true blood, have stood in his place in Westminster Abbey today, George saw Charles Edward's lips move into a grim smile.

'I envy you the least of any man alive,' the Pretender said—and then he added something else beneath his breath.

George felt a shiver go through him and he stared over his shoulder to where—his coach having now gone past—the sinister figure had stood. But it too had vanished into the crowd.

'I think that man was Charles Edward Stuart,' said the King. 'And I think he cursed me. Dear God!'

'Oh no, Sir,' the equerry answered soothingly. 'The Young Pretender lies a drink-sodden hulk in the Duchy of Bouillon. He will never set foot on these shores again.'

But the simple stubborn George was not convinced. He wondered if the curse on the House of Stuart—which he had often hear discussed—could, with the putting on of their crown, have been transferred to him. He wondered if his reign would be a glorious one—or if it would be fraught with tragedy.

Fortunately for him his stalwart character knew nothing of premonition or destiny. He had no idea that that very crown would weigh so heavily upon him that for twenty years he would know recurring fits of madness that would cause him to wander the solitary galleries of Windsor crying out aloud with pain and despair. He had no glimpse that his eldest son would turn against him; that he would go blind; that he would be the King remembered throughout history as he who lost the American Colonies.

Poor George—he rode on to his coronation banquet with his big face glum. Poor Charles Edward—he was helped into Garnet Gage's carriage, his frame weakened by years of excessive drinking.

'For you, sir,' said Pernel, holding out the champion's gauntlet.

He smiled at her.

'We have taken up his challenge, haven't we? He has not heard the last of us.'

'No, sir.'

But he knew even as he spoke—as did Garnet and his daughter—that they were empty meaningless words. And Pernel, with her ancient gift, also knew that not only was the third Hanover George doomed to an agonising life but that her Sovereign Prince would return to Europe and shut himself away as a recluse; that the days of Bonnie Prince Charlie, the pride and hope of all the Jacobites, were dead and gone forever.

'To Dover, Highness?' said Garnet.

'Yes, yes.'

'There is nobody you wish to see before you depart?'

Just for a moment the vision of the great Beauty he had once loved—the sparkling eyes of Melior Mary—flashed before Charles Stuart. Then he moved savagely in his seat.

'No, nobody,' he said. 'Drive on.'

CHAPTER 22

Over the unruffled surface of the River Wey a kingfisher skimmed effortlessly, passing over the head of a heron that stood one-legged in the shallows; in the fir tress of the autumn home park the October birds sang their crisp midday song; in the falling masonry of Sutton Place a departing swallow circled round the Gate House Tower, where he had built his summer nest, and then flew south. It was the end of a cycle, the fading of another year into mezzotint. Soon it would be 1778 and George III would have sat on the throne of England for seventeen years. Time was passing rapidly now for all those left from the long-ago drama of the great house.

And almost intrusively, for there had been no company there—except for an occasional tradesman or calling doctor—for twenty years, a carriage was slowly wending its way up to the overgrown drive. Melior Mary Weston was to have a visitor at last.

'All right, Miss Seward?' shouted the driver as the horse stumbled over some bushes that were threatening to close the way off completely at that point.

And the poetess Anna Seward called back, 'Yes, thank you,' and peered out even more curiously to see what extraordinary forest they had ventured into through the huge and reluctant gates that bore the inscription Sutton Place, beside the emblem of a once-guilded Tudor rose.

Before her and overhead the trees grew so thickly that the glowing ember of the seasonal sun was blotted out and the carriage moved as if in a tunnel of shade. The only life came from the river which they had crossed by means of a rotting and precarious bridge and with the way ahead curving to nothing in front of them, the poetess—just for a moment—felt a slight tinge of fear. But she straightened her back resolutely. Anna Seward was not only a celebrated writer—a woman of letters as opposed to a blue stocking and literary entertainer—but she was also the daughter of a clergyman, the Canon Residentiary of Lichfield Cathedral. She had been brought up in a bishop's palace amongst the gentle spires of the dreamy town, and her faith in the presence of God was unshakeable.

She was a beautiful looking woman. About thirty years old, her mental alertness shining in a small heart-like face dominated by a pair of large and serious grey eyes. She had earned herself the title of 'Swan of Lichfield' and was a friend of both Dr Johnson and Boswell. This, she considered modestly, was a reasonable achievement for one who lived in the cloisters of a cathedral town and rarely ventured forth to London.

But recently her romantic imagination had

been fired by a poem about the rising of 1745—
and her research had turned up a curio. An
elderly friend of Canon Seward's—whose political
leanings were quite definitely in sympathy with
the Jacobite cause, though this was something
never spoken of in the family—had said, 'There's
one of them still alive, you know.'

'One of what?'

'One of the Prince's mistresses—begging your
pardon! It was kept very secret at the time, but
there were rumours of course. They say she lives
like a hermit in a crumbling ruin beyond Guildford.'

'Who is she?'

'Weston's the name. Melior Mary Weston.
However she must be very old now. It's said that
she's completely mad.'

It had not been an encouraging picture that
Miss Seward possessed that intrepid sense of
determination, combined with English good
sense, only to be found in gently raised daughters
of clerics. She had donned a travelling cloak of
plaid, packed a box with enough clothes for a few
days journey, and set forth with no-one except
her coachman as companion.

And if she had been anyone else other than
Anna Seward she would have turned back as the
carriage rounded the bend and the sight of a once
magnificent mansion house, now rapidly falling
into ruin and giving a most sinister impression
outlined as it was against a blood-red sun, came
into view. In fact, as she drew nearer, she stared

in amazement. Four enormous poles—like battering rams—were propping up what must have once been a stately gate house and tower. If they had been pulled away, the entire facade would have come tumbling. Furthermore the arch of the tower had been boarded, only a small door in it giving access. The carriage could proceed no further.

'I can't get round the wall, Miss,' said the coachman. 'We'll have to go on foot. Do you want me to come with you?'

'Yes please, Thorne,' she answered a fraction too quickly. 'It doesn't look very prepossessing.'

'No!'

He was a thick-set man of about forty and, without realising it, he squared his shoulders as he said this and grasped his whip more tightly in his heavily gloved hand. Miss Seward stretched out a timid knuckle and knocked nervously on the door. It swung open beneath her touch revealing a dim and shadowy courtyard.

'Hallo!' she called out. 'Is there anybody there?'

Nothing stirred except for the startled beating of birds' wings.

'Oh Thorne, what shall we do?'

'Go in, miss. She's expecting you, isn't she?'

Anna looked down at the tips of her shoes.

'Well, I wrote—but she didn't answer. But then she's always in. She leads a solitary existence I believe.'

'Then come on. We must at least try.'

What had once been a beautiful courtyard with

terracotta brickwork decorated by the carved initials R.W. and the design of a tun, to say nothing of grinning amorini and fruit and flower mouldings, was now strewn with falling masonry and it took concentration to manoeuvre to the hugely arched front door.

'This hasn't been opened for years!' said Miss Seward anxiously.

'Look, miss. There's another door to the right. Try that.'

A rotting bell pull snapped beneath the poetess's grasp and Thorne was reduced to beating on the door with his whip handle.

'Hullo,' he called out loudly. 'Miss Seward to see Miss Weston, if you please.'

There was a movement at one of the upstairs windows and, as they craned their necks, both of them had a glimpse of a wild-headed figure staring out for a second.

'Oh dear,' said the Swan of Lichfield. 'What was that?'

'I think we'd better go,' answered Thorne.

But too late. The door had opened an inch or two to reveal a short, squat nose straddled by a broken pair of glasses.

'Yes?' said a man's voice.

Anna cleared her throat.

'Miss Anna Seward calling on Miss Melior Mary Weston. I did write.'

Rather surprisingly the door opened a foot or two to reveal a short, fat, anxious-faced priest.

'I'm Father Gage,' he said. 'One of Miss
431

Weston's cousins and also her personal chaplain. Come in, come in! She *is* expecting you.'

Rather slowly the visitors stepped over the threshold.

'I'll see if she is ready,' said the priest—and scampered off.

They found themselves standing in a small entrance hall from which, through an archway slightly to her right, Anna could glimpse an enormous hall which—as she looked—was suddenly suffused with light, the afternoon sun being then at just the right angle in the courtyard. It was in such contrast to the gloom and rot all about her that, unbidden, the poetess went in. From a myriad of stained glass old escutcheons of ancestors long dead gleamed about her with the colour of ruby, of sapphire and of gold.

'How beautiful,' she said aloud and then jumped as a voice behind her said, 'Look at the floor. See, they are little islands of colour.'

She wheeled round and stared in amazement. Arrayed in the splendid style of twenty years earlier, Melior Mary Weston stood before her. A large brimmed hat, from which feathers trailed almost to the ground, shaded a face quite skull-like in its thinness, whilst the frail body was robed in a hooped dress very much too large.

Anna Seward dropped a curtsey. 'Miss Weston?' she said.

Melior Mary laughed and, just for a second, the poetess saw it; saw the flash of vivid beauty that must once have been; saw the unusual colour of the eyes as they lit up with some long-ago gaiety.

'Yes, yes. I am she. What do you want with me? There's nobody about any more, you know. They all went a long time ago. Only I live here now—and Father James Ambrose Gage.'

'But it's you I came to see. I rather hoped to talk over the old times. The days of the Young Pretender.'

A claw-like hand shot out and grabbed the poetess's arm.

'You've come from him? You have a message from the Prince?' Her face changed to that of a forlorn robin, beady of eye and anxious. 'Don't tell him how I have decayed. He loved me once, you know. But I was a fool. I let him go that I might keep this accursed house. And I am alone as a result.' Now she was an old vixen—cunning and wicked. 'But I had my revenge. I have killed Sutton Place. Soon it will fall down into ruins and good riddance to it. But come—see for yourself what was once Sir Richard Weston's pride.'

She took Anna by the elbow and led her up a staircase the walls of which were hung with damp and mouldering family portraits interspersed with those of a morbidly religious nature. Anna Seward stared in horror. The whole house was crumbling. The smell of decay was almost as powerful as that of the incense which clouded the atmosphere like a pall.

And dimly, at the top of the stairs, she could

433

glimpse what had once been a magnificent Long Gallery turned now into a faintly lit chapel.

'See,' said Melior Mary, 'all the old folly gone. Giles must cry to God these days.'

Anna had no idea what this meant but to her poetic eye the conversation of such a superb piece of Tudor architecture into a gloomy and miserable place of prayer went against her whole idea of glorifying the Creator.

'It's very dark,' she ventured, staring at the windows which had been totally enclosed by ivy.

'That's how I want it. I don't like the light on my face any more.'

'But surely it is a tragedy to let such a glorious house disintegrate.'

Melior Mary threw Miss Seward an angry glance, her face a death's head beneath the broad brimmed hat.

'You don't know what you are saying. Sutton Place is accursed—accursed by things evil and pagan. I have put on the armour of the Lord—'. She gazed round the terrible chapel with a kind of triumph. '—but there are others who have not. It is better that the place returns to the elements and is never lived in again.'

Anna Seward looked at her in pity. It was obvious that the old woman had totally lost her reason.

'But who will it pass to? What of their wishes?'

Melior Mary put her finger to her lips.

'Don't speak too loudly. You see—it is always the heir that suffers. Death, madness and

434

despair—that is what he or she must bear.'

'But who *is* your heir?'

'First it was my fat cousin William and his three little boys. But the house killed all of them, one after the other. So then I had a choice. Viscount Gage's son or my aunt's great-nephew John Webbe or—Garnet Gage.' She gave a breathless little laugh. 'But the Viscount is not a Catholic and Garnet—well, I could not inflict such a thing on him—so it is John Webbe. He means nothing to me. I have barely met him.'

She genuflected before the white and gilt altar.

'I am at peace over that, Miss Seward. Webbe will pull down what remains of it—and that will be an end to the wretched place.'

The atmosphere in the chapel had grown suddenly cold and right behind Anna Seward—so near that logically she should have felt his breath upon her—a man sobbed in despair. She spun round but the dim—and somehow sinister—light revealed nothing. And then she heard a rattling —as if a stick was being run along the walls of the chapel. She turned enquiringly to Miss Weston but the old woman had either not heard the noise or was pretending ignorance.

'So what is the message?' she said, bowing again to the altar and turning back towards the staircase.

Startled, Anna said, 'What message is that?'

'From the Prince. That is why you came, isn't it?'

'I'm afraid not. Really I just wanted to talk

about him.'

'I see.'

The mistress of Sutton Place relapsed into silence as she led the poetess back down the stairs, past a carved and coloured wooden statue of the Virgin Mary.

'I am powerfully protected,' she said, nodding in its direction. And then she added quite inconsequentially, 'Will you stay for a few days? We are very dull here and you have a beautiful face.' She peered at Anna closely. 'Are you sure you're not the Prince's daughter?'

Miss Seward smiled. 'Yes, I'm quite sure. And I will take a dish of tea with you and then depart. I'm afraid that I cannot be your guest though it is kind of you to invite me.'

She had an overwhelming urge to quit the house immediately—only politeness forbade it. The noise in the Long Gallery—or the chapel as it had now become—had unnerved her. She knew that she must lead Sutton Place before nightfall if her courage was to hold out.

'A pity,' said Melior Mary, pulling a bell rope that had once been made of stiff and fine brocade. 'I should have enjoyed your company. Now what shall we talk about?'

'Prince Charles Edward Stuart,' said Miss Seward firmly.

'He too came from a cursed family.'

'Oh?'

'Yes. Have you not heard of the curse on the House of Stuart? Do you believe in curses, Miss

436

Seward?'

'I am a Chrisitan but I am also a poet—so I think that I do.'

'If you were a Weston you would be sure. Now when you have drunk your tea I shall show you the rest of my mansion house.'

The emotions of fear and curiosity raged in the delicately nurtured breast of Miss Seward as—an hour later—she followed Melior Mary's stalking form through room after room of decay. Rotting bedhangings festooned chambers in which the walls were springing damp and the curtains were strips of grime; ancient tapestries disintegrated above Tudor carving so encrusted with cobwebs and dust that it was no longer possible to see their shape; mullioned windows that had once been thrown open to hear the laughter of Henry VIII's Court in the gardens below, were sealed forever by interweaving tendrils and foliage.

Anna's poetic soul was in torment. To her the house was being desecrated, a victim to an old, mad woman's notion that it had ruined her life. Yet she could not find it in her to dislike the wreck of humanity that had once been a Beauty of Bath and mistress to the Jacobite Prince. There was something about the gaunt face, the great hollow eyes, that held, still, a spark of their former splendour. The toss of the head with its strings of silver hair had, yet, an air that long ago would have raised every quizzing glass in the room. The writer in Miss Seward could see

437

beneath the ravaged facade to the spirit of the storm bird that fluttered pitifully within.

And when it came to her final glimpse of Melior Mary, standing in the archway of the great door that she had insisted on opening and which it had taken six servants—including Anna's coachman Thorne—two hours to prise ajar, the poetess's warm heart was rended. A skeletal hand waved a kerchief, the head in the huge and over-bearing hat was tipped back, a smile played about lips that twitched involuntarily with old and forgotten griefs. The last of the Westons was a sad and crazy figure as the coach rounded the bend in the drive and was lost to view.

And that night, sitting in her room in The Angel in Guildford, Anna Seward wrote a verse for posterity:

Where lofty oak-trees form a lonely shade,
Where no sun gilds the solitary glade,
A castle rises to the curious eye,
And ruins speaks its former majesty.
The folding gates (on hinges loth to move),
Are seldom op'd and never op'd to Love.
Within, an aged pious lady dwells;
High walls her mansion and her form conceal.
With her no laughing Grace, no Pleasure strays,
Her youth long past, in age she reads and prays.

The Swan of Lichfield sighed deeply as she put down her pen, blew out her candle and included Melior Mary Weston's immortal soul amongst

438

her night-time prayers.

★ ★ ★ ★

'Oh damme, damme—mind out there! You're disturbing me prinkum-prankum, so you are.'

Joseph's long hand flapped in the air to where his two great-grandchildren ran about his feet, shouting for joy as they felt the sand of the beach beneath their toes. One either side of him, his twin grandsons, on whom he was leaning heavily, chuckled to themselves but Pernel, who walked behind him lest he should totter over backwards said, 'Children, be quiet. This is Great Grand-papa's outing as much as yours.'

He was ninety-four years old and, for this rare treat of a visit to the coast with the younger members of his family, he had put on a suit of fuchsia satin, a cravat of lace, a waistcoat of peri-winkle blue and a full white wig. On his feet, adding to his difficulty in getting along, were shoes with pinchbeck heels and one of the two children carried his walking cane a-swirl with taffeta ribbons. The great rake was turned out in fine style for the occasion.

'I must say, Grandpapa, that you're got up very grand,' said the twins—almost in unison.

They were dressed, very dully in his opinion, in breeches and cambric shirts and—with no sense of style—had taken off their shoes. But for all their lack of fashion sense he adored them. Not quite as much as Pernel, of course, and

439

certainly not as much as Garnet—but nonetheless a great deal. They were dark-haired, with those grape blue eyes that had singled Matthew Banister out, and they stood very similar in build to their true grandfather. They had entered the Spanish Army together—as was now the family tradition—and had both been made captain during the previous year. But, unlike Pernel who had married Brig Linden—another Jacobite exile —they were still single. Joseph sometimes thought that it would be difficult for any two girls to take them as husband. Was it fanciful of him to believe that the brothers shared the same soul?

Jacob—the elder by five minutes—was putting out a folding chair that had been carried down the beach by a servant, and Joseph sank into it with a groan.

'I'm getting old,' he said.

Together the twins said, 'You will never be old, sir.' And James added, 'The great rakes of this world are always young.'

But as he sat in the sun Joseph knew that he was, in truth, at last ready to leave behind him the cavalcade of his incredible life. He had been born when that merry man Charles II had sat on the throne of England and he had lived through seven reigns—eight if one counted William of Orange's solitary rule. He had seen the Stuarts banished forever and the House of Hanover take their place; he had seen the English way of life alter to an age of elegance; he had seen the American Colonies take up arms against

George III and Spain join the war against England. In fact Major Garnet Gage was out there fighting now and the twins were soon to join their father.

Joseph poked his face further into the warmth like an old tortoise: he had been called Fortunatus twice in his own lifetime; he had taken on another man's child and through him had founded a dynasty; he had conquered despair and poverty and returned in triumph. Of the many remarkable men that the eighteenth century had produced, Joseph Gage ranked amongst the leaders.

In his ears was the laughter and joy of little Joseph and his sister Elizabeth—Pernel's two children; in his nose the sweet harsh salt of the waves; in his mouth the taste of a honeyed comfit he was nibbling. He was perfectly content. The circle of his life had just swung into place. He was ready to go, in the sunshine.

He opened his eyes. Standing in the water—bare legged and with her skirt tucked into her sash—a young woman stood with her back to him, bending over, like as not to look at a shell. Her blonde hair seemed almost pink in the sunshine and when she turned in his direction it became a dazzle about her head. So much so that he could not see her face. But she knew him all right for she waved her arm in a friendly manner.

A little wind had come from nowhere and was ruffling the tiny white froth that lapped at the very edge of the sea. Pernel felt it and looked up, where she knelt on the sand building a castle for her son and daughter. She saw that her two brothers were also propping themselves onto their elbows from their recumbent slumbers in the sun. Garnet's children looked at one another, Pernel's clearwater eyes enquiring from the identical blue of the two boys.

'Yes,' said Jacob. 'He's dying.'

'Should I go to him?'

'No. Watch.'

'Is it Sibella?'

James said, 'Yes it is. It's our grandmother.'

Pernel said wonderingly, 'Look, he's getting up out of his chair.'

'And he's young again. See him stride out.'

Joseph did not notice how strong he had become. All he could think about was that the girl was waving her hand in a beckoning motion and—though he still could not see her face—he knew that she was smiling. His pinchbeck heels were a nuisance so he kicked them off and walked into the waves but the sea did not strike him as cold or wet.

'Hullo Joseph,' said the girl.

'Who are you?'

'Don't you know?'

'I can't see your face.'

'You will in a moment. Here, put your arm round me. I want to walk with you on the beach.'

The three magic descendants of the house of FitzHoward hardly breathed as they saw the great rake encircle Sibella's waist and begin to strike out towards the sun.

'He'll never be forgotten,' said Pernel.

'Oh no. The name of Joseph Gage will go into the history books now. He will be known as one of the mighty English eccentrics.'

'I suppose he's the last of those connected with that great house in England. The one where Father was born.' This from Jacob.

'No,' said Pernel slowly. 'There's one left. A woman. One day we must go to her.'

'He's almost vanished now.'

A sea mist was blotting out the sunshine.

'I love you, Joseph,' said Sibella. 'There's no need to explain any more, is there?'

'No need at all,' he said.

'Then hold me tightly.'

He had never been happier than at that moment. Behind him he could see his family on the sand and beside them an old man sitting motionless in a folding chair. He did not want to return.

'Goodbye,' he said.

And holding Sibella closely in his protective arm, he walked with her out of life and into legend.

CHAPTER 23

So at last the web—the threads of which had been gradually enclosing Melior Mary Weston since the minute of her birth, as it must all those singled out to inherit or own the ill-starred Manor of Sutton—had her almost enmeshed. Every actor in her strange, sad charade was gone. Sibella in the morning of her life, Brother Hyacinth restored merely for a moment to himself, Mitchell full of savage unrequited love. Only Joseph and Sootface had finally escaped the strands that had threatened their existence. They had cut loose from Sutton Place and—refusing to set foot in the place again—had avoided the evil that threatened those closest to the heiress.

But now the sand of Melior Mary's own life was running out fast. And she, growing weaker, did not care. Every day of her existence was a prison; she had known madness and despair as had been predicted.

But nonetheless she prayed before the altar in the ghastly, rotting chapel that had once been the Long Gallery.

'Hail Mary, Full of Grace, look upon your unhappy servant who fears dying solitary. Send someone to hold me at the last, to give courage for the journey to you. Help me I beg you. I am all alone with my enemy—Sutton Place.

And the sad and terrible thing was that she had forgotten why she hated it so much; why her entire life was devoted to the destruction of her mansion. She did not know any more the reason that caused her to neglect Sir Richard Weston's beloved dwelling in order that it might collapse before she did.

'Help me!' she said as she turned away from prayer. 'Please—don't leave me by myself much longer.'

And, as it does in every situation, the counter balance began to swing. The Law of Libra—ever present, every watchful, demanding only some effort on the part of the person in need—took command. The scale quivered and then began slowly to rise in favour of Melior Mary. And with it came enormous power—power that could defy even a curse born seven centuries before. The force for good was about to challenge that of blackness.

And—just as their ancestors had done two hundred years ago—the magic descendants of the house of FitzHoward heard the call. The power of Sibella Hart and Matthew Banister—which had skipped their son Garnet Gage—was fired in all three of Garnet's children. Without the aid of ancient glass or cards, they knew what they must do.

'We must go to our cousin Melior Mary,' said Pernel to her father.

He looked at her very surprised.

445

'Why do you say that? You have never met her—you know nothing of her.'

'She is dying.'

The twins also stared at him; two identical pairs of eyes fusing in force.

'It's true, Father. She is alone and afraid. Let us go to her.'

Brig Linden, Pernel's husband—who was as sturdy and sweet as his name—said, 'They must go if they feel like this, sir. They are never wrong.'

He had not lived with his magic wife nor shared hours with his extraordinary brothers-in-law without realising that there were great unseen strengths in the universe.

And Sarah, Garnet's wife and mother of them—still bearing the assurance that had singled out all the Missetts—said, 'Come, come Garnet. You know your heritage. If the children feel this so strongly, you must agree. For did Cousin Melior Mary not befriend my mother Tamsin, when together they rescued Queen Clementina? Why, it was told me, that she put out her hand and welcomed me, where I danced in my mother's womb.'

They all turned their gaze on him and he was lost.

'Very well—though I believe it to be foolishness. Brig and the grandchildren shall stay here and you may go. You will find her in a great house near Guildford called Sutton Place.'

'We know,' said Pernel.

446

And so they had left Spain and gone first to London on the business of Garnet, who had inherited the silver mine from Grandee Joseph, and there they had wandered in the sweet clean June rain and looked at the names of Melior Street and Weston Street which lay to the south of Southward Bridge.

Once she owned all this,' said Jacob.

'Yes. She was the Belle of London and a vast property dealer.'

'What happened to stop her?'

'She loved unwisely—but then what human being does not? No more than that—the curse which lies on her land caught her up and she has forgotten.'

'But Melior Street will be there long after she is dead,' said Pernel. 'A constant reminder.'

But the twins did not answer her. They had already turned their horses away from the city. The time was beginning to run fast.

★ ★ ★ ★

Every day of her life Melior Mary would rise, dress, and breakfast alone. She would walk in the gardens, she would pray. She would keep vigil at the window of the chapel—which had once been the Long Gallery—watching for...she could no longer remember. But nonetheless she would do it. Staring out into the twilight...waiting.

But this night when she was so weak that she could scarcely crawl, there *was* somebody riding through the home park. Threading through the trees, horsemen approached Sutton Place. Melior Mary's eyes were anxious knots of violet as she stared beyond the splashing arcs of the summer shower to a flash of brown velvet riding habit, a glimpse of lace. A woman with two outriders was on her way.

Her poor tired heart beat faster. Her prayers had been answered. In the five years that had passed since Anna Seward's visit not one person had called on her. But now hooves crunched in the quadrangle. The visitors had pushed their way through the rotting planks which sealed up the Gate House arch and were waiting impatiently before the Middle Enter. Somewhere in the depths of the dying house a bell rang.

There was no servant to answer. Squinty Tom had died of quinsy and Bridget Clopper had finally gone at a ripe old age. And that had seen the end of her son Sam. He had stuffed a handkerchief with hunks of cheese and headed off through the forest. Only a farmer's wife from the estate came in to feed Melior Mary now—and then bolted back to the comfort and cleanliness of her own kitchen.

And yet—to her amazement—with nobody on the inside to unbolt it, Melior Mary heard the Middle Enter swing open and footsteps traverse the Great Hall. She crouched back against the altar, afraid of what might be coming towards her.

And then a woman's voice called out, 'Cousin

Melior Mary—where are you? We are Garnet Gage's children. Do you remember Garnet?'

The inexplicable fright caused her to freeze where she stood.

'No,' she shouted. 'I don't know him. Go away!'

But too late. Three figures stood at the top of what had once been the Great Staircase. And, as they drew nearer, even in the shadows of the ivy cloistered windows, she saw the gleam of curls beneath a veiled riding hat and the smile of clearwater eyes.

'Sibella?' she said uncertainly. 'Sibella, is it you?'

But the woman was close to her now and she saw that the hair was black. And then her gaze was pulled to the two men who looked at her from identical faces. She saw the dark-fringed eyes, the blaze of wild hyacinths. She began to cry in that raking, tragic way that old people have—her fingers wiping piteously at drawn cheeks, her hair wisping into her mouth.

'Don't weep,' said the woman. 'Come Melior Mary—put your hand into mine.'

And one of the two men kissed the feet of the altar's crucifix muttering an inaudible prayer, while the other said, 'Great Force, let our cousin not die in sadness. Let the magic of the house of FitzHoward challenge old, wild power.'

There was a sudden hush after that broken only by the sound of Melior Mary's sobs—and then from downstairs in the Great Hall the lone

449

voice of a fiddle struck up. She looked at her cousins in amazement—the Long Gallery was ablaze with five hundred candles. Before Melior Mary's tremulous feet a Fool danced; the rotting chapel had vanished—and all the while the sweet sad voice of the violin cajoled.

And then, when she looked into a full-length mirror—its frame candle-lit—she saw that she had been mistaken about herself. She had not grown old at all. The Beauty before whom Beau Nash had gasped—she who had conquered not only Bath but London—stared back. The silver hair was piled ringlet high, crowned by a triumph of ostrich feathers; the eyes were violets from a springtime brook; the gown sparkled with a thousand million crystals. And on her fingers and throat the Weston diamonds blazed like glittering rainbows.

The Fool knelt to kiss her shoe.

'Who are you?' she said.

'Giles, my Lady. I've seen you a hundred times—but never as beautiful as tonight. Shall I play my lute?'

'Yes, yes,' she answered, clapping her hands. 'And I shall walk down the staircase between the two twin boys—and you shall follow behind.'

And so they proceeded—but when the little cavalcade rounded the bend in the stairs she saw such a sight. A fire blazed in the hearth of the Great Hall before which slumbered two of John Weston's mastiffs, regardless of the chattering throng that clustered about them. It seemed that peasants and gentry rubbed shoulders alike for she saw her fat cousin William chattering to a farm girl, and her parents—John and Elizabeth—talking to Tom of the squinting gaze.

'But I thought they were all dead,' she said to Jacob—upon whose left arm her fingers rested while those of her other hand rested on James's right.

'Death, life—past, present,' he said, 'there's only a curtain between—thin as veil—and tonight you can see through it.'

'Then who is that man in dress of long ago? He with the eyes spaced wide.'

James laughed.

'That is your ancestor, Richard Weston. See, dancing over there to the fiddler, is his son Francis.'

There was no need to ask the identity of the girl who twirled in Francis's hold, giggling as her headdress slipped to reveal a flying mass of red curls.

'It's Rose,' she said.

'Yes—they're all here.'

And they all were? Even people in clothes of another time. A man who muttered to himself that he could not sleep and whom a servant addressed as Lord Northcliffe; and old man named Getty with a wintry one-sided smile, surrounded by fawning artificial women; a Duke in a lounge suit who laughed a lot; a host of young men in the uniform of Hussars; a girl with apricot hair and jade green eyes who whirled a curtsey

451

in Melior Mary's path and said, 'Lady Horatia Waldegrave at your service, ma'am.'

She saw the old fiddler who had played at the Christmas barn dance where Hyacinth had held her in his arms—and who had led the people of the estate to Sibella's wedding at Holy Trinity—scraping for dear life, seated upon a high stool. He had a black hood masking his face, yet he must have peeped round its folds as he saw Melior Mary coming down the stairs, for he changed his tune to 'Sir Roger de Coverley'. Everybody looked up to where she came and there was an exclamation and then a burst of clapping.

'It's the Beauty,' said somebody—and others took up the cry.

She stood on the bottom step and smiled at Sir Richard, at Francis and at Rose. She nodded her head to the Duke, to Northcliffe and to Getty. She extended her hand to the brilliant young soldiers, to her Cousin William, to Lady Horatia. But all the time her eyes were searching. The people she most wanted to see were not there.

As if knowing what she thought Jacob said, 'Be patient'—and took her in his arms to join the dancing throng. Accidentally one of the Hussars bumped into her. 'Captain John Joseph Webbe Weston, ma'am. Imperial Austrian army.' He clicked his heels. 'May I have the pleasure of the next dance?'

And just as she was smiling at him she heard Mitchell's voice announcing from the Middle

Enter.

'Miss Sibella Hart and Mr Joseph Gage.'

Her head spun round and she ran with arms outstretched. The two of them stood laughing in the doorway—Sootface just behind them. Joseph was examining the assembled company through a quizzing glass but Sibella had smiles for only one person—for her, for Melior Mary.

'Oh my dear, dear friend,' Sibella said. 'I shall not leave you again.'

'Then I will never be lonely?' answered Melior Mary.

'No—not any more.'

'But where is Brother Hyacinth?'

'Oh, he's somewhere in the crowd. But you will have to look carefully.'

Kissing Sibella on the cheek she broke away from her and began to thread herself a path through the twirling dancers, peering into their faces as she passed them. The identical twins were suddenly at her elbow.

'If you find him he'll want you to go with him,' said one of them.

'I don't mind.'

'However far the journey?'

'However far.'

'Then look over there.'

She stared to where the magic trio pointed—for Pernel had come to stand by them—but could see nobody.'

'There's only the old fiddler.'

'Look again.'

She gazed once more and saw that the cowled head was staring in her direction.

'Play "Haste to the Wedding," ' she called.

'Certainly, my Lady.'

His bow swirled onto the strings fiercely kissing out the sound. She walked towards him and as she did so the concealing hood fell back. She saw the halo of damson curls, the finely made nose, the grape blue eyes—and just for a second it did not occur to her at who she was gazing.

Tremulously she whispered, 'Hyacinth?'

His head went back, the exuberant laugh filled the room.

'Do you not know me? A fine welcome!'

'Oh my darling,' she shouted and hastened towards him, people scurrying to the right and left of her as she pushed her way down the length of the hall. And he, in his turn, jumped from the high stool and threw down his violin that he might catch her to him. At last they were together —friends, lovers, childhood companions.

'Dance,' he said. 'Dance with me.'

She knew then that this would never end. That she and Hyacinth would spin through eternity— bright as any star.

'You're not afraid?' he said.

'Is the circle done?'

'Yes, my storm bird, it's done. Fly free, wild girl.'

Her laugh was a cry of joy, a song of ecstasy.

'Then we shall never leave Sutton Place shall we? It will always know the strange story of

Melior Mary Weston—and her beloved Brother Hyacinth.'

'Always,' he said—and they smiled at each other as the curtain finally closed.

EPILOGUE

'But it's a ruin,' said John Webbe Weston despairingly. 'It's too far gone. I shall pull it down and start again. It's the only way.'

He stood with his wife Elizabeth, his two-year-old son and baby daughter, in the crumbling quadrangle of Sutton Place, staring round grimly at his newly-inherited manor house.

'But John, you cannot,' she answered. 'It is of great historic interest. It was the family seat for two hundred years and more.'

'Damn the family,' said her husband shortly.

He felt no sentiment for the Westons at all. He was no blood relation whatsoever. He was descended from the sister of old William Wolffe who had married John Weston's sister Frances. He was a Webbe—through and through. In fact he couldn't think why his remote and lunatic connection, Melior Mary, had left him her fortune and estates. She had been far closer to the Gages. In fact, she had died in the arms of those frightening identical twins, who had been calling at the time with their sister—or so they said!

He had not taken to them at all. They had not even stayed to attend the funeral which he had arranged with no thought to expense. Nor had they seen the fulsome monument which he had

456

had erected to Melior Mary in the family vault at Holy Trinity.

'She was the last immediate descendant of an illustrious Family which flourished in this county for many successive generations, and with the ample possessions of their ancestors inherited their superior understanding and distinguished virtues.'

He had thought her a crazy old woman living in squalor but it had showed him up in a good light to raise that stone. John Webbe Weston of Sutton Place—gentleman and respecter of the dead.

'Shall we go in?' his wife was saying.

'Yes—it cannot be any worse than outside.'

But it was. Damp rotted the air with its stench, woodwork crumbled beneath his touch.

'Dear God,' he said. 'And I had to adopt her name just to inherit this?'

'But there is the money as well, John. I know we had hoped to move straight in but we can afford now to make do with something else while the new house is built.'

'So you agree Sutton Place must come down?'

'Quite definitely.'

'I think I shall consult that Italian architect—what's his name...?'

'Bonomi?'

'Yes, that's the fellow.'

'Wouldn't that be very expensive?'

John squeezed her arm.

'That is not of paramount importance these

457

days, my dear.'

They had traversed the Great Hall, glancing cursorily at the stained glass, and were ascending the dilapidated staircase that led up to a dim and depressing chapel.

'What a terrible, terrible house,' said Elizabeth. 'It is almost as if she was insulting us in leaving it to you.'

John laughed shortly and kicked a crumbling floorboard which fell apart beneath his touch.

'When I was a small boy some old relative talked of it being cursed. That was when Melior Mary had left it to the Wolffes.'

'Strange how they all died.'

'Yes.'

'Perhaps there is something in it.'

John laughed again.

'We'll see how a curse gets on in an Italian villa—that's what I fancy. Somewhere with classical columns and pediments.' He turned to his wife enthusiastically. 'We could convert that monstrous Great Hall into two stories—full of small modern chambers. What do you think of that?'

'A wonderful plan. And what about this dreadful gallery?'

'Oh, it will have to come down with the rest of the wings.'

They stood gazing about them with distaste.

'It's very cold, isn't it?' said Elizabeth—and at that both the babe she carried in her arms and her toddling son burst, for no apparent reason, into tears. Behind them there was a noise like a stick being rattled along the wall.

'What was that? Be *quiet*, John Joseph.'

'A bird in the chimney I expect. Come along, my dear. I've see enough.'

Elizabeth followed her husband's stolid form down the Gallery.

'Well,' she said, 'I think it's hateful. It should be pulled down—every last brick of it!'

Her words died on her lips. Behind her a voice like a million sighs said, 'Wait and see!', and a cold little hand seemed to paw at her shoulder. She spun round but there was nothing there. Nothing, that is, but the house looming round her like a vast and relentless shadow. Elizabeth Webbe Weston was glad to hurry into the comfort and apparent safety of daylight.